Rebel
Born

Books by Amy A. Bartol

The Secondborn Series

Secondborn
Traitor Born
Rebel Born

The Kricket Series

Under Different Stars
Sea of Stars
Darken the Stars

The Premonition Series

Inescapable
Intuition
Indebted
Incendiary
Iniquity

"*The Divided*" (short story)

Rebel Born

AMY A. BARTOL

Published by 47North, Seattle

www.apub.com

Amazon, the Amazon logo, and 47North are trademarks of Amazon.com, Inc., or its affiliates.

ISBN-13: 9781503936935 (paperback)
ISBN-10: 1503936937 (paperback)

Cover design by Shasti O'Leary Soudant

Printed in the United States of America

For Tommy, Max, and Jack, the loves of my life

Prologue
Gilad Sword

I'm not gonna watch the Opening Ceremonies of the Secondborn Trials.

Everyone needs to shut up 'bout it, too, especially the Diamond-Fated announcers with their fancy clothes and celebrity gossip. I glance at the three-dimensional visual screens dappling the walls as I make my way from the shower closet to my locker. They installed these holographic monitors just for this tragic event, so none of us secondborns will miss just how insignificant our lives are to them. It makes me wanna puke. I feel a scowl wrinkling my nose when I look at the images of the bubbleheaded news anchor standing beside her counterpart with the high-pitched voice and glittering lashes. Neither of them would last a day as a Sword secondborn soldier. Not even for a minute.

Water drips from my hair. I slump down on a steel bench. My muscles ache from dragging metal boxes of ammo cartridges after the supply-chain vehicles broke down today. I still have titanium shavings under my fingernails. Annoyed by the prissy chatter, I toss my wet towel at one of the nearby life-sized holographic projections, hitting it just right so that the light skews and cuts everything in half. The reporters now resemble severed bodies. The images' shrill voices prattle on, though, 'bout Roselle St. Sismode—'bout her ascension to heir after the death of her firstborn brother, Gabriel.

"Ahh, Gilad!" Hazel gripes from her locker, several units down. She slams it shut with a bang. "I was watchin' that!"

"Nothin' to see but a bunch of secondborn competitors at the Silver Halo," I mutter. "They'll be dead in a few days, and if we're lucky, we'll still be alive."

Hazel ignores my lack of enthusiasm. "They're about to start the exhibition—Roselle St. Sismode and some firstborn dope from Stars are going to duel on a platform in the arena. She's gonna crush him. She's got the new Salloway Dual-Blade X17!"

"She's gonna be The Sword one day," I snarl. "You'd think they'd play it safe with her."

"But Roselle's already *a* Sword anyway! She was one of us. Badass." Hazel flexes, showing me her rippling muscles. She moves to the visual screen's projection port and snatches my towel away. The hologram becomes whole again. "She doesn't need anyone's protection from anything."

"You never met her mom."

The coverage pans to the crowd in the sky arena above the Fate of Virtues. For a few minutes I can't help but aggressively scan it for Hawthorne. I haven't heard from him since he left our Base. We were best friends when he was secondborn. I'd thought he'd find a way to contact me—tell me he's okay, ask me how I am. I was wrong. I've heard nothin' from him. He ghosted me the minute his brother, Flint, died. He's firstborn now. Traitor. He's probably at The Trials tonight, even though he used to hate it. Once upon a time, he'd be anywhere Roselle was. He lost his damn mind for her at one point, thought he was in love with her, but then he ghosted her, too. I saw her around after he left. Like me, she took it hard. Now she's firstborn, too. I wonder if she'll forgive Hawthorne. I won't. I would never have lost touch with him if our situations had been reversed. I hope he's still in love with

Roselle and that he has to watch while she marries that Salloway creep who the announcers say she's engaged to, because karma. Suck on it, Hawthorne.

My stomach aches. Hurriedly, I dress for sleep. I just want to go to bed and not have to think about any of these people ever again. I slam my locker shut and pass a horde of orange-uniformed locker-room attendants. They move down the aisles, opening lockers and pulling out armor, tossing it into hovering collection receptacles. I grab an attendant by the arm, startling him. "Hey," I growl at the young Stone-Fated secondborn, "where're you takin' our armor?"

"You're getting new requisitions—Burton Weapons Manufacturing's upgrading 'em."

My eyebrow quirks. "Yeah?"

"Yeah. This is our last air-barracks of the night. We were supposed to be done with our Tree by this afternoon, but we fell behind."

"When do we get the new stuff?"

"In the morning—first thing."

I smile and let go of his arm. My armor was starting to smell like dead rodents. I could use a new liner at the very least. I exit the locker room. The catwalk leading to my capsule is practically barren. Everyone's either in their capsules watchin' the Opening Ceremonies or in the airship's rec room watchin' it together. I don't go to the rec room anymore. It reminds me too much of Edgerton and Hammon.

An ache caves in my heart. I clench my teeth and pant a little to work through the pain. I don't know what happened to my friends. Hamm and Edge were here one day, gone the next. No explanation. No good-bye. No nothin'. That creepy freak, Agent Crow, thought I might have had somethin' to do with it. He took me down into Census's hole beneath this Tree Base and interrogated me. I thought he was gonna kill me, but he must've realized I knew nothin' 'bout where they'd gone or why they'd left. I think he kept me alive so he could watch me to see if they'd contact me. So far they haven't. Whatever happened to them,

I hope that steel-toothed, psychopathic Census agent never finds 'em, because if he does, they'll probably wish they were dead.

Exhausted, I climb the ladder to my capsule, crawl inside, and close the hatch and stretch out on my mat. The small space is a cozy cocoon, and I'd stay in it forever if I could. I just want to be left alone. I hate people now. Well, I don't hate them. I just don't want to be friends with any of them. It's nothing personal; it's just that they all die or leave. It's not worth it—friendship. I scrub my hand over my scarred face.

I resist turning on the visual screen embedded in my ceiling, for a little while, but then I think about Hamm and Edge. What if, somehow, they show up at the Opening Ceremonies? Before I know it, I turn it on, blinking as my eyes adjust to the bright light. The scene is chaos. People running—screaming—in every direction. It takes me a second to understand that an attack of some kind is taking place in the Silver Halo. People are slaughtering each other. I sit up on my thin mattress and throw aside my blanket, knowing I should do something, but what?

My nose wrinkles. An acrid scent burns my nostrils. I lift my hand to cover my nose and mouth. Hissing clouds of white vapor fill the air through my capsule's vents. My eyes water, but when I wipe them with the back of my hand, I find a streak of blood, not tears, on my skin. Sounds of coughing and moaning erupt in the airship. I clutch my blanket and try to cover the vents. Blindly, I fight to open the capsule's hatch, but it won't budge. Kicking it does no good, even with both feet, as hard as I can, over and over. Light-headedness overwhelms me. My lungs feel like they're melting. Through the slit between my swelling eyelids, I witness the end of the world play out on the ceiling of my capsule until my last, dying breath.

Chapter 1
The Poison of Our Age

My wrists are bound with steel cuffs.

Hawthorne viciously prods me forward. I stumble behind Agent Crow, through the blue banners, and exit the Sword balcony at the back of the Silver Halo suite. I glance over my shoulder, but it's not the ache of betrayal that wrenches my heart. It's fear that whatever has happened to Hawthorne is irreversible. Silver light beams from his eye. I might have caught a glimpse of it the last time we were together, but I can't be sure. I can hardly process what's happening now.

Screams of terror echo throughout the colosseum's corridors. I'm surrounded by no fewer than a dozen Zeros. Fast and ferocious, these once ordinary people pounce on the scattering spectators fleeing the Secondborn Trials. Switchblade-sharp claws extend from the monsters' fingertips. The flesh of their victims rips. Blood, slick and gory, blooms in patches of red everywhere I look. I tug against the cuffs on my wrists. Hawthorne clamps his hand on my nape and squeezes until I wince. A warning that he can snap my neck in seconds if I resist. I stop struggling and stumble to keep in step with my captors.

Through the chaos of the ensuing massacre, I study the Zeros. On the back of these predators' hands, zero-shaped monikers suck in light like black holes. Silver beams extend from their left eyes. They move as an otherworldly pack, in an intricate choreography, without fatigue or missteps. Like one machine, they slaughter with precision everything that moves, everything that isn't one of them or part of Census. *All except me.* I shudder. They must be communicating, but in a language that only they understand.

None of the other marauding Zeros approach the team surrounding me. Instead the monsters busily butcher everything with a pulse. Unafflicted firstborns and the secondborn competitors attempt to escape from the floating colosseum and are immediately pursued.

My training and experience as a soldier keeps me from being sick. *I can't help anyone!*

Another shove compels me forward. We pass a gondola station that leads to the training field below. Blood and carnage litter the platforms. Some firstborns jump to their deaths rather than be caught by the Zeros. The hairs on my nape stand on end.

"Why are you killing firstborns?" I growl at Agent Crow.

"Why not?" he replies in a blasé tone, reaching to brush wisps of my hair from my face as we walk. I recoil from his touch. "They won't do well in our new society, Roselle. We're doing them a favor." His mouth curves up, exposing the steel teeth that stand in stark contrast to his supple lips. The black disc adhered to his temple blinks with eerie blue light. It must be how he manipulates the silver-eyed cyborgs. Their obedience to him seems absolute. He doesn't have to say a word. He somehow just *thinks*, and they respond.

He's depraved.

The inky tattoos near his temples and on his throat are deceptive. Although hundreds of the so-called kill tallies are visibly etched into his skin, they only represent a fraction of the deaths he's caused. His skin would need be covered from head to toe in order for it to accurately represent all the people whose slaughter he brought about tonight.

Agent Crow guides us to a staging area where a nondescript medical-supply airship awaits with its ramp down. The Census agent enters the front of the ship, while I'm shoved up the open ramp by the killers behind me. Inside the tail, I find that the airship doesn't have any cargo, nor any seats. The monster that was Hawthorne flings me to the metal floor. Sitting up, I push myself to the wall, lean back against it, and draw my knees up to my chest and rest my forearms on them.

I'm not sure how smart these Zeros are when they're in Black-O mode or whatever it was that Agent Crow called it back when we were on the Sword balcony. The woman who'd cuffed me made the mistake of securing my arms in front of me. If I can reach a sword, I'll have no problem cutting them off. But there aren't any swords. No weapons of any kind here in the cargo hold. It's just me and the Zeros.

The airship door closes, sealing us in. My throat tightens. Dim lights come on, but it's still dark. The Zeros' eyes glow like small moons in the night sky. Gore mottles their mouths, their clothes, and their fingers. The steel claws seem to have retracted into their fingertips, but I know they're there.

The vessel rumbles and lurches upward. The Zeros don't move. They don't talk. They gaze straight ahead. They seem barely alive. Hawthorne sits across from me and several bodies over. He isn't smeared in carnage like the others. I don't think he was in the fight at the Silver Halo, which means Agent Crow wants to use Hawthorne some other way. More than likely against me.

My wrists tremble on my knees. Or maybe it's my knees trembling. Or maybe it's both. I thread my fingers together, but the trembling doesn't stop. Panic seizes me. It's hard to breathe. I feel dizzy. Sweat soaks the back of my white sparring outfit. Wisps of damp hair cling to my cheek.

I have to wait for several minutes in the grip of the panic attack. When it finally subsides and my breath isn't coming out in hacking pants, I try to get up, and all the creatures look at me at once. They're ghosts; the real people are gone, and these demons are what's left. It's like I knocked back a shot glass full of pure adrenaline. My stomach roils with fear. I press myself against the wall and rise. Carefully, I walk between the Zeros until I'm across from the ghoulish Hawthorne.

I kneel in front of him. He stares, but it's as if he isn't really seeing me. "Hawthorne." I try a normal tone, but it comes out in a breathless whisper. "Remember when we first met? It was in Swords, when the airships fell from the sky. Remember?" My voice quivers. Tears spill down my cheeks. "You tried to help me, and I hit you in the nose?"

He doesn't even blink.

I sit down and cross my legs. "You rescued me when I was Crow's prisoner in Census. You were so brave. Nobody in my family lifted a finger to help me. It was you." I touch his hand, wanting so badly for him to hold me.

Suddenly he focuses. He pounces, wraps his hand around my throat, and squeezes. My face burns hot. My windpipe feels crushed. I hold up my hands to him, palms out, in surrender. He lets go.

I cough and sputter and gulp breaths, gasping when I finally get my voice back. "Okay, so no touching." I wipe tears from my cheeks with my sleeve. My fingertips glide over my ravaged neck. "I know you're in there somewhere, Hawthorne. We're a half-written poem, you and me. Wherever you are—whatever basement in your mind they've got you trapped in—I'll find you. I won't leave you down there alone."

As if it's just the two of us here, I remind Hawthorne of everything we've shared together. Every stolen moment when we were secondborns. Every kiss. Every caress. My throat aches, but still I talk.

Hawthorne stares straight ahead. No reaction. No indication that he hears me or understands me. Hours pass with no sign of recognition. The pain of it is too much. It's too real. It threatens to bury me. I hold my head in my hands and give in, sobbing quietly.

The cargo ship begins to descend. The touchdown is smooth. Wiping my face with the back of my sleeve, I try to pull myself together.

The tail opens. Humid air rushes in. The sky is still dark, but tall lamps loom above us, like those that line the secondborn military Bases in Swords, throwing stark white light on everything.

Hawthorne stands in unison with the other mind-controlled monsters. He grabs my arm and roughly hauls me out of the hold. Agent Crow waits on the hoverpad. The black beacon on the side of his head blinks blue. Around us palm trees sway in a salty breeze. Balmy air blows loose strands of my hair.

"Pleasant trip?" Agent Crow asks. He smiles, baring his wretched steel teeth.

Normally I try to have something scathingly sarcastic to say back to him, just so that he remembers he hasn't beaten me. This time I don't. This time he has destroyed me, reached inside me and torn my heart out, and I know this is only the beginning.

"Where are we?" My voice is gravelly.

"A little place we call The Apiary," he replies. "It's a small island near the Fate of Seas, one of the first military Bases to have Trees. It's been decommissioned, as far as most people are concerned. Not a lot of people outside Census know of its existence."

I can just make out the ocean in the distance. All around us lie the relics of a decrepit military Base. Ancient airships that I've seen only in holographic history files rust out in the open. Everything is at least a few hundred years old. The only lights shine from the Base's Trees and infrastructure. Nothing but water lies beyond the Base, from what I can tell. Behind us, rough, tree-lined, rocky crags dapple the horizon. No other signs of civilization.

Viable airships hang from the Trees' branches, but they're not current models. I wouldn't know if I could fly one unless I got inside the cockpit. Behind me the cyborgs form two lines, equally spaced. Efficient. Mindless. Controlled and manipulated by a psychopathic Census agent.

Agent Crow strides ahead of me into a Tree's trunk. I'm prodded to follow. A familiar dimness greets me inside the Tree, but the smell isn't the same as the military Trees I inhabited as a soldier. Energy thrums and snaps in the air. There's an overcharged, singeing scent that, if I licked my fingers, I could probably taste on my skin. As it is, I feel it in my chest. The hair on my skin rises, from the smell and from fear.

This structure, a docking station for military air-barracks that was tantamount to a small, thriving city for soldiers, has been resurrected to fit the needs of madmen. We enter a warehouse for hundreds of thousands of adult-sized canisters—cylindrical tanks filled with fluid. Blue neon light glows from the tops and bottoms of the transparent capsules. Inside each is a person, curled in a fetal position, floating. Some resemble modern *Homo sapiens*. Others don't. Some are amalgamations of different species. Others are unifications of human and machine. Above us are levels of canisters as far as I can see, arranged in concentric rings like the cross section of a real tree.

Agent Crow teeters on the edge of mania. His insolent smile cuts through my haze of disbelief. "Would you like a history lesson of the Fates Republic, Roselle?" he asks. "Not the one you've been taught in Swords, about the nine Fates forming for the common good to create perfect symmetry between the classes. That's mostly propaganda. I'm talking about a *real* history lesson."

"Enlighten me," I reply.

He clasps his hands behind his back, and we stroll together through a ring of the glowing tanks. "Unimpeded progress in technology and medicine has always driven our civilization forward. Some advances came with unpleasant side effects, though. Years ago, the average life expectancy expanded exponentially in a very short period. Our population was exploding. We were on the brink of exhausting all our natural resources, of bringing catastrophic destruction to the planet. We were wasting away. Something had to be done. At the same time, a powerful ruler by the name of Greyon Wenn the Virtuous came into power. Have you heard of him?"

"Of course," I reply. Like lurking rats, we continue between the glowing containers. "Greyon was a ruthless warlord and a brilliant strategist. Brutal in his tactics, he slaughtered his rivals when they surrendered, and he set about systematically toppling every other government until he became the first supreme ruler to dominate the world. He formed a single unifying government and presided over it with unmerciful aggression."

A sudden spasm of motion explodes in the cylinder next to me. I lurch away. Hands press against the transparent surface. An open mouth with sharp fangs gropes the glass. Black, glassy orbs bulge from the creature's head. Gills cover its neck. Webbed fingers paw at us through the fluid. Hawthorne shoves me away from the tank, propelling me in Agent Crow's direction.

Agent Crow snickers and keeps walking. "You surprise me, Roselle. You know our true origins. Your mentor, Dune, taught you well. You're not as ignorant as most people I encounter."

"Dune always said, 'Know your past so you can avoid it in the future.'"

He chuckles. "What else did he teach you about Greyon Wenn the Virtuous?"

"Grisholm Wenn-Bowie was said to be a direct descendant of Greyon," I reply numbly.

"Yes, you could trace his family line all the way back to the supreme ruler . . . but the same could be said about you, Roselle. The St. Sismode line directly descends from Greyon. Some say that the Wenns and the Bowies have the name, but it's your family that has the blood."

"They're all dead now," I say. "You and your minions decimated them."

"All except for you and your mother. But the Wenn and Bowie lineages lost their nobility and intelligence years ago. We simply rectified the genealogical error. We relegated them to where they belong—a foot-note in history. But getting back to Greyon . . . The world was stagger-ingly overpopulated and growing more so in peacetime. Greyon Wenn decreed that restrictions be enacted on procreation. His government began issuing birth cards, a rudimentary way to give permission to a couple to have a child. Firstborns weren't the only ones allowed to have birth cards. It was based purely on genetics. Once undesirable traits were expunged, it became an issue of privilege. Cards were dispensed at higher and higher prices. Families died off. Inherited wealth became a way to ensure the survival of the family name. Finances were pooled and given to firstborn heirs to keep family lines alive. Only the elite could afford to have children.

"The government began issuing cards for secondborn children, but with the explicit provision that the child be given to the government when the secondborn reached adulthood. And voilà! The Fates Republic was formed. Of course, there will always be rule breakers, and enforce-ment of laws is essential—so Census was born."

I consider trying to choke him to death, like I did with his own belt when we first met. I could probably do it. Hawthorne lingers so near, though. It wouldn't take much for him to break my arms. I contemplate other killing scenarios as we pass more tanks. The beings inside these appear more human, despite having machine parts grafted onto them. The fine-boned lines of one woman's face are covered in a shiny coating of metal. Her left pupil has been replaced by a protruding lens. She doesn't move as we pass.

Agent Crow drones on. "Over time, the population scales tipped, and we slid back the other way. Our low birth rate threatened us with extinction. Depressing the birth rate was never meant to be a permanent solution to overpopulation, and even though we were living longer, the population was declining. So again, something had to be done."

He has led us to a Census bunker. He scans his moniker under a blue light near the security doors, and they roll open. We walk a short corridor to the lifts and enter a car. The last time I was in a Census elevator, it filled with lake water and I almost died. I feel like I'm drowning now, too. The doors close, and we descend.

And still, he continues his history lesson. "Scientists were put to the task of finding a solution to our complex problem. Cloistered away from society, they lived like kings and queens on this island oasis, creating generations of offspring we affectionately refer to as zeroborns. A harvesting plant was built right here on this military Base."

I scoff. "Why not just repeal the laws and let everyone repopulate the world naturally?"

He scrunches his face like I've said something distasteful. "Bah! I never took you for a simpleton!" He looks down his nose at me and sneers. "You'd let every dirt farmer have as many brats as he wanted, wouldn't you? You'd let the lawbreakers go unpunished?"

"My way would make Census obsolete."

"Your way will never happen."

The elevator doors open. Before me sprawls a state-of-the-art laboratory. It's eerily dim, lit by a low blue haze that seems to come from the floor. Incubation capsules resembling giant wombs hang from tubing in neatly lined rows and columns. I stand frozen, mouth agape. Agent Crow exits the car, turns, and gazes at me, his hands still clasped behind his back.

"Beautiful, isn't it?" he asks. Technicians in gloves and black lab coats tend to the wombs. "The next generation of zeroborns. We use zygotes taken and produced from captured thirdborns before we execute them. We used to genetically engineer our batches through cloning, but we're getting much better results now—from diversity, of all things. Diversity has been the key to hiding our progeny. Clones don't blend in well, but clones *are* useful in running our secret facilities."

Hawthorne shoves me in the back, and I stumble from the elevator. Agent Crow turns and continues walking, passing rows of swollen, veiny, synthetic-flesh bladders filled with fluid and floating fetuses.

"Once the first generation of zeroborns was created," he says, "the operation became self-perpetuating. Zeroborns manufacturing zeroborns to work in the embryo centers, as caretakers, as population-insertion specialists—chemically mapping the brains of our progeny with false memories so that individuals can be inserted, undetected, into the population in any Fate we choose." The technicians resemble one another, some right down to their freckles. They have zero-shaped monikers.

"How did you keep the zeroborns a secret for so long?" I ask.

"The zeroborns who are inserted into the population receive new monikers representing whatever Fate they're assigned to. Take, for example, zeroborns earmarked to become Sword soldiers. We create them here, in our underground facilities. Other zeroborns care for them. They leave this facility when they're infants. The zeroborn soldiers are raised at other secret military facilities, where they're trained and given false memories of a life and family in Swords that never existed."

I can't believe what I'm hearing. "How do you give someone false memories?"

"Reality and perception are easy to manipulate. Your eyes, as it happens, aren't the best way to perceive the world. They're horrendously inadequate filters. We don't perceive most of what there is to see. Perception is a guessing game for the brain. Once you understand that, then you know that everything you perceive with your senses can be altered and manipulated, especially your visual perception. Take our cornea implants—the silver shine results from an alteration to the visual acuity. The Black-Os aren't seeing what you and I see. They're being fed a virtual reality on top of the world at large. Their cornea implants, coupled with alterations to the chemicals and electrical impulses, override their higher cognitive reasoning, replacing it with artificial intelligence that we control. We can implant any memory we see fit."

I glance at the black disc on his temple. "How do you control them?"

He pauses next to a fleshy womb. In the translucent sack, a fetus floats, blissfully unaware of its very unnatural environment. "The Virtual Perception Manipulation Device, or VPMD, began as a toy," he explains. "It was a form of amusement—tricking our brains with enhanced optics. Recreational visual deception. Eventually, Census created our own virtual worlds by implanting devices into the brains of zeroborns. The implants, once embedded, create their own unique neural pathways. Biochemically, we manipulate visual and aural perception, and with implants in the cornea, show them images they perceive as 'real.' We have complex programs and protocols. When we send Black-Os out to perform a mission, there are 'laws' that they have to follow, but the program also incorporates artificial intelligence. How the collective reaches the goal is almost entirely up to them. They just have to adhere to certain rules."

"Rules like 'Don't kill Roselle. Bring her to the Sword balcony while you slaughter everyone else'?"

Amusement dances across Crow's lips. "We gave them your scent. Did you know that? They smelled you, like maginots would."

"So they have olfactory enhancements?"

"And so much more."

"You use that device on your temple to communicate with the Black-Os," I say. It's not a question.

"That information isn't part of the tour, Roselle," he admonishes. "We've already created our own population—our own elite forces. The time for a great change in power has begun. No longer will we be subject to the idiocy of the Clarities of the Fates Republic. Census will make the laws now. Your mother, of course, is the exception."

"It always comes down to power, doesn't it?"

"Everything is about power, Roselle. The war between the Fates Republic and the Gates of Dawn has accelerated the transfer of power. Census has been hiding our declining population with zeroborn replacements masquerading as Swords, but we've been having trouble keeping up with your mother's production demands. If things continue at the current rate, secondborn Swords will go extinct in a generation. The Gates of Dawn keeps throwing their martyrs at us, and we can't grow new organic soldiers from infancy fast enough. We had to find a way to convert existing assets."

"Assets?" I spit. "You're talking about *people!*"

"Oh, you don't know the half of it, Roselle."

"If the ban on procreation were lifted," I snap, "Census would lose its power. So instead you kidnap people like Hawthorne and insert VPMDs to make them obey you?"

"It's called *conversion*, Roselle. We implant devices that allow us to control the host. Let the Gates of Dawn throw as many bodies at us as they want. We'll just keep killing them and producing enhanced reinforcements until there's no one else left."

"My mother knows?" I can barely contain my rage.

"We needed each other, Census and The Sword."

"How long will that last?" I ask him. He smirks but doesn't answer. "How long has Hawthorne been your convert?"

"Not long. A few weeks. We grabbed him at his home after that little stunt you two pulled at the Sword social club—the Rose Goddess Massacre. We had to wait until after he gave his testimony of the event to The Virtue at the Halo Palace, but our patience paid off. I must admit that I was impressed with how you handled our non-converted zeroborns. It showed just how weak they are compared with our enhanced AI versions."

"Non-converted?" I ask.

"None of the assassins you fought at the Sword social club had cerebral enhancements. It was too risky. If the implants and other enhancements had been found before we were ready to unveil them, it could have ruined everything."

"Other enhancements?" I think of the steel claws that sprang from the Black-Os' fingertips.

"Lethal enhancements, Roselle. We're on the cutting edge of tapping into other perceptions, what some would call a sixth sense. The new neural pathways that the VPMD creates have presented us with some tantalizing opportunities. We've commissioned Star-Fated engineers to help us with our research—only the brightest." I haven't seen these Star-Fated technicians around.

"You've commissioned them, or you've kidnapped them?" I ask.

"'Kidnapped' is such an ugly word, Roselle. Most of them are secondborns. We appropriated them."

We leave the room and enter a stark-white corridor. The light hurts my eyes. Windows afford a view of a nursery. Swaddled in temperature-controlled cocoons, infants rock gently in nestled bins. Above them, holographic images of faces hover, talking and smiling, giving the impression that a real person is attending to the infant. These are interspersed with other images, flashes of light that I can't make out.

"They haven't gotten their cornea or other implants yet," Agent Crow says. "The holographic images simulate mothers and fathers or siblings—all of them obedient to Census."

Thousands and thousands of cocoon cradles fill the nursery. It reminds me of a morgue. "Cranston Atom, the mortician at the Halo Palace," I surmise, "somehow figured out that something wasn't right about the assassins at the club."

"He was clever. At first he was fooled into believing the assassins never had monikers. Protocol for missing monikers demands that Census investigate. It was how we planned to recover all the assassins' bodies before any other agency could investigate. But Cranston was too good at his job. Later, at the Halo Palace morgue, the mortician noticed the zeroborn monikers were once present in the assassins. He figured out that they'd all been cut out of the Death Gods from the Gods and Goddesses Ball and they'd undergone skin regeneration, but the zeroborn moniker had left behind unique imprints inside the corpses' flesh. The markings were different than normal Fates Republic monikers. Cranston contacted me after my initial meeting with him to tell me about his discovery, which meant I had to kill him."

"How did you get away with that?"

"We're Census. No one questions us."

We've reached the end of the corridor. Another elevator opens before us. Agent Crow steps in. I have no choice but to follow. Hawthorne enters after me, the doors roll closed, and I'm relieved to feel the car rising.

Hawthorne's sandy hair lies over his eyes. I want to brush it away, but if I touch him, he'll hurt me. He gazes straight ahead, emotionless. My heart aches with sorrow.

"How is it that Hawthorne was converted weeks ago?" I ask. "I just saw him yesterday in the war room of *Upper Halo*."

Agent Crow laughs. "Hawthorne has no idea that he's a Black-O when he's not being actively redirected. Unless his VPMD is turned on, you'd never know he's one of us. His eyes have the implants, true, but they won't shine. You'd have to examine him closely. He's the perfect spy because he's unaware that he's spying."

"You're disgusting," I growl.

"And you'll make a fine Black-O, Roselle."

A cold tremor slips down my spine.

We return to the trunk of the Tree. I'm escorted to a heartwood in the center of the facility. Agent Crow gestures for me to enter the heartwood with him. I clutch the pole and step onto a rising star. He is on the step beside mine. We're lifted together through the tube.

"There is something I want to show you on level five," he says.

We pass storehouses of neon cylinders containing people—his experiments. On level five, we step off the heartwood and walk together to the area that, in a normal Tree, would be used for the intake of new Transitions. Inside, secondborn Atom- and Star-Fated technicians are busy at work. They don't appear to be mind-controlled. No silver light shines from them.

Agent Crow commands the attention of the nearest Star-Fated man in an ebony lab coat. The tall, handsome man stops what he is doing on his holographic screen, climbs off his chair, and walks toward us. Dark hair falls over his brow. His eyes are focused on his moniker, but his inattentiveness doesn't seem to bother Agent Crow.

"I need you to prepare Roselle St. Sismode for Black-O conversion," Agent Crow says.

My heart pounds in my ears. I turn to bolt, but I'm caught and restrained by Hawthorne and several other Black-O soldiers. I struggle, but they're ridiculously strong.

The technician doesn't miss a beat, ignoring my outburst. "I just need a requisition, and I can take her back to an exam room now. I'm sending you the appropriate files." His fingers swipe the light of his star-shaped moniker.

Agent Crow uses his moniker to send the requisition. They're still using the Fates Republic communication system. They must have ways of blocking access by nosy Star-Fated firstborns like Reykin, but for my sake, I hope not.

The technician draws a tranquilizer gun from the holster on his thigh. I kick him in the stomach and try again to get loose, but I'm immediately tackled by the nearest Black-O. He growls in my ear until I exhaust myself and stop struggling, and he hauls me back to my feet. I pant in frustration.

Agent Crow leans in, touches my cheek, and smooths my hair away from my eyes. "I'm looking forward to your conversion more than I have with anyone else's, Roselle. What will it be like when you fall into my arms instead of trying to rip them off?"

I spit in his face. He scowls and pulls a cloth from the pocket of his black leather coat. Methodically, he wipes away my spit. "Hand me the gun."

The technician places the tranquilizer gun in Agent Crow's palm. He places it directly over my heart. My eyes defy him, even as the dart penetrates my skin. I jerk at the impact of the needle against my breastbone. My eyes blur. My ears ring. Everything mutes. A dreamy, faraway feeling sets in.

"Let her go," Agent Crow orders. It sounds distant.

I'm released. My knees weaken, and I almost collapse, but the technician reaches out and catches me, clutching me to him. He smells like lemongrass.

"Opa," he groans. "It must be too much. You're such a little thing."

His deep voice sounds so familiar.

"Don't be deceived," Agent Crow warns. "She's a killer."

"Oh, I know who she is," the technician replies. "Everybody knows Roselle St. Sismode."

"Her mother expects her conversion to begin as soon as possible," Agent Crow growls, "so quit the rhetoric. Prep her for conversion, and tank her. Alert me the moment she's ready. I'm leaving the Black-Os to guard her. Don't let her out of your sight, or you'll regret it."

Agent Crow leaves, and the technician says nothing. My head lolls on his shoulder. He lifts me in his arms and, followed closely by Hawthorne and several other Black-Os, takes me to an examination room.

The technician lays me on an examination table beneath a bright-white spotlight. Beside it is a tall tank filled with briny fluid, like the ones I observed earlier. I drift in and out of awareness, trying not to succumb to the tranquilizer. The technician removes my cuffs. I feel him tug off my clothes and wrestle me into a wet suit. He inserts IVs into my arm. Using a powered sprayer, he coats my exposed skin with something.

Then he takes my hand and lifts it.

His thumb rubs over my palm.

He pauses and lifts my hand higher, inspecting it closely.

He rubs his thumb over the small star again.

"That's—" He leans over the table, his head blotting out most of the white light above. A halo remains, ringing his face with its aquamarine eyes, which bore into mine. "How did you get this star?"

I recognize the chiseled lines of his face, the way his dark eyebrows slash together. My pulse jumps as he lays a hand on my shoulder and shakes me.

"The star is unique to *my* family crest," he says. He holds it before my eyes. "Seven points—a seven-three prism, with three long points that form a *W*. And my brother's initials in relief—mirrored? What *is* this?"

My lips curl into a dopey smile. "Ransom . . . Winterstrom." I squeeze his hand. "Reykin is . . . looking . . . for you . . ."

Chapter 2
While Everything Burns

I feel a *pop* sensation inside my head—the world turns on.

I blink slowly. My head aches. I'm outside. It's cold. Night. Flickering light. My mind, sluggish and heavy, stumbles over sensory cues, attempting to make sense of my surroundings. A shiver slips through me. I inhale the acrid scent of embers and taste it on my tongue. Wood hisses and crackles. Thick black smoke hovers above gray stone walls like an enormous spider. It blots out the stars in the night sky.

Someone's home is on fire.

It's an older home—if the building material's any indication—but it's much more modern than the Sword Palace, where I grew up. It seems familiar, but I can't place why.

Think, Roselle.

My mind struggles in confusion, and my head throbs with pain. The beautiful architectural lines of the structure crumble. Windows shatter and melt in the intense heat of the inferno. My eyebrows draw together. The home is fast reducing to a soot-black shadow of its former self.

It shouldn't burn, I think, my mind racing. I gape at the destruction. *A beautiful estate like this should have protections against damage by fire, unless it has been purposefully torched . . .*

The flames dance. The night's still. No airships above. *Strange.* I realize I'm trembling and run my hands over the sleeves of the inky-black uniform I'm wearing. The material is luxurious and supple. My fingers touch my long hair. Soft brown tendrils of it slip over my shoulders and arms. I almost never wear my hair loose like this. It's usually in a ponytail or a bun. My nerves tingle. Fear creeps over me. I have no memory of how I came to be here or where here is or why I'm dressed like this.

I lift my left hand toward my aching forehead, but it stills halfway there. Startled, I examine the crown-shaped moniker on my hand. It swirls like a black hole, outlined by the flames from the burning building. My identification processor seems to suck the light into it. My muddled mind tries to make sense of it. I study the holographic emblem, wondering how and when my silver-sword moniker was replaced.

No, that's not right—my moniker was a firstborn's gold sword, not a secondborn's silver one. Gabriel's dead. My chest heaves and aches for the loss of my older brother. Soon, though, my sorrow turns to panic. *I'm firstborn now, aren't I? I should have a golden-sword moniker, shouldn't I?* One that tells the world I'm the heir to the Fate of Swords—the next in line to inherit the title of The Sword.

I've seen this kind of moniker before—during the massacre. Black-O. It's supposed to be O-shaped, but my diadem-shaped birthmark has distorted it. I swallow hard against the rising lump in my throat. The last thing I remember is the blinding-white laboratory lights above me in a sterile operating room. Ransom Winterstrom was looming over me, whispering about the star on my palm—*or did I dream that?*

Disoriented, I glance around. On the lawn surrounding the inferno, other figures stand, staring at the coruscating ashes, as if transfixed. They have similar uniforms—more costume than combat—although with lightweight plating over the chest, torso, and thighs. My black trousers are tight, molding to me like a second skin. The top is the same, with long sleeves.

I gape at the mob ringing the collapsing home. Two words come to mind: "death squad." The men, women, and in some cases mutant creatures—amalgamations of human, machine, and beasts—are so still that small, white curls of fog from their respiration are the only signs that they're alive. My own breathing grows labored. I've been in the Sword military for a while, trained in formations, but this is different. These rows of soldiers are mathematically precise.

The diversity of the creatures astounds me. Most are human-shaped, but some have a light dusting of fur, like woodland creatures. Others have metallic veneers, like gleaming chrome cyborgs, while others have translucent flesh, lit from within by some phosphorescent form of energy. The sterling glow of their mind-control devices suggests artificial intelligence capable of the grisly and cunning problem-solving capabilities that I witnessed during The Trials massacre.

I search the estate grounds over my shoulder. More precise rows of mind-altered warriors stand motionless as far as I can see. The devices implanted in their brains radiate light from their left eyes into the night. The luminosity of so many soldiers rivals the lambency of the moon. Full-blown fear, raw and blinding, envelops me.

Deliberately, I lift my jittery palm up near my left eye, holding my breath and hoping that my hand doesn't reflect a silver light. To my immense relief, no light from an implant in my brain shines on my hand. My knees grow weak.

Screams of outraged anger pierce the air. My head snaps in the direction of the feminine bleating. Two Black-Os drag a woman from behind the burning house. She struggles against them, in vain. The mind-controlled soldiers can no more stop what they're doing than she can. The men drag her nearer to me. My mouth falls open in surprise when I notice the skin of one of the soldiers. It's scaly, like a fish—no, that's not right. It's more like a dragon's scales—armor-like. The shifting light from the fire shimmers off it. From what I can tell, the rest of him is human. He has black hair, human features—except, of course, that one of his pupils illuminates with silver light, and his ears are a bit pointier than normal.

The woman's screams turn to fierce growls. She sees something ahead of her and drives her feet down, digging her heels into the lawn, leaving divots in the sod. The Black-Os simply lift her higher by her forearms and continue. She kicks them. Her hands ball into fists.

They come to rest only a few yards away from me. Other soldiers part, and I'm able to see what I'd missed earlier. An ornate throne has been placed in the center of the formal garden. It's made of gold—I've seen it somewhere before. Recognition dawns.

It's Grisholm's throne—from the observation deck of his training facility at the Halo Palace! My mind reels. *Is Grisholm here?*

My focus narrows on the slouching occupant of the throne. His profile shows high, chiseled cheekbones and sharp angles. His blond hair is slicked back, not a hair out of place. Dark, notched, tattooed lines—kill tallies—mar the skin of his face and neck. A small black disc with a flashing blue light protrudes from his temple.

It isn't Grisholm. No one, having met Agent Crow, could mistake this Census agent for the heir to The Virtue. And then I remember why it could never be Grisholm. The firstborn heir to the Fate of Virtues is dead. He was torn apart just yesterday at the Opening Ceremonies of the Secondborn Trials. *It was yesterday, wasn't it?* My mind falters, scouting for cues to evaluate how much time I've lost. *It's so cold here. Winter . . .* My fingertips have reddened from the chill.

In front of Agent Crow, the woman shakes away the hands of her captors, but only because their intent was to let her go. She straightens her winter cloak and readjusts the flat cap on her head. She lifts her chin in a show of bravado.

"You, Census agent," the woman shrieks in rage, "are a filthy coward!" She spits in his face before he has a chance to address her.

As if in a fog, I recognize Reykin Winterstrom's housekeeper. *Mags! It's Mags!* My attention darts away from her small frame to the burned-out shell of Reykin's home. I hadn't recognized it from the outside—I'd seen it only through a haze of pain and a brutal concussion. The once beautiful facade is now nothing more than an inferno. The elegant bedroom where Reykin nursed my wounds, after saving me from a raging mob of Gates of Dawn soldiers, is no more. A dull ache pierces my chest.

The malicious blond psychopath wears a mask of calm. His body still slouches in a negligent pose on his royal seat. Slowly, he extracts a white handkerchief from the pocket of his black uniform trousers and unfolds it. He wipes the sputum from his cheek before folding and tucking the fabric away. Cold blue eyes assess the woman in front of him.

"Where's Reykin Winterstrom, Stone?" he asks. A growing grin exposes his steely front teeth. I know that smile well. He's never more satisfied than when he has his prey cornered.

The brown mountain range of Mag's moniker gives off the dull glow of a Fate of Stones secondborn. "You'll never find Reykin!" she declares. She has the rich, lilting accent of a non-aristocratic Star instead of a secondborn Stone. It lacks the blandness of the Stars aristocracy. It's probably because, even though she's a Stone, she grew up here in Stars before her Transition Day. It's her home.

Agent Crow rises from the ostentatious chair to tower over Mags. "I find *everyone*."

"The resistance will bury you!" she sneers.

Agent Crow's eyebrows shoot upward. "Will it? I don't think so. It's much more likely that they'll all be made to turn on each other, one by one. They won't find you, though. There won't be much of you left to bury when we're finished here—maybe a few bones." He snakes his hand out to encircle Mags's delicate throat and lifts her from the ground. Her eyes bulge, and her fists pound against his forearms. I'm struck by his speed and strength. He has always been a fit man, but he was never this strong. Not many people are. He isn't even straining to hold up Mags's struggling body.

The palms of my hands run down my sides, searching for a weapon. My fusionblade is gone. I have nothing on me with which to fight him. Frustrated, I ball my hands into fists.

It doesn't matter. I can kill him without a weapon.

I shift to take a step toward Agent Crow. It's harder than it should be. My feet want to remain rooted to the lawn. I'm a statue coming to life. With supreme effort, I break the stillness and manage to inch forward. The next step is a bit easier. My momentum carries me. I near Agent Crow and break into a run. Lowering my shoulder, I lead with it, aiming for his knees and plowing into the psychopath with all the force I can muster. The impact of my tackle knocks him sideways. His grip on Mags breaks as he careens to the rocky garden path. I land on top of him. He wheezes from the unexpected contact. The blue light affixed to his left temple emits a series of flashes, illuminating the side of his face, turning his flesh aqua in waves—pale, blue, pale, blue, pale, blue.

I reach for a rock and curl my fingers around its rough surface. With all my might, I lift it and bring it down. The stone smashes against Agent Crow's head. Blood spatters outward from a jagged cut on his chiseled cheekbone. His groan turns into a growl of rage. The blow should've rendered him unconscious, but he's still very much awake.

My knees dig into his abdomen, holding him down. I clutch the rock tighter. The uneven surface of the stone abrades my fingers. I raise the rock over my head again before plunging it down, aiming for the blinking light on his temple, but Agent Crow's hand lashes out and latches on to my throat with alarming strength. Startled and unable to breathe, with my fingers weakened, I drop the stone. I'm ripped from my perch on the idiot's chest as he stands, lifting me with one arm.

My face must be turning blue. I meet his gaze. His pupils dilate, letting me know just how much he's enjoying hurting me. His hair is uncharacteristically tussled. I grow dizzy from lack of air, and my vision distorts. Just when I think I might pass out, the pressure on my throat eases. He opens his fingers, and I fall from his grip.

On the ground, my arms and legs sprawling, I'm unable to do anything other than cough, sputter, and gasp for breath. Smoke from Reykin's burning home stings my lungs. "Hold her, Cherno," Agent Crow barks. Bulky arms with the tough-textured skin of a dragon catch me and drag me to my feet. My back slumps against a soldier's chest. When I can, I struggle, my hands gliding over cool, jagged skin. Smoldering-brimstone breath warms my neck. The thing behind me squeezes tighter. I can't move more than a few inches, no matter how hard I kick or jerk. I groan in sheer frustration.

Agent Crow probes his cheek gingerly. Blood wets his black collar. He eyes me with a vicious snarl. "How are you awake, Roselle?" His jaw tenses, and he moves closer.

The implication of his question sends a chill through me. *Was I asleep?* I glance at the mob of unmoving, brain-altered soldiers. *Was I one of them?*

Blood trails down the Census agent's cheek and drips from his chin. The area around his wound swells like a budding horn, forming an angry red welt. "How is she awake?" he roars, spinning to glare behind him, addressing the sea of statuesque soldiers he finds there. No one answers. Their faces remain expressionless—inanimate. He latches on to one soldier by the front of her uniform and lifts her onto her toes. "Fetch Roselle's technician from my airship!" When he lets go of the trooper's collar, she doesn't move. Agent Crow gnashes his teeth. Reaching up, he touches the disc on his temple with two fingers, maneuvering it a millimeter or two, settling it back into place. The blue light flashes again, reflecting off of the ashes that fall on us like snow. The woman animates and bounds away from us through the crowd. Agent Crow turns and faces me.

"I'll kill you," I growl with another heave against my captor's arms—I'm hardly able to move at all.

A smug smile curls his lips. "How will you do that? I'm so much more powerful than you are—I've been enhanced."

"Enhanced?" I laugh, shaking soot from my hair. "The only thing that will improve your personality is a lobotomy."

"I'd hoped that we'd found a solution for your sharp tongue, Roselle—maybe the only cure is to cut it out."

"You already did that to my father."

"That was your mother's idea, but I did enjoy the result."

"You're next. I promise."

"Always so sure of yourself, aren't you? I've missed your wicked disobedience, Roselle." He fixes me with a sinister stare. "I find that surprising, seeing as how your mouth usually makes me want to smash all of your teeth in. Still"—his head cocks to the side—"I've missed your feral nature. No one resists me quite like you do, especially now, when I can make them do whatever I want—whenever I want. When you're in a state of compliance, an altered state, it's almost no fun hurting you." He leans near my ear and whispers, "Almost." The feel of his breath on my skin, along with his scent, makes me want to retch. He pulls away so he can see my face.

My stomach twists in knots. *What does he mean? Wasn't I just with him minutes ago in the Fate of Seas? How has he hurt me—and when?* "How could you miss me? You just gave me a tour of your asylum."

His bark of laughter makes my flesh crawl. "That was over a month ago, Roselle. But I'm told time is meaningless to Black-Os."

"I'm not your drone!" I can't help the harsh cadence of my speech. Fear suffocates me.

Shadows cast by the fire slither over his cheeks, hollowing them, but his lips curl with humor. "Ahh, but you are. You're a Black-O, but 'drone' works as well. You do everything I tell you to, Roselle."

I buck against the arms that imprison me, but on the inside I'm recoiling in horror. "Order me to do something!" I retort. "I promise you I won't obey!"

Blue light strobes on his temple in a serpentine silhouette. I shrink away, expecting to feel something—the burn of high voltage, a hostile takeover of my brain, the vicious bite of snake venom—but seconds pass and I feel no different. His face strains. A vein pops out on his forehead; his face flushes. With a huffing pant, his fingers move to the device receiving messages from his brain. He tries to readjust it. He glares at me again until his eyes narrow and darken further.

"Something's wrong with your device!" he bellows. "You're supposed to integrate when I command it." The blood, drying on his face, resembles an inkblot of a unicorn.

"Did you break your toy?" I ask, pushing out my bottom lip in a feigned pout. "You're always the reason why we can't have nice things, Kipson." I use his first name to rile him, but my heart's racing.

Has he made me one of his mind-controlled assassins?

"How is *she* resisting me? My implant should dominate hers." He's talking to himself.

What he's saying spooks me. If I could raise my arms high enough, I'd search my scalp for scars or any other indication that they've tampered with my brain. My distress gains Agent Crow's attention. His expression softens.

"Does that scare you?" he asks. "I've missed crushing your unfettered ego." His palm lifts to my hair. He entwines his fingers in the thick, brown mass of it. Clenching his hand, the spiteful psychopath jerks my head back so that my face tilts upward. "I like that you're awake. I can do whatever I want to you and you'll feel it. No one will stop me. You're going to take the pain I give you. Every time I awaken you, you'll know there will be no mercy. Ever."

In my need to avoid any contact with this monster, I jerk my face back from his, and my hair rips from my scalp. Movement over my shoulder captures his attention. His lip curls in anger. "The Stone is running off!" he barks. "Stop her!" His hand untwines from my hair and drops from me. The light on his temple blinks in rapid flashes.

Mags sprints across the lawn toward the burning house. Black-O soldiers chase after her. Some of the creatures drop to all four limbs and hurtle across the lawn like maginots. It's frightening, especially because they appear mostly human, save some chrome embellishments. The genetically modified soldiers close in on Mags. She reaches the stone walls of the house and leaps through a broken window. Flames engulf her. Her agonizing screams are the music she dances to before the heat melts her body. She crumples and disappears in the smoke.

I hold my breath, desperate to keep my emotions in check. My throat aches from having been strangled and from the effort to restrain my tears. Several Black-Os follow Mags inside the inferno—whether ordered to or not, I don't know—and like Mags they become part of the ferocious destruction. Mags killed herself to protect Reykin, and possibly everyone in the Gates of Dawn. I bite my lip to keep from sobbing.

A howl of frustration tears the air. Agent Crow seizes my jaw and squeezes it hard, forcing me to look at him. "Tell me where he is! Where's Reykin Winterstrom?"

I swallow back my tears of anguish and force a hollow laugh instead. "If you need to ask, then you don't know. If you don't know where he is, it's because you can't see inside my mind. That means I'm not, nor have I ever been, one of your Black-Os." He slaps my cheek hard enough to turn my face. My focus snaps back to him in defiance. He snarls and punches me this time. My skin burns. The inside of my cheek bashes against my teeth. Tasting blood, I manage to grin anyway. "What's wrong? Too much wicked disobedience?" I mutter.

Agent Crow grabs my upper arms, even as I'm still held back by the dragon-scaled Cherno. "Tell me who Winterstrom's allies are," he demands. "Who would he run to? Where would he hide?"

Trying not to wince, I simply stare back at him.

Someone clears his throat behind Agent Crow, but he keeps well back from us. The Census agent straightens and whirls on the man. The dark-haired newcomer wears a uniform similar to my own, except with an iridescent pin on his chest, in the shape of a slim rectangle through a triangle. His silver shooting-star moniker indicates that he's a second-born from the Fate of Stars.

"Come!" Agent Crow orders.

I sense reluctance in the other man's body language as he moves toward us. I study his face and swallow against the bile rising in my throat. I think for a moment that it's Reykin himself, but then he enters the light from the fire, and I know it isn't the firstborn Star, but his secondborn brother, Ransom.

A new burst of fear wends through me. My heart, aching from Mags's suicide, now thrums harder. I wonder if Agent Crow will make the connection between Ransom and Reykin—*or maybe he already knows?* Agent Crow's superpower is observation. He cannot possibly miss the resemblance between the brothers. It's so obvious—at least, it is to me.

Ransom appears to be thinking the same thing. The lines around his mouth tighten. He watches Crow straighten, and his Adam's apple bobs in a deep gulp. He bows his head in a show of respect to the menacing Census agent. "You wanted to see me, Your Grace?" Ransom asks.

"Your Grace?" I repeat with a snort. "Is that what you make them call you?" My reaction is as much a distraction to divert Agent Crow's attention from the newcomer's face as it is a jab at his arrogance.

Agent Crow tenses. "As you can see, Roselle St. Sismode has awakened from our control. I've told you before that her implant is an utter failure. I still cannot access all her memories or one single relevant image from her dreams!"

A knot coils in my belly when I realize that there truly *is* something installed in my brain, and Ransom Winterstrom put it there. The betrayal I feel at the hands of Reykin's brother is almost as bad as the heavy dread of knowing my body has been infiltrated. The only solace is that, for some reason, the technology malfunctioned. Agent Crow may be searching for Reykin Winterstrom, but it isn't because he found out anything from me. Maybe he's looking for Reykin because the firstborn

Star was part of Grisholm's advisory council? Or because Reykin managed to escape from the massacre at the Silver Halo? Whatever the case, I haven't betrayed him . . . yet.

"You can't pry your way into my memories," I gloat, interrupting Agent Crow's interrogation.

His mouth spreads in a grim line. "I don't need to access your mind, Roselle, to know what you've been up to. You're quite the little Fate traitor, aren't you? At least, that's what Hawthorne thinks of you."

A spasm of fear sharpens my voice. "Where's Hawthorne? Is he here?" I force back tears of rage.

"Hawthorne. Now there's an interesting story. You think you know him, don't you? I'd wager that you believe you're the only person that Hawthorne Trugrave dreams about. As it turns out, he doesn't dream of you at all. Do you know who fills his mind?" I can't answer. If I do, my voice may crack and betray me. "He dreams about Agnes Moon. You remember her, don't you? She was his lover before he met you—before I beat her to death for helping you escape me. Hawthorne obsesses over every shape she's ever taken." Agent Crow leans near my ear, whispering, "Every time he ever touched you, he thought of her, and it stopped him from wanting you. Are you sure he ever loved you?"

"I'm not surprised," I lie, swallowing past the lump in my throat. "Hawthorne cared about her. I promised him I'd help him kill you to avenge Agnes."

"Hawthorne will never have revenge. He'll die fighting *for* me."

"You should be worried. Your devices aren't infallible. Your control is slipping—it has already failed with me."

Agent Crow's look turns sour. The light on the side of his head flickers. Cherno's grip on me tightens. I wince, finding it hard to breathe. Agent Crow's attention whirls back to Ransom. "You promised me that her device would correct itself in time!"

Ransom doesn't flinch. "Typically, an implant requires weeks to adopt neuropathways in a subject's brain," he replies matter-of-factly.

"In some cases, it can take months to capture those connections. You've insisted on taking the subject from the lab too soon. She isn't ready for this type of operation yet. Her device hasn't had a chance to integrate fully."

"Nonsense! I've taken several subjects from the lab with far less recovery time, and I've never had a problem!"

Ransom doesn't waver or show weakness. "As I've said before, every mind is unique, and every subject responds differently to the device—"

"No one has ever awakened on their own before!" Agent Crow seethes.

Ransom's shoulders round a bit. "You're right. It's unusual."

"I know I'm right!"

"I'll take her back to the lab with me and run some tests."

Agent Crow's scowl deepens. "My first inclination is to turn my soldiers on you now, Star, and let them devour you." The threat hangs in the air for a moment. "If I didn't have assurances from other agents that you're the most gifted scientist and innovator in your field, you'd be dead right now. As it is, I'm giving you one last chance. I want full access to Roselle's mind. Anything less and you won't live to regret it."

Ransom grimaces and hunches his shoulders. "I'll make certain she's ready soon."

"Do," Agent Crow says. The crowd of transmuted soldiers remains unmoving, watching the flames. Agent Crow turns and walks away from Reykin's demolished home, through one of the precise rows of soldiers, toward a waiting Verringer in the distance. The luxury airship resembles the one Clarity Fabian Bowie owned. It wouldn't surprise me if it is one and the same.

Cherno's brutal grip eases. He turns me loose but remains close enough for me to feel his brimstone breath on my neck. All the Black-Os—the entire field of them—animate at once. My flesh crawls at the sound of the garbled ticks and pops of their speech, which is indiscernible as *language*, and yet, at the same time, a tingling in my spine somehow suggests what they're communicating. They're negotiating. I look toward the golden throne, and I *know* what they're haggling over. They're devising a means of returning the monstrous thing to the airship. Several nearby soldiers lift the heavy, gilded seat from the ground, and hoist it over their heads. It's then passed to the next soldiers down the line, who pass it on further, until it disappears.

Beside me, Ransom extracts a small disc from his pocket. It resembles Crow's mind-control apparatus. He touches it to his temple. The disc adheres to his skin like a magnet would to metal. It strobes with green light.

Cherno's expression changes from a blank, emotionless mask to one of confusion. He seems conflicted. His arms open, releasing me, and the towering soldier takes a step away. He pauses, then walks until he reaches the mossy bark of an oak tree. His back to us, he stops so close to the bark I'm sure his nose presses to it.

My gaze meets Ransom's. "You can control them?" I stutter.

"To a point," he replies. "You saw how he resisted me. It won't take long for his directives from Agent Crow to overtake mine again."

"If you can do that, how could you let them burn your home to the ground—kill Mags?" I ask with a harsh whisper.

He looks as if I slapped him. "Mags is dead?"

My eyes narrow. "She threw herself into the fire."

He swallows hard. "Like I said," he replies, his voice hoarse, "my control's limited. I didn't know what Agent Crow planned, and by the time I did, it was too late. You couldn't stop them either."

"At least I tried," I hiss.

"It was my home once." His eyes are baleful, but he doesn't look at the wreckage. "I grew up with Mags. Do you think if there were any possible way of stopping what happened, I wouldn't have taken it?" His expression reminds me so much of Reykin's.

"I don't know what to believe. Whose side are you on?"

"There are no sides, Roselle. There's just survival and revenge."

35

We've gained Cherno's attention. He has turned back to face us. The draconic demon takes a struggling step in my direction, fighting whatever control Ransom cast over him.

"We don't have time to talk now, Roselle," Ransom whispers, his eyes following Cherno's progress. The Star's attention turns back to me. The green light coming from the device on his temple flickers. Buzzing in my ears makes me dizzy. I sway—my brain vibrates. I hear myself speak involuntary words: "Am I yesterday?" His arm around my shoulders, Ransom braces me against his side. I want to resist him, but I feel so lethargic.

"You're the future, Roselle," he whispers in my ear, "and it's time for you to awaken."

I feel a *pop* sensation in my head—the world becomes as shiny as a star, and I'm falling from the sky.

Chapter 3
Altered

I open my eyes to dawning sunlight filtering into the bedroom.

The long, golden rays grow sharp like knives on the wooden floor beneath the windows. The linen sheets covering me are impossibly soft. My fingertips smooth over the fabric. I close my eyes again, and I lie on my side, savoring its silkiness. Smiling, I stretch my legs. The toes of one foot slip from the rumpled folds. My other foot shifts in the opposite direction until it meets the warmth of a hairy, masculine shin. I press my heel flat against his leg and curl my toes around the muscular calf. A quick gasp of air sounds from the pillow behind me. A large hand slides over my side to rest on my hip. Soft, rumbling laughter vibrates. He snuggles into me, his bare chest against my back—his lips press against my hair. Delicious warmth spreads through me. He inhales. His stubbly cheek shifts and brushes the sensitive skin of my neck. Desire for him kindles an inextinguishable fire.

"Your foot is freezing," Hawthorne complains in a whisper while he moves my hair to nuzzle the sensitive skin of my nape. I shift my exposed foot back beneath the sheets, letting it join the other in pressing against his fuzzy leg. His grip on me tightens. "Okay! I'm awake and at your mercy."

I giggle and turn over on the mattress to see him. For a moment, I'm caught off guard. Reykin! I stare at the face of the man who wants to change

*the world, and feel the kind of painful relief that comes only when you real-
ize someone you love is safe. Staggering disorientation quickly follows—a
mixture of hope and renewed fear—but why? I'm awash in loneliness and
misery; it's like the ache to go home. My mind drifts, slow to process.*

*Reaching out, I touch the dark stubble on his cheek and trace it to his
lips. He's a little over a handful of years older than me, but that doesn't
matter. Responsibility, and the fact that I'm secondborn, compels me to
feel older and more mature than most firstborns I know—except for him.
Reykin's different. Intense. He makes me feel as if I don't understand the
world like he does. Aquamarine eyes, with their predacious tilt, study my
face. His arm snakes around my waist to draw me even closer. Our bare legs
entwine. His hand takes mine. He kisses the backs of each of my fingers. I
lean my forehead against his.*

*"I need you to do something for me." His soft tone holds a note of
urgency.*

*"What do you need?" I ask, but a flicker of light distracts me. The rays
of golden sunlight in the bedroom shift, dancing. The windows sizzle—glass
pops and melts. Thick smoke creeps through the cracks in the broken panes,
darkening Reykin's bedroom. Ashes drift down and land like snowflakes on
our cheeks and hair. It stains the sheets. The elegant wooden wainscot that
encircles the room catches fire. Smoke chokes me. My throat grows raw.*

"Fire!" I gasp between coughs. I clutch him, tears wetting my cheeks.

*Reykin seems unconcerned with his burning bedroom. He reaches out
and cups my cheeks with both his hands, forcing me to look at him. "Lead
your army."*

*"What?" I gasp. The flames grow higher. I remember what happened—
the fire, his estate in the Fate of Stars burned to the ground. I stifle a sob.
"Mags is dead, Reykin!" Panic overwhelms me. I can't breathe!*

*Reykin hugs me to him and whispers in my ear, "Life is lost without
love."*

I blink. The bedroom is gone. I'm awake—alone. Shrouded darkness replaces the smoldering room—lit only by an eerie red glow of

filtered light. A cavernous airship's hold lies before me now. I'm suspended in an upright position by compressed air and some form of antigravity device, and I'm staring through the glass of a transparent, cylindrical capsule. My dark hair blows upward, tickling my face with occasional errant wisps. Unable to stifle my urge to cough, I bend forward, hacking as if I just emerged from a burning room. The small space traps the sound, but it's muffled by the force of air surrounding me. My hand presses against the wall of the glass cylinder, leaving a smudge of fingerprints on it.

Disoriented, I turn my head. Cold, stiff neck muscles protest with aching pain, and my brain feels on fire, as if it's still in the burning room. I wince. My fingertips go to my forehead and rub it gingerly. Through a haze of soreness, I peek to the left, then to the right. More capsules like the one I'm in smolder with rose-colored light. Inside each capsule, a soldier stands—unconscious—unmoving except for respiration and the upsweep of hair caused by compressed air. Metallic catwalks line rows and tiers of capsules that go on for as far as I can make out. The containers curve around a bend. The high steel walls of the airship form the perimeter of the immense hold.

I try to swallow, but my throat constricts around a tube inserted into my esophagus. The cold, tinny taste of it against my tongue is enough to make me retch. I grip the segmented hose and yank it urgently. I drool a slimy residue when it slides free. It triggers my gag reflex, and I retch uncontrollably, but nothing but mucus emerges. The gunk blows upward in the compressed air and spirits away through a vent in the ceiling of my glass pod. The tubing retracts and disappears behind me through holes in the iron spine of the capsule.

Tears run from my eyes while I take deep breaths. I wipe them away with the back of my hand. My palms move to my bare upper arms and clutch them to try to still my trembling body. Smaller tubes, intravenously attached to my left arm, ache dully at the insertion points. I straighten my arm, grasp the IVs with my right hand, and snatch the needles from my wrist as I grit my teeth. My wounds sting. The tubing retracts and disappears through holes into the spine of the capsule, just as the other had. Small droplets of my blood, blown by the compressed air that holds me aloft, crawl up my arm. I bend my elbow so they don't spatter everywhere.

Thin, black underwear with a matching bra covers my otherwise naked body. Its coarse fabric is nothing like the sheets on Reykin's bed. *Was I there? Was that real, or is this real?*

Beneath the underwear, there's one more tube—a catheter. I pull it free and let go of it. It retreats into the spine of the capsule as well.

Confusion gives way to panic. I'm shivering uncontrollably now—my teeth chattering—partly from cold and partly from the trauma of waking up here. I have no idea where I am. My hand against the glass, I feel for a seam in the surface. A holographic display comes to life and glows red. Scrolling through the options it offers, I select "Terminate Hibernation." The compressed air beneath me lessens, as does the anti-gravity in the capsule, and I lower. My bare feet settle against the chilly metal floor of the capsule. The glass reveals a door. It unlatches and opens with a sigh of air. The pressure change is instant. On wobbly legs, I climb from the capsule and latch the door back into place.

Outside the door, a dull hum of energy pulses through cables in the grated floor. The wires supply life support to the capsules. On my row, soldiers of all types dwell—the scaly one nearby has a flat face with full fish lips. Next to it is an unconscious warrior with a gray-and-black-furred dog head with a long muzzle. An elongated pink tongue hangs loose from its mouth and flaps in the breeze inside its capsule. Its feeding tube covers its black nose like a cap. The containers remind me of a collection of life-sized dolls waiting to be unpackaged.

Is Hawthorne here somewhere? I scan the containers near mine, but I don't find him. I'm compelled to run down the metal catwalk, screaming Hawthorne's name and banging on capsules until I find him, but I don't. I don't even know if Hawthorne's aboard this airship. I need a plan if I'm going to find him and free us without getting caught. *Where can we go if we succeed in escaping?* My throat aches, and I swallow back tears because I don't know if there's any place to hide from Census and Agent Crow. *Maybe we don't hide. Maybe we decimate Agent Crow and any other entity that tries to make us slaves.*

The din of running boots against the metal grate of the catwalk breaks the silence. I pause—my heart leaps into my throat. A quick search of my immediate surroundings leads me to the only area remotely feasible for cover. I climb to the tiny alcove between the capsules in my row and slink back into its shadow. My position doesn't afford much camouflage. I'm better off facing the threat head on, but I don't move. Footsteps draw nearer, and then they slow.

A soft beam of white light passes over the capsule I vacated, shining on a set of numbers made of frosted glass on the side of it. Someone swears. "Roselle," a familiar voice hisses low. Ransom ducks closer, shining a penlight around. Small droplets of perspiration slip from his dark hair near his temple and trail down his taut cheek. With the black leather sleeve of his uniform's long coat, he swipes at the moisture on his brow. He pants as if he's been running for a distance. Splashing the beam around, he acts as if he can't see me, but I know he must be able to, because I can see him. I'm standing almost right in front of him.

Ransom moves closer, then kicks and stubs his toe on the edge of the capsule. He swears again and points the small flashlight at the floor. "Roselle, it's me! It's Ransom." His tone is soft and urgent. He turns the penlight on himself and looks around in every direction. It gives him a sinister air. "I've been monitoring you, waiting to see if you'd wake up. I've turned off all the security monitoring systems in this area, so it's safe—no one will know." He pauses, like he's listening for me. "We need to talk! You need to listen to me—we don't have much time! Agent Crow is taking you to the Fate of Swords—to the Sword Palace!"

The mention of Agent Crow chills my already-frigid body, as does the knowledge that I'm going to be transported to my mother's home. I hesitate to come forward, though. I watch Ransom instead. He's standing right in front of me, his eye searching.

Is he blind? Is this a game? Indecision roots me in place. *Is Ransom friend or foe?* And then I remember. *He put something in my brain.* Anger grips me. *Foe. Definitely foe!*

"You're a dead man," I snarl at the laboratory technician, sounding like a feral badger, my throat sore and cracked. I take a step in his direction, intent on making good on my promise by any means necessary.

Ransom shines his flashlight at me. "Wait," he snarls back. "I'm on your side!"

"'There are no sides,' remember? 'There's only survival and revenge,'" I quote him. Enraged by my circumstances—the circumstances that *he* made possible—I lunge at him. Ransom doesn't even move to avoid me. My hand strikes out and grips his throat. I lift him off his feet with one arm, as if he's a vase I'm placing on a high shelf. His cheeks turning red, his eyes watering, he clutches my forearm.

My stomach spasms with dread at my raw strength. It's incomprehensible. It terrifies me. I let go of the secondborn Star. He drops to the grated metal walkway, gasping and sputtering to catch his breath.

"What's happening to me?" I ask, flexing my fingers.

He wheezes and coughs. "You're upgrading."

"You made me a Black-O!" I hiss, looking down at him. "You implanted a device in my head. You made me Census's slave!"

"No, I didn't!"

"Don't lie to me!"

"I'm not lying. I mean, I did implant a device in your brain," he concedes with a guilty look, "but it isn't the same kind as Black-O soldiers would get—or the temporal master devices that Census agents use to control them. It's completely diff—"

I snatch a fistful of his hair and drag him up to his feet. He leaves his flashlight on the ground. I seethe, still holding his hair so that he's bent sideways with his neck wrenched. "You *violated* me!"

"I had no choice." He winces in pain. "If I didn't operate on you, they would've killed me and gotten someone else to do it! Another lab tech would've implanted a standard VPMD into you, and then you'd be mind-controlled, unable to resist them, just like everyone else."

"That's what I am now!"

"Not for long. I gave you a weapon! You just used it. You're awake, and your strength—it's unbelievable. Cyborgs are strong because they've been torn apart and rebuilt to make them that way. You—something's happening to you."

"*What's* happening to me?"

"It's biotechnology. I not only enhanced your adrenal glands to improve strength, but I improved your heart, lungs, and other organs so they can withstand it without frying out." He removes a thin disc from his black uniform pocket. He touches the device to his temple, and a green light on it winks.

Let go of me, Roselle, Ransom's voice booms in my mind.

My fist, entwined in his hair, opens on what seems like its own volition, letting go of him. I hold my hijacked wrist with my other hand and take a few steps back. Flexing my fingers, I find it has returned to normal—mine to control once more.

"You can control me with a thought." My disgust for what he's done to me leaves me feeling sick. "I'm your puppet!"

Ransom straightens. "I can control you only until you stop me. You're growing stronger by the day—strong enough to wake yourself up." He doesn't sound upset about it. On the contrary, his words hold a note of pride in them. Still holding my errant wrist, I take another step back from him. He's not looking at me. He's looking in the direction of the space I'd occupied a few moments ago. It dawns on me why.

"You can't see me, can you? Am I invisible or something?"

His face turns toward the sound of my voice. He lets out a small sigh before his lips form a grudging smile. It's gone in seconds, but my heart pumps harder because Reykin has the same smile. "No, you're not invisible. It's pitch black in here. I can't see you because my eyes aren't special, like yours. Your vision has been enhanced. I can't see anything without my flashlight, but you can see in the dark." He points to the dim light of his flashlight on the catwalk.

"Don't you have an implant, too?"

"I do, but mine's different—temporal like the Census agents', but unlike theirs, which are almost omnipotent, a lab-tech implant only gives me limited control over most implants and never any control over Census agents. Rumors are swirling that we'll have even less control soon—the artificial intelligence within Spectrum is evolving . . ." He trails off as a worried crease between his eyebrows deepens.

I hold my palm up near my left eye. Nothing shines on it. "Why don't I have the silver shine?"

"You were programmed for hibernation with the rest of your Black-O squadron. You're not *active* right now, so your eye wouldn't have a silver shine, but you can't go by that anyway. The Black-Os' silver glow can be turned off remotely so that the soldiers avoid detection. Census usually only turns the silver light of a Black-O's eye on when they want their soldiers to terrify their victims." My mind reels. I barely hear him add, "But your implanted device's silver light is a simulation anyway—nothing more. Your moniker is different as well. It can be changed to reflect anything we wish. It can project a Black-O hologram, or a silver sword a moment later—or any of the symbols from any of the Fates, in any birth order."

"I'm—" My voice is weak. I swallow hard before continuing in a stronger tone, "So I *am* one of them—a Black-O?"

"Yes," he replies with a worried look, "and no. At least, you were part of the collective consciousness we call Spectrum up until a few moments ago. It's an augmented reality controlled by Census through AI technology—but that's just the surface of what it is. It tailors programs specifically for everyone within its web so that you never even know your reality has been altered. Then it uses your mind and your body at will. No one, once unified, has ever escaped from it . . . until you."

"What about you?" I ask.

"I'm not part of Spectrum . . . yet. It won't be long, though. I'm becoming obsolete. It's only a matter of time before they kill me."

"Kill you? Why wouldn't they integrate you, too?"

"It's not efficient. They'd have to change my technician's implant— swap it out. The procedure would probably kill me anyway, and why would they go through the trouble when they believe their programs to be cleverer than I am already? I may have a way into their world, though. It's a huge risk—a last resort."

My strongest impulse is to leap onto the railing overlooking the dark chasm of the cargo hold and hurl myself over its edge. The fall would kill me. It would be a quick death. I'm a monster now. I should kill myself, like Balmora did, before they use me as their weapon, but I need answers before I do anything, so I ask in a shrill tone, "How long have I been asleep?"

Ransom cringes, holding his palms out and pressing them toward the floor. "Shh, keep your voice down!" He turns his head and peers over his hunched shoulder, as if searching for enemies. He faces me again. "Do you want to alert Census agents to the fact that you're awake? I've already had to creep into Spectrum's system beyond my security clearance and hide the alarms going off when you deactivated your pod. And after that, I had to deal with this ship's monitoring systems. Don't blow this opportunity we have to talk."

"How long?" I ask again, quieter.

"It's been a little over a month since the night we were at my family estate."

"A month!" *I've lost another month of my life! Gone, in a blink of an eye.* My stomach twists in knots because even as I search my mind, I have no memory of anything that happened in that time. "What have I been doing for an entire month since the fire?"

"Now isn't the time to talk about that."

"Why not?"

He sighs. "You don't want to know what's been happening. I prom-ise I'll tell you later, but for now just trust me that you're better off not knowing."

"Did you just ask me to trust you?" I scoff and jab my index finger near my forehead, even though I know he can't see me. "You shoved a machine in my head without my permission. You granted them access to my mind—to me."

"Yeah, I did, and it's going to save our lives! You don't know how amazing the technology is that I gave you!" he says with a note of sat-isfaction. "You're not broken, Roselle. You're exactly how I made you."

My hand reaches out to the railing beside me. I grip the cold, metal bar to steady myself because my knees feel weak. I glance over the edge of the catwalk. Capsules filled with soldiers go on and on as far as I can see—and I can see farther than I ever could before. "Exactly *how* did you make me?"

Weary, he sighs and runs his hand through his thick, close-cropped hair. It's the color of midnight in this light. "That question requires a long, complicated explanation."

He turns, retrieves his flashlight, and sets the light on the ground between us with the beam pointing up so he can see me. He's not much older than me, but he's much taller. My lower lip trembles from cold. He swears and shrugs off his black leather coat. The garment screams "Census agent," except it's styled a little bit differently. It has a subtle lab-coat look rather than a hunter-killer one.

"Here." He holds the material out to me. Bitter about what it repre-sents, I eye it with suspicion and make no move to take it. "It's warm." He draws it nearer to me and, when I don't back away, drapes it over my shoulders. The residual warmth from him comforts me, but I'm disap-pointed that the leather doesn't carry with it the scent of lemongrass—like Reykin's clothing does, or like it had when I first met Ransom in the laboratory. The coat has a piney scent, which is probably from the soap provided for him by his overlords. It's pleasant enough but not as nice as the other Winterstrom's lemongrass.

I'm pulled from my musing by Ransom's next words. "I don't know where to begin to explain things to you, Roselle. I think I need to gain your trust. I need to tell you what happened to me after my Transition Day, and why I've done what I've done to you—so you understand I did what I thought I had to do."

"I'm listening," I reply, but inside I'm trying to decide if the fall from this height would smash my head in enough to leave no chance of being resurrected.

Ransom shoves his hands in his pockets. "How much do you know about my family?"

"A lot."

"Then you *do* know Reykin well?" He eyes me under his lashes with a hopeful air.

I shrug, noncommittal. Tears sting my eyes. I force them back, trying not to think of how Reykin and I parted. He had told me that he loved me. He thought he was going to die at the time, so it sounded more like a confession than a profession, but still, I hadn't known that he'd felt that way until it was too late. I don't even know if he survived the assault at the Opening Ceremonies. Agent Crow seems to think he did, though, which eases the ache in my chest just a little.

Ransom looks at his feet. "Well, if you know Reykin, then you know that he can be a pain in the ass most of the time."

I blink, forcing back more tears. "He *is* an ass," I agree, "but when it really counts—when all hope is gone—he finds a way to come through for you."

"Yeah, you know him all right. From my earliest memory, he was always pushing me to work harder. When we were just little kids learning how to duel with fusionblades, he'd beat me mercilessly, never giving me an inch, never easing up on me. I could barely hold a sword, and he would pester me, show me how to grip the hilt better, demonstrate defensive maneuvers, perfect my form. The same was true about coding and systems architecture. He goaded me to try harder. I figured it was because he thought he was better than me, because he was firstborn. But then, a few days before my Transition Day, I heard Reykin and my father arguing. Reykin was pleading with my father to stage an accident—to fake my death. He insisted my father contact the underground resistance and procure me a new identity as a firstborn."

"What did your father say?"

"Rasputin Winterstrom is a smart man. Have you met him?" Ransom asks, his eyebrows rising. I shake my head, realizing that he doesn't know his father is dead. Ransom goes on. "He said it wouldn't work. It would look too suspicious—me supposedly dying before my Transition would only serve to bring Census to our door. He told my brother that they had to let me go—that I was the price they had to pay to keep my other brothers safe."

"Reykin didn't take that well."

"No, he didn't," Ransom replies with a half smile like his brother's. "He told me he'd always be looking for me, and when he found me, he'd free me. He said, in the meantime, I needed to learn everything I possibly could, wherever I was placed, to bring down the Fates Republic, only . . ." He hesitates and looks around at the containment units. "I wasn't assigned to anything resembling the Fates."

"Have you always been on the island in the Fate of Seas?"

"Yes, I've always been isolated. Being your personal technician is the only reason I'm able to leave it. When I first arrived, I didn't think I would survive. We were tested, you know, for aptitude and moral ambiguity—a lot of us didn't survive the first few weeks."

"Why not?"

Something that looks like shame twists his lips. "They made us do things, experiments that caused pain to our subjects—intense pain, sometimes death." His voice wavers under the strain of saying the words. "If you couldn't do it, they took you out and killed you in front of everyone."

I thought my Transition with Agent Crow was harrowing. It was nothing compared to Ransom's. "Hopeless," I whisper. Enduring pain isn't much of a choice. You either do or you don't—embrace the suck or die. Inflicting pain is a choice. It comes with a certain amount of acceptance, and the decision, once made, has consequences.

"That's why he doesn't know who I am," Ransom admits.

I lift my eyebrow.

"Agent Crow—he doesn't know that I'm Reykin's brother, or even a Winterstrom. As soon as I could break into Spectrum, I killed Ransom Winterstrom and took on the identity of one of the other Star secondborns who didn't make it. Everyone thinks I'm Calvin Star. If anyone views my fake profile, they'll find my image attached to the Ekko family line."

"Why did you do that?" I ask. "Reykin might never be able to find you."

"You think I want my brother to find me after the things I've done?" His voice is taut. His hand goes to his nape, and he grips it. "I mean I want it more than I want anything in the world, and at the same time it's my worst nightmare. The shame and dishonor of the things I've done will never go away." His other hand clutches his nape as well. His chin tilts upward, and he winces. With a snarl, he drops his hands to his sides. "The only thing I want now is to annihilate Census. I made you to change an existing reality, Roselle. Census is the new world order. They're in control of almost everything now. They have the most powerful army the world has ever seen. *That's* reality. They can engineer humanoid beings, and they can control them. They couldn't be stopped, because their army couldn't be stopped—until now."

"You've come up with a way of making them obsolete?"

His brow furrows with uncertainty. "Maybe. I've thought about it from every angle. To make their army obsolete, I had to engineer an even better soldier, so I built a prototype device unlike any that had come before it. It's biotech that I created in secret. It's not like theirs. I made only one. I wanted to use it on myself, but it's been impossible to execute a plan to insert the RW1 Device into my own brain. For that, I'd need help, but here"—he lifts his hands and gestures to our surroundings—"I can't trust anyone. Anyway, I already have a technician's implant. The RW1 device and my technician's implant probably wouldn't have integrated with each other in the optimum way necessary to combat a Census master-level device."

"Can you upgrade your device to a master-level one?" I ask.

"Again, in theory, but there's a huge risk of something going wrong. And how would I hide it if I did? The moment Census discovered it, I'd be dead. No, I had to find someone I could trust—someone who's strong enough to take on an entire legion of Census's madmen. Then you arrived with that scar on your hand, and I thought"—he scrubs his face with his hands—"I don't know what I was thinking." He drops his hands to his sides. "Maybe I wasn't thinking, but everything I've ever seen you do is noble—maybe even chivalrous. I'm desperate to stop them, and I saw your scar as a sign."

"A sign of what?"

"A sign that maybe you're the one who's supposed to bring down Census."

"Me? Just me?" I ask with a dark scowl.

"Theoretically, you're all we need. If I can hide you long enough—"

"Have you *seen* what they're doing? Do you *know* about the population they've infected with their technology?"

"I've been forced to *help* them do it since my Transition Day. Do *you* know what that's like—to be forced to do horrific things that make you a monster in everyone's eyes, especially your own?" His sorrow and rage are enough to silence me.

I think of the death-drone beacon I attached to Reykin on the battlefield in Stars. *If he hadn't spoken to me, would I have let him die?* I can't say. I hope not, but I can't be sure.

"What if I asked you to take the prototype out of me?" I probe.

He shakes his head. "I can't—even if you beg me to." His frown deepens. "If I tried to extract a standard VPMD, the subject would most likely suffer complications. We did that for an attack on the Fate of Virtues. Most of the soldiers we took it out of died before we were even halfway through the procedure. They'd stroke out—shaking and twitching on the table. Those that made it, they didn't have a long shelf life—a few days, just enough time to complete a mission, and then their brains crumbled."

I wonder if he's alluding to the Rose Goddess Massacre, but Agent Crow had said those assassins had been non-converted zeroborns, so I don't interrupt him.

"Your implant is different, Roselle, and possibly far worse in that regard. In theory, it's even more powerful than the master-level devices integrated in Census agents. The ones they use sync with Spectrum to take over internal systems of a drone subject, suppress their sense of agency, and lock them down so the collective consciousness can gain control. Master-level devices issue directives to Spectrum or sometimes to these subordinate devices. The orders act like the subject's own impulses, or, if given to Spectrum, they can rely on the collective AI to find the best way to accomplish a goal they've set forth."

"So it's true—soldiers never know they're being controlled."

"The AI programs are so advanced that subjects who are being controlled don't even know they're not operating in the real world most of the time—and when they are in the real world, they sometimes don't know that either. The one you have acts like a living organism that couples with your tissue and expands your mind. With time, it will grow and form billions of unique neuropathways, not only in your cerebral cortex, but much deeper to areas that have never been infiltrated. There's no telling what you'll be able to do. I have theories, but—"

While listening to him talk about his theories, I develop one of my own. *How can one person defeat an army made up of monsters that don't possess a shred of empathy—defeat an army that's operated by Census and a unique intelligence that expands its knowledge base?* "I'd need to have dominion over the master-level devices. If my prototype could control Agent Crow's device and the like, then I'd control the army."

"That's the idea. You'd be their Virtue—their overlord—but in a way that Fabian Bowie never was. You'd be more like a goddess."

I laugh with a strange-sounding derision. "Yes, of course! A goddess—why not?" I want to cave my own head in. No one should have that much power, least of all me. "There's just one problem, Ransom."

"What?"

"It doesn't work."

"What doesn't work?"

"Whatever you put into my brain—it doesn't work like that." I growl with a mixture of relief and frustration. "I'm trying to make you slap yourself, but your cheek isn't red."

"You expect to be able to employ the weapon in your mind with no practice? Were you able to defeat Dune in a duel the first time you tried to use the fusionblade?"

My eyes narrow. "I've never mentioned Dune to you—you've been creeping around in my memories, haven't you?" I was probably around three years old when I wielded a fusionblade for the first time.

"I've watched you grow up—same as everyone else," he replies defensively.

"So you haven't been poking around in my brain?"

His expression turns sheepish. "I had to, but it's not what you think. I was trying to keep Agent Crow out. In the beginning, your memories were easy to access, like the ones you have of your early years with Dune. Others, from your Transition Day onward, are murky.

Those of my brother you guard ferociously, but still I could've remote-viewed them, and I didn't." He says the last part quickly, trying to reassure me. I must appear mortified, because I am.

"What's remote-reviewing?" I ask.

"I can attach a probe to your cerebral cortex through an incision behind your ear and access your memories by what we call memory mapping. Whenever I found ones containing my brother, I used a neurochemical to insulate and inhibit them from being accessed remotely. The inhibitors wear off, though, so I had to try to keep one step ahead of Agent Crow."

"Why didn't you remote-view my memories of Reykin?"

He sighs. "Because I wanted to know too badly, and stealing that information from you makes me one of them—and I'm *not* one of them!" His eyes narrow. "Instead I've been helping you keep your secrets by throwing up blocks against Agent Crow for the past month, diverting him to other memories. He mostly focuses on the ones with Hawthorne Trugrave and Clifton Salloway because he cannot locate the ones with Reykin, but it's been difficult to outmaneuver him, and I'm in constant fear that he'll suspect something's still wrong and give you to another technician for evaluation. If he does that, we won't survive it. They'll discover the differences in your implant, and they'll have no other choice but to destroy you."

"What does Crow know about my relationships with Hawthorne and Clifton?"

"Everything." Ransom's mouth curves in a dismal frown.

"I have to warn them." I rub my temples, hoping to jar my memory, but there's nothing. "What have I been doing for the past month?"

He reaches out and touches my arm in a placating way, like he's done it a thousand times—and maybe he has. I've been his experiment for weeks. His expression is sympathetic, though. "You've done what you've been ordered to do. You were too weak to resist. No one can blame you . . ."

Alarm rages inside me. "Ransom . . . have I—have I hurt people?"

His palm cups my elbow. "It's not your fault that Agent Crow used you." His expression beseeches me. "You couldn't stop him. You were like an infant. You just needed time—and still do. You have to look at the long game."

I yank my arm away. "Who have I hurt?"

He shakes his head. "It doesn't matter. Nothing matters but the endgame."

I can't catch my breath. Violent tremors weaken my knees. Light-headedness accompanies the cold rush of fear, but unlike every other time this has happened to me, I don't completely lose it. Something inside me is different. After the wave of crippling anxiety washes over me, a second, calming wave comes close behind it—like my brain's awash with dopamine.

Ransom reaches for me again. I shrug off his hand and turn to grip the metal railing with both of mine to steady myself. The steel bar dents from the pressure of my fingers. I swing up onto the metal ledge and poise on its edge. My leg muscles twitch. I look down.

The fall should kill me beyond repair.

I feel relief. I teeter on the edge, leaning forward just enough to maintain my balance.

"Don't do it!" Ransom begs.

I glance at him. "I don't know what I've done, or who I've slaughtered for them, but if you won't tell me, then it's probably pretty bad." I clutch my chest above my heart. The ache is something I can't ease. I feel dirty, used. I need this to end.

"Wait!" Ransom pleads. "You've awakened, Roselle! You're not theirs anymore! Now we make a plan that eradicates Census from existence. I can't do it alone. I need you! I need your help!"

I hesitate. Something in his voice stops me from taking the final step. It had the same note of desperation mine had when Balmora walked off the wall of her Sea Fortress and plummeted to her death. I think for a moment about what she did then, and what I'm prepared to do here. She thought she had nothing left to live for anymore. That's not why I'd do this. Unlike Balmora's, my death would prevent Census from using me as a weapon, but I do have something to live for—I have vengeance. The need for revenge burns me to my very marrow. Agent Crow doesn't get to exploit me and go free—he doesn't get to win.

The decision to remain—to fight—is more complicated than just revenge. I carry a desperate ache to see Reykin again, to play out the dream I had of being in his arms. He represents home to me. *When did he become so vital?* I can't imagine being happy without him. He's the real reason I'll stay.

"Ransom," I say, not looking at him. "If your theory doesn't work out and I'm their assassin, I need you to find a way to make sure I never hurt anyone again."

"I will," he replies without a second of hesitation.

"And if we do this, we never stop until every Census agent is dead and Spectrum's destroyed."

"I promise."

I look up from the levels below me and meet his eyes. "Then let's begin."

Chapter 4
Containment

Violent judders rattle through the airship's hold.

Sounds of thunder echo. None of the soldiers inside the capsules near us awaken. Moments before, I'd climbed off the catwalk railing overlooking the hold. If I hadn't, I might have fallen to my death. My eyes dart to Ransom's. He clutches the railing with his long fingers. He swallows hard.

"Where are we now?" I ask. "In what Fate?"

Ransom consults his moniker, anxiety etching lines around his clean-shaven mouth. "We just crossed over into the Fate of Swords. We're passing above the Brontide Ridge."

"We'll be in Forge in two hours—maybe less, depending on our airspeed."

He tries to disguise a shudder.

"Are you okay?" I ask.

An uncertain frown deepens the creases around his mouth. "No— not really. First off, you nearly jumped. Everything I've been working for would've gone with you. Second, the airship just shook like it's going to fall out of the sky. Third, they'll be mobilizing all the Black-Os shortly. I'm not even sure you can pass for one now. Fourth, I'm in

Swords—a place I've never been. I know the Census Base in Seas. I know parts of the Fate of Stars. I don't know this place. And fifth, there's also that little nagging fear I have that Agent Crow will recognize me as Reykin's brother at any moment." Sweat drips from the hairline by his temple. I can relate—fear has been my life lately.

"We won't crash," I explain, attempting to calm Ransom. "I've been on worse flights. Cold wind slams hard against a large airship like this one, but it isn't enough to cause a significant drop in altitude. It'll be okay. It was probably just a wicked west wind off the mountains." Then I lean closer, like I'm telling him a secret. "As the story goes, Tyburn, the Warrior-God of the West Wind, froze the sea when Hyperion, the God of Water, raised it against him, forming the Brontide Mountains. The peaks resemble cresting waves. That noise you heard—the one that sounded like distant thunder—was tectonic plates beneath the mountains shifting. That's what makes the rumble."

"You don't believe that demigods formed those mountains, do you?"

I shrug. "I don't know. I wasn't there—and neither were you. It's just a bunch of oral history handed down for what seems like forever."

He frowns again and pushes his hand through his hair. "Okay, we'll arrive at the Sword Palace soon. When we do, they're going to give orders to the Black-Os through Spectrum. All the capsules will open."

"What will they order?" I ask.

"I don't know. Nothing has been explained, and no directives have been logged, so I'm in the dark." He looks around and adds, "Literally."

"The soldiers will be in an altered state, right? Technically, they're all 'asleep'—mind-controlled or whatever." My hand lifts, indicating the capsules near me. "I'll be expected to be the same—to follow whatever orders I'm given. How am I supposed to pretend that I'm asleep?" A part of me is numb. Another part knows this is the worst plan ever because it's not even a plan—just a set of impossible circumstances piled on top of impossible circumstances.

"You'll have to pretend to be integrated, Roselle. They need to believe you're an active Black-O."

I raise my hands, palms up. "Yeah, but how?"

"I made something for you—for the moment you woke up. It's an enhancement. Your implant should adopt it. I created a program based on the master-level-unit protocols. I used something like it for gathering intel, but mine isn't advanced biotech like this." He smiles like he made a joke and leans nearer to my jacket pocket. "May I?"

"Yes."

Ransom reaches in, fumbles around, and extracts a tiny black case. The case is security locked. It opens when he holds it to his eye and it scans his retina. Using the flashlight, he finds and selects a small glass ampoule of gin-clear liquid. "Drink this, but let the liquid settle under your tongue for a few moments before you swallow."

I hold the ampoule up in front of my eyes. "What is it?"

"Most of it is water, but inside is a tiny bit of your DNA and neuro-enhancers. Did you know that a single gram of DNA can store hundreds of petabytes that will last for hundreds of thousands of years? I stored your upgrade in it. It will be absorbed by the—"

As Ransom explains, I open the ampoule and allow the water and DNA to slip into my mouth. I hold it under my tongue while he maps out how this all works.

"You can swallow now," he instructs, allowing me to clear my mouth.

"How long will it take?"

"I don't know. A few hours? A few days? I've never tested it."

Panic has me pacing along the grated catwalk. I study the stasis pods closest to mine. My jaw tightens when I recognize the dragon-man a few units down from me. I pause in front of him. His chest is bare. He seems unbreakable—genetically enhanced.

"Cherno," Ransom whispers near my ear, and then he shivers. "He's going to be a problem."

"Why?"

"Agent Crow has made him a permanent part of your protocol. Wherever you go, he goes. His orders are to shadow you—and under no circumstances is he to let you escape alive."

"Who is he?" My attention roams over the brutal figure who almost doesn't fit in the capsule. He looks as if he could chew rusty swords with his teeth. "Where did he come from?"

"He's partly from a museum in the Fate of Stones. Crow extracted DNA from a dragon egg few people believed was real."

"You're kidding," I reply, glancing over my shoulder at Ransom. "I'm not."

"What's he like?" I analyze the impossibly strong creature. His shoulder-length dark hair dances in the compressed air of his capsule. Thick, bristly eyebrows, the same hue as his hair, contrast the scales of his flesh. His skin expresses as more human without the shimmer of the fire to turn it golden in places, and in this non-light, it has the appearance of an intricate tattoo.

"I don't know. He's a drone. I've never spoken to him unfettered from the Spectrum. He was never part of my division."

"We could use some allies. Do you know which one of these capsules is Hawthorne's?"

Ransom's Spectrum apparatus, attached to his temple, blinks with erratic flashes. "He's not racked."

"Racked?"

"He isn't in a capsule," Ransom explains. "He's part of a security detail on the main deck protecting Agent Crow."

Rage flares in me. "Why does he keep Hawthorne so close?"

"I don't know. Why does he do half the things he does?" Ransom grumbles. "You'll drive yourself insane trying to figure out reasons behind the things Census agents do. Most of the time, they act on some maniacal impulse to spread terror around like it's a virus and infect the world with their particular brand of fear."

I'm about to agree when something in my mind triggers. A burst of energy surges through me, akin to the explosion of a fusionmag pulse, but without the pain of being shot. Everything shimmers with golden light. My eyes wander, literally *seeing* energy glimmer in a heady brilliance of liquid gold along the channels that provide power to the capsules. Large concentrations of charged atoms dance in the air and cover everything like a thin layer of sparkling diamond dust. Walls and images form from the golden pixie grime. They're shapes and outlines of invisible worlds that project from the soldiers nearest me. Maybe these are the memories that agents can remote-view or the AI constructs that keep soldiers passive?

Golden, frost-like energy covers Cherno. The impression of dragon wings sprawl and twitch from his back—phantom wings. I peer at him closer and can "see" inside his mind. Or it projects from him—I don't know. Visions of flying over rugged crags and whitecapped ocean waves push their way into my mind. The images are cut short by whispering voices—soft at first, stringing together patterns that are more like thoughts. They're familiar, like déjà vu, maybe because I have been here before. I've been in this world for over a month without knowing it—maybe this is somehow a part of that?

Voices surround me. Quiet at first—just mumbling. They're coming from all angles, from the sleeping soldiers in the airship's cargo hold. They grow louder and louder, attempting to pull me into the sound. Some of them are wailing, screaming out for help, but those soon fade to the background while other, much more aggressive voices attack—latch on to me—attempt to siphon information from the chemicals swirling within my cerebral cortex.

I groan, holding my head in my hands and bending at my waist. I'm dizzy from it. I reach out and catch myself with my palm against the glass of Cherno's capsule. "What did you do to me?" I writhe for a few breaths, listening to the wretched wailing, before something within my mind roars to life and defends itself against the frequency of the waves bludgeoning me. The assault rages, and I fight to handle the onslaught of the chorus. Something's trying to take control of me—of my thoughts.

It's a few more moments before I can discern Ransom's voice among the snarling growls raging in my head. "What is it? What are you experiencing?" he asks with clinical detachment, a question that reeks of self-preservation. He touches my elbow and holds it.

I wince as I whisper, "I-I'm being bombarded by—thoughts? Shrieking, painful pleas for mercy—darker images." The assault rages. My eyes narrow to slits, and for a moment I think I meet Cherno's fiery gaze through the glass, but when I open my eyes wider, his are closed.

"That's Spectrum—the collective part of the AI. They want you back in with the horde—to use your knowledge and your reasoning to further their goals. The upgrade I gave you is something I'm hoping will help you connect with them but allow you to rise above the collective and give you power over them, or at least help you maintain autonomy within its program, because we need you to be able to slip in and out of Spectrum at will. Here, let me take you to your capsule." He places his hand on my hip and guides me. We walk together, my knees wobbling. "I couldn't give you master-level protocols within Spectrum, like the ones Agent Crow has. They'd know it if I did. I hope you'll be able to master Spectrum on your own. I just gave you a little back door into it."

"We need to destroy this thing," I whisper. Shrill cries from the tortured minds inside the collective conscience have me cringing.

"Impossible," Ransom grumbles. "If it were in one place, it would be doable, but it isn't. The program houses pieces of itself everywhere, in just about everything where it has a connection. Sure, you could torch the Base on the Fate of Seas where it originated, but it's no longer just there. It resides in everyone who has ever had an implant. It hides itself in machines that don't even have AI."

"Then we make a virus and we annihilate it that way."

"Yeah, I've thought of that. I just can't figure out how to kill it without killing everyone. Mass murder isn't my thing, contrary to what's said about me. And it's not just going to lie down and take it. It has defensive systems that I've only narrowly avoided for the past few months. Our time is running out. It's going to find the trail of what I've been doing sooner or later." He looks me up and down. "Anyway, you're in no shape to plan an attack on Spectrum. Let's take it one step at a time. We focus on surviving the next few hours." Ransom opens the containment unit's door and helps me inside it, then sets aside his coat outside the capsule. With deft fingers, he reattaches me to the capsule, inserting tubes into me like it's second nature. "I'm going to turn this back on. It'll make you stronger. We can make a plan later."

I gasp as he reaches for the feeding tube. "Wait, what am I supposed to do when we get to the Sword Palace?"

"Improvise. Pretend if you have to. Anything so we don't get caught."

"But—"

Ransom reaches to the ceiling of the capsule and pulls down the metal feeding tube. He puts the device near my mouth. It animates and latches on to me with steely pinchers, prying open my jaws. An inner hose snakes out and spirals down my esophagus into my stomach. Tears stream from my eyes as I choke. Straightening, Ransom backs away and closes the unit's glass door. The compressed air and antigravity device lift my body into stasis. If I thought I was in control in this relationship, I was mistaken. I control nothing that happens to me until I learn how to fight them.

On the other side of the glass, Ransom puts on his jacket and rakes his hand through his hair. Words echo from his mind: *We're so screwed!* The secondborn Star is freaking out inside, but outside he has a serene expression. His thought pattern has a desperate urgency to it but still sounds like his voice—maybe because I know the timbre of it. It floats above what seems like millions of other voices. They fall back to create a kind of white noise. *I screwed up!* Ransom continues. *They're going to find her and shred her. This upgrade better work—does it even have enough time to work? We're dead!*

His terror reaches out to me, clutching me in a choke hold. Ransom's shooting star–shaped moniker alerts him to an incoming communication. He backs away from my capsule and taps the back of his hand. "Yes?" he responds to the small holographic screen. I see his lips move. I can't hear his voice with my ears, not the way one would hear a normal voice, not with the noise of the compressed air and the thick glass surrounding me. The sound is in his head. I hear it telepathically.

"Where are you?" a stern voice replies. "You're not at your post!"

My eyes slip out of focus, and my head pounds with pain, trying to filter out all the noise. Ransom turns and creeps away on the grated catwalk, back the way he'd come from earlier. I close my eyes and try to strategize how to survive in Swords. The only plan that comes to mind is "Fake it until you make it."

Chapter 5
Heads Will Roll

Hours later, a hot mist infuses my capsule, drenching my skin and opening my pores.

Pine-scented disinfectant mixes with the humid air, clinging to everything. The warm steam vents. Cool, dewy air pipes in from above. Droplets of water form on me and run down my limbs. A rush of warm air blasts from above and below, forcing the moisture from the capsule and drying me. The intravenous tubing attached to me retracts, leaving a stinging reminder.

All the capsules on my level open. AI programming, disseminated through Spectrum via the implanted device in my head, takes over. A rush of neurotransmitters floods my brain with a tingling sensation. Electrical impulses fire inside my head and down my spine, causing me to shiver. The command of the neuro-enhancer feels tenuous, but still it has some hold over me. My left foot lifts, without me directing it, and takes a step forward onto the grated catwalk. More AI-generated impulses fire, and I'm all the way out of the capsule, turning, and walking in the same direction as everyone else. We all move with precisely the same gait, as if we're one entity instead of thousands of individuals.

I don't have to think or pretend to be a part of Census's world. I'm integrated—one of them—but my thoughts are my own, which makes me different. I'm simply floating in a current, moving and shifting by the will of an outside force—on autopilot. It's a struggle not to fight the alien impulses. I've conditioned my body to perform as if it's dancing on a pinpoint. The anxiety of being out of control now may just get me caught. I focus on slowing my breathing, on letting go.

I calm somewhat when I reason that I can resist these impulses. The proof is in the way I direct my eyes to scan the surroundings. More proof is in my autonomous thoughts. I'm only partly engaged with Spectrum. Outright resistance now could be suicide.

Wide tubes loom ahead, reminding me of heartwoods. The soldiers in the line in front of me each enter the transparent tube and fall from sight. My heart flutters faster than a hummingbird's wings, but I don't defy the programming directing me forward.

I step off the catwalk and fall. Compressed air from holes along the tubing blasts me. It slows my decent along with an antigravity device.

I reach a lower deck and land on my feet with almost no impact. The air forces me out of the transport tube. The colossal metal hull of the airship dwarfs me. Massive automated machinery whirls and clangs nearby. A silver orb the size of a man's head whizzes up to me. It has a face of a thousand tiny blue lights. It bobs toward the Black-O moniker on my left hand and scans it. A floating hoverboard darts from a waiting line of them to pause just in front of my shins. Still on autopilot, I'm made to step on it. The hoverboard shifts me sideways across the complex. From the corner of my eye, I see Cherno make it to a hoverboard and follow me into another industrial room awhirl with machinery.

My arms lift and outstretch. I pass through a halo of blue lights. My holographic image, a mirror image, shimmers in front of me. Measurements are assessed—the machine processes a multitude of numbers and lengths, the digits spinning so fast I can hardly track them as they float by on the side of my likeness. Steel robotic arms from sinister-looking contraptions rise around me. A huge bolt of black textile surges up from the floor. Chrome pincer hands unwind a length of it. Shiny material whirls and sheers from the bolt in midair. The pincers drape the fabric on me. Red lasers cut my silhouette from the cloth. The heat from the laser melts the material so that when the burned edges meet, they mesh without a seam. It's self-healing fabric. With my Black-O uniform complete, my hoverboard whisks me down the line.

A layer of black liquid puddles on my sleeve. At first I think it could be something disgusting, but glancing up I find it came from an iron cauldron suspended above. Warm to the touch, the liquid polymer forms fibrous strands as it spreads over my arm, crawling and weaving until it covers my hand and fingernails, forming a protective glove. Machines mount cylindrical bands and clap them onto my wrist. The silvery metal sinks into the polymer, becoming a cuff to detach the combat glove. More drips of polymer fall on me and spread over my shoulders and back until I'm covered from my toes to my neck in hardening armor. The final machine on this line stamps the breastplate with a large crystal ring. From it, a holographic black O projects outward, appearing to suck at the surrounding light and draw it in.

My arms fall to my sides. The hoverboard makes a ninety-degree turn. A new chrome-plated machine awaits me. Its mechanized arm has a bristle attachment on the end. The brush whirls, catching my hair up with its quills. It gathers and winds silky strands into a long ponytail, then secures it with a rubbery fastener. Picking up speed, the hoverboard careens from the room with me atop it. It chauffeurs me through a series of towering archways and halts at a troop-assembly room. Rows and rows of mind-controlled Black-O soldiers stand, like effigies, with their backs to me.

Spectrum-generated impulses launch in my head; I step down from the hoverboard under their direction. My precise, robotic steps resound. I'm the only animated object in this cavernous hull. I pass by the perfect rows of the cerebrally shackled soldiers. Their combat-jacked bodies resemble acres of cornstalks. Shoulders and biceps swell with cyber-genetic enhancements in the form of bulky chrome-plated limbs. Machinery augments bone and sinew beneath skin in some places, but in others wires and circuitry stand exposed.

A shiver prickles down my spine. It raises the fine hairs on my nape. The cognition of the AI program drives me forward, but something else inside my brain triggers with a *pop* sensation. My flesh turns hot. My vision changes to note energy patterns—auras, heat signatures, like the ones I'd see with night-vision technology. A soldier near me shivers, too, but not physically. It's his aura. It's as if his spirit lifts from his body. With a ghoulish snarl, the spirit flashes toward me in a rush of glowing hellfire.

More Black-Os' feral spirits break off from their collective in the same way. They tug themselves out of their physical forms. The phantoms lurch and attach to me, like leeches to swollen flesh, siphoning my strength. My mind lashes out at these ghostly parasites. I disrupt their thought patterns with a surge of high-intensity energy that comes from within. It expels them from me. They retreat.

During all of this, I never miss a robotic step forward. As they disappear back into their bodies, my vision clears and returns to normal. I analyze what just happened. Spectrum has at least two distinct facets. The first is a set of standard protocols—instructions that control individuals by directing impulses through the implanted devices. The second is the AI that feeds from an individual's knowledge. This is by far the more fearsome aspect of Spectrum, because it tortures as it takes. It imprisons minds as it binds itself to bodies.

I arrive at the front of the vast cyborg assembly. The program compels me to make an abrupt right turn, walk to the center of the unit, make a sharp left turn, and face the hatch of the airship, with the demonic soldiers behind me. Spectrum stops me there. At arm's length, Cherno pauses, too. I side-eye him. His jaw tenses, but the rest of his expression remains emotionless. The hatch opens. A crack of brilliant sunshine pierces the hull. It's blinding, but my vision adjusts to it in seconds. The door lowers, creating a ramp. It comes to rest with a jarring thump. With just a glance, I know where I am. The airship now occupies the grassy mall in front of the Sword Palace, known as St. Sismode Gardens. The grounds are a dull shade of brown and green—the last gasp of color before snow falls.

I battle my impulse to run. My fingers twitch at my sides. I have no weapon. I scan the area without moving my head—it's an open space. *I'll be cut down before I manage to slip away. There's a horde of armed soldiers behind me. Even if I do manage to escape, where would I hide? My moniker will bring them right to me.*

I take a longer breath than the ones synchronized by Spectrum and recite some of Dune's strategy lessons in my mind. I must trust that my mentor's training will allow me to create an opportunity. The crisp scent of pinecones and scarlet winterberries bring my attention back to my surroundings. I know this place like I know a well-practiced sword maneuver. This area of the St. Sismode Gardens opens part-time to the public. Discussing the art of war, Dune and I used to walk its paths on the days it was closed to everyone else. A painful stab of grief slices through my chest. Tears well up in my eyes, but I force them back. I haven't mourned Dune's death. If I think about him anymore, I might fall apart, and they'll know I'm no longer one of them. I focus on what he taught me instead, studying the outside of the airship. It's an enormous flying fortress, encompassing most of the block. It must've crushed whatever was unfortunate enough to have been underneath it.

Under the influence of shadowy mind control, I step forward. The army behind me capitulates as well. We skirt a golden fountain containing Hyperion, the God of Water, and his frolicking, naked nymphs. I pass under the garden's wide archway, made from wrought iron fashioned into an immense bowed sword, and turn right onto a cobbled street of Forge. A tall iron sign indicates this is Whetstone—one of the main thoroughfares of the capital city. This area is called Old Towne.

The Sword Palace itself isn't far from here; it's just up ahead. Hawthorne's estate home resides only a few streets away, but I know he isn't there. I wonder if his parents know about his abduction by Census—the violation he has suffered at their hands. If they do, will they try to help him? Are they worried about him, their secondborn turned firstborn?

I march down the center of the thoroughfare, the unit of soldiers behind me. The old-world style of residential buildings—mostly beautiful gray stone facades; dark, slate-tiled spires; twisted bell towers; and rooftops—line the left side of the street. On the right, the St. Sismode Gardens swim in a sea of wintergreen behind the black iron fencing forged to look like broadswords. Golden fountains speckle the gravel pathways and rosebush topiaries.

No vehicles occupy the roads, or the airspace above us. On the sidewalks, Sword citizens stare horror-struck at our procession. A tall woman with cherry lips, the same color as her hair, clutches a small child to her side. Her fingernails dig into his indigo serge sleeve. The man with them doffs his hat, but not as a sign of respect—there's terror in his eyes. His fingers worry his cap's woolen brim. I want to feel sorry for him, but his golden-sword moniker means he sold his secondborn for a better lifestyle, so . . . I don't.

Our boots stomp the ground. People in the street scatter. Ticker-tape words slither around sharp-edged cornerstones and over elegant architecture while a booming, tinny voice from somewhere above us barks out dire warnings. "We are Census. We are everywhere. We are inside your sons, your daughters, your parents, your neighbors, and your friends. We are in firstborns. We are in secondborns. Do not resist us. The Fate of Swords is dead. Report to the Census Bureau nearest you to receive your new moniker today! Become a number!"

I'm not sure what scares Swords most—Census's appalling new social order, the uniformity of the cyborg army, or me, their symbol of Sword piety, sporting a Black-O moniker and leading the charge to the Sword Palace.

We reach the security gate. Spectrum sends a signal for me to stop, so I do. Cherno and I stand at attention in the street. The bracing wind lifts wisps of my hair against my cheek, but I don't raise a hand to brush them away. The metal-infused men and women behind us form single-file lines and take up positions against the Palace fence facing the street.

I feel the cagey mental pacing of these enhanced Black-O minds stalking me. The mental barrier I've erected against them keeps them back. Spectrum's inaudible siren wailing slips through to me uninhibited, because I'm not trying to block its programming . . . yet. Wordlessly, my body reacts to its influential call.

Following the summoning of the AI, only Cherno and I turn and traverse the street to the guard post. Our steps are much less stern or pounding now—but the gait isn't mine. It makes me feel like a stranger in my own body.

We climb the stone steps of the dark, foreboding Sword Palace in synchronicity. Doors held by servants I don't recognize swing wide for us. Cobalt-blue light glows up from the doorman's left hand. It's a moniker identification I've never seen before—numbers at least twenty digits long hover above pale flesh, turning it a cadaverous hue. It takes my entire focus not to turn my head and study it further.

Cherno and I cross the Grand Foyer, desecrating with our sharp bootheels the Fate of Swords crest inlaid in the marble floor. Everything I look at invokes vague childhood memories, until we get to the St. Sismode elite's private family residences—Mother, Father, and Gabriel's personal living and entertaining quarters. I've rarely been permitted inside their hallowed walls.

Verdant and gray stones line the passageways. Thick tapestries soften the walls and deaden the sound. Weathered weapons stand behind gleaming glass at equal intervals. Military armor spanning the millennia act as tour guides through the St. Sismode legacy, embodying our dominance and ability to endure change over time—to evolve when necessary.

The passageway forks. The one we take funnels downward, winding around and around on a spiraling ramp. We descend several levels. The dizzying snail's-shell structure flattens. We walk along a cold, damp hallway. Finally, we come to a part of the Sword Palace that I never knew existed. The Spectrum programming stops us in front of a colossal golden broadsword with the sharp point directed into the stone floor. If it were a real sword, it could be wielded only by a giant. It stands at least a story high. The crease down its middle indicates that it's a huge entryway. One side of the golden sword swings open, shaking the ground and revealing a medieval throne room and hall where behemoths could sit and hold council.

The summons by Spectrum become almost irresistible. The urgency of its draw now has a sickening, sinister feeling woven into it—a coldness. My instincts tell me to resist, to not be drawn into the trap almost certainly awaiting me ahead. The alternative would be to run. I already know it's too late for that—it's been too late for that since the moment I was hurled off the platform into the arms of a Black-O at the Silver Halo. Whatever this is, I have to face it alone.

Cherno and I share the same rhythm as we enter the great hall as one, our steps echoing in unison. My jaw tightens, and my fingers ache to reach for a fusionblade that isn't there.

The walls are carved stone, depicting ancient battles. The stunning renditions must have been done by masterful artists. They remind me of the ornate carvings that decorate the floors high above us. In front of the murals stand several rows of Black-Os. Their savage minds hack at mine, fighting to force me into their mental horde. My mind fends them off, just as it did the others—with fierce aggression. I beat them back with a powerful frequency that pierces their minds, causing them pain. Their ghostly spirits cower from me as I continue to move.

I focus on the hall. The broadsword-shaped glass ceiling allows slanting sunlight into the mystical chamber. The light wavers in watery patterns, throwing diamonds everywhere. My heartbeat quickens.

I know where we are! We're beneath the sword-shaped water feature in the formal gardens! It lies between the Sword Palace and the St. Sismode family shrine.

The pool itself is protected from trespassing by an invisible energy barrier, allowing in only small robots with limited AI programmed to clean the pool. Signs posted around it warn pedestrians of the lethal security measures. Even with that, several Stone servants die each year attempting to reach it—maybe they can't read and want to swim, or maybe they no longer want to live. I believe it's the latter.

Ahead of us, a dais with two enormous gilded thrones occupies the hilt of the great hall at the far end. My mother and Agent Crow occupy the glimmering metallic seats. Each of the newly minted monarchs wears a golden crown. Agent Crow bears the one belonging to The Sword. The sharp points of its metallic blades circle his ashy hair, lending him height. Othala wears my father's crown—the Fated Sword's—upon her dark, flowing hair. The crown's smaller blades are ringed by golden halos. It takes everything I have to keep my face expressionless.

Othala St. Sismode sits on the inferior throne, her red-velvet dress barely touching the flat metal blade of the grand chair's backrest. The design of her dress isn't "her." It's too heavy somehow. I'm surprised my mother let it near her slender frame. Bloodless knuckles protrude as she clutches the claw-shaped armrest with one hand. Her other hand, almost hidden by the bell sleeve of her garment, forms a fist in her lap.

In contrast, Agent Crow is the picture of ease, his back resting against the throne's golden sword blade, the point of which travels well over his head—a metaphor, perhaps. He raises one eyebrow as he observes our approach. With every step, it feels as if there's an invisible noose tightening around my neck.

Agent Crow's attention shifts to his seated audience. Census agents in long, dark coats occupy carved wooden chairs before him. They're positioned on either side of a center aisle to face the dais. The water on the other side of the glass above our heads gives their faces a bluish tint.

Through the carved holes in the tall mahogany seatbacks, they leer back at us, reminding me of eels ready to spring through gaps in coral. But I forget all this the second I notice Hawthorne standing behind Agent Crow's gleaming throne. I nearly lose my mind.

The relief I expected at finding Hawthorne never materializes. Instead I'm destroyed by his blank stare. I swell with unshed tears until I think I might burst. If I were to let them loose, the flood would drown the world. Instead I fight back the tears and bite the inside of my cheek to keep myself from blurting out his name. Tasting blood, I'm compelled to break all pretense of being Spectrum-integrated and run to Hawthorne's side, but the impulse vies with my reason.

The silver light of Hawthorne's left eye stops me from dropping my charade. Another thing I notice is Hawthorne's resemblance to Agent Crow. His hair, slicked back in much the same way as the Census agent's, accentuates the hollowness of his cheeks. He's lost some of the youthful fat in them, hardening the lines, aging him. The supple contours of his lips are the same, but they don't smile or turn up when he sees me—if he sees me. I can't tell if he knows who I am at all. Statuesque, his powerful body never twitches. He doesn't make a sound. He's a beautiful, life-sized tin soldier awaiting someone else's will to propel him into war. I sift through the melee of AI frequencies thrashing about the room. If Hawthorne's is one of them, I can't sense any difference from the rest.

My attention darts back to Agent Crow. The maniac leans over the gilded arm of his chair. His new kill tallies cover more of his skin. It gives the illusion that his face is being consumed by a shadow.

I'm too close to the dais now to have errant thoughts. I choose a focal point on the wall behind my mother and Agent Crow and blur my sight so that I can maintain my guise.

"Ah," Agent Crow simpers. "Here they are—my favorite swine."

There's a swift change in the Spectrum directives. Cherno and I come to an abrupt halt in front of the dais. I'm still out of striking distance. Behind me, the council members' conversations hiss like the sizzle a fusionblade makes when it touches water.

An ominous trickle of energy stings my nostrils. The odor buzzes with the sharp burn akin to ammonia. The shape of Agent Crow's mind reaches out to me and rakes against the mental barrier I erected. His energy, too, has a scent—burning, acrid. The coiling uproar of current he creates triggers my olfactory sense. I lose focus, wheeze. Something almost tangible enters my mind. I feel the pinch and burn of it. Invisible, sharp, mental talons scratch and abrade my brain, causing horrific, stabbing pain. I flinch. My face screws up in a grimace. My hands ball into fists. I resist his skulking psychic energy and, with an internal force of my own, push against his telepathic bludgeoning. Maybe the device in my head is defending itself. I don't know, but my scalp tingles. A shock of energy releases in an invisible pulse.

Crow scowls at my resistance. He grits his teeth and winces, but then he touches the device on his temple and drives a searing wave of energy into my frontal lobe. My defensive barrier melts; my brain inflames. I try not to scream, but a shriek issues from me anyway. My head in my hands, I sink to my knees before him. The surface of my mind throbs in agony. Agent Crow strokes the glowing veneer of the master-level beacon with his forefinger. It pulsates blue light in slow waves.

His face flushes with bitterness. Cords stand out on his neck. "You're *still* different from my other followers, Roselle. I feel it whenever I'm around you! What have you done? How have you beaten Spectrum?" Spittle flings from his lips.

His ability to have me on my knees petrifies me. "Followers?" I groan. "You mean slaves? No one would follow you willingly."

"Explain to me exactly what you've done to escape integration!"

"I don't know what you mean," I reply, gasping and straining to repel the increasing viselike grip he has on my mind.

"Don't lie to me!" he retorts through his shiny metal teeth. Another searing razor talon punctures my mind. A drop of blood falls from

74

my nose and spatters on the floor. Just when I think my head might explode, the pressure eases a fraction as Agent Crow withdraws his energy. Still on my knees, I drag my forearm across my nose, blotting away more blood with my dark uniform sleeve.

"You're a murderer." My mother's soulless voice, corroding my already chaotic thoughts, carries to me from her lofty perch. "You slaughtered your own brother."

The accusation leaves me feeling as if invisible letters sear into my flesh: *M-U-R-D-E-R-E-R*. I bridle against the label. "I tried to *save* Gabriel," I snarl, "but he killed himself so he didn't have to live with the monsters you helped create."

"Liar!" my mother screams, her bloodless face now reddening and contorting with rage. "You were always so jealous of him! You craved his power. You wanted to be firstborn."

"I craved his love—and yours! That's my crime. I loved you both, and I bought into your useless propaganda—the role that you wanted me to fit into. But Gabriel never could stomach his. No matter how hard he tried, he couldn't make himself what everyone expected him to be, and *that* ruined him." My head still throbs with pain. It's probably why I didn't censor my response. I just said more words to her at one time than I ever have in my life. She's stunned, but she gets over it.

Othala points her bony finger at me. "You never accepted your role as secondborn. You always had to try to be the best at everything."

"I'm sorry I couldn't lie down and die like you wanted me to, Othala. It's not in my nature."

My petite mother springs to her feet. "Fate traitor!" she declares, venomous. "You stole my son from me! You butchered him!"

"No." I shake my head. "He killed himself because he wanted me to become firstborn so I'd stop you!"

"Give me a sword," my mother rails at Agent Crow and extends her hand. "I'll finish the job you were supposed to do on her Transition

Day." When he scowls at her, she snatches at the fusionblade—*my* St. Sismode fusionblade—that he's wearing in a sheath on his hip.

Agent Crow's hand shoots out and encircles her delicate wrist, staying her. "Enough! Sit down, Othala."

She wrests her arm away and staggers back, clutching her wrist. Then she whirls back at him like a cobra. The skirt of her red dress flares out, revealing her ankles. "I want her *dead*. You promised years ago that you'd kill her, but she's still alive. Why haven't you done it?"

Glowering at her, Agent Crow rises to his feet. "I said *sit down*." His words are almost gentle until he barks, "Now!"

Othala quails. The only people I've seen raise their voices to my mother were my grandfather, my father, and Fabian Bowie. No one else would dare, until now. I expect her to have a meltdown. I'm wrong. She backs away, returns to her seat, perches on the edge of it, clears her throat, and stares straight ahead into the distance.

"Why have you brought Roselle here if you aren't going to kill her?" she asks.

"I need to question her," Agent Crow replies, sinking back into his own throne. "She has resisted integration. I need to find out how she's doing it."

"She's obviously defective. You should execute her *before* she finds a way to destroy you, Kipson." A slap to my face would've been kinder, but I steel myself for more of my mother's vitriol.

The excruciating vise on my mind eases a bit more with every moment that Agent Crow's attention strays from me. Another drop of blood slips from my nostril. I wipe it on my sleeve.

Agent Crow steeples his fingers. "You have no love for secondborns, do you, Othala?"

"No. And you have no sense of the danger my daughter represents, do you? She's hope to these peasants that surround us, in Forge and beyond. They want her to rule the Fate of Swords."

Agent Crow straightens in his gilded seat, his eyebrows slashing together. "There *is* no *Swords*, Othala. Swords was conquered. *I* rule here now. I've earned my power—unlike you, who simply inherited it. You're no better than them." He flicks his hand toward the gathered Census agents.

Has he turned against Census?

A ripple of uneasy murmurs comes from the council of gathered Census agents behind me, as if that thought just occurred to them, too.

Do they know he earned his power by killing his older sister? He's a deluded hypocrite who can't be trusted in any deal.

Agent Crow's seething words have the magical effect of cowing my mother. Her attitude changes in an instant. With a tone meant to placate, she says, "I only meant to give you sage advice from my vast experience as the leader of a Fate. My daughter's cunning and manipulative nature shouldn't be underestimated. She plotted against me when I was The Sword, because she coveted my power."

I want to scoff. I don't. Bringing attention to myself is lunacy. I glance around, noting the weapons nearest me. They all hang from sheaths on the armor of Black-Os, who stand lifeless throughout the gigantic hall. The soldiers have been physically altered with implanted weapons—small versions of fusion cannons mounted to forearms, robotic hands, and legs that have arching blades instead of feet. Their numbers are such that should they all come to life, they'd be able to pile on top of one another and reach the water on the other side of the towering glass ceiling. And then there's Cherno with his hulking body right next to me. Curiously, he has no weapon.

"Don't worry about me underestimating your daughter," Agent Crow purrs to Othala, his humor restored. "I still control Roselle. I'll show you." He pulls a small disc from his pocket and tosses it toward me. The device bounces on the floor and rolls. "Do you know what you've been doing for the past month, Roselle?"

Amy A. Bartol

Slowly, I rise to my feet. "I've been building my strength up to kick your ass," I reply, wishing it were true.

"You've been on *my* team. You've been my Goddess of War." Light projects up from the disc on the floor, blurring my view of Agent Crow and Othala. It's a recorded hologram.

The glowing steel of my former penthouse apartment appears. The sword-shaped tower was constructed by the Rose Garden Society to replicate the birthmark on my hand. A cloudless sky allows an unobscured view of the crown-shaped quarters circling the sharp peak of the blade.

Drone cameras provide aerial views of the tower. Ants surround the massive structure, or so it appears at first. The flying cameras' lenses zoom in, revealing dark-clad figures. Black-Os in heavy combat gear dapple the shore. Thousands of Census soldiers surge over the sand, wielding implanted metal claws they use to scale the shiny silver girders of the building's bladelike shaft.

Salloway security men, occupying the penthouse level, fight the marauders, firing state-of-the-art weaponry. The powerful munitions fail to eradicate all the Black-Os, who seem to outnumber the stars. The horde isn't attacking only from the walls; they're striking from the air with Burton-manufactured airships. One such troop carrier releases a rain of assault soldiers from its hold. Bodies hurtle toward the penthouse. Golden blasts of energy pour from the defensive cannons mounted to the rooftop and incinerate them. Ashes fall like snow.

The cameras focus on the rooftop. Amid the carnage, a figure wields a Salloway dual-sided fusionblade. Her fighting form mimics Dune's. The hairs on my nape rise. I recognize my image among the violent invaders. Vicious and emotionless, the bloodshed I perpetrate with my fusionblade is without equal. There's no hesitation, just blind savagery. I watch as the mind-controlled me executes every Salloway rebel and Rose Gardener in my path. Droplets of blood soak my image's three-dimensional hair and run in red rivulets down my cheeks. The bodies pile up, but still I press on, killing with no remorse. I watch myself slash a path to the far edge of the conflict—to my target, Clifton Salloway.

"There he is, Roselle, your betrothed," Agent Crow chuckles jovially from the dais. "Watch closely. This is my favorite part."

My hand aches to reach out and touch the light that projects the image of Clifton's golden-blond hair, tousled and matted with streaks of blood. I'm unable to see the shine of his green eyes, but they seem to hold mine in a desperate plea. The Black-O image of me neither pauses nor holds back when she comes face-to-face with her former commanding officer. Clifton checks his sword thrust when he recognizes me, and his face becomes a mask of pain. He lowers his sword and kneels before her—before *me*—in surrender. Instead of accepting his defeat, I wind back my sword with an effortless sweep before swinging it forward to sever Clifton's head from his neck.

Bile rises in my throat and burns my mouth. I swallow hard, trying to stifle the need to retch. The recording only gets worse. It shows me picking up Clifton's head by his hair and holding it aloft, as if it were some trophy to the gods on high. Devastation, raw and unrelenting, pierces my chest. The agony is unbearable. Breath shudders from my lungs, forcing past my constricted throat. My carefully constructed facade crumbles.

This is the thing that Ransom couldn't tell me. I slaughtered Clifton. I'm a traitor to everyone—even myself.

"You see, Othala," Agent Crow says, "if I'd killed her earlier, we wouldn't get to have this exquisite moment with her."

"You're a disease," I growl between clenched teeth. I feel something slide down my cheek, and I know it's a tear that I couldn't hold back any longer. Several more follow. All I can do is wipe them away. I can't stop them. I'm an overfilled pitcher of sorrow, spouting wretchedness. In my fury, I can't even think of a better epithet than "disease."

Without thinking, I take a few menacing steps toward him, my blurred vision searching for any weapon I can use to kill him.

Hawthorne snaps out of his statuesque pose, pulls his sword from its sheath, and ignites the fusionblade. Golden light glimmers with the thrum of power from its hilt. The hollow husk of my friend blocks my way with his broad, armored chest. The breastplate's dark sheen displays a large Black-O emblem. The insignia appears to cave in his chest where his heart should be. Hawthorne's lips stretch in a grim line. One of his gray eyes shines with unnatural silver light. I wonder if he sees *me* or just a threat to his master. The thought makes my bottom lip quiver. I bite it to stop it and try to sidle around him. Hawthorne moves with me. I can't get past him without hurting him. Instead I back away toward Cherno and pause to reassess the situation.

My retreat signifies that the threat to Agent Crow has been eliminated. The fusionblade in Hawthorne's hand extinguishes. He sheaths it and returns to his post.

"Come now, a disease, Roselle?" Agent Crow tsks, enjoying my tears. "Don't you mean a god?"

"You're an infection." I seethe, breathing hard, my face hot. I tilt my chin upward and wish I could bathe my flushed cheeks in the icy water behind the glass ceiling.

"I merely strive to annihilate weakness. Isn't that the very purest form of evolution?"

"True power is leading people by their hearts, not imprisoning their minds."

"You should've made her kill herself right after she slaughtered Salloway," my mother interjects. "Salloway was her friend. She'll exact revenge—she'll find a way to outwit you. It's what she does. She's exactly like her grandfather, a direct descendant of Greyon Wenn—the man you revere."

Agent Crow gives Othala only a cursory glance. "Greyon's interesting," Agent Crow replies, "but I'm much more intrigued by the story of *his* lineage."

My mother thinks for a moment. "You're referring to the legend?" she scoffs. "Don't tell me you're simple enough to believe that Greyon descended from the gods?"

Tittering escapes from the crowd behind.

Agent Crow's jaw twitches angrily. "Quiet!" he roars. The other Census agents go mute. He prowls off his throne, pacing the dais. The golden crown on his head shifts. He reaches up and adjusts it before turning back to glare at my mother. "You must believe it on some level. You named your daughter after the war goddess."

Othala's sharp nails drum on the arm of her throne. I notice a new ring on her finger—an amethyst. It's strange—she hates purple, and it clashes with her gown. "You do know it's propaganda, don't you, Kipson?" My mother can hardly contain her condescension. "We tell the simple folk that we're descendants of the Goddess of War, and they don't question our right to rule them. It's an antiquated notion, but my father insisted that I adhere to it with Roselle. She's no more a descendant of the gods than I am."

"Ah, but you are, Othala. You're just so distant that the immense power the deity possessed has been bred out of you. It seems to be the theme when it comes to the first families. They chose inferior spouses— except for you. Your spouse was different. Your father chose well for you, genetically speaking." He says this with a thoughtful air, but he doesn't elaborate further. "Greyon studied the lineage of the gods because he *was* a descendant of Roselle the Life-Taker."

My mother's nails stop drumming. She sits up straighter. "Where's your proof? You'd need DNA from a myth. You'd need to have located Roselle's remains."

"And what makes you think I haven't?"

"Have you found Roselle's tomb?" my mother asks pointedly. "Many have searched, but none have found it."

His face contorts in anger. "Not yet, but I *will* find it. I've already located several false ones."

Othala's expression twists into one of extreme irritation. "You haven't found it because it doesn't exist."

Agent Crow gives her a condescending smirk. "No one creates false tombs to hide a myth. You lack imagination, Othala. Have you ever wondered what drives people to have more children than their allotted two offspring? The ban on thirdborns is a simple rule. Why break it?"

Othala's nose wrinkles in disdain, her fingertips tracing the gilded arm of her throne. "I'm not a Census agent. I cannot fathom why anyone does it. I was loath to have even my secondborn." Othala's eyes bore into mine.

"You're not the nurturing type, Othala. Even so, I believe it's the pursuit of perfection—the need to create life, to create a perfect being. We are all trying to find our way back to immortality—to being gods."

My mother's fingers still on the armrest. Probably wondering, like me, if insanity runs in his blood, she glances at the madman. "We bear children because it's required by law. Anyone who has more than two is simply an anarchist."

"Are you an anarchist?" he asks.

Othala shifts in her seat. "Of course not! I follow the laws."

"Which laws?" he asks. "The old Fates Republic rules, or the new Census ones?"

"I'm your partner, Kipson. I have proven my value to Census. You know that. The only threats left to its rule are the dwindling rebel incursions and my daughter."

Agent Crow takes the seat beside hers again, slouching into it. His hand reaches out to hers idly, and his fingers caress her skin. She doesn't move her hand away, but her entire body grows rigid.

"Are they the *only* threats?" he asks. He studies her hand next to his. My skin prickles. He's playing with her.

"You're implying that I'm a threat, but I've been loyal. I kept Census's secrets for years. I've helped when you've asked. Isn't that enough?"

"That was before. What have you done for me lately?"

"I've provided you lodging in my Palace," Othala sputters.

"Whose Palace?" he asks. His eyes narrow. "I seem to recall telling you that it's mine now."

"That was never the agreement! A St. Sismode has resided in the Sword Palace since its inception. We agreed that I would help the transition to a new form of government, and in return, Swords would remain intact and under *St. Sismode* leadership."

"Swords will remain as it is, with a few minor adjustments."

"You promised that the St. Sismode line will continue."

"I did, and it will continue—maybe even better than it was before."

"And you promised me that my daughter dies."

"And she will die." My mother visibly relaxes, until Agent Crow adds, "Eventually."

Othala stiffens and turns her chin in his direction. "What do you mean? How long do you plan to keep her?"

Agent Crow shrugs. "Well, if I kill her now, I can't study her the way I'd like to, or fulfill my other promise."

"What other promise is that?"

"The promise I made to allow your line to go on. If I kill you *and* I kill her, then the line ends, unless I artificially continue it, but that's tedious and time consuming, and the results are often fraught with complications."

Othala gasps. "Kill me?" She snatches her hand away from his and brings it fluttering to her throat.

"You're no longer much use to me, especially because you've been plotting with Edmund and Malcolm Burton and my High Council"—he gestures to the crowd in front of him—"to assassinate me and take back your supposed power."

Her cheeks darken. She glances in the direction he indicated. "I have no idea where you've gotten such a strange idea, Kipson." Her voice quavers. "I assure you, my only interest has been in helping you assimilate to your new role as leader—"

His finger shifts to his temple. The blue beacon throbs. A female Black-O with limp, dark hair marches from the crowd to the dais and stops near the thrones. My mother recoils as the soldier opens her bland lips and speaks. "'You're certain that this poison will kill him instantly?'" the soldier says, but the voice is unmistakably Othala's. The mind-controlled woman's timbre changes to a male voice as she answers herself. "'It's a fast-acting aerosol. One inhalation and his lungs will vaporize along with everything else inside him.'" Then my mother's voice comes from the soldier again. "'When can I administer it to Crow?'" The soldier's voice deepens to a male's. "'This evening—after he kills Roselle for us.'" The soldier closes her mouth and stands in dreary silence. My mother's betrayal hangs like a stain in the air.

After a long pause, Othala clears her throat. "I—I'm under orders from the Census High Council, Kipson. Marius and Claudia know of your escapades of late, and your refusal to follow their directives. Your own people at Census ordered your death."

"Yes," Agent Crow replies, "I know. Marius Cabal, Claudia Anubis, and their sycophants have lost control of Spectrum—or rather, they've been shut out. The AI has outgrown them. Even Marius, the all-powerful Master of the Hunt, can no longer manipulate the army with his master-level implant."

"But you can still influence it," Othala states.

"Of course. I've adapted along with the program. The rest of them have remained stagnant."

"How did you do that?"

"Genetic enhancements. My scientists know that if they fail me, they die."

"Census believes that once you're gone, it will be a simple matter of reinstating governorship of the machine."

"The *machine!*" Agent Crow laughs with true amusement. "It ceased to be a machine a decade ago. They think they can just flip a switch and obtain dominion over Spectrum! The only way to gain control of it now, Othala, is to become a part of it."

"What do you mean 'become a part of it'?"

He smiles. "I would tell you, but it's pointless. You'll never understand."

"You plan to kill me, Kipson?" Othala plays with the amethyst ring on her finger, twisting it around and around.

"I think it's only fair, don't you?"

She worries at the jewel on her finger more and more frantically, gouging her nails into the ornate filigree around the gem, trying to pry it open. Her glossy nails break and bleed.

"Are you looking for this?" Agent Crow opens his palm. On it lies an identical ring. "It's a heavy stone, but then, it has to be to contain the mechanism that will release the aerosol poison."

My mother's fingers still.

"They must not have explained to you how this poison works. If you were to use it like this—open the mechanism—it would surely kill us both."

"They gave me an antidote."

Agent Crow snorts. "There's no antidote to this particular poison. You've been deceived."

Blue lights flash a pounding beat on Agent Crow's temple. The dark-haired female soldier reanimates and kneels before her master. She opens her mouth and sticks out her tongue at him. Crow places the ring on it. She pulls her tongue back into her mouth and closes it, pursing her lips. Standing and backing away from him, she turns to face us, and then she bites down hard on the gem. An involuntary sound wheezes through her larynx. Then her cheeks turn gray and cave in—dehydrating as if all the moisture is evaporating from her body. Her eyes dry up and shrink into tiny beads in hollow sockets. Dropping to her knees again, she shrivels. Her hands wither. By the time her head collides with the floor, her skin is leather over bones. The atrophy is such that she's half her size in seconds. A gruesome mummification.

Agent Crow chuckles. "I so enjoy seraphinian. Witnessing its power never gets old. As poisons go, it has no equal."

My mother's eyes have grown wide. Her hands tremble. She somehow looks boneless—a slumping, sullen sack of skin in a red-velvet dress, the armpits of which have darkened with sweat. As for me, I'm rotting with fear from the inside out.

"Kipson," Othala says, wavering, "I—they ordered me to kill you. I had no choice. They've lied to us both." My mother's lower lip vibrates. She looks toward the assembly in desperation.

"Don't worry, I'll take care of them," Agent Crow promises. The crowd of seated agents behind me breaks out in low murmurings. The Black-Os don't stir at all.

"What are you going to do?" Othala asks.

"This," he says. From behind Agent Crow's throne, Hawthorne comes to life. Prowling forward, he moves to stand in front of my mother. With a quick flick of his wrist, he extracts his fusionblade and ignites it. My heart leaps into my throat. I take a lurching step toward the dais, but I'm brought up short by a powerful, scaly hand clutching my wrist. I make eye contact with Cherno. His golden irises show the gleam of intelligence. His head gives a slight shake. If I weren't staring at him, I wouldn't have noticed.

My mother's shriek of terror chills me to my marrow. Hawthorne swings his glowing fusionblade with perfect form, striking Othala's delicate neck with the blade. It separates her head from her body. Her head and part of her throat, cauterized by the heat of the fusion energy, tumbles through the air bloodlessly, traversing Agent Crow's throne. Her limp blue eyes stare at me in death, and Agent Crow's face breaks into ecstasy. My mother's cranium hits the dais and rolls. Her crown clatters loudly off the ornate floor and bounces, traveling off the dais to land at my feet, sounding the death knell of the Fates Republic.

Chapter 6
Exes for Eyes

I'm frozen with shock, listening to Agent Crow's peals of laughter.

"That was righteousness!" he gloats. "That was justice!"

I stare at the golden crown at my feet while Black-O soldiers, animating around me, clear away my mother's sagging, lifeless body and severed head. Her head passes by me first. It's handed off from soldier to soldier, who, as they come to life, pass it before freezing into motionless figures. It's barbaric in its efficiency. The pieces of my mother quickly disappear to the entrance of the hall, as does the shriveled corpse of the poisoned soldier.

"What will you do with my mother's body?" My voice doesn't seem like mine. It sounds like it's coming from someone else—from a distance.

Agent Crow bends to pick up the Fated Sword crown from the floor and comes closer to me. He toys with it, turning it to examine its ornate detail. "I'm not sure. I could reanimate her—put her head back on, bring her back to life. Would you like that? She won't be the same, though. I haven't perfected the procedure yet. She'd be no more than a performing monkey."

My stomach lurches in revolt. I barely keep myself from vomiting. "Leave her be."

"She would've had your head on a pike for killing your brother, Roselle." It's probably true. She would have tortured me if she had been allowed, but she won't now.

"I didn't kill my brother. Gabriel killed himself."

"He was weak. You're not weak, are you?"

I feel weak—insubstantial, flimsy, brittle, inadequate, helpless. "I'm not weak," I repeat numbly.

Agent Crow bends to whisper in my ear. "But *I* will break you." A tremor of fear slips through me.

From behind us, a thin, troubled voice interrupts. "You must allow me to make amends, Your Grace!"

I recognize the deep resonance I heard just several moments before, from the corpse-girl—the voice of the other person in the poison plot to kill Agent Crow. He straightens, gazing into the rows of seated Census agents. The hunter-killers appear to know that their days are numbered. Sweat pours from some. Others are as white as winter. Agent Crow turns his back on them and returns to his throne. He sits and places the Fated Sword crown on the center of the throne next to his.

Footsteps echo from a young man trudging up the aisle to reach the dais. With the icy water from the ceiling refracting the sunlight onto his face, his grin resembles that of a shark swimming toward us. He's tall and regal looking in his elegant black Census uniform and shiny black boots. Pausing before Agent Crow, the young man bows. A Burton fusionblade gleams in its black leather sheath on his hip, secured there with a ruby clasp.

Agent Crow's top lip forms an ugly twist. The newcomer glances at me before he addresses the psychopathic tyrant. I narrow my eyes at Firstborn Malcolm Burton—a warning to shut his mouth. It's Grisholm's ex-mentor, the man The Virtue made me fight for the job at the Halo Palace. Malcolm returns a snarl before addressing the despot on the dais. "I'm Firstborn Malcolm Burton. My father supplies munitions to your army, and he—"

"Plotted against me with Othala St. Sismode," Crow interrupts. "I know who you are. You're the voice in the exchange my soldier interpreted for us. Othala invited you here today to witness my death."

"You're quite right," Malcolm admits. "It was done, as The Sword said, through coercion from the Census High Council."

"Othala's no longer The Sword. She's nothing." Agent Crow's calm tone is a mask. He's seething.

Malcolm winces. He raises his hands in a placating motion. "Of course, she's . . . Of course she's not The Sword. You have all the power now, Your Grace. What I propose is that you spare our lives, and in exchange I'll—we, my family will—continue to supply your army with the highest quality munitions."

"Am I to understand that if I don't agree to your terms, my army will lack the proper means to defend itself?"

"I wouldn't be so crass as to use extortion as a negotiating tactic." But he would, because he just did. "Suffice to say," he continues, "your army would be at a severe deficit without us, now that you've eliminated Salloway Munitions Conglomerate from, well, existence. The rebels are still a threat. They comprise Stars and Swords who are more than capable of manufacturing their own weapons."

"So you're saying that in exchange for your life—"

"And the life of my father, Edmund."

"And the life of your father," Agent Crow adds, "Burton Manufacturing will supply weapons and assault vehicles to me?"

"Yes. However, we would ask one more concession." Malcolm pivots from Agent Crow to gaze at me. "Allow *me* the honor of killing Roselle St. Sismode for you." With growing confidence, he moves away from the dais in my direction. He stops in front of me. "She is the last symbol of the past—she's now The Sword."

"Why do you want Roselle dead?" Agent Crow asks.

"I owe her." Malcolm sneers. "Don't I, Roselle?" He trails a long finger down my arm before reaching up and grasping my chin with his soft fingertips. A smug smile creases his lips. "Not so proud now, are you—"

The dragon-skinned creature next to me stretches out his massive hand and catches Malcolm's face in his enormous palm. Cherno squeezes, muffling Malcolm's screams of agony in his talons. The firstborn releases me. Cherno's scaly biceps bulge. He rips Malcolm away from me. The thinner man sprawls across the floor and writhes, cradling in his hands what's left of his bloody face.

Chaos explodes in the great hall. Desperate voices echo off the watery ceiling. The assembled Census agents run for the exit, weaving through the Black-O soldiers. Bodies pile up at the golden doors, which won't open to allow the Census agents to leave.

Above the cries and commotion, a hysterical male voice screams, "Call off your monster!" Edmund Burton, Malcolm's father, rushes to the edge of the dais, extracting a fusionblade from its sheath. Deep lines frame his mouth. He moves his thumb over the ignition switch. Power seethes forth, forming a blade from the strike port. The weapon crackles. This sword has a dual-blade, like the one I helped design for Salloway Munitions, but its energy ignites from a single strike port, so that the silver hydroblade and gold fusionblade appear to be conjoined. Edmund swings the blade, but he's too far away from Agent Crow to hurt him.

Hawthorne stirs out of his stillness in a rush. With a few strides, the shell of my friend, his fusionblade ignited with golden light, stands in front of Agent Crow. He strikes the stiff-kneed man, forcing him to stumble back from an onslaught of vicious swings.

The once powerful and privileged gentleman can't defend himself against the brutality of Hawthorne's AI assault. With a panting, high-pitched voice, Edmund pleads, "Call your creatures off! I'll give you anything!"

A look of fascination crosses Agent Crow's face as he stares not at Edmund, but at Cherno, who picks Malcolm up again and continues to throttle him. "Why should I? I already have everything you own. I appropriated your intellectual property days ago. I took over your factories today. You have nothing."

"Please!" Edmund begs.

Hawthorne pauses.

Agent Crow chuckles. "I haven't ordered this attack on your son, Edmund—well, not in any sort of direct way." He stands and moves toward us to get a closer look at Malcolm, whose face has progressed from an agonized red to a mottled purple. Our new despot flashes Edmund an impish grin. "Protocols were written into Cherno's programming. He's to monitor Roselle and make sure she doesn't somehow escape from us—under her own power or through the power of another. Cherno must see Malcolm's behavior as menacing. If she were to die, that would be an escape of a sort, wouldn't it?" He seems delighted by this prospect. "The brute is defending her from death! I didn't foresee that result."

Cherno's making pulp out of Malcolm. Hawthorne resumes his assault, hacking at Edmund with the vengeance of a scorned god. Agent Crow watches them. No one pays any attention to me until the fancy Burton fusionblade rattles to the floor with the old man's severed fingers still wrapped around it. It stays ignited as it skids into the aisle.

I dive for it before any of the Black-Os move. The hilt is slick with sweat. Burton's fingers loosen and fall off. Somersaulting, I come to my feet in a crouch. Hawthorne cuts Edmund Burton in half. My ex-boyfriend stands between me and Agent Crow. I'll have to stab Hawthorne if I have any hope of killing Agent Crow with this sword. But I know I can't do it. I can't hurt him like that, even though we're both dead anyway.

A raging burst of energy from Agent Crow's mind crashes into my brain, sending me reeling. My knees weaken. I stumble backward from the impact. Blood oozes from my nose. Agent Crow's sinister temporal device blinks blue. I narrow my eyes at my oppressor and allow my blood to drip from my chin unchecked. The soldiers surrounding us all come to life and surge toward me from every angle. I can't possibly reach Agent Crow on the dais before they grab me and tear me apart.

It's okay. I don't need to reach him. I just need to wait a few seconds for his monsters to come to me.

A husky cyborg hurtles at me. I swing Burton's sword. The blades lop off the Black-O's cannon-enhanced arm. I pivot to catch the severed arm of the soldier while I avoid the rest of his body. The black metal arm is heavy. It has been fortified with a Burton Series-7 fusion cannon, according to the coding on the alloy.

I aim the weaponized arm upward and, with the embedded manual lever, trigger the cannon several times. The flashes of golden fusion energy careen toward the ceiling and shatter the transparent barrier holding the water back. Crouching, I cover my head with my arms, inhale deeply, and hold my breath.

Soldiers jump me, piling on top, covering me. Crushed and disoriented, I hear pounding water—like the downpour of a waterfall against rocks. Panicked cries cut off abruptly. Frigid liquid drenches my face and stings my skin. In seconds, I'm submerged. Bodies float off me.

I kick away from them and swim toward the surface, bumping into chairs and loose weapons, dodging flailing arms and legs. My hair swirls in my face. I kick as hard as I can, but the water just keeps coming, filling the room. The harder I swim, the faster I sink. My temples throb as I ache for oxygen. Bubbles of my breath escape, but I won't. Suddenly that's as clear as dawn.

My lungs burn. I wheeze and retch, vomiting water. It comes out of my nose, too, and flows down my cheeks into my ears and hair. I spit it out, almost choking on it, and gasp for air. Halos of bright white light blind me and sting my eyes. With some effort I'm able to lift one arm to shield my face, but my muscles feel as if they're tearing. I grimace and moan at the ache. I'm trembling, and my fingers are tinted blue. I'm nearly frozen solid. My armor is gone. Only the uniform the machines created for me remains.

With my other arm, I feel around on the hard surface beneath me. Smooth metal. I turn my head a fraction. Shooting pain in my neck makes me pause. My breath comes out in watery pants. When I resume moving, I go slower, until my cheek rests against the cold metal surface of a laboratory table that hovers legless above the floor.

I recognize the room, with its barrel-vaulted ceiling held up by stone pillars. It's the morgue located beneath the Round Ballroom of Sword Palace. Hovering bright lights center over a hall full of floating examination tables. There are so many hovering units—intended to serve as a triage ward if there were ever an attack on the Sword Palace. Now it contains a legion of drowned soldiers and Census agents. Not all of them fit on the units. Bodies are stacked in piles. Glass walls enclose the morgue's hall on the far side—the front. Toward the back, where I am, it's all stone.

I've been here only a few times before. The first was when I snuck down here to see my grandmother, the Fated Sword, before she was set to be interned. I was very young—no more than seven. The circumstances had been unusual. Firstborn aristocracy usually live well past their hundredth birthdays. With our advanced medical technology, such as it is, they look and feel young for decades. This wasn't the case with my grandmother. She'd been relatively young, and sick on and off for spells, but no one would say why. Then she'd died quite suddenly in her sleep. The Stones of the Sword Palace whispered about poison—my grandfather and grandmother hadn't been close. Theirs wasn't a love match, much like my parents' marriage. They say she outlived her usefulness. It makes me wonder if any of them knew how to love.

Maybe no one ever loved them, so they didn't know how?

Othala didn't allow me to attend my grandmother's formal wake—
it had been for firstborns only. So instead I brought my grandmother
a single red rose and said my good-byes to her here, without Othala's
permission. I didn't stay long. The Sword Palace is ancient, and even
though this part has been modernized, it still has a medieval architecture that makes it easy to believe that ghosts reside within its stone walls.
And now the room is overflowing with bloated, wet corpses.

Am I dead?

Every cell of my body aches. If this is death, it's not what I'd hoped.
The only thing I like about it so far is that it's quiet. Nothing stirs,
except me, but I'm not merely stirring, I'm quaking.

I need to get warm—get to a safe place.

I scan the other side of the room, but the exam table next to
mine demands my attention. The unmistakable, waterlogged profile
of Firstborn Agent Kipson Crow—His Grace, the ex-Census warlord
and maniacal tyrant—lies rigid, possibly from rigor mortis, beside me,
under intense circles of lights and a mortician's embalming apparatus.

Agent Crow's skin is even bluer than mine. Wet clumps of ashen
hair rest in swirls on his cheeks and forehead. The kill tallies marring
his face and neck seem darker, more pronounced. He isn't breathing.

Did he drown? Did I? I feel as if I had—I feel mostly dead. Stiff and
icy. To-the-bone cold.

It takes me a few tries, but I ease my leg off the side of the metal
table. The rest of my body slides with it. Water drips from my Black-O
uniform. My fingers catch the edge of the dull-silver slab, and I grip
it until my feet feel steady on the floor. Shuddering wracks my body.
My teeth rattle. I glance at Agent Crow beside me. His eyes are closed,
his blue lips frozen in a condescending snarl, showing his metal teeth.

Squish. Water makes my boots burble. I inch a step, still holding
on to my tabletop. I let go, shift abruptly, and catch myself on Agent
Crow's examination slab. I haul myself across the small aisle to him

and steady myself against the table's edge. Poking his shoulder, I ready myself to shove away if he stirs. He doesn't. I press my fingertip to his damp eyelid, pull it back, and reveal his pale eyeball's dead stare. When I snatch my hand away, it remains open—a sinister stare.

The thrill of vengeance percolates inside me. *This can't be happening. He's dead! I've beaten him! I've won!*

Then another thought: *Is this something my brain is selling me—a part of Spectrum? Is this real?* I sober instantly.

I slap my cheek as hard as I can. The sting is everything it should be. Glancing at my palm, I zero in on the raised star. My thumb glides over it, feeling its familiar ridges. My elbow grazes something sharp. It's the metallic hilt of a fusionblade sheathed on Agent Crow's belt. I reach for it, wrap my hand around the silver metal, and slide it from him. It fits my grip because it was made for me. It's mine. The raised rose vines wind to my family's crest. The fusionblade ignites from the strike port. Golden energy growls—a familiar sound.

Agent Crow's corpse glows from the sword's reflection. My eyes narrow.

They're not bringing him back. Not if I can help it. I want maggots to make a feast of his heart—eat it from the center out.

I twirl my wrist, and the fusionblade spins. I lean away from the table and balance on my own two feet. Viciously I drag my glowing blade down the center of Agent Crow from head to foot, cutting him in half along with the hovering table upon which he lies. The bisected unit, each containing half of Agent Crow, caves in. I lurch back and scarcely avoid getting slimy, sloshing pieces of dead Crow on my boots.

Staring at the mess on the floor, I wonder, *Will this be enough to make sure he never rises again?*

I glance up at the cadaver just beyond Agent Crow's severed body. All the breath leaves me. Panic kicks in. "No," I whimper. My fusionblade falls from my fingers and extinguishes. My heart drums his name in frantic beats, *Haw-thorne. Haw-thorne. Haw-thorne.*

I slide forward, not caring about the awfulness I'm stepping in. Using the corners of the tables, I drag myself to the examination unit adjacent to mine. A rush of pure adrenaline courses through my body. I hesitate and hover over him, too afraid to touch him, because then this might be real.

"Hawthorne," I croak, and then cover my mouth with my jittering fingertips.

Involuntarily, I reach for his cheek. *Glacial.* His flesh is colder than the blood in my veins.

"No."

It comes out as a plea. I sob. Hawthorne's bangs curl over his forehead, just like I've seen them do a thousand times after he's taken a shower. His hair is cold and soft and smells like him. I touch his lips, hoping that he'll start breathing.

"You can't go," I rasp. "Please don't go, Hawthorne. Please."

I kiss his cheek, then brush my lips over his. He doesn't move.

Another choking sob catches in my throat, and with it all the fight drains out of me in a wave of emptiness. I'm like the dead trees on a battlefield, sheared off at the heart and splintered all the way down. I crawl up onto the wide silver slab next to Hawthorne's body, cuddling to his side. My cheek rests against his neck. I close my eyes that refuse to stop weeping, the salty trails running off my jaw.

"Take me with you, Hawthorne," I beg him. "Please . . . I want to go with you." But I know he can't hear me. He's already gone.

Chapter 7
Speaking in Genetic Code

A jarring noise startles me.

I flinch. Adrenaline pumps into my bloodstream. "That one's alive!" a male voice shouts in terror, having dropped the metal tray he was carrying.

"No, she's not," replies another deep voice from farther away. "Someone probably just moved her to mess with us." Shuffling feet creep closer.

I open my eyes and wipe tears and snot from under my nose. Then I liberate the fusionblade from Hawthorne's sheath. Igniting it, I sit up and snarl at them. The two lab technicians scream in terror, backing away.

"You said she was dead!" the round technician in the black lab coat yells.

"She was dead! I swear it!" the other yells back. "I checked her myself—so'd Calvin!" He skids into a lab table, falls onto it, and, wiping his hand on his sleeve, pushes back up from a dead soldier. He readjusts and continues to move away from me. The wide glass door slides open behind them, and they exit. The door slides closed. On the other side of it, they call for help into their monikers.

The sudden sound of pounding feet has me on mine, though I'm still stiff. On the table across from Hawthorne's lies a drowned cyborg Black-O. I stumble toward her, thinking to liberate her arm so I can use her Series-7 fusion cannon. Then the glass doors shatter, along with all the glass walls at that end of the morgue. A unit of combat-armored Black-Os swarms in. They want me alive; otherwise they would've simply rolled a grenade in here.

The Spectrum soldiers hesitate, assessing me. They're not speaking aloud, and yet I can hear them negotiating, planning my apprehension. I'm dialed into them—through telepathy, maybe, I don't know—and can follow their negotiations like I'm a part of the team. I'm eavesdropping on a plot to capture myself.

I'm also operating on my own autonomous frequency, but I'm aware of the rapid-fire orientation of tasks each of them plans to execute—I know their game plan. Protocols still exist that dictate I'm not to be killed. I'm unsure if they're residual orders left over from before I flooded the throne room, or if they're new. I also don't know why they want me alive—none of the chatter indicates where the directives originated. I try to search other frequencies, but it's difficult to focus when they're so close. Their physical threat takes priority.

A shuddering exhale escapes me as I locate a directive indicating that maiming me is an option. A part of me wants them to come—wants them to tear my limbs from me and rip my flesh until there's nothing left but bones. But some instinct will never allow that. The fight hasn't gone out of me—it's roaring back with a vengeance.

Who's controlling them now that Agent Crow is dead? Maybe no one. Maybe Spectrum has outgrown the paltry human minds that made it. I ignite Hawthorne's fusionblade and sever the arm from the dead soldier nearest me.

A few Spectrum soldiers leap up onto corpse-ridden tables. They hurtle from one hovering slab to the next, overturning the deceased in their paths. Others use their steel claws to climb the stone walls. Another wave fans out. They're trying to surround me.

Movement to my right catches my attention. Cherno sits up on a hovering table near me. Bare-chested, he rises. His golden eyes meet mine. Water drips from his shiny, black hair. The dragon-man nods once, acknowledging me, like an ally would. I freeze, my heart lurching faster. He turns away and focuses on the charging horde. Without a word, he stands. I aim my Series-7 cannon at him. The fearsome creature tears a cannon-armed limb off a corpse on the slab next to him. I flinch, expecting him to aim at me. Casually, he angles it at the encroaching Black-Os instead.

With my focus on Cherno, I fail to fire on the Black-O who's now about to pounce on my chest. Cringing, I brace for the impact. *Boom!* The Black-O's body in front of me explodes, careening sideways from the fusion pulse Cherno pumped into it. I take a shaky breath. Cherno obliterates another Spectrum soldier that dives at me, and then another.

I have no more time to think, so I just react, leveling the fusion-cannon arm at the invading Black-Os and catching one midair near me. A solid strike to the head blows his skull apart. Still, the ones behind him come, undaunted by the powerful weapon in my hands. They're not individuals. They exist as one—they're *everyone*, and because of that, they're no one.

Is Hawthorne's consciousness still in there among them?

Another wave of Spectrum Black-Os nears me, forcing me behind a stone pillar for cover. Cherno moves with me and braces behind an adjacent pillar. I fire in bursts at the Spectrum soldiers who approach me, blowing their heads apart. It's a massacre. Cherno and I keep shooting, and they keep falling, but more and more take their places.

Bodies pile up in front of us, forming a wall of gore. We shoot down our enemies who scurry across to the ceiling, the ones that come at us from the sides, and the ones in front of us, until the first wave is all dead and the air reeks of charred flesh and exploded ions. The next wave comes, almost without pause. My weapon's charge rapidly depletes. I need to rearm soon—literally.

Cherno isn't so fortunate when it comes to Spectrum's protocol. No rules bar the soldiers from returning fire at him. In the next wave, he catches a fusionmag strike to the chest. It bounces off him, repelled as if by Clifton's Copperscale material. It leaves a dark, scrawling mark resembling a lightning strike on his dragon-scale flesh. Cherno reels back, bending at his waist and shielding his chest with his hand. I target the soldier that shot him and fire until I blow a hole in her.

"Are you hurt?" I bellow at Cherno.

He scowls at me with disgust. "These puny human-halflings cannot harm me!"

I gape at him. The timbre of his voice sounds like a volcano rumbling. I hadn't expected him to speak—at least not in my language. A nod, maybe, but not this. I'd expected to hear Spectrum's garble—the abbreviated, often symbolic, guttural, more efficient, higher-echelon code that they spout for everything seen and unseen.

"You understand me," I reply.

He doesn't look at me but continues tracking and destroying our enemies. "It isn't difficult. Yours is a simpleton's language."

"Oh." We whittle down the few Spectrum soldiers left, but behind them another wave stands ready to enter the room.

Cherno growls. "Do you intend to kill them until we run out of ammunition and get crushed? Or should we do the intelligent thing and find a way out of this tomb?"

So dragon-men are prone to sarcasm. Lovely. "There's a hidden door."

"Where?"

"Ceiling." I point above us with a motion of my chin. "This used to be an ancient oubliette. Do you know what that is?"

He glances at the outline of a door at the peak of the arching ceiling, a story or more above us. "Is it a place to hold your enemies?"

"Yes."

"In my time, we called it a *gaolgahl*."

"Your time?"

"Can you climb?"

"The walls?"

"Yes."

"No."

Another wave of Spectrum soldiers advances. Cherno dives behind my pillar, joining me.

"Climb on my back," he orders.

"What? No!" I fire on the soldiers.

"Climb on my back, and I'll get us out of here." He grasps my elbow and pulls me nearer to him.

"We'll never make it," I balk, shooting off target.

"We'll make it. They don't intend to kill you, so you can be my shield." He turns away and hunches down. I'm out of options. My weapon misfires. It's dying. Soon I won't be able to scorch holes in these careening monsters, and then they'll have me. I choose the lesser evil and jump onto Cherno's back and wrap my arm around his thick neck. He springs from his crouch and sprints toward the wall at the back of the morgue. His talons screech against the stone fortress's dull-gray granite, finding purchase. Rapidly, we ascend the rough surface.

Claws extend from the flesh-covered fingertips of the Black-O soldiers below us. They scramble up the wall. I use what's left of the fusion power in my weapon to kill as many as I can. When Cherno reaches the barrel-vaulted ceiling, I'm forced to drop my weapon and clutch him with both arms. My legs wrap around his waist. My cheek rests against his scaly flesh. It's cool like armor, but softer and suppler, like butterfly wings, with scales and ribs that refract the light and appear iridescent.

At the high point of the ceiling, Cherno punches his fist against the trapdoor, almost dislodging me with the jolts. My feet dangle.

"Hold on tighter," he grunts.

I grab him more firmly, and he heaves against the trapdoor. The hinges grind and shriek, but the stone door opens like a hatch. Cherno reaches his palms up onto the floor above and pulls us out of the morgue. I let go and tumble onto the sturdy floor. I crawl to the trapdoor and force it closed, pushing with all my might. It falls shut with a bang. Sprawling on top of it, I pant and stare up at the rosette-shaped glass ceiling a couple of stories above me. Moonlight shines on my face. It must be dark in here, but my eyes compensate for the lack of light.

We're in the Round Ballroom, aptly named for its shape. It's near my former wing of the Sword Palace. The trapdoor lies at the core of the marble dance floor. Inlaid with intricate glass tiles, it looks like the center of a stained-glass rosette. Few guests or residents have known about the door as they glided across the ballroom at one of Mother's lavish soirées. They'd comment on the clever way the pattern on the floor reflected the light of the eight stained-glass rosette windows ringing the room, and of course, the one forming the ceiling.

Cherno pants as he climbs to his feet. The trapdoor jolts upward, and I'm nearly thrown before it closes again.

"Cherno!" I squeak.

He runs to one of the curved silk settees in the room. With a powerful shove, he sends it gliding across the dance floor, scattering the round bolsters. I crab-walk backward off the trapdoor just before the divan settles onto it.

The enormous crystal chandelier above us glows golden, dispelling the gray with brilliant color. "You're alive," Kipson Crow, incredulous, calls from the balcony above us.

What I see next makes me question my reality. Two figures, both of whom I know to be dead—one by cyanide poisoning and the other by throne-room drowning—stand near the balustrade on the floor above. Seeing Kipson Crow and Flannigan Star together is like having a pin in the back of my head pulled and feeling my mind explode.

"Returned from the dead, have you, Roselle?" Crow asks. He aims his feral sneer at me.

His teeth gleam white and straight in the shine of the chandelier. Not a mark mars the supple veneer of his youthful complexion. His ashen-blond hair is combed back in his usual style, but it's glossier, and there's more of it. The kill tallies—gone. He's handsomely dressed in dark, elegant evening attire.

"I could ask the same of you," I reply. My fingers ache for a weapon.

The young woman beside him holds his arm like a lover would, leaning against his side, with a curious smile for me. The velvety black waves of her hair reach only to her chin. Her emerald-colored silk gown complements her every curve. The room is lovelier with her in it.

"You killed the old version of me," Kipson's voice echoes from above. "Do you want to know what I thought about as I was drowning?"

"No. I don't care."

"My final thought," he continues through clenched teeth, "was for my firstborn sister, Sabah. I'd often wondered if she'd felt pain as I drowned her. Now I know what it's like. It has left me conflicted as to whether I should bring her back." Fear trembles down my spine. "Maybe I should thank you, Roselle, for killing me. I was dreading suicide. Nostalgia for my old body—you know how it is."

"Oh, you're welcome. I'm happy to keep killing you until it sticks."

He squeezes the marble balustrade. "I feel the same way about you, Roselle. I'd kill you again and again. But I wasn't resurrected. Bodies are merely something to wear now—like this suit. I've been growing this one for a while. I have several more just like it." He strokes a hand over the fabric on his chest. "I'm immortal, and soon I'll be able to access every living person in the world."

I grit my teeth. "Was I dead?" I ask. I'm starting to think that I really did drown.

This elicits a soulless grin. "You were as dead as this one here, not too long ago." He indicates Flannigan with a gesture of his chin. "I checked you myself in the morgue when I came to inspect my corpse, but unlike Flannigan Star"—he runs his hand over the bare skin of her slender arm—"*I* didn't bring you back to life. How are you here?"

"Magic, Kipson." I use a playful tone that's the opposite of how I feel. "For my next trick, I'm going to make you disappear." It's a boast I can't possibly make good on. I don't even know what happened to me, let alone how to dismantle him *and* his artificial intelligence.

He knows it, too. "As if you could, Roselle."

All the ballroom doors rip open at once. Several units of Spectrum soldiers swarm inside and surround the perimeter of the dance floor. None of them try to touch Cherno or me. Cherno draws closer to my side.

Kipson notices. "You're no longer under my control, beast."

"Did you think you could own me forever?" Cherno replies with a bitterness that makes me like him more.

"Did you remove your implant?"

"It melted."

"How?"

"Puberty."

"Puber—why didn't you tell me? I'm your creator."

"You're not my creator," Cherno retorts. "Do not sully the term. A true creator makes something where nothing exists. You simply found a way to fuse two types of beings together. That doesn't make you a god. That makes you a scientist."

"You're angry with me so you decided to help *her*?" Betrayal weakens Crow's voice. His fingers skim over his heart.

"It's ironic," Cherno answers. "In my time, I would've ripped out her throat if she'd dared to speak to me, but now, here, Roselle the Conqueror is exactly what this world deserves."

"Roselle the Conqueror? You're referring to *her*?" Agent Crow snorts. "She isn't a goddess. She's a secondborn nothing with an exquisite pedigree." But his expression turns to grudging fascination. He doesn't seem to believe a word he just said.

"She resembles the goddess I knew," Cherno says.

"The goddess you knew? That's not possible. I created you from a petrified egg."

"You spliced. You manipulated. You did not *create*. And that wasn't an egg. That was the form I took to await my next lifetime—a form imposed on me by my enemies."

Agent Crow grips the balustrade with both hands and leans over it. "I *made* you!"

"No. I already existed! But you *changed* me. I will return the favor by *unmaking* you!"

"I'm a god!" Kipson roars.

The handsome figure above us thrusts his palm toward Cherno. The power of an invisible airship collides with the ancient being beside me. The dragon-man jerks off his feet and hurtles backward across the ballroom. He bounces a few times when he hits the ground before skidding to a stop on his back. Spectrum soldiers converge on him. For a moment, I can't see Cherno, but in the next second, fire engulfs the Black-Os at the bottom of the dogpile. Cherno forces the burning legion off him. Back on his feet, he spews scorching flames from his mouth. More soldiers ignite.

My attention volleys to Crow. *Kill him while he's distracted.*

The psychopath thrusts his palm out again. Cherno jolts from the floor, rising in midair. An invisible force sends him flying into the far wall. The stone behind him shatters. Huge cracks shoot in all directions. Cherno winces and moans.

Before I make it to the stairway, Black-Os jump me. I punch and kick. Overwhelming numbers pile on top of me. I'm wrestled to the floor. It's excruciating just to breathe. Knees dig into my spine. Their weight crushes my lungs. When they finally pile off my torso and pull me to my feet, Cherno's head hangs motionless. Four Spectrum soldiers hold him up. Others haul me back beneath the balcony. Kipson Crow—the god—peers down with a satisfied smirk.

"How are you alive?" I ask, tasting blood in my mouth.

"I'm not merely alive, Roselle," he replies. "I'm replicating myself in everything. You didn't think you actually killed me, did you?" He laughs and leans over the balcony's ornate balustrade. "You can't kill me. I *am* Spectrum."

The young woman next to him places her elbows on the railing and with one hand cups her chin in her palm. "Kipson, why is this woman so familiar to me?" she asks, her innocent eyes absorbing me.

"You stole monikers from Census with her on a Sword military Base," he replies.

She straightens in surprise. "I did?" Her smile's impish.

"Yes." Crow's indulgent grin spreads. "You helped to blow up the vault and flood the Census Base. Do you remember that?"

"And you made me a new body and reconstructed my mind, didn't you?" she replies, like a child reciting a story she'd heard thousands of times.

"I did." He taps her nose with this fingertip.

"And you breathed life back into me, right?"

"That's correct."

"But I don't remember any of that." Her pout is seductive.

"Maybe one day you will. I mapped the undamaged portion of your original mind." He caresses the hair near her temple with the backs of his fingers. "It may still form the connections you need to remember your past."

"But she knew me?" Flannigan turns to face me again.

"She's the one who got you killed."

"Did you get me killed?" Flannigan 2.0 asks me.

I shiver. "The Flannigan I knew," I reply, "would never ask that question. She was cunning and brilliant. She went into those underground tunnels to destroy the thing you're standing next to and others like him. She killed herself rather than be taken alive by them. So, no.

I didn't get you killed. Flannigan was a leader. You're just a pathetic, doe-eyed copy of her."

Apparently I hurt her feelings. Her bottom lip starts to tremble, and her eyes well with tears.

Kipson Crow sneers, just like his old body would've, but without the steel teeth or the kill tallies, he isn't as scary. "Don't listen to her, Flannigan. She's nothing. You and I are going to pay a visit to Marius, Claudia, and the rest of the Census High Council in Virtues. They believe they still have the right to exist. They're wrong. When we return, Roselle's little technician friend, Ransom Winterstrom, will show me exactly how he created the device he implanted in Roselle's brain. Then he and I are going to dissect her together. Won't that be fun, Roselle?"

I lick the blood off my lip and smile. "Can't wait," I reply confidently, but inside I'm quaking with fear.

Kipson Crow places a gentle arm around Fake Flannigan's shoulders and leads her away from the balcony. She casts a look over her shoulder at me before she exits the ballroom.

Sad eyes. She has very sad eyes.

Cherno, still unconscious, gets dragged away by a few well-built cyborg soldiers. Several more force me to move, too. At the junction that leads to my former wing of the estate, a mechadome with a black metal veneer idles in the shadow of the wide hallway. Its red eyes glow from an iron head fitted atop a nearly neckless Class 5Z Mechanized Sanitation Unit. I'm dragged past the squat bot and stumble into an adjacent corridor.

At the top of my lungs I yell, "Census is dead! It's just Crow! Only Crow! Ransom, the Sword Palace! Ransom, the Sword Palace! Phoenix, relay my message!"

Chapter 8
Phoenix to Flame

I moan and try to lift my cheek from a pool of my own vomit.

"I didn't hit you that hard," Kipson Crow taunts, standing over me. "Aren't you supposed to be a prodigious fighter, Roselle?"

I spit blood onto the stone floor of a square, dim cell in the Sword Palace detention center. "Aren't you supposed to be killing Census agents in Virtues with Fake Flannigan?" I ask, to buy myself some time. I lift my face. It's not Agent Crow's body that I glare at through my swollen, half-closed eyelids. The soldier who struck me looks nothing like Kipson. He has a goatish face—creepy eyes that angle in odd directions, an elongated jaw with an underbite, and garishly crooked teeth. His torso is brutish, and his fists are bludgeoning tools.

"Oh, I *am* with her. We're just now arriving in Virtues. It's only that I have a theory, and I'm curious to see if it bears out."

I shudder at his ability to be two places at once. "I have a theory, too." I wince, resting my hand on my broken ribs. "My theory is that you're insane." I take a shallow breath before I add, "I don't need to test it any further. You've already proven it."

"Why do you try to be funny, Roselle?" the soldier asks me in the exact timbre of Agent Crow's voice. He's not looking at me, though,

I don't think. It's hard to tell with his cockeyed leer, but I think he's looking at the golden glow of the fusionblade in his brutal grip. "Why don't you ever beg me for your life?"

"Because that would give you power." I manage to pull myself up to my knees and sit back on my heels.

"But I already have all the power, Roselle."

"Maybe so, but I didn't give it to you."

"Ah, and there it is. The reason of reasons. Are you ready now?"

"For what?" I ask, before gnashing my teeth in pain and hanging my head.

"To die."

"Yes," I reply.

The soldier frowns. "You take all the fun out of everything." With a clumsy thrust of his fusionblade, the soldier stabs the searing point of energy through my chest, piercing my heart. The sizzling scent of burned flesh assails my nostrils. I gasp in pain and collapse. His scuffed boots move away as everything grows dark.

I blink a couple of times. The heavy ache in my chest tempts me to clutch at it. My fingers glide over charred, crusty fabric. The self-healing material of my uniform has failed, unable, it would seem, to stand up to burns from a fusionblade. I cough and taste blood—old blood. The bitter flavor makes me retch, which hurts my chest. The skin is tender and burned over my heart. My eyes take a few moments to adjust to the darkness. I try to sit up, but I'm wooden. I smell bad—extremely bad. It's a mixture of vomit, blood, and urine. I groan.

A chair leg scrapes against the floor near the wall of the cell. The sound of slow, bootheeled steps and the high-pitched whine of metal chair legs dragging across the floor trigger goose bumps to rise on my flesh.

Amy A. Bartol

"You're alive." It's Agent Crow 2.0's voice—the one I haven't killed yet, the pretty, younger one—but the sound comes from the goatish soldier with the cockeyed stare and mangled teeth. The goon sets his chair right next to me. He takes a seat, rests his forearms on his knees, and stares down at me.

"So are you," I reply in a gravelly voice.

"How is that possible?" he asks. "I killed you yesterday."

"I remember."

"Look what you've done to yourself," he says.

I smell like death.

"What've I done?" I slur.

"You've *remade* yourself."

"So have you."

"Not like you." Jealousy simmers in his tone. "I created a new body—grew it in an accelerator, remapped it. You did none of those things. You regenerated."

My mind whirls. I try to rise. He doesn't attempt to stop me. My legs shake like a newborn colt's. I slump against the wall and rest my cheek on its cool surface. "What now?" I ask.

His eyes dart in a couple of directions. "Now we see how many ways you can die . . . and come back."

I brace myself with my elbow and swallow past the growing lump in my throat.

The creepy creature rises from his seat and lurches toward me. The fervent expression on his face turns my stomach. I stretch my hand out to ward him off and scream, "Stay away from me!"

Something expels from my palm—a fiery, invisible energy that singes my fingertips. I fall to my knees while the goatish fiend rockets off his feet and flies backward into the stone wall. His bones shatter, and he slides to the ground and slouches into a heap. Blood streams from his nose.

Is this real?

Hacking pants judder from between my lips. My hand tingles as if from the horrific recoil of a high-caliber weapon. Weak, and on my hands and knees, I crawl past the broken body of Agent Crow's henchman. My aching heart bashes my chest from fear that the creature will somehow awaken. The door of my cell opens, and Black-Os swell over the threshold. One of them, a beautiful young woman, smiles at me. Her silver eye glows brighter as she says in Agent Crow's voice, "My, you're stronger than I thought, Roselle. But not strong enough."

Kipson reaches toward me with her delicate hand. I eavesdrop on the frequency they're dialed into and decode the garbled stream driven by Kipson's orders. With my mind I push Crow's consciousness out of her. His energy rages all around us like a dark, menacing storm. I smell him in the ether. Quickly, I interrupt the Spectrum negotiations between the remaining Black-Os and drive one of my own thoughts into the stream of consciousness: *Help me up.*

The soldier beside me hesitates. A sharp pain attacks my mind as Kipson rebels against my hostile takeover of his drones, but I mentally fend him off. He's weaker than I am when it comes to the soldiers in the cell. Maybe his signal isn't as strong as mine? Proximity must matter.

The female soldier clutches my elbow, helping me to my feet. She holds me erect. The other soldiers converge on us in full-on pounce mode. I close my eyes and concentrate on sending them a task.

Bring me Ransom Winterstrom.

I hold my breath. Everyone stops, turns, and stomps away. Following them, I limp out into the wide containment area. The walls are dull metal, and transparent security walls divide other cells. A monitoring station with holographic displays occupies the center of the room.

All the cells in this area are filled with Sword diplomats and firstborns. Some I recognize. Others are unrecognizable, tortured to bloody pulps. I hobble to the command center. The station has hundreds of individual cells in its monitoring grid. Touching an image enlarges the hologram and brings it to the center. I scan through hundreds of them, using my fingers to enlarge and then swipe them away, sending them back into the grid. It takes me several minutes to locate Cherno. His smoldering golden eyes catch my attention. He's in the corner of his cell, his scaly flesh blending with his surroundings. I unlock the door to his cage. It opens.

"Cherno," I speak into the communicator, "we gotta go!"

I trip the emergency release, triggering all the cell doors to open at once. The prisoners who can walk emerge from their chambers on shaky legs. Cherno's among them. He wastes no time joining me. The others scatter, scuttling to the exits at the far end of the detention center.

"Finally." Cherno takes my arm with the familiarity of someone who's known me for years. "Which way?" he growls, scanning the detention center. Blood seeps from slashing knife wounds on his arms and chest. Some are scabbed over, but some appear fresh. He's been tortured, too. Bruises mar his jaw and cheeks. Those are harder to see on his rough skin, but they're there. He drags me in the direction of an exit.

"Wait." I resist. "We need to wait!"

My desperation makes him pause. "Why?" he growls.

"Because I can't leave without my friend."

"You have a friend?" His eyebrows rise, as if this is the most shocking news of the millennia.

"He's a Census technician. He—"

"Technicians are not friends. They're hideous monsters who will steal your soul." Cherno latches on to my forearm again and tugs. My toes curl under and drag across the stone floor as he hauls me toward the open door that leads into an underground corridor.

"Wait! He's not a normal technician. He's special. He gave me a tactical neural implant that allows me to—"

"To what?" Cherno pauses, glancing back at me.

I wrench my arm from his grasp. "To hack their systems. Eavesdrop on their frequencies. Seize control of their soldiers—" Movement at one of the entrances has me diving to the floor and towing Cherno with me. We crouch and watch.

Spectrum soldiers converge at the entrance, led by a towering cyborg with arm-mounted cannons. The creature, who's covered in black body armor, has nearly lidless eyes, and its neck and skull have a transparent layer of skin. A visorless helmet encases its head.

The skeletal head opens its mouth and speaks. "Roselle." Agent Crow's voice emanates from the gigantic soldier. The vocal chords vibrate visibly. This creature is a genetic mutation of Crow. "Did you really think you could get away?"

From the opposite end of the detention center, the horde of Spectrum soldiers I'd sent out earlier troops in, carrying the unconscious body of Ransom Winterstrom.

A sigh of hope issues from me. I stand up and reveal myself, to distract Crow's attention from Ransom. Cherno stands as well. "I didn't really think I'd get away"—I turn to face Crow—"until now."

The cybernetic Crow clone lumbers toward me. I lift my hand and thrust it in his direction. The creature roars. A shuddering crack of energy releases through my fingertips and palm. It slams into the cyborg, crushing the ebony casement of his armor. Blood and flesh squirt out of the armor's crevasses like dough squeezed in a fist.

The power it takes leaves me almost unable to stand. Blood drips from my nose. Without missing a breath, Crow emerges in the soldier next to the mess of his vile clone, just as it crumples to the floor.

"You think you're more powerful than me?" his voice rages from this newly claimed body. He waves the soldier's hand. The other Spectrum soldiers, who were carrying Ransom toward us, stop and stiffen into statues. Ransom tumbles from their grasp and slips to the floor, his limbs flailing. He doesn't move. I can't tell if he's alive.

"Proximity, Roselle, is the only reason you can control these soldiers better than me. I'm on my way back to my Palace, and when I arrive, you'll wish you'd stayed dead. I'll make you suffer for your crimes against your god."

"You're not a god."

Cherno nudges my arm and whispers in my ear. "Withdraw. We need allies. I know where to find some."

"Your revolution is too late!" Crow bellows. "You should've remained loyal to me, Cherno. Now you'll die a traitor's death."

Cherno's expression darkens. "Come," he urges. The energy around us swirls. The body of the Crow soldier sparks with it. Cracks of light form in his armor and flesh. It radiates so brightly, I squint, shield my eyes, and turn away. Cherno collects Ransom from the floor and hoists the technician's limp body over his massive shoulder. Flaring shafts of heat and light stab out from the Crow soldier in sharp beams that break apart and form birdlike images that glide around us and dive in harrowing swoops.

Cherno hollers from over his shoulder, "Roselle, let's go!"

I stagger in his direction, following, chased by Agent Crow's deep-throated laughter. In the corridor, I hobble after Cherno, watching Ransom's head sway back and forth until, *boom*, the building shakes and rock dust overtakes us. I'm thrown forward, sent crashing and sliding on the floor. My ears ring. Dizzy, I get to my feet and balance myself with a hand on the wall. I choke and stumble in the haze.

"Cherno!" I call out.

"Here," he growls just ahead of me. "Find us a way out of this maze."

I clutch the dragon's enormous hand. His skin's cool, but his breath's steamy. He carries Ransom as I lead him, by feel alone, through a series of corridors. I know where I am. I've walked these hallways thousands of times. We're near the kitchens.

The garbled voices of Spectrum soldiers sound ahead. I veer into a prep area. The haze of dust lends us cover. The kitchen staff, all Zeros, file out in emotionless order. Still, I back away, afraid that Crow might recognize me through them and claim one's consciousness.

Intent on not drawing their attention, I don't notice the squat bot hovering motionless in front of me. I bump into it. Cherno collides with me.

"Phoenix!" Its name comes out of me in a breathy rush. I let go of Cherno's hand and crouch to peer at Phoenix's metal face. The red, glowing orbs of my automated assistant scroll the words, *You're alive.*

"Reykin?" I whisper. My voice hitches as I ask Phoenix if he's being controlled by Reykin now.

Phoenix's lenses nod yes. Tears cloud my vision. I hadn't allowed myself the luxury of thinking about Reykin. I wanted to protect him from Crow.

I'm everything Reykin dreads. My stomach twists in knots. *He can't possibly love me anymore. I'm a monster who kills her allies. I'm a mindless drone—at least, that's what he must think—one that has said good-bye to her good side.* I know I'm right when Phoenix's cannon arm slowly raises toward me.

"Reykin, I found Ransom," I blurt out. "He's hurt." I indicate Ransom behind me. Deep cuts in his skin seep blood, soaking his uniform. Dark bruises and swelling mar his face. "We need a way out. Can you help us?" I bite my lip. My heart aches. Phoenix's cannon arm hesitates, and then it lowers. The iron-rimmed lenses nod yes again, glowing a darker red. The bot extends its claw hand to me. I take it and rise from my crouch. It hovers its way to the back of the food-prep area, leading me to the garbage chutes. Cherno's just a step behind. With a wave of its cannon arm, Phoenix opens the automated chute doors. A putrid odor rises from below. My nose wrinkles.

"I will not fit through there," Cherno grumbles.

Hovering in midair, Phoenix turns, evaluates Cherno, and then faces the opening to the garbage chute again. It raises its cannon arm and fires a couple of hydrogen pulses into the chute. The blasts widen the sluice's opening. Sprinklers turn on. The metal channel transforms into a water slide. I waste no time in helping Cherno shove Ransom down it. I go next, hoisting myself in feetfirst and sliding into the darkness. The sprinklers in the metallic tube drench me all the way down to the receptacle at the bottom. I land on top of Ransom's legs, which lie atop slimy vegetable peels. My eyes water at the smell.

I scurry off Ransom and tug him from the middle of the pile just in time to avoid the massive dragon-man emerging from the slide. Potato peels stick to his skin. The waterfall drenches everything.

Cherno stands in the muck and sloshes toward me. "Are you hurt?" the giant growls. It's dark in here, but my vision adjusts. Cherno must have nocturnal vision, too, because he stares at me, awaiting my answer.

"No." It's a lie. I ache everywhere, but I know he means, "Can you still move?" I cradle Ransom's head above the rising water and slimy waste.

Phoenix materializes from the chute, glistening with beads of water and hovering above the muck. Its glowing red eyes lend an even more sinister ambience to the composting tank.

"What is that thing?" Cherno asks.

"It's my mechadome."

"What's a mechadome?"

"A robot assistant."

"It appears the furthest thing from helpful."

"It was designed to clean up sewage."

"Why would you have an assistant that—"

"I'll explain later. We have to go, before this tank fills up and we drown in peels."

Cherno turns and splashes around the perimeter until he finds a hatch. Using his considerable strength, he ratchets the lever open. A gasp of putrid air belches from the tank. Cherno shoves the door wider. Water flows out, taking me with it. I spill onto the floor of a huge underground warehouse. Heavy equipment and rows of similar composting tanks go on for as far as I can see. Water from the hatch washes into a grate in the floor. Cherno takes Ransom from me and heaves the technician's limp body onto his shoulder.

Phoenix hovers at my side and reaches its claw hand to take mine. The scrolling words *Follow me* show in Phoenix's red glare.

"My mechadome wants us to follow it."

"Do you trust it?" Cherno asks.

"It will lead us out of here," I reply.

It's not what Cherno asked. The real answer is that I don't trust Reykin, so by extension, I don't trust Phoenix. He must believe that I'm his enemy. That breaks my heart. I choke back my desire to sob. As circumstances dictate, though, Reykin's still the best shot we have of getting out of here, but only because Cherno and I have Ransom. Reykin won't kill us until his brother's safe. Even knowing this, my heart wants to follow Phoenix with its every ragged beat, even when my head knows my hope is misplaced.

My limping gait's less pronounced than it was a few minutes ago. I allow the short bot to guide me away from the warehouse. We enter the mouth of an arching tunnel made of stone. Few zeroborns occupy this part of the Sword Palace. Instead it's awash with automated security checkpoints, camera drones, and roaming maginots. Reykin must have infiltrated the Sword Palace systems, because doors unlock and slide open for us when we approach.

All the hairs on my nape rise when I hear the sharp tap of metal claws against the damp stone floor. A ferocious howl pierces the air of the tunnel, echoing. My breath catches. A maginot model I don't recognize emerges from the shadows ahead. Steely blue eyes from the redesigned wolfhound home in on me. Nothing about it can be described as "cuddly." It's pure metal. The shape of its muzzle resembles the former model, but it's not designed to look like a real animal. It's hairless—a cold, robotic frame.

Its ears prick back. Spiky metal hackles rise on its neck and withers. The killing machine snaps its jaws open and closed a few times before it throws its steel nose in the air, sniffing our strange scents. It charges toward us.

Phoenix levels its cannon arm at the maginot's shiny veneer and emits a powerful pulse from the barrel. It strikes the maginot and electrocutes it, scrambling its circuits. The gigantic wolfhound glitches several times before tumbling onto its side. Phoenix tugs me forward. We creep past the shorted-out maginot.

Other mechanical sentinels suffer the same fate when we encounter them in the winding passageways. The drone cameras are different, though. It's like they don't even see us. Reykin must be controlling them, too. I gave him access to Sword industrial systems when I uploaded his virus into my favorite maginot. He can hack into everything in this city now, maybe even all of Swords.

Distant thumps and whirls break the silence now and again the farther away we get from the Sword residences. Automated machines and mechanical drones go about their work, and the air grows damper and cooler with each step. The fabric of my tattered uniform dries, but my core temperature doesn't improve all that much. I shiver and my teeth chatter.

To distract myself from how wretched I feel, I ask Cherno, "Who are you?"

"Who are you?" His scaly eyebrow arches. "You look like the god I knew, but you don't act like her."

"Who do you think I am?"

"You're Roselle—Torturer of Men, Destroyer of Dragons, Harbinger of Death."

I snort with derision. "I'm not that Roselle. I'm Roselle St. Sismode. Secondborn Sword—now a firstborn heir to a Fate that no longer exists. The fatedom died with my mother."

"Your mother was unworthy of power, like you used to be. If you were still a narcissistic tyrant, I would annihilate you."

"How do you know what I'm like? You don't know me."

He snorts, and smoke plumes from his nostrils. "I watched you kill yourself to stop Crow—saw you rise from the dead, curl up next to your enemy, and weep for his demise."

I hold back fresh tears. "Hawthorne wasn't my enemy. He was my best friend, and I killed him."

"You did what had to be done. Our only regret should be that it didn't work. You were too late to drown the monster in an abyss. Like you and me, Crow has many lives now."

"Many lives, what does that even mean?"

"You drowned . . . and yet here you are asking me questions and denying that you're a god."

"I'm not a god."

"So you say."

"How come you didn't drown in the throne room?"

"I'm part dragon. I can hold my breath a long time—slow down my heart, stop it when necessary. But also, it's because I'm a god."

"Right," I reply, trying to keep the sarcasm from my tone, "because you're someone who knew the original Roselle. When was that again?"

"Eh?"

"When was your last life, when you knew the other Roselle?"

"I don't know time. All I know is that it was vastly different from the squalor I've been subjected to here."

"How do you know that's real? How do you know your memories weren't given to you at some stage of your development, by a technician?"

"My memories are authentic," he replies defensively. "I can recall every one of my lifetimes. I was there when you tore down Hyperion's temple on the Cliffs of Agamaya. You slaughtered all his followers. It was gruesome and ugly, like everything you do."

"*Did*—like everything I *did*. If you're going to insist that I'm somehow Roselle the Death Maker—"

"The Harbinger of Death."

"Yeah, her—then let's talk about it in the past tense, because I'm not a god anymore. I'm just a woman."

"Who drowns and comes back to life, who conjures weapons from thin air, who controls others with her mind."

"But I—that's not *me*. I mean it *is* me, but I'm not doing it. I mean, I'm doing it, but I have this *thing* in my head."

"I had a *thing* in my head, too, until it melted. It did not give me the powers you possess."

"Yours was different from mine, or so I'm told."

"Well, if you see Hyperion, I wouldn't tell him you're not a god. He might still be angry about Agamaya. In fact, don't tell him I'm helping you. You're our sworn enemy. It will reflect poorly on me."

"What?" I pause for a moment with my mouth hanging open. I snap it shut, and then I hurry along the tunnel for several miles beside Cherno, badgering him with questions. He's completely delusional, like insane times infinity, but some of the things he tells me raise goose bumps on my skin. Before long, the air blows colder and the tunnel slopes upward. The stone walls roughen as the passageway narrows. We can no longer walk side by side, but must go on single file. The cries of gulls break the silence. Ahead, a transparent force field covers the opening to the beach. The hum coming from the force field gives it away, along with the faint, shimmering reflection of us in it as we near. On the other side of the fortification, waves surge upon the shore at mid-tide.

Phoenix pauses before the security wall. It's the type of barrier that allows air to pass through it, but not living beings. Gusts of bracing wind billow in, lifting and twirling my hair. The sun's light on the water wrings a small breathy sound from me. Dangerous, what it does—instilling hope that my life can go on after all this. Reykin must have control over the force field, because the security wall falls away, allowing us to pass through the crag onto the shore.

I yank off my wet boots, even though it's cold. Sand presses between my toes. I stagger toward the frigid surf foaming onto the beach. Waves steal around my ankles. Hawthorne's face floats in my memory. The first time I saw the sea, I was with him, in an airship, on our way to war.

I killed my best friend. Heart-wrenching emptiness envelops me.

"What now?" Cherno asks, joining me in the tide. He left Ransom sprawled behind us on the sand.

"We wait."

"For what?"

"For them to decide if they want to take a chance on us."

"Them?"

"The resistance—if they even exist anymore."

"We don't need them. We have allies."

"Who?"

"Gods."

"The sleeping ones?"

"Yes."

"You're going to awaken gods?"

"Not me. You."

"Why do you think they're sleeping?"

"They would never allow Crow to exist if they were awake."

Behind us, Gates of Dawn soldiers materialize from alcoves in jagged rocks along the bottom of the cliff. I knew they were there. I'd felt them—their life forces, energy. It's all connected. And as with all things, I'm one with it. High-powered weapons train on Cherno and me. From the shadow of the rocks, a figure emerges. At first I convince myself it's Dune, my mentor, even though I know it's not. Daltrey Leon, Dune's older brother, strides toward Ransom alone. His dark hair catches the ocean breeze and stirs around his shoulders. His combat armor isn't the same as when I fought the Gates of Dawn on the battlefield. It's newly issued and bears the signature lines of a designer I know well. Clifton. The etching in the breastplate's armor forms gates.

The soldiers with Daltrey hang back. Their weapons aim at me. They know I've been Crow's assassin for a month at least. They probably believe I'm still mind-controlled—that this is a trap to draw them out into the open. Wariness in Daltrey's sandy eyes confirms it.

I feel Reykin nearby—the essence of him. I can detect his scent on the breeze. My senses are heightened. I've changed. Death has given me a new understanding of life. I feel the blue of the sky—not the color, but the *frequency*. I feel *all* the frequencies. *They* can be my armor.

Daltrey kneels beside Ransom in the sand and assesses his injuries. He waves his men forward. Gates of Dawn soldiers rush in, lift Ransom, and carry him off the beach. A watercraft emerges from the surf and beaches like a suicidal whale on the shore. The belly of the craft opens like a gaping mouth, revealing more soldiers ready to attend to Ransom. Phoenix sidles over to me, its eyes glowing brighter. It takes my hand in its claw and raises its cannon arm at Daltrey, as if in warning. My mechadome tries to shield me from the weapons trained on me, but it can't possibly cover all the angles.

I pay Phoenix and Daltrey little attention. My mind seeks Reykin. I feel his rage and distress. He needs to speak to me, but they're keeping him from me. He's here somewhere, but he's restrained. I need to see his face. I need to confess everything to him—tell him I'm an angel of death, ruthless, that I'm somewhere between me and infinity now.

Daltrey approaches us and nods a cautious greeting. "Roselle."

"Daltrey." I return the nod. How this goes is up to him. I wait for the leader of the Gates of Dawn to make the next move.

"Will you introduce me to your friend?"

"This is Cherno. He's a . . . well . . . he's a . . ."

"I'm a god."

"He's a god," I manage to say without grimacing.

Daltrey blinks in disbelief, but his manners prevail. "Cherno." He gives the dragon-man a curt nod and edges nearer to us.

"Your services are not required. We're on a quest. Heal the technician. Roselle has a special connection to him. The death-harbinger and I will collect him later."

Daltrey frowns. "The death-harbinger?"

"Your gods have returned to save your miserable lives from—"

"Cherno, please let me handle this," I interrupt.

Cherno's eyes narrow at Daltrey. "Why haven't they brought tributes and laid them at our feet?" Smoke huffs from Cherno's nose. His golden irises flicker with internal fire.

"I said I'll handle it." Cherno growls at me, but I ignore him and face Daltrey. "Will you walk with me? We only have a few minutes. Kipson Crow is on his way here. He's aligned with Spectrum—part of the AI. I don't know if I can protect you."

"You know I can't let you live," Daltrey replies.

Behind Daltrey, Reykin screams, "Run, Roselle!"

Reykin sprints toward us over a dune. He doesn't have armor. Pit stains darken his white shirt. The diagnostic headset he uses to control Phoenix juts out from his ear and shadows his mouth. Shackles bind his arm.

A vestige of grief in Daltrey's look gives way to determination. He yanks a grenade from his belt and triggers it. The fusion weapon flashes yellow, orange, red.

Without me moving, an invisible force from my mind strikes the grenade from Daltrey's hand. Strobing red, it hurls away from us into the ocean. The bomb detonates. A geyser erupts, spewing salt water and sand into the air. Fear and surprise rattle through me. Something in my mind seized the grenade, moved it. It was an unconscious act—a survival instinct.

"You did that!" Daltrey accuses. "You're telekinetic!"

With a deep snarl, Cherno lurches toward Daltrey. I step between them. "Wait!" I put my hands on Cherno's chest, staying him. "Don't hurt him, Cherno." Then I spread my arms wide so they stay apart. "Daltrey, I'm on your side."

"You're Crow's assassin," Daltrey retorts. "You can't be trusted."

"Roselle!" Reykin yells again. Just over the crest of the dune behind him, an army of Black-Os surges. The swarm of cyborgs fires on Daltrey's soldiers. The rebels' weapons finally swing away from me, and my former allies open fire.

Airships converge above the sand and water, and the Black-O invasion of the beach commences. Cherno reaches for Daltrey's combat belt and plucks a grenade from it. Winding back, he hurls it into the air. The small fusion bomb collides with a Burton fighter. It detonates, blowing a hole in the nose of the spiraling airship. Smoke and flames burst from it. Careening, the Winger screams over our heads, plunging into the sea.

The ground trembles. Daltrey flinches. I scream, "Get to shelter!" and shove him aside.

Two beefy Burton Rapier airships target Daltrey's men. I thrust both my palms up toward the soaring fighters. I feel connected to them, like I'm wielding toy airships on strings of energy. I clap my hands together, and the two Burton jets smash into each other and explode. Flames and burning debris scorch the beach where they crash.

My head feels on fire, ready to explode. Something seeps from my ear. I touch my fingertips to it. *Blood.* Dizzy, I try to regain my balance. The world tilts sideways.

"Roselle!" Reykin shouts. He runs headlong to me and falls into my arms. I catch him and drape my hands around his nape. He's wet with sweat. The dark stubble of his cheek abrades me as he pants against my neck. "You're alive!" he repeats over and over.

My throat's too tight to speak. My hands run over his damp shirt. I locate the cuffs restraining his wrists. Concentrating, I gather to myself an abundance of scattered energy from around us and channel high-frequency pulses from my palms to pry the metal apart at a molecular level. The alloy cracks and shatters, freeing him. Reykin throws his arms around me and lifts me off my feet for a sticky, somewhat painful hug.

An explosion nearby brings Reykin to his knees. He shields me with his body as sand rains on his back. A second later, he's on his feet, dragging me to mine. He yanks me away from the Spectrum soldiers pouring over the terrain.

"C'mon!" he yells.

With Reykin's tugging hand on my wrist, I sprint after him, not knowing where he's heading, but trusting that he has a plan. Cherno follows right behind me. Beside him, Phoenix and Daltrey keep pace. A squadron of Spectrum soldiers churns up the sand, trying to catch us. They're gaining, fast. Their cybernetic limbs bounce off the sand, propelling them forward almost effortlessly. As they reach Daltrey, Cherno pauses. The dragon-man opens his mouth and breathes fire at the encroaching cyborgs. The exposed flesh on the closest metal-veneered soldiers ignites. The metal itself turns molten. The soldiers behind them leap through the fire onto the giant half-breed, tearing at his flesh with their extended claws.

I jerk against Reykin's grip on my wrist. He slows and stops when I dig my heels in the sand. I tug my arm from him and raise my hands toward Cherno. I throw precise bursts of energy at the Spectrum horde, striking the soldiers piling up on my friend. They fall off him—short-circuiting and glitching—onto their backs. Cherno reels, but he catches himself and turns toward us.

My world tilts sideways again. I lose my balance. Reykin grasps my shoulders and steadies me. Cherno joins us and hauls me up with a hand beneath my armpit. "Move!" he bellows. "Crow's here. Do you have a way off this beach?"

Panting, his gaze tense, Reykin's eyes dart from the beach, to the cliffs, the surf, the sand, to the enemy closing in, but he pauses on

Phoenix. "Maybe," he replies with a grimace. "Get together." He prods us into a disjointed cluster.

Another wave of soldiers gushes toward us, rushing in a weird-shaped formation. I squint against the setting sun, trying to make out what they're carrying. My eyes widen when I realize it's that gaudy throne, with Kipson Crow lounging on the imperial seat. He's riding the crest of a wave of soldiers. My heart leaps into my throat.

"Reykin, hurry!" I say.

Sweat drips from Reykin's brow. "Phoenix was a sanitation unit." He breathes heavily. "It's equipped to handle hazardous waste—evacuate people from hazardous environments." He readjusts his headset and orders Phoenix to activate protocols for a toxic-environment rescue.

My iron-sided mechadome reacts by lifting its cannon-shaped arm and launching a clear, plastic-looking ball into the air. The moment the material hits the sand, it inflates in seconds, transforming into a hazmat-protection bubble that looks a lot like a giant hamster ball.

Reykin scrambles to me and shouts, "Get in!"

He shoves me as I squeeze through the slit on the side of the inflated ball. I feel trapped rather than saved once I'm inside it, but I move away from the opening so Daltrey, Cherno, and Reykin can crawl in. The bubble is so big it could probably hold a few more people.

Reykin seals the opening. "Phoenix, drag us under the water and out to sea!"

My mechadome grasps the tether of the translucent orb with its claw hand and clamps it to its torso. Once it's secure, Phoenix hauls us toward the surf. The ball rolls—we sway on our feet and are forced to move with it or fall.

Suddenly an invisible force lifts me off my feet, as if I'm a kite, and I crash against the wall of the clear bubble. I wince in agony. It feels as if I'll tear in two at any moment. The energy engulfing me carries with it Crow's scent. The ball stops rolling but drags across the sand under

Phoenix's powerful hover mode. It inches off the ground, lifting like a balloon.

Cherno reaches up and with his large hand grabs my arm. He pulls me toward him so I don't rip through the material. From the look on his face, I know the soldiers are closing in. They haven't fired, though. Crow must believe we can't escape.

"Resist Crow's will," Cherno barks at me.

Pain sears my brain. "How?" I moan.

"Fight him!" he retorts through his clenched teeth, grasping my wrist with both his hands to anchor me. I try to resist, but invisible claws dig into my brain. I bite down to keep from screaming.

The bubble elongates with my body being the opposing force, but Phoenix continues to yank me and the ball anyway. We move from the sand to the water. Waves lick the bottom of the orb. Just when I think the bubble is about to burst, my mechadome submerges and drags our enormous ball just inches beneath the waves. The water diffuses Crow's power. Our bubble slingshots beneath the waves, and Phoenix tugs us into the deep.

Chapter 9
Rogue Wave

Everyone in the bubble loses their footing and falls onto one another.

I'm at the bottom of the pile, crushed by Cherno, Reykin, and Daltrey, until the orb shifts and I wind up on top of the pile, lying on Reykin's chest. Water sloshes all around us. The liquid outside of our stretchy orb pushes against it as we submerge.

"What is this thing?" Cherno groans, throwing his elbow to try to right himself. It connects with Daltrey's stomach, and the smaller man's breath comes out in an "Oof."

"It's a hazmat-protection device," Reykin says, "but they're also a lot of fun at birthday parties and outdoor picnics. Do you like it?" He grunts. Daltrey's foot presses on his head.

"No," Cherno replies.

"Phoenix has a beacon," Reykin says. "One of our ships will locate us soon. We just need to hang on until then. Can you stop moving so the bubble doesn't burst?"

Cherno growls at him and then stills.

"Are you okay?" Reykin asks me. His arms are around me, protecting me from the knees being thrown my way as Daltrey shifts. I manage to nod, then rest my head against Reykin's chest.

The smell in these close quarters borders on obscene. Cherno and I both still reek from the compost pile. I probably smelled horrendous even before that, having died and risen recently. His heart throbs in my ear like he's still running from monsters. In minutes, an aquatic, whale-like vessel swims up on our rubbery bubble and swallows Phoenix and our balloon whole.

Within the hull of the enormous submarine, oxygen pumps into the chamber and forces water out through drainage pipes until our womb-like vessel settles on the wet metal floor. Cherno and Daltrey get to their feet and touch the rubbery walls. I try to roll off Reykin, but his arms tighten around me.

My face feels warm. "Hi," I say, because I can think of nothing else. "Hi," Reykin replies.

He's larger than I remember him. Stronger. Before, he was elegant and lithe from fusionblade training—every muscle stretched and poised, like an extremely strong Diamond-Fated ballet dancer. Now, battered by war, he's taken on a warrior's build. If I didn't know any better, I'd think him a Sword. He's always seemed to me much older because of his polish and sophistication. As I gaze at him, he somehow looks a little younger now, maybe because he's trying so hard to be gentle with me.

Phoenix punctures the material. Stinky air escaping, the walls collapse in on us. Cherno tears at the material, stretching to free himself from its strange confines. Phoenix cuts bigger pieces away, exposing us to a launch hold with blue metallic walls, ceiling, and floor. Smaller aquatic crafts hang nearby. Pipes run along the ceiling. Reykin shimmies from beneath me and stands before pulling me to my feet. His left hand no longer has a golden shooting-star moniker. It has a small scar, though. It's just like him not to get the scar removed—or maybe he installs a different moniker from time to time, to hide among the masses?

Reykin's warm grip shifts in mine. He turns my right palm faceup. The pad of his thumb moves over the small star scar he finds there—his star—a seven-pointed star with three longer points that form a *W* with a backward *R* beside it.

"It is you," he says.

"It's me." I wonder why my scar never healed like the rest of me. Maybe it's timing—pre- versus post-implant? I don't know, but it's still there.

Reykin lifts my left hand, peering at my Black-O moniker. The ugly dark spot consumes the light around it. "Forgive me, but I need to take this out."

The tenderness in his voice makes me want to weep. I can't have him talking to me like that or I'll lose control and degenerate into a blubbering mess on the floor. "Why are you being so polite? The old Reykin would be forcing the chip out of me with a rusted piece of lead, telling me to hold still."

That's good. Be tough.

Not a hint of a smile curves his lips. "Yes, well, that was the old me. This is the new me—the one who has had the arrogance beaten out of him. The one who knows he has made promises he could never keep."

The rawness of his voice almost breaks me again. I blink away tears, and my throat aches. Reykin calls Phoenix forward. My little bot opens a hinge on its chest, revealing a compartment. Phoenix selects a moncalate, the tool for surgically implanting or extracting a moniker. I wonder if this is one of the devices Flannigan and I stole. As Phoenix offers it to Reykin, I blurt out, "Flannigan's alive—only it's not the real Flannigan. I mean she's real and has some of the same memories, but she's a clone, and Crow keeps her close, and he's trying to get her to remember her predecessor's past."

Reykin just stares at me for several breaths, the moncalate in his hand hovering idle above my moniker.

From behind me, Daltrey asks, "You're sure it was her?"

I glance over my shoulder at him. Tension etches lines in his face. "I'm sure. Crow told me he mapped all the memories he could recover from Flannigan onto the clone Flannigan's new brain. He's even calling her Flannigan. She *thinks* she's Flannigan."

"He's trying to find us." Reykin stares at Daltrey. "He's using *her* memories to rout us and eradicate us. It wasn't Roselle providing him with intel—it was Flan."

If his suspicious look's any indication, Daltrey doesn't seem to be drawing the same conclusions as Reykin.

"I think it's even more than that, Reykin," I reply. "I think Crow's in love with Flannigan Two. The way he looked at her, spoke to her, took her to Virtues with him to kill his enemies—he needs her close. He's making her his Fated One."

"Then he has a weakness," Cherno adds. "If we get to her, we might be able to get to him. She could be the key to discovering the chink in his armor."

A small frown touches Reykin's lips for a second and then disappears. He bends his head and moves the moncalate to the surface of my hand. "I'll be as quick as possible, Roselle," he says. He delicately positions the tool on the skin over the implanted identification processor, near my thumb and finger. He activates the moncalate, and it goes to work, sterilizing and then laser-cutting a small incision and extracting the blood-coated chip.

Reykin grimaces, worrying that he's hurting me. He has no idea that I died for the second time yesterday, pierced through the heart by a goatish man with a fusionblade. This feels like a pinch, maybe less.

"It doesn't hurt," I assure him.

The moncalate sucks the chip into a chamber attached to the device. The laser seals my skin so that only a small scar remains, but the pink line rapidly fades, like most of my other wounds. Reykin doesn't seem to notice the fading scar as he triggers the device again. The tool compresses the moniker until it shatters into small pieces.

He glances to Cherno. "You're next."

Cherno gives Reykin a bored stare while he slits his skin with a talon and digs out his own identification processor. He drops it to the floor and presses his bootheel to it, crushing it.

Reykin turns to me. "Where did you find him?"

"He's my bodyguard."

"Have you earned another heart?"

I blink, unsure what he means. "I don't think so. He believes I'm Roselle, the Goddess of War—his sworn enemy."

Reykin must have been listening to our conversation in the tunnels, because he doesn't seem the least bit surprised. Instead he replies, "You have a way of making your enemies sticketh."

"Only one Star ever did that . . . and one is all I need," I say.

Daltrey moves closer. "There's still the matter of her neural implant, Reykin."

Reykin scowls at his Gates of Dawn commander. "You saw what she did on the beach. She resisted Crow's mind control. She fought them in ways I don't even understand. She brought down airships!"

"It could all be a ruse to make us trust her enough to bring her into the fold," Daltrey replies. "Or maybe she can control it but Crow can find a way to reinstall her in his ranks. What, then? Crow has a direct link into her head. He could be watching us now."

Reykin snarls, "Do you want to destroy the best chance—maybe the only chance—we have of saving our lives?"

"Daltrey's right." I rub my temples. "I woke up once before this and was pulled back into Spectrum. No one's safe around me. I have to talk to your brother. I need him to show me where we were—the Sword Tree Base in Seas where I was implanted. I need to stop the manufacturing and implantation processes—or at least slow them down. After I see Ransom, Cherno and I can make our own plan. We won't stay and put you at risk."

"You're going to take on Crow?" Reykin glowers at Cherno. "Just the two of you?"

"No." Cherno glowers back. "First we will awaken the gods. Then we will destroy Crow."

"Is he insane, Roselle? I mean I was listening in the tunnels when he was explaining his supposed history to you—I'm just not so sure if he really believes it, or if he's programmed to believe it."

"I don't know," I reply, eyeing Cherno, "maybe he isn't programmed. Maybe it's real."

"Maybe it's real?" His tone oozes skepticism.

"I'm not programmed," Cherno huffs. Curls of smoke smolder from his nostrils.

"You don't know everything that's happened, Reykin," I reply.

"Then tell me. Everything."

"I can't tell you." I cover my face with my hands.

"You can," Reykin insists, gently lowering his voice.

I drop my hands and glare at him with tear-blinded eyes. "I really can't. Huge chunks of time are gone—pieces of me have disappeared. I don't know what I've been doing. I woke up once about a month ago, and I was in your garden in Stars. Your whole estate was an inferno. And Mags"—my voice catches—"Mags was there, and Crow—h-he was questioning her, but she broke away from him and she threw herself in the fire. And I-I *envy* her because maybe now he can't ever get to her. Crow can't bring *her* back to life to torture her over and over. He can't—"

Reykin pulls me to him, and I bury my face in his chest. I can hardly hold back my tears.

"I'm sorry," Reykin's deep voice rumbles in my ear. "You need rest." Then he tells Daltrey, "Keep us away from the main ship as long as you can."

"You think they'll *want* her on the main ship?" Daltrey asks.

"I don't care what they want. Follow my orders, Daltrey. You're not in charge anymore. You transferred leadership of everything to me when you made your suicide plan to kill Roselle, remember? Everyone reports to me now. Just keep us away from them while Roselle rests. And get a status report on my brother."

Reykin's arm shifts around my shoulders. He leads me away from Cherno and Daltrey, toward a hatch door. We enter a narrow corridor together. The dull-blue ceiling and metallic walls echo his booted footsteps. My bare feet make almost no sound. Heavy footsteps ring behind us.

Reykin pauses and turns to confront my gigantic shadow. "Why are you following us?"

"Where she goes, I go," Cherno replies, pointing from me to his chest.

"I'll give you a room, but I need to speak to Roselle alone."

"Try to make me leave her side," Cherno challenges with a malicious grin.

Reykin's hand twitches near his belt—to a fusionblade that isn't there.

"Can you find him a room near mine?" I ask. "One where he can check in on me if he needs to?"

Reykin, the epitome of poise, replies, "Of course."

We continue through the small halls. Cherno ducks his head at every junction and hatch so he won't get brained. Gates of Dawn soldiers flail like startled birds and gape in fear at Cherno and me as we slip by. At the end of one hall, we pass through doors that reveal a narrow locker room with shower closets to one side. On another wall is a small vanity area with a row of sinks and a long mirror. Moving farther in, Cherno catches his reflection and walks to a mirror. He gazes at himself for a few moments before driving his fist through it. The glass shatters. Shards fall in the sinks and fragment on the floor. He grips the edges of a basin and bends the metal. It whines and echoes.

"What's wrong?" Caution rings in Reykin's voice. He pushes me behind him. "It's not going to steal your soul or anything. It was just a mirror."

"I will crush your *soul* if you don't stop talking," Cherno replies between his teeth. "I know what a mirror is."

"Then why'd you break it?"

"I was once one of the most powerful dragons in the world. Now look at me, trapped in this hideous human form."

"You're not ugly, Cherno," I tell him softly, taking a few steps forward. Reykin puts his hand on my elbow. I shoot him a look, letting him know it's okay.

With his head still bowed, Cherno replies, "Says you—the most gruesome creature I've ever beheld. I look like one of you."

"You really don't," I reply. "You look like a dragon."

"Crow's stolen my wings from me." He's wretched—a wounded beast. Smoke billows from his nostrils and collects above his head.

"I'm sorry."

With his back to us, Cherno, still gripping the metal sink, asks, "How do I bathe in this underwater leviathan?"

"Phoenix will show you," Reykin replies. "Just follow it."

Phoenix eases forward and glides to one of the private shower compartments. My mechadome must be in butler mode, because it holds the door open for the brooding dragon. Without looking in our direction, Cherno trudges to the private compartment.

"Do not leave this room without me, Roselle," Cherno says. With that, he closes the door.

"Do you have clothes that will fit him?" I ask Reykin.

"I'll have some made—for you as well."

I move to a separate shower. Closing the door behind me, I'm at a loss for a moment, staring at my left hand. It's bizarre not to have a holographic image glowing up from it. It's empty. My hand feels lighter, if even just a fraction. It's probably psychological, but it's as if a piece of me is missing. It's strange to think I'll have to learn to live without it after it has controlled my life since I was born. Now all that's left is a scar through my crown-shaped birthmark.

A holographic display panel illuminates when I get close to the showerhead. I set the temperature. Steam fills the small shower closet. I strip off the ruined Black-O uniform and let it soak on the floor. With my head bowed beneath the showerhead, water drips from my chin. I wash my hair and body. Where I was stabbed through the heart feels bruised and sore, but my skin's smooth.

What does that mean? What am I? Am I a god? Am I Ransom's science experiment? Is this some conjured reality created by Spectrum?

Minutes later, with no answers to my questions, I turn off the water and order a robe through the holographic panel. A compartment door slides open beneath the showerhead. Transparent material that feels like tissue paper covers a folded white robe atop a rollout shelf. The package juts toward me. I take it and unfold the paper. It evaporates into a small plume of smoke. I shake out the white robe and shrug it on. The fabric's nicer than it should be for military-issued clothing, especially on a rebel ship. The tails of the belt hang to my knees after I tie the length around my waist. I wipe my face and hair with the accompanying towel. The shower slippers are flimsy and too big, but I put them on anyway. Combing my hair with my fingers, I use mouthwash to dissolve the plaque on my teeth before spitting the excess into the drain.

When I exit the closet, I find Reykin showered. The firstborn has changed his clothes to an athletic Gates of Dawn uniform and is waiting for me, with Cherno next to him. They're not talking. Each has his arms crossed over his chest, and each leans against the lockers facing my shower closet, stern expressions on their faces.

"Everything okay?" I ask.

"Yes." Reykin pushes off the locker and walks to me. "I have something for you. It's a communicator." His dark hair hangs over my wrist as deft fingers clasp a golden cuff to it. His proximity feels heady. The scent of him, now that we've both showered, makes me want to wrap my arms around him. He feels like safety to me, and I crave that more than anything. He lifts his sublime face, and I stare at him. "This way," he says, "we'll never be out of touch. Do you like it?"

I glance at my wrist. A holographic projection of red light shines from the bracelet—a blooming red rose. "Did you design this?" I move my fingers in the colorful light. The rose changes into rose-colored menu screens. The concept is based on monikers but coupled with the wrist communicators of old.

"Not the communicator itself—it's one our network uses. I designed your identifier." Reykin shows me his communicator, a spinning, star-shaped moniker, but it's *his* star, the seven-pointed star with his initials. He notices me staring. "Everyone gets their own individual identifier. You can change yours to suit you."

"No, I like it. It's pretty." I touch the bracelet and admire the detail of the rose. My brow wrinkles in confusion. "When did you do this—create the identifier?"

"A while ago."

He must have made it after I was implanted—when I was Crow's assassin. "You must've known I was—that I'm . . ."

"I knew."

"Then why would you make one for me?"

A raw, shattered look chisels his features. "Survival. I had to do something." The pulse in his neck throbs harder, hammering like mine.

"I will have a dragon identifier," Cherno states. "When will it be ready?"

"I'll get right on that," Reykin replies sarcastically, without looking at him.

"Do," Cherno's deep voice rumbles.

"Would you like to rest?" Reykin asks me.

"Yes, please."

Reykin leads us out of the locker room and down a twist of corridors. He stops at a door near the end of one corridor. Instead of using the control panel, he touches a screen on his wrist communicator, triggering the door to slide open. "This is your room, Cherno." He gestures with a wave of his hand. "I'll send someone to assist you with ordering clothing." He eyes the blanket covering Cherno.

Cherno's eyes narrow at the small bunks in the walls. He probably won't be able to sleep in either one, but he says nothing about the accommodations. Instead he asks, "Roselle, would you like to stay with me?"

"I'm putting her in the room next to yours," Reykin explains, pointing to the wall. "She'll be right here."

Cherno's attention turns to me. "Is that what you want?"

"Yes," I say. "We could both use a little privacy and some sleep."

"Beat on this wall if you need me," Cherno says, and indicates the adjoining one.

"Okay. You do the same."

His textured lips twitch in a faint smile. "You're not like yourself at all, death-harbinger." He enters his room. Reykin closes the door.

We walk to the next door, and Reykin opens it. He stands aside for me to enter. It's not a very large room. On one wall nestle two small sleeping bunks. The other contains a small washing and dressing area. The largest wall, opposite the door, has a round window that fills almost the entire area. I go to it. The water outside the vessel lacks illumination at this depth, but with my vision I can see marine life teeming around us. Reykin joins me at the window.

This ship's shape leads me to believe that it would be just as comfortable flying in the air as in the sea. It doesn't resemble a whale, like I'd thought. It's much bigger than that. The hull takes on the colors of the water, camouflaging it. We appear to be operating within a pod of whales. The large aquatic mammals swim in formation around the entire structure.

"How do you get the whales to do that?" I ask, trying hard to act normal despite the growing awkwardness between us.

Reykin blinks. "You can see the whales?"

"Yes."

He leans his hip against the window frame, pretending to look at the water, but he's really watching my face in the reflection of the glass. I know because I'm watching his.

"Well, those aren't really blue whales," he says. "They're robotic simulations. We use them to explain the mass of our ship if we're somehow spotted from a satellite or sonar. Outside the *Sozo One*, you can hear the replicated whale sounds."

"That's clever, unless a whaler finds you. Do you own this ship?"

"No, but I know the captain fairly well. He owes me a favor." He smiles, but then he looks puzzled, squinting at the window before us. He turns his attention back to me. "How are you? Do you need to see a physician?"

"I don't think a regular physician can help me. I need to speak to your brother."

"My brother? Why?"

"He's a technician. He knows things about me no one else does."

"What things?" A note of suspicion, or maybe jealousy, is in his tone. He sounds angry. "How did you even find Ransom?"

"He found me . . . Well, that's not really true. He . . . he put—I should let him answer that question."

Frustration draws Reykin's eyebrows together. "Where was he when he found you?"

"We were in the Fate of Seas, in what was once a military Base long fallen out of use by Swords. I'm betting my mother, knowing what Census was doing, gave it to them. It was all a cover. It contains labs where they design and test implants, do genetic experiments, create generations of new beings from incubators. I don't know if they do other genetic enhancements there or somewhere else, but their cyborg soldiers are well equipped with state-of-the-art weaponry in place of some body parts."

"I'll find the Base. We have access to old military terrain maps and training Bases. We know about cyborgs. We've been fighting them since I left you. They're mostly a separate division of Black-Os. They're harder to fight than the zeroborns. There's another new threat, too. We were calling everyone zeroborn, but the zeroborns are really the ones who Census created in their human farms. 'Numbers' are the new acquisitions acquired after the initial attack on CTD—Census Transition Day. Numbers are firstborns or secondborns who grew up in the Fates Republic and received their implants and numbered monikers after CTD. Numbers get new monikers now that have unique digits assigned to each. Normal citizens who report for their new monikers are getting VPMD-implanted at the same time, against their will. They don't know it. They leave a few weeks later with devices in their heads. The technology isn't activated right away—not until whole areas are implanted. Then they assimilate them all at once, like flipping a switch. The only symptoms they have are extreme headaches. Those who resisted the moniker appointments find themselves in the middle of a conspiracy once the Numbers are triggered and the implants are activated in Census's network. Implanted family members hunt down and murder resisters in the streets."

"Have you figured out a way to extract the Spectrum mind-control device from a host without killing the victim?"

His head bows.

"I see."

"I'm sorry." The skin of Reykin's neck darkens. The color travels up and spreads over his cheeks. He reaches for me but hesitates and crosses his arms over his chest instead.

"What are you sorry for?"

"I should've jumped. If I had, you would've escaped."

"You don't know that."

"You would've had a chance." His jaw clenches.

"I did have a chance. I lived, sort of . . ."

"What does that mean?"

"I'm different now, Reykin."

He has a searching, tender look on his face. "You look the same, Roselle." He reaches out to me again, but this time he cups my cheek in his hand and turns my face toward his. He rubs a calloused thumb over my soft skin.

"I'm not the same." I activate the silver glow in my left eye. The light casts a metallic sheen over his face. Reykin winces, and his hand drops from me, retreating. His response almost breaks my will. A tremor enters my voice: "I can control it, this thing in my head, for now. I can't promise you that it will always be true. Crow's horrifically powerful. He's part of the collective consciousness they call Spectrum, and he can take over anyone with a VPMD implant—inhabit their bodies. His control is absolute."

"Except over you." Reykin's response is restless and angry and . . . hopeful.

"I don't have a VPMD."

"You don't?" He's staring at my silver eye.

I extinguish the light. "No, mine's different. I have a prototype developed by a rogue technician who wants to defeat Census."

"*Ransom* put that thing in your head," Reykin growls, his dark eyebrows shooting together in downward slashes, "in the Fate of Seas." He has figured it out. It wasn't hard. I all but told him. Dread and remorse color his expression.

"I should let Ransom explain it. He had reasons." I choke on bitterness. I know I'm a freak, but Reykin's reaction all but buries me. I'd almost rather face Crow and accept his oblivion than wither under this exposure.

His fists clench. "I don't care about his *reasons*."

"You should care. At the very least, Crow would've murdered your brother and had someone else implant a VPMD inside my brain if he hadn't operated on me. It was at great personal risk that he did what he did. Ransom could've just implanted me with the standard device. If he had, we wouldn't be having this conversation now. I'd be one of the many Black-Os still hunting you."

Reykin grasps my upper arms. "He made you their pawn."

"I'm no one's pawn now."

"But you said yourself that it could change."

"It could," I admit. "You should never drop your guard with me."

His hands fall from my arms. He looks devastated. "I see."

From the corner of my eye, something moves in the sea outside. When I glance that way, Hawthorne's there, staring at me through the glass. I gasp and place my hand to the cold surface. By the time I do, he's gone, evaporated.

"What's wrong?" Reykin asks, reaching for me. I put up my hands to stay him while staring at the dark water.

"Did you see anything outside?"

"You mean, like a ship?" Through the glass, Reykin studies the darkness, too.

"No, not a ship. You didn't see Hawthorne?"

"In the water? No! It's impossible—not at this depth. It would crush him."

My eyebrows draw together. "I just . . . I'm just tired." I rub my forehead with a shaky hand.

"You're sure you're all right?" He touches my hair, smoothing it away from my cheek.

My heart thrums faster. My palms are damp. Being near Reykin makes me light-headed. For me, it's as if I had left him only days ago, not months. "I'm glad you made it out—that night—on the platform," I blurt out. "I'm glad you didn't die—or have to go with Hawthorne and me." I can't say more. Emotion chokes me. I'm blinded by tears. I turn away to hide them from him, my shoulders rounding.

"I tried to find you . . . I couldn't . . . I got close once, but I didn't make it in time."

I feel sick. "When?"

"The attack on the Salloway stronghold in Swords." He touches my shoulder, a gesture meant for me to turn and look at him.

Shame burns my cheeks. I can't face him. "Never drop your guard around me, Reykin."

"Roselle—"

"I mean it! Don't let me in."

Reluctantly, Reykin withdraws a step. "I'm going to the bridge to contact the other ships and locate which one has Ransom. I'll give you an update on his status when I know something. Try to get some rest." He moves toward the door. "I have to lock you in this room. Contact me with your communicator when you awaken," he calls over his shoulder, and then exits. The door slides closed behind him and locks.

"I am awake," I reply softly to myself. "I just hope it's forever."

Wet, puppy-scented kisses assault my cheeks and nose, bringing me out of a dream. Rogue's black-and-white tail beats Reykin's pant leg before the little furry maniac hops onto my bunk and continues to bathe me in adoration.

"Rogue, you're so big!" I try to hold him back from licking my face, but he's so squirmy and excited that I just have to endure it. "Hi, you," I say, rubbing my cheek against his small head. "How did you get so big?" He isn't big by any standard of the word; he's simply bigger than when I was taken from the Fate of Virtues.

Reykin crouches down so that he's eye level with me in the bottom bunk. "Rogue eats everything you put in front of him, which includes the occasional boot, and he likes to snuggle."

I stare into Reykin's ocean eyes, and I completely get the wanting-to-snuggle-Reykin part. Heat flushes my cheeks. Ruffling Rogue's floppy ears, I ask, "How did you rescue him from the Halo Palace? You couldn't have gotten far on that platform."

Reykin moves closer to sit on the edge of my bed. He reaches over and pets Rogue. "I didn't. That ridiculous platform crashed just past the Trial Village. I almost didn't make it to the cover of the secondborn training camps—you know, the ones we toured with Grisholm on our hoverbikes?"

"Yes."

Tension forms lines around his mouth. He drops his hand from Rogue. "I hid out in the woods—in a bunker that one of the secondborn survivalists had erected during their training sessions. It was good camouflage—hard to see, made of moss and bark. Roving bands of zeroborns who looked like normal citizens from Virtues hunted in packs, preying on most of the people they stumbled upon. I infiltrated the industrial systems in the Fate of Virtues and acquired street footage from the drone cameras of the night you were taken."

Reykin uses the hologram on his wrist communicator to project images of the war-torn streets of Purity. Roaming the sidewalks and pavement are groups of once ordinary looking firstborns with beams of silver light coursing from their eyes. Some are in tattered ball gowns and high-heeled shoes, others in expensive, frayed suits or blood-smeared robes and slippers. Still others are barefoot in torn negligée. All their expressions are the same snarling mask.

Reykin extinguishes the hologram. "I knew I had to lose my moniker—it was a beacon. I cut it out that night and destroyed it. My phantom orb kept my body temperature low, so the infrared scanners didn't find me." He digs in his pocket, extracts the small silver orb, and extends it to me.

I take it and roll it around in my palm. The device feels icy. My skin adopts its temperature, which slowly spreads over my hand and down my wrist. I shiver and hand the device back to Reykin. He takes it and shoves it in his pocket.

"I had my headset communicator with me, so I could control Phoenix," he says. I know what he's talking about. I've seen him use the compact headset while upgrading Phoenix, back at the Halo Palace. "I had to boost the signal, using the energy from my fusionblade and a hidden camera uplink that I discovered in the forest of the training grid, but finally I managed to connect with your mechadome. I took control of Phoenix, and by manipulating the bot remotely from the camps, I gently stuffed our furry friend inside Phoenix's hull, along with supplies I needed, and then I guided Phoenix to me. Without your Class 5Z, I never would've made it out of the Fate of Virtues alive."

"No one ever challenged the mechadome?"

"Well, it was chaos in Virtues, but no. Nothing challenged it. It's like they don't even see it. The zeroborns were too busy murdering everyone to notice a sanitation unit. And Phoenix is lined with lead, so it can transport just about anything, because scanners have a hard time seeing inside it."

"So Phoenix made it to you in the woods?"

"Yes. Rogue thought it was a grand adventure." He ruffles Rogue's floppy ears. "At first we survived on the supplies Phoenix gathered from your apartment. Then we lived on whatever Phoenix foraged during forays into the nearby Trial Village. In the days after that initial night, zeroborns were either slaughtering or capturing everyone. Birth order didn't matter. Wealth didn't matter. Political connections didn't matter, unless they were Census connections. Similar things were happening in other Fates to varying degrees, but nothing like what went on where we were. High-level Census agents made the city of Purity their own."

"What about Quincy," I ask in a terrified rush, "the little Stone-Fated girl who used to attend to Balmora? I promised her I'd take care of her. She was in my suite in the *Upper Halo* on the night I was captured! Maybe you saw her?"

Reykin's expression turns bleak. "She didn't make it."

"How do you know?"

"I sent Phoenix to look for her. The zeroborns didn't take prisoners, Roselle. She died with everyone else."

"How do you know for sure?" I challenge, desperate not to believe it. "She could've made it—gotten out somehow. She could be hiding in the Sea Fort—"

"She's dead, Roselle. I hacked into the surveillance logs for the *Upper Halo* and recovered the records from CTD. She died the night of the initial attack."

I swallow the bile in my mouth. "Let me see it."

"No. Not even if you beg me, Roselle. You don't want to see what the zeroborns did to her. Please, trust me on this."

I can hardly keep from crying, so I ask, "How did you escape Virtues?"

"Phoenix helped me avoid the legions of mind-altered soldiers and citizens scouring the streets and shooting down aircraft. Your mechadome has very old maps of the sewer systems in its files—for every fatedom, city, town, and residence in the Fates Republic. It guided me through an underground network of tunnels, city by city, until we were out of Virtues. From there, it became a little easier. We just continued underground until we made it to Stars."

"Did anyone resist Census's takeover, beside the Gates of Dawn? What about secondborn Sword soldiers?"

"There was a massive purge."

"What do you mean by 'purge'?"

"Census knew that secondborn soldiers, when they discovered what Census was doing, would more than likely rebel, even with your mother in control of Swords. Census had a plan for that. At the same time as the Opening Ceremonies of the Secondborn Trials were commencing, secondborn soldiers were being eradicated in the Fate of Swords."

My breath catches. "How?"

"Your former Base, Stone Forest, was hit the hardest, probably because it was close to Forge and your mother couldn't have seasoned warriors mounting an attack on her city, or against Census. She was complicit in the deaths of hundreds of thousands of secondborn Swords. Census led the slaughter. They already occupied the Census underground facility of every Tree. It was easy for them to pump lethal gas into the ventilation systems of those Trees' trunks, and into the hanging air-barracks docked on the branches. Most secondborn soldiers died in their sleeping capsules while watching you and me spar during the Opening Ceremonies of the Secondborn Trials."

Panic and the urge to vomit hit me simultaneously, but then something else happens. It's as if I've eaten a chet, because the nausea dissipates, along with my trembling. I still feel horror and disgust, but it's not making me dizzy or allowing for any of the other symptoms that accompanied my panic in the past. I think the device in my head is compensating for the neurochemicals in my system by releasing others to neutralize their effects.

I'm able to calm myself enough to ask, "What about Twilight Forest Base, or Platinum—Darkshire?"

"Twilight Forest Base was treated the same way. Some Trees in Platinum Forest and Darkshire weren't gassed at all. Instead they were overrun by zeroborns. The captured secondborn soldiers were taken for VPMD implantation and then surgically altered with military enhancements and enlisted into the cyborg ranks. What we know is that the device implantation was performed on most Bases from predetermined Trees. Some of the soldiers who managed to escape found their way to the Gates of Dawn resistance, but it wasn't many."

"How many other Bases survived?"

"Out of the thousands? A few. Some of the military Trees survived—the gas failed to deliver in some of them—but most Trees on all the Bases are now filled with rotting corpses. They're mass graveyards. This is no longer a struggle for power, Roselle. This is an all-out war for our existence."

I'm numb. I think I'm in shock, even though I'm not at all surprised by what Reykin's telling me. I've been a part of them. Deep down, I know how they operate. Efficiency. It's about achieving goals in the least amount of time and with the least amount of effort. It doesn't matter who dies or how many or what's destroyed. Immediate, uncompromising results are all that matter. I know I'm like that now, too. In the end, I didn't hesitate to kill everyone in the throne room—even myself—to achieve my goal of killing Crow. It just didn't work as I'd planned.

"Census and their High Council deserve everything that Crow's bringing them," I say.

"What's Crow bringing them?"

"Death. The Census High Council ordered my mother to murder Crow with seraphinian, a poison. She failed. Crow had already locked every Census agent out of Spectrum. Their master-level devices no longer work. They can't control the VPMDs anymore, and that means they can't control any zeroborns, including Black-Os. Census agents are adrift now, existing outside of Spectrum. Rudderless."

"That coincides with our reports of the past two days. The Census High Council is just . . . gone. Virtues is in chaos again. Bodies lie dead in the streets—we're getting intel that they're all Census agents."

"Crow's vendetta against Census is probably the only reason I escaped. Had Crow been in residence at the Sword Palace when I was still in my cell, I wouldn't be here now. You saw what happened on the beach when he returned. He's telekinetic, too, and he's in all of them, but the proximity of his true body matters for some reason. He's stronger in it than when he's occupying someone else's."

"Maybe he's not bypassing their consciousness?"

"Maybe, or his own body has been genetically altered to give him his power. I'm not sure. He doesn't seem to be able to move things with his mind when he's not in one of his own clones, but when he is, I've witnessed him project Cherno across the room as if the dragon-man were a hologram."

"You move things with your mind, too, don't you?" Reykin replies. "Or did we all just hallucinate that grenade flying out of Daltrey's palm and out to sea?"

Fear ties my stomach in knots. "I'm not like Crow. I don't know how I did that. I think it was some sort of survival instinct."

"But it was you, right? You made that happen."

"It was me, but I was afraid," I reply with a reluctant sigh.

"And the Burton airships that crashed?"

"Also me." I hug Rogue closer for comfort. The puppy licks my hand.

"Can you move something for me now?"

"Why?" I feel defensive. I don't want him to think I'm a monster.

"Just to see if you can."

"I don't know."

"Try."

"What do you want me to move?"

"How about you pass Rogue to me?"

"But what if I hurt him?" I snuggle my dog closer to my chest.

"You won't."

"How do you know that?"

"I know you."

Attempting to calm my racing heart, I exhale and loosen my grip on Rogue. The last thing I want to do is demonstrate to Reykin just how big a freak I am. "Maybe we shouldn't do this in the middle of the ocean."

"Please?"

"If something goes wrong, I'm blaming you."

"Okay."

I concentrate on the small mass of fur in my lap. My eyes adjust to the energy that comprises everything. The world outside the window is dark and murky, but everything inside this room is golden light and airy and within my "reach." I don't have to move my hands—I simply *will* the lifting of the puppy. Rogue levitates off me, about a tail's length or so.

"How are you doing that?" Reykin whispers.

"You know when you prepare to pick up something heavy, you sort of grasp it and clench your abdomen in preparation?"

"Yes?"

"It's a little like that at first, but then, when I breathe out"—I exhale—"it's lightness that lifts Rogue, not heaviness. Do you know what I mean?"

"No," he replies. "I have no clue what you mean." But he seems impressed.

"Oh, I wish you could feel this. It's a little ticklish." Rogue's tail wags furiously as he floats above my lap. He barks at me with his little puppy voice, like we're playing a game he doesn't really understand.

"Can you pass him to me?" Reykin asks.

"Hold out your hands so you can catch him if he starts to fall."

Rogue's tail wags in earnest, as if he's filled with airy happiness. I float the small creature to Reykin's waiting arms. The moment Reykin has him, I let go of the lightness it took to move him. In Reykin's hands, Rogue squirms, trying to get away from him and back to me. Reykin stares at me wide eyed, holding Rogue close to his chest.

"Say something," I order with a frown, feeling like the freak I am.

"What else can you do?"

I don't know how to tell him that I might be immortal, so I don't. Instead I ask, "Can I have my puppy back?" He hands me Rogue, who happily licks my face again. I cover him with kisses of my own.

"When did this ability come about? Did you develop it over time, or . . . ?"

"It just happened today."

"We found you yesterday. What was different about yesterday?" Reykin asks. He lets nothing go at face value. He's inquisitive and, quite frankly, extremely nosy.

"You found me yesterday? How long did I sleep?"

"Longer than normal. I was worried, so I brought Rogue with me to check on you. Why are you avoiding the question?"

"What question?"

"What was different about yesterday?"

"I don't know." I shrug. "I was scared."

Reykin frowns. "You've probably been in a state of constant fear whenever you're conscious. Was that it, do you think? Do you think fear triggered something in your physiology and made you develop a defensive trait?" He looks skeptical.

"Maybe," I hedge.

"You don't think that's it. What's your *real* theory?"

"I don't have a good one."

"C'mon." His eyes narrow as he chides me. "Yes, you do. I can see it in your eyes."

I set Rogue aside and rise from the bunk. "I should get dressed. Are these clothes for me?" I ask, even though I know that the package must be mine because it wasn't there before. I tighten the belt of my robe, pick up the package, and clutch it to my chest. Rogue sits at my feet, looking up at me like he wants me to hold him again.

"Here." Reykin scoops up Rogue. He presses a button, and a partition unfolds from the wall and arches around the small vanity area, separating it from the rest of the room. "You can change behind this privacy screen."

I forget he's not a secondborn Sword trained not to need privacy. "Thank you," I reply, and duck behind the divider. I close my eyes and exhale for a moment, then unwrap the parcel. It contains a Gates of Dawn military-issued training uniform. The top is midnight blue and made for a female, with support built in. The matching athletic bottoms look like they'll fit me just right. I set the boots aside, tug my robe off, and drape it over the top of the partition.

"You were about to tell me your theory of how you developed your telekinesis," Reykin reminds me from the other side of the partition.

"No, I wasn't," I say under my breath. "I was?" I ask, loud enough for him to hear me as I tug the top over my head and smooth it into place.

"You said you were afraid?"

"I was afraid . . . I'd just woken up."

"From the collective, err—from Spectrum?"

"No, I'd been awake—out of Spectrum's control—for a couple of days. This was different." I pull on the pants.

"How was it different?"

I pick up a military-issued boot, struggling with what to say. Inside the boot, the label bears the Salloway logo. It brings tears to my eyes. I force them back, tugging one boot on, then the other. I straighten, covering my face with my hands and wiping an errant tear on my sleeve.

"Roselle?" Reykin asks, and waits.

I choke back more tears.

I come to a decision. If he wants to know so badly, then he must hear everything. I won't spare him any details. Just like when we trained together with fusionblades. It'll be brutal and threaten to kill us both. Squaring my shoulders, I move around the partition. Reykin's leaning against the shelf, staring at me, a handsome mask of concern.

I exhale slowly, my throat tight with emotion, and say, "I was dead. I'd just awakened after dying, for the second time."

His brow wrinkles. "I don't understand."

"I died, Reykin."

"You died? Like *dead* died?"

"Yes, I died twice." I hold up two fingers. "And each time I came back to life."

"How is that possible? Did they restart your heart?"

"No. I think I healed myself—my body regenerated in a way that's not . . . normal."

"Can you explain what happened?"

"I drowned, the first time. We were in the secret throne room of the Sword Palace. My mother and Crow were there. Hawthorne was there. Othala was involved in a plot with the Burtons and the Census High Council to murder Agent Crow. They planned to poison him, but she failed because she didn't understand that he isn't *Agent* Crow anymore. He's much more than that. He knew what she was planning, and he made Hawthorne cut off her head. Then Crow turned on all his allies and announced that he planned to kill everyone on the Census High Council.

"I didn't have a weapon that could kill him, but the ceiling of the secret throne room lies beneath the mall of the Sword Palace. The water feature there is the length of the cove's beach at the Halo Palace—you remember it?"

Reykin nods.

"I realized that if I shattered the ceiling, the room would fill up before it could drain. So I borrowed a cannon from a cyborg, and I broke the ceiling."

"And you drowned?"

"Yes. I killed Crow, too—his body anyway. But he's a part of Spectrum, or maybe he *is* Spectrum now, I don't know. All I know is that he reanimated himself in a new Kipson Crow clone he'd been growing."

"What about Hawthorne?"

My chin wobbles. I can hardly speak, so I whisper, "He died, too, except he didn't wake up."

Reykin sets Rogue on the floor. The puppy prances over to the round window and watches the whale simulations, his black nose pressed to the glass. Reykin moves to me. He wraps his arms around my shoulders and pulls me to him. My arms glide around his waist. I lay my head on his chest and listen to his heartbeat thump wildly against my ear. Tears roll down my cheeks.

"You don't have to tell me any more right now. I'm sorry I pushed you," Reykin says softly before kissing the top of my head.

"No, you should know. We never lie to each other. I want you to hear everything so you understand." I move away from his chest and wipe my cheeks with my sleeves again.

Reykin's lips are set in a grim line. "Okay. What happened after you woke up?"

"I was in the morgue. Cherno was there, too. He was still alive because he has a dragon heart or something like that and he doesn't need oxygen the same way we do. He and I tried to escape. That's when Crow caught us. He was with Flannigan. They were about to leave for the Fate of Virtues to destroy the Census High Council. Cherno tried to defend me from Crow, but we were both recaptured. That's when I saw Phoenix."

"You told me Ransom was in the Sword Palace and that Census was dead."

"You understood my message."

"I received it. I didn't understand it right away—Census wasn't dead—but I realized that Ransom was there somewhere. I started looking for him, but nothing came up when I analyzed monikers in the area, because he changed his name and moniker to Calvin Star. Why would he do that?"

"He had to—to survive. If he hadn't, Crow would've found his connection to you and used him against you."

"Did Ransom know that?"

"No. Ransom changed his name for his own reasons. You'll have to ask him yourself."

"I knew they'd taken you to the detention center. I wanted to use Phoenix to get you out, but we had no way to extract you at the time. We were scrambling to assemble a unit that could go in from the beach. It took several hours just to transport the team. That's when they restrained me. I was going to come get you."

"It wouldn't have mattered, Reykin. Agent Crow had left the Palace, but a part of his consciousness was still there—in the body of a Black-O soldier. He used the soldier to interrogate me. Agent Crow had a theory. He'd checked me out himself in the morgue the first time I died, when he came to inspect his own corpse. He knew I'd come back to life somehow, and he wanted to see if I could do it again."

"What did he do to you?" Reykin asks with a grimace, as if he really doesn't want to hear my answer.

"He wanted to see if I could heal myself after death, so he tortured me, and then he drove a fusionblade through my heart."

Reykin's jaw tightens. He grips my shoulder and squeezes, almost involuntarily.

"Are you all right?" I ask.

He winces and looks up. The pressure of his hand eases, but he doesn't remove it. "Am *I* all right? Who cares how I feel?"

"I care."

"How long were you dead?"

"I don't know—it took me maybe a day to regain consciousness?"

His eyebrow raises slightly. "Is it possible you're somehow mistaken?"

"About being dead?"

"Yes."

"No."

Neither of us speaks until Reykin clears his throat and asks, "When you came back to life, what state were you in?"

"Not great," I reply. "I woke up in a pool of crusted blood and vomit. My chest ached—it was tender, felt burned—but it had healed."

"Was that why your uniform was charred over your heart?" Reykin demands. He's seething now.

"Yes. When I woke up, Crow was waiting for me—it was his consciousness inside the body of my torturer. He was prepared to kill me again, to see if I could keep healing myself, to see if I'm . . ."

"Immortal."

I nod. "The Crow-possessed soldier came at me again, but this time I held out my hand and I . . . I stopped him. An invisible pulse triggered from my palm and through my fingertips. The power tickled at first—like the vibration of a fusionblade powering up. But it was nothing like a fusionblade when it hit. It was more like a hovercycle striking him. The impact forced the soldier against the wall and shattered him."

"You didn't have that power before you died the second time?" Reykin asks.

"No. Something happened to me when I died. I think when my body healed itself, it *upgraded*."

"Do you think it has something to do with the device in your head?"

"How could it not?" I rub my forehead in confusion. "I need to speak to your brother. How is he? Have you seen him?"

"I haven't seen him yet. He's on a different vessel. The reports are positive, though. They believe he should wake up soon."

"I want to see him as soon as he does."

"Me, too. What is he like now? Did you and my brother talk much? Are you . . ."

"Are we friends?" I finish for him. "I hardly know Ransom. We're more allies than friends. He seems to know me much better than I know him. He has been my personal technician since the day you and I parted, Reykin."

Reykin grimaces. "'Parted.' That's a poor choice of words." He's angry, but I know it's not directed at me. "We weren't parted. We were shredded."

My heart misfires, aches like it still has a hole in it, as if it's filled with air bubbles instead of blood. "I don't know who had it worse, you or me. You had to watch the decimation of our world. You'll never be able to forget it. I, on the other hand, went to sleep and had my body violated so I'd massacre everyone they ordered me to. Crow showed me some of what I've done. I could hardly look at myself. I'm sure everyone knows I've been his assassin. No one can ever trust me again." Emotions choke me into silence. I can't talk about Clifton to Reykin or anyone. I can't allow myself to think about what I did to him or I might go mad.

"I trust you."

"Don't trust me!" I snarl. "What I've done is unforgivable. I killed for them. I might do it again."

"It wasn't you. You would never—"

"But it was *me*—*my* skill, *my* combat training." I thump my chest with my fist. "When I witnessed a recording of me fighting for Spectrum, I knew. I'm not innocent. I saw Dune in me, *his* techniques that I've spent years mastering. I didn't follow Spectrum's contrivance. They followed mine. The planning of the attack came from *me*. It's strategy I'd employ today if Crow were the target under the same circumstances. I'd kill him the same way. Don't you get it? Spectrum harvested my mind. Without me and the training I brought them, it would've been different."

"You don't know that."

"Yes, I do. If they reinsert me into Spectrum, I'll be their assassin. You can't let that happen. You need a weapon on you at all times in my presence."

"Why?" His eyebrows come together, and he growls. "You think I can kill you?" He's offended.

"What's wrong with you? You always threatened to kill me before! I may be immortal, but you can incapacitate me and figure out a way to destroy me if I turn into Crow's henchman again."

He shakes his head incredulously. "Even if I could figure out a way to kill you, I won't."

"Why not?" I seethe. "You could before."

"Before, I was a stupid, arrogant boy. I believed myself capable of sacrificing everything for my ideals. But now I know that I could never have ended your life—not for anything in this world, not from the moment you saved my hide on the battlefield. I was yours then. I am yours now."

I choke back a sob. "Haven't you been listening? You can't let Crow get me back. He'll take control of my mind, and I—if I kill you, too, I'll—" Reykin gathers me to him. I cling to him, even when a part of me wants to beat on his chest and wring the promise from him. "The torture will never end. Never," I whisper into his chest.

"You can't say these things to me, Roselle, not when I just got you back. Find a way to sticketh, remember? We'll find a way to annihilate Spectrum and Crow."

He draws away a little and then presses his lips to mine. Perhaps it's the new neuropathways in my mind, or maybe it's him, I don't know, but the ocean of sadness I've been sailing in stops roiling. I'm breathless and dizzy. My knees weaken. Reykin's mouth opens. I taste him on my tongue. His kisses burn away the soreness around my aching heart. My hands splay in his dark hair, ruffling it before trailing along the light bristle of his cheeks.

The door to my room slides open. Startled, I immediately shove away from Reykin. He holds onto me, though, not letting me out of his embrace. My heartbeat ratchets up another level, probably because I was raised as a secondborn, and getting caught kissing anyone, especially a firstborn, was treason. Cherno looms large in the doorway. He's wearing an athletic Gates of Dawn uniform that makes him seem unconquerable.

"You are mating?" the dragon-man half asks, half accuses. "Now? In the middle of the sea, while we are at war?"

"Yes," Reykin replies at the same time as I say, "No."

My face is on fire. "We're not *mating*." I run my hand down my side to smooth my uniform.

Cherno holds up his sharp-taloned hand against my denials. "I don't care how you behave with your slave, Roselle. If you want to do hideous things to him with your body, I will not stop you. I only ask that you do so *after* we awaken the gods and destroy Crow." Cherno gazes at us and then shudders, like we've grossed him out.

"Is he serious?" Reykin asks.

"I think so," I reply.

Cherno changes the subject. "I need to see your maps."

I slip out of Reykin's hold, even though he doesn't want to let me go. Rogue barks and trots along the steel floor to me. I pick him up as he wags his tail and howls at the newcomer.

"Is this a tribute for me?" Cherno asks, eyeing Rogue.

My eyebrow arches. "A tribute?"

"Is it breakfast?" he replies with a slow smile.

"No!" Reykin and I answer in unison.

I hold Rogue closer to my chest. "Cherno, if you eat my dog, I'll kill you."

"Then don't starve me," he replies. "I require sustenance and maps that show terrain, preferably from an aerial view."

Reykin sighs heavily. "Follow me, and we'll find you maps and something to eat." With his hand on the small of my back, Reykin guides me past Cherno, into the corridor, and down the narrow hallway.

Chapter 10
Intrinsic Memory

The chaotic bustle aboard the underwater vessel, the *Sozo One*, feels strange.

Unlike Spectrum, there's very little unity to the movements of the soldiers I encounter as I follow Reykin. No complex rhythm or synchronicity rules these people. The lack of uniformity comforts and annoys me at the same time. The commotion feels disjointed, multidirectional, and confusing. In many ways, I'm an alien here. And they view me like one. Suspicion and outright fear burn brighter than any silver light.

Reykin doesn't notice, or if he does, he doesn't let on that anything is amiss. He gives me a tour of the vessel with Cherno by my side. Every so often, Reykin's hand accidentally brushes mine. His finger strokes a column of skin, sending quivering jolts of slow-burn desire through me. It makes it hard for me to concentrate on anything other than the myriad sublime half smiles and side-eyed glances he bestows on me.

With Reykin as our escort, we cross the threshold to the command center of the vessel. The firstborn's large palm touches the small of my back. Holographic instruments throb from glass walls at workstations.

Although the diagnostics are advanced—nothing I've ever studied in flight school—they somehow come across to me as elementary. As we stroll, charts flash with readouts of life-support systems. At a glance, I notice the CO_2 level in a forward compartment rises above an acceptable level for respiration.

I pause. "Your carbon dioxide level is high."

"What was that?" Reykin asks, leaning nearer to hear me over the conversations from the sailors around us.

"I said your CO_2 level is high in this compartment." I point to the tiny line of the offending readout. "It's one of the greenhouses."

Reykin squints at it. "How can you even read that?" A moment later, the line flashes red and the system corrects the imbalance by adjusting a few valves automatically. The levels drop, and the red line returns to a soft blue.

"Ah," I say, "all fixed."

Confusion etches lines in Reykin's brow. He knows I don't have training in this area.

Maybe I shouldn't point those things out.

I stroll onto the thick, transparent panels that give us a panoramic view of the underwater terrain. We skim along the bottom of the sea, in a rocky canyon. Its walls rise to skyscraper heights around us as an ancient civilization reveals itself, a kingdom fallen into the sea. Some of it has crumbled to sand. Clinging to the rock are bioluminescent coral, their gentle lights like stars in the night sky.

It could be a city on a distant planet for how different it appears from everything I know. Enormous warrior sculptures lie in broken pieces on the sandy floor. Others still hold their weapons aloft from arching niches in the stone.

"What is this place?" I whisper, watching whorls of sand kick up at the edges of exotic rocks we pass. The ambition of the structures that remain rivals the cutting-edge architecture on dry land.

"We don't know," Reykin replies.

"It's Gildenzear," Cherno says. "You claimed dominion over all this, Roselle. You gifted it to Cassius for safekeeping."

"Cassius? The Lord of Raze and Ruin?"

"The same," Cherno replies.

"Is he fer real?" a familiar voice asks behind me.

Cherno bears his teeth, turns, and growls at the newcomer. "I am authentic."

That *voice*. "Edge," I exhale. Whirling around, I find Edgerton standing by the helm. He stares at Cherno. Trying to read the dragon-man, he tilts his head and squints at him.

Finally, he gives up and turns to me. My long-lost friend. His brown eyes widen, and he grins. "Erebody said you was one of 'em, 'cept me and Hammon," he says. "We knew if there were a way back from zombieland, you'd find it. Them fools don't know you like we do." The brim of his uniform cap dips at a jaunty angle, nearly hiding all his left eyebrow. It gives a criminal cast to his pressed uniform. The ex–Sword soldier's wiry build has filled out somewhat. He's still slim and fit, but his cheeks aren't hollow like they used to be.

"I'm not sure I've made it back, Edge," I manage to say, just above a whisper, trying to hold in my emotions.

He moves forward and, embracing me, lifts me off my feet in a fierce hug. "You may feel lost at sea, Roselle, but we gotcha. We ain't gonna let nothin' happen to you."

I hug him back with the same fierceness. "What are you even doing here?" I ask when he sets me on my feet.

Edgerton gestures to Reykin. "He set us up in the Fate of Seas, which was a blessin', but you know I cain't sit still, which makes me a horrible firstborn. I cain't pass for an aristocrat, what with my mountain accent and all. It sinks like a stone in the ocean there. I had to get me a job that I could do without lookin' too suspicious. I were already a pilot, so I learnt to fly underwater ships instead."

I glance at Reykin. Finding out my friend isn't just surviving, but thriving, swells my heart with gratitude. "You did that for Edge?" I hold up my hands, indicating the watercraft.

Reykin shakes his head. "I set him up in the Fate of Seas. You can thank Salloway for Edge's position on this vessel. Salloway contacted Daltrey several months ago, before Census attacked, and told him he wanted to help after he found out that you were okay—after we put you on the vessel deporting from Stars."

Clifton's name fills me with remorse. My heart twists and feels broken. I swallow past the growing lump in my throat and nod. "He never told me that."

"I captain the *Sozo One* for the Salloway fleet," Edgerton explains, "which makes the job damn awkward when I've been ordered by another friend to avoid the other vessels in the ship's fleet." Edgerton looks pointedly at Reykin.

"Roselle needs rest, not an interrogation," Reykin replies in a low tone.

"Burnin' bridges ain't wise," Edgerton scolds.

"Bridges won't burn underwater," Reykin replies with a shrug. "Neither will reprisals."

"Thermite burns underwater," Cherno states with an aloof look. Both Reykin and Edgerton scrutinize my bodyguard.

"They weren't being literal about the bridges, Cherno," I explain. "They're arguing about some sort of orders regarding me."

"No one orders us." Cherno's chest puffs out to accompany his hubris. "We are gods."

"Are you hungry, Roselle?" Reykin asks, smiling. His nearness intoxicates me. I nod. "I've made arrangements for Hammon and Edgerton to join us for brunch. Would you like that?"

"Hammon is here, too?"

"Of course my wife's here," Edgerton replies. "Where else would she be? She's on the other end of the vessel, negotiating a trade with another ship."

A wave of nervous excitement and gratitude washes over me. I hadn't allowed myself to hope that they'd both survived the massacre of Census Transition Day.

Edgerton throws his arm around my shoulder and hugs me to his side as if we'd never been parted by time or circumstance. "It's been almost impossible keepin' my wife away from you so you could rest. The only way was to have Reykin talk to her. She listens to *him*. When he told her you needed sleep, she agreed to wait. She keeps askin' me a million questions, though, 'bout you and Hawthorne. I keep explainin' that I don't know anythin' more than her."

My smile fades. *Hammon will want to know about what happened to Hawthorne.*

My initial euphoria at the prospect of seeing her dies. A ball of dread bubbles up inside me. Hawthorne and Hammon went through secondborn Transition together. I murdered her best friend.

How do I tell her that?

My head throbs. A part of me wants to disappear again, never to be tormented by the truth of what I've done. Oblivion. It's seductive. A place with no shame, remorse, or regret. Spectrum is like that. Integrated in it, I'd feel nothing. My conscience would evaporate from the world along with my consciousness. But I'd rather die than go back. Facing up to what I've done is now my only option.

"When can I see Hammon?" I ask. I don't know what I'll say to her. I can't even rehearse the conversation in my mind. It's too painful. Dark despair, and with it an underlying rage, blooms within me.

"She'll join us later," Edgerton replies. "There was a problem with another ship. She's dealin' with it."

Reykin's face flickers with concern before he can hide it. It's deep-seated worry. Maybe he's wondering, like me, if it's possible for me to come back from killing someone I love—to go on living. "If you're ready, Roselle, we can go get something to eat," he says with a slight bow.

"Yes . . . of course," I reply. His offer feels like a stay of execution.

Edgerton escorts me from the command center. Reykin and Cherno follow. After passing through a few corridors, we come to an executive dining room. The two-story hall, shaped like an exotic lagoon, has a glass stairway that ascends to a balcony level. Black mother-of-pearl floors with peacock coloring cast my reflection in them. White mother-of-pearl tables in the shape of oyster shells dot the room. One transparent wall has a view of the sea. The husks of an ancient underwater city, illuminated by exterior lighting from the *Sozo One*, float by us.

A host greets us, his mouth agape as he looks Cherno over. After he recovers from shock, he leads us to the center of the room. Conversations cease. I pretend not to notice the silence, but my chin rises a notch nonetheless. We come to a table beneath a black-coral chandelier on the main floor.

"The captain's table," the host announces with a sweeping gesture of his hand. He pulls out a chair for me. His hand on the seatback trembles.

"Thank you," I reply, taking the seat. Every pair of eyes in the place is riveted to Cherno and me. Whispers and the chinking of cutlery gradually commence.

Reykin sits to my left and leans his handsome face near my ear. "You'll find the daily meal selections in your communicator's menu." He displays the hologram on his own communicator. I lean closer, pretending that I can't see the menu well, just to be nearer to him. I know it's dangerous. I should be putting distance between us.

"I do not have a wrist communicator," Cherno churlishly growls beside me, seating himself on my right-hand side and glaring at Reykin.

"We don't have beagle on the menu, if you had it in mind for brunch," Reykin replies with an adorable smile.

I shoot him a look of censure before turning to Cherno and asking, "What do you like?" I pull up the selection of food and show him the hologram pictures.

"Meat." His large head dips near my face. Golden eyes scan the hologram above my wrist. The intricate texture of his skin fascinates me, but I try not to stare too long at it. He has a scent of campfire and mountain air. It reminds me of cool nights in the woods as a second-born soldier, on patrols between battles, looking for wounded.

"Will fish work?" I ask.

His dark eyebrows pull together over his golden, glowing orbs. "Yes, but they have to be fresh."

I scroll through options. "They have a lovely tuna."

"That will be a nice start."

"Oh." My gaze darts back to the menu. "Okay . . . the eel looks fresh."

"I will have that as well." I begin to close out the menu, but Cherno stays my hand. "And the squid"—he quickly scrolls through the menu—"the octopus, sea bass, and the halibut—"

"Should I just have them bring everything they have on the fresh-catch menu?" I tease.

"Yes."

Reykin studies us.

"Is that—can we have all that?" I stammer.

"Of course," Reykin replies. "I owe him a debt. Cherno carried my brother from the Sword Palace—he helped you. You can both have whatever you want, in whatever quantity you desire."

I sigh in relief. I'm responsible for Cherno. I brought him here. We have a bond. We escaped Crow's torturous nightmare together—from Spectrum's mental and physical slavery.

"Okay," I say, "how would you like your entrées prepared, Cherno?"

"What do you mean?"

"How would you like your fish to be cooked?"

"I don't like them cooked. I like them raw."

"Oh." I smile to cover my faux pas. "Of course."

"With scales."

"With scales . . . How about the heads? Do you like the heads still on?"

"That's the best part."

I order a simple breakfast of eggs and toast along with Cherno's selections. My eyes gravitate to Edgerton. A weird shyness invades my body, and I pluck at the hem of my sleeve with my fingernails.

He notices my unease. "Hey, it's just me, remember? You don't need to be wary. We're past that. We both took the beatin' of our lives together."

I don't doubt that the beating we received at the hands of the Gates of Dawn rebels was the worst of his life. For me, it's only in the top ten, somewhere behind drowning and being murdered by fusion-blade. Reykin's grimace says he's thinking the same thing, or maybe he's remembering the day he saved Edgerton and me from his fellow soldiers.

Our drinks arrive. After a host sets a steaming mug of coffee in front of me, I wrap my hands around it, letting it warm them. "How have you been, Edge?" I ask.

"Leaving Swords was the best thing that ever happened to me, Roselle. Hammon and I—we still cain't thank you enough."

"That's not necessary, Edge."

"It *is* necessary. You do realize that you saved my life a thousand times over, don't you? You saved us from war against the Gates of Dawn. You got us out of infantry. You know we wouldn't have lasted another year. If you hadn't come up with that plan to rescue Hammon from Agent Crow, he'd've gotten her. She'd be dead—along with my baby—or worse, one of them Numbers they're convertin' everyone into.

"Assumin' I'd survived all that, Census would've gassed me to death in my capsule on CT Day had I still been livin' on a Sword Base. Instead we were floatin' around the ocean, outside their reach. They cain't get to us down here with them inferior Burton seafarers. They cain't reach this depth—not yet anyway. Them ships cain't hack it. They fold in, or the people in 'em die from decompression sickness when they surface. We're safe fer now."

"You can't count on that," I reply. "Spectrum's a collective AI. They'll find a way. It'll only take one person who understands this technology to integrate and change its perspective."

"We haven't seen nothin' like that yet. This ship's self-contained. Barrin' any major catastrophes, we can live down here forever. We produce our own oxygen, food, purify the water for drinkin', and we answer to no one 'cept the rest of the fleet. No more firstborns and secondborns. We're encouraged to have children—lots of children if we want."

"It sounds like utopia, Edge."

"It is. Reykin and Salloway made it possible."

Clifton's aesthetic graces every line of the design of this vessel.

"We plan to get our people back up to the surface eventually," Reykin explains with a serious look. "Although these vessels have long-term capabilities, they're only meant to be temporary. Once we figure out a way to beat Crow and his killers, we can all go back."

"How many ships do you have?"

My question is met with silence. Reykin drops his eyes from me. I catch on. They don't want me to know in case I get assimilated back into Spectrum. I can't be offended—I warned Reykin not to drop his guard around me—but I am somewhat wounded, even though I try not to be.

I smile and change the subject. "You haven't told me about your baby, Edge. Did you have a girl, or a boy?"

"We had a girl! This is our Roselle—Rosie." Edgerton grins and fumbles with his wrist communicator. "We call her Rosie because she's sunny all the time—so happy. She looks like me, but with Hammon's dark hair." He projects hologram pictures of Rosie from his wrist communicator onto the table. The images "stick" to the surface and roll to me. I use my fingers to enlarge them.

"You named her Roselle?" I whisper, scrolling through the various images of a tiny infant, then a plump-cheeked toddler with pigtails and a sanguine smile.

"After her auntie Roselle." Edgerton gazes at me across the table. "Because there ain't nothin' I won't do for her auntie Roselle in this lifetime, or in the next. You hearin' me?"

I nod, wiping the corners of my misty eyes on a napkin. I continue to scroll through the images. I flick a cute picture of Rosie and Rogue over to Reykin, who catches it with his finger before enlarging it and chuckling.

"Rogue adores her," Reykin says softly.

Edgerton laughs, every bit the proud papa. "We're not sure who she loves more, Rogue or Uncle Reykin."

"She loves me more," Reykin assures him with a gentle smile that makes me melt a little.

Beside me, Cherno appears not to be listening to us but instead studying the world outside the window. Then plate after plate of our meal arrives. When it's all laid out on the glistening table, entrées surround Cherno. I half expect the dragon-man to pick up his food with his hands and devour it, but Cherno has definite table manners. He lays his napkin in his lap and lifts the cutlery. The knife and fork look dainty in his hands. It makes me wonder what his life with Crow has been like. Has he suffered at the psychopath's hands? Can he remember any of it? All of it? Or are these manners common to all ancient dragons? I find that last thought doubtful.

We begin eating. I ask Cherno, "How is it?"

He chews slowly and swallows before answering, "It's better than a feeding tube in my capsule."

Goose bumps raise on my arms. "It does taste like freedom, doesn't it? You have lovely manners for being force-fed in a capsule all your life."

"I acquired my table etiquette through long, grueling hours of training with technicians and the sadist himself." Cherno draws the

Amy A. Bartol

plate of raw octopus nearer to him. Its pinkish suction-cup arms jiggle amid a parsley garnish on the white porcelain dish.

"Crow taught you to dine like this." It's not lost on me that Cherno's the only being here who has gone through the same kind of torment that I have. In that way, too, we're connected.

"He did. If I did something wrong, he would withhold my meals for days."

"I hate him," I blurt out, pushing my eggs around the plate, my appetite lost.

"I hate him, too," Cherno states, like it's a fact he has long made peace with rather than an emotion that festers like it does in me. "As I matured, Crow awakened me from Spectrum's control to consciousness, from time to time. Sometimes he'd run experiments on me—interviews—both from inside Spectrum's world and outside of it, in the real world. He's obsessed with gods. He wants to steal our traits. I refused to give him the answers he wanted."

"How did you know to resist him? He raised you from infancy, didn't he?"

"Yes. In body, I was a child. In mind, I was not. I have memories of my lifetime as a dragon. I had been in a dormant stage—a hibernation, forced upon me by my enemies. Given a few more eons, I would've returned to the form I once held, but Crow stole my life from me and trapped me instead in this weakling's body." Disgust oozes from him. "Childhood with him was harrowing. Crow tried, but he couldn't scrape information from my mind, because he doesn't understand my innate traits. He knew just enough about me to be able to control me. I inadvertently gave him some information early on. He has found some minor priestesses' tombs because of me, but nothing of real value. I now know why. Everything he's searching for is submerged beneath the sea." Cherno gestures to the transparent wall. Kingdoms slide by us. A magnificent world, dormant—the vanity of ancient beings.

170

I do the math on the timeline. It doesn't make sense when I consider our physiology and Crow's age. "Cherno, how old are you?"

"In this body, I am almost three."

"Three decades?"

"Three years."

"How is that possible?"

"The technicians have ways of accelerating the aging process. They also have made advances in slowing it down and, in some cases, suspending it. Do you know how old Agent Crow's body was before you drowned him?"

"Twenty-five, maybe?"

"He told me he was well over two hundred years old. His sister, Sabah, died two centuries ago. Census manipulated his identity and that of his family's. He's the ultimate chameleon. And I should know—I've met quite a few."

"How long have you been awake?" Reykin asks. "Out of Crow and Spectrum's control?"

"I became the master of my own body, such as it is, a fortnight or so ago," Cherno replies. "It has been a gradual process—disconnecting. It took a while for the device in my head to melt. Spectrum reclaimed me on and off in the weeks leading up to my device's final demise."

"Your technician didn't notice the changes in you—that your device was melting?" I ask.

"He noticed. That's when I incinerated him. Census believed he jumped from the airship to his death. They couldn't recover footage of him after he left my capsule. It's because I gouged out his eyes before killing him. Technicians don't have advanced vision. They can't see in the absence of light. That means they cannot visually record what happens to them for the collective to view. The instant offline status of both his neural implant and his moniker was consistent with him plummeting to his death."

"So at the end you were just pretending to be assimilated, like I was?"

"Yes, I managed to fool Spectrum for several days. I understand its world and know how to pretend by simply following you, as your bodyguard. It helped that they were distracted by other matters—your mother's plot with Census for one. Had I had Crow's full attention, like I did when he first started studying me, then I'd never have gotten away with it. His focus waned from me when you arrived. He spent less and less time with me, and I became conscious less and less frequently, until my device failed."

"I replaced you as his favorite toy?"

"You became his favorite *assassin*. He liked to use you against anyone who ever slighted him—intentionally or otherwise."

"I remember none of it," I whisper with a painful ache in my belly.

"I saw you inside."

"Inside?"

"Inside Spectrum. You were locked away in the box."

"The box?"

"Agent Crow's private, inner sanctum—his palace of horrors. Most of the poor souls in that place believe it's the real world. Be grateful you cannot recall it."

"Why? What happened to me there?"

"I was always under the impression that he wasn't interested in anything you could tell him about the outside world."

"What was he interested in?" I hold my breath, because I already know the answer.

"Hurting you."

A deep exhale comes from Reykin. His leg bounces in agitation. He has his hand wrapped around his water glass, and I'm afraid he might shatter it at any moment. Pain clouds his eyes. I reach out and brush my fingers over his.

"I don't remember any of it," I say. "Nothing."

He lets go of the glass and threads his fingers in mine.

Cherno's deep voice resonates as he says, "I've been called 'monster' numerous times in the span of my vast life, but after what I've seen inside Spectrum, I know that no one has ever embodied the term more egregiously than Crow."

"Not even the goddess Roselle you once knew?" I ask.

"Not even her."

Edgerton grimaces. "Woo, this is some freaky crap you're slingin' here." He whistles low, then scowls and slaps his palms on the table. "Are we gonna hunt that blackbird or what? Cuz I'm personally offended that he's still alive."

Cherno levels a sinister stare at Edgerton. "Yes, let us hunt that bird."

I reach for my glass of water. "We can't hunt him until we have a weapon to fight him with." They all gaze at me as if I'm missing something. "What?"

Reykin studies me. "We have a weapon," he says tentatively. "We have you."

Chapter 11
Cassius Cometh

I nearly choke on my water.

"You think I'm your weapon?" I utter the question in a normal tone, but my clenching teeth, the downward slash of my lips, and the sharp daggers of my stare convey my outrage at Reykin's suggestion.

"Ahh, hell," Edgerton swears under his breath. He's studying his wrist communicator with a frown. "I can smell a fight comin', and as much as I want to get in on it, I have to go see what's keepin' my wife. She should've been here by now, and she switched her communicator to 'Do Not Disturb.' I hate it when she does that. It was a stupid option to put on these things, Reykin. We never had privacy before, and now I know why. You cain't never get no one to answer you when they oughta. I'll be right back." Our captain sets aside his napkin and rises from his seat, gives me a conspiratorial wink, and retreats from the dining room.

My hostility grows. "Umm, were you not on the beach with me?" I hiss at Reykin. "Crow yanked me right off my feet—*with his mind.*"

"You didn't even attempt to fight back," Cherno interjects.

I gaze between him and Reykin. They've been talking without me. *When did this happen? When I was resting?*

"You need training to prepare to battle Crow," Cherno says, "but you're not ill equipped. We need to find Cassius. He has awakened."

"Cassius—the god Cassius?"

"The same." Cherno stacks yet another empty plate on the pile and moves on to the next entrée. "Although, it may be impossible for me not to kill him the next time I see him. He's the one responsible for the form I had to take."

"The so-called egg?" I ask, remembering that Ransom said the DNA they had extracted had been from an egg.

"It wasn't an egg!" Cherno hisses back. "It was me. The Lord of Raze and Ruin used his considerable power to crush me into that form."

"I'm sorry. I didn't mean to offend you. But what makes you think the Lord of Raze and Ruin is alive?"

"He made this ship, did he not?" Cherno asks. He gazes around at the dining hall. "It bears his crest everywhere."

"I'm not following . . . I thought Cassius's crest was a rose. All I see are clamshell-shaped tables."

"Walk to the top of those stairs. I will wait."

Over my shoulder, the glass staircase sparkles with reflected light. "Why?" I ask.

Cherno ignores me and continues chewing. I slide from my seat, walk to the steps, and climb to the top, where more diners converse around their tables. Reykin follows me closely. The balcony's twisting wrought-iron railing has a black-coral feel to it, but I peer closer and notice its blunt, thornlike nubs. Leaning on the cool metal, I peer at the floor below—and I see it. The clamshell tables reveal themselves to be rose petals. They're arranged to form a lush white flower.

But, it's coincidence, right? It must be. Clifton isn't a god. He just pretended to be Cassius at the Gods and Goddesses Ball in Virtues. If he were a true god, I never would've been able to kill him, would I?

"Is Clifton Salloway dead?" I ask Reykin, who has joined me at the railing.

175

His eyebrows lower in confusion, and he frowns. "No, he survived the massacre at the Secondborn Trials. I thought you knew that. You never asked about him."

"Did I kill him after that?" I demand with growing anxiety, and even worse, hope. "I was told that I murdered him during a battle at the penthouse suite, where I used to live." My breath comes out in shallow pants.

"He was wounded in that battle, but he survived it. He escaped through a subterranean passage into the sea. What is this about?" He reaches for me and holds my upper arms.

Dazed, I stare at him as if he might turn out to be a stranger, too. "No one thought to tell me Clifton was alive? He's my fiancé."

Reykin's eyes narrow. His strong fingers tighten on me. "Is he your fiancé? I thought he was your *ex*-fiancé. The Fates Republic no longer exists. The betrothal contract he made with The Virtue is irrelevant."

"You have to know that I never believed my engagement would get that far. The Gates of Dawn plans would never have allowed my marriage to Clifton, but that's not the way things turned out, was it?"

He shakes his head.

"Does Clifton know I'm here?"

Reykin sighs in frustration. "Yeah, he knows. He has been threatening us hourly. He's demanding that we bring you to him. We don't know how much longer we can keep him away. Hammon's working the problem as we speak, or else she'd be here with us by now."

"Why didn't you tell me?"

"I wasn't aware that you thought he was dead. I was trying to give you space so you could rest before having to suffer reprisals from Salloway."

"Reprisals?" My chin rises a notch. "You think he wants to hurt me?"

"You did try to assassinate him, Roselle," Reykin replies with a half grin, like he approves. I don't find it funny. Losing control of my mind and my body is harrowing. Reykin sees it on my face, and his smile slips away. "I'm sorry."

"According to Crow, I *did* assassinate Clifton. Crow showed me a hologram of me cutting Clifton's head off."

Reykin's eyes widen. "Do you remember killing Salloway?"

"No. I know only what Crow showed me, but it was compelling."

"But was it real?"

"Clearly I did something to Clifton if he's demanding reprisals."

"He's not exactly demanding reprisals. He's demanding you be returned to him."

"Returned to him? I don't know how to take that."

"Neither did I. You think you assassinated Clifton Salloway?"

"That's exactly what I'm saying."

Reykin lifts one hand from me and rubs his forehead. "I wasn't there for the battle. We didn't make it there in time, so I don't know all the details of what happened. I arrived afterward. The place was destroyed—bodies everywhere. So what you're saying is that you think you *killed* him, but he's not dead . . . so you think Clifton's . . ."

"Cherno believes he's a god. He said whoever made this ship is Cassius."

Reykin drops his other hand from me. "Cherno also believes *you're* a god."

I chew my bottom lip. "Let's go back to the table and find out what else the dragon-man thinks he knows."

Reykin slides his arm around my shoulder and guides me back to the stairway. We descend together. When we reach the captain's table, Cherno lifts his napkin from his lap and pats at his lips with the rose-embossed white linen. He sets it aside just as I take my seat next to him.

"How did you know it was Cassius's rose?" I ask, indicating the arrangement of tables.

"My perspective's different from you ground dwellers. Most of my former life was spent in the air. I have a natural predilection for understanding the whole instead of just the parts."

"Roselle," a voice says from behind me.

I look up from the table when I hear my name, and see Hammon hurrying across the dining room. My heart catches in my throat. *How do I tell her the truth about Hawthorne?*

She casts a wary glance over her shoulder, and her long brown braid waves in the air. She has a haggard expression when she turns back again. I lurch to my feet, and so does Reykin. There are at least two kinds of shared intimacy that bind people together. Love is one. Pain is another. But the latter is also destructive. Pain, like the loss of Hawthorne, is sometimes the knife that hacks the bond of love until it snaps.

Running the last few steps, Hammon engulfs me in a fierce hug and whispers, "I'm sorry, I couldn't keep him away any longer."

"Who?" I whisper into her ear.

"Salloway," she replies, panting.

She must have sprinted here from the other side of the vessel, but her ferocious hug conveys pure love—complete acceptance. Fighting back tears, I squeeze her, too. I missed her so much—the way she included me in everything she did when we were soldiers, the way she'd taught me the skills she learned as a mechanic, the way she treated me like I was her sister. She's a new mom now, and I missed all of that. I want her back. I need her.

"I missed you like crazy, Hammon." My voice is breathless.

"I missed you, too," she replies. "I can't believe you're here." She lets me go. Her eyes are misty. Mine, too. She takes my hand in her sweaty one.

A commotion of raised voices from the entrance to the dining area draws my attention, and then the room grows quiet.

"I'll never let him hurt you," Hammon whispers.

Through the crowd, I can just make out Edgerton blocking a very annoyed Clifton Salloway. Beside me, Cherno emits a low, menacing growl. The sound of it makes me feel threatened and defensive.

And then comes the unmistakable sound of Clifton Salloway's voice. "I don't care if it isn't safe. I'm going to speak to her, so get out of my way."

"What if Roselle kills you this time, huh?" Edgerton challenges him. "All them assassins were sent for you. The only reason they quit lookin' is they thought you was dead. Now you're runnin' in here like a ninny, riskin' 'em findin' out you still exist, and that doesn't help anyone."

"Move, Edgerton!" Clifton orders.

The captain's shoulders round in defeat. He gets out of Clifton's way but calls after him, "She's dangerous! I'm keepin' this ship if she does manage to kill you this time!"

"She managed to kill me last time," Clifton sneers over his shoulder. That last bit does the trick and silences Edgerton, whose mouth hangs slack jawed as Clifton marches toward me. "Everyone clear out!" Clifton yells with a wide sweep of his arm.

Diners rise and bolt for the exits, leaving half-eaten meals on their tables. I stand my ground, though my knees feel weak. Hammon and Reykin do, too. The crowd parts, and I get my first unobstructed view of Clifton Salloway. His intense green eyes flare with ire when he sees me. His look of hatred takes me aback. I swallow against the tightness of my throat. I don't know how to make amends for what I tried to do to him, or whether it's even possible to atone, but as Clifton grows nearer, I realize his glare isn't for me. It's for Cherno.

Cherno's grumbling voice stirs the air. "Cassius the Unrelenting, the Sacker of Cities, the Slayer of Dragons. I should've known that wherever Roselle was, you'd not be far behind."

"Chernobian the Fierce," Clifton spits with definite sarcasm. "Escaped the tar pit I threw you in, have you? Well, a part of you has."

He scans Cherno from the floor up. "You may be even uglier now than you were before." His usually smooth and flawless brow creases. He shoulders me behind him protectively, getting between me and Cherno, and his possessive grip lingers on my hip. Hammon lets go of my hand.

Anger and embarrassment color Cherno's expression. "You recognize me in this monstrosity of a form?"

"It's your eyes—your eternal fire has a particular smolder I could never forget. And"—he leans toward Cherno and sniffs the air—"a reek that I loathe."

Smoke curls from the dragon-man's nostrils. "I hope Roselle decides to cut off your head for a second time."

"Okay, enough!" I move around Clifton to get between them. I'm a runt compared to them, but they stop.

Clifton gives me a seductive look. He cups my cheek and rubs my skin with the pad of his thumb. "Who are you?" he asks.

His question startles me. "I don't know anymore."

"Nor do I," he admits. "I thought I did. I thought you were just some beautiful, genetic mishap."

"What do mean?"

"In form, you resemble the Roselle I knew." He lifts my left hand. "You even bear her mark, but you had no natural powers. We'd hoped you'd be like her. That was the Rose Garden Society's purpose, when we formed— to see if a goddess could awaken. We watched and we waited, but your latent traits slept, so we believed you weren't one of us. You did have courage, though—courage enough to take down a government. We saw your potential in helping us reclaim our society. Then you devastated every one of your enemies at Valdi Shelling's social club, and I thought, 'Ahh, maybe the Goddess of War's descendant inherited some of her traits after all.'"

"You're joking."

Clifton chuckles. "About what? About you being a goddess?" He gazes toward the transparent wall. "No. I'm not joking. The cities we're gliding through belong to me, such as they are now."

I pull away from his grip, and his hand falls from me. Turning, I stare out at the ancient, crumbling kingdom.

"And, I'm beginning to believe that you, Roselle, are a sleeper."

"What's a sleeper?" I ask.

"Someone who has all latent genetic traits of a god," Clifton replies, "but none of the raw power."

Cherno laughs humorlessly. "I would rethink that assessment of her if I were you. The goddess Roselle has awakened. Your severed head should be proof enough."

Clifton scowls at Cherno and absently touches his neck. If I cut his head off, it healed well. His skin's flawless.

"It wasn't Roselle St. Sismode who killed me—it *was* her body, but it wasn't *her*. I didn't see the person I knew in those eyes. They were devoid of emotion. Roselle was a shell—a machine—when she tried to take my life."

"Did I hurt you?" I whisper.

"I've had worse."

"Have you really?" He must be lying. Dying is excruciating. It wasn't just the physical pain—it was the massive fear as my body struggled to resist the cold.

"I planned for it to happen the way that it did. I knelt before you, knowing what you'd do. I needed Crow to believe I was dead. I knew I was Census's target. We set a trap. I was bait. I'd hoped Crow would send someone else to kill me, but he didn't."

"I'm sorry." My lower lip quivers, and tears brim and overflow. "I have no memory of it—of the slaughter."

Clifton wipes a tear from my cheek with his thumb. "Don't be sorry. I know it wasn't *really* you . . . and maybe it's what I deserved for not saving you when Census attacked us at the Opening Ceremonies of the Secondborn Trials." His guilt is written all over his face.

My heart feels swollen and bruised. "It was chaos that night. Zeroborns were murdering everyone. You had to leave."

"I prayed you'd be able to escape the Silver Halo." His gaze moves pointedly to Reykin, whose jaw tenses. "I did manage to locate the platform later, but it was abandoned on a practice field. You were gone."

I don't want to think about that night, so I quickly ask, "How did you survive without your head, Clifton?" In my mind it isn't possible.

He has the audacity to smile. "Had you taken it with you, I wouldn't have survived long, but you dropped it, so my body reclaimed it, put it back on, and healed itself. Well, with some help from deft physicians and technology."

The world I thought I knew was merely a fantasy.

"Why are you hiding from Crow?" Cherno interrupts. "Why haven't you laid waste to him and his tyranny?"

Apparently it's the Lord of Raze and Ruin's turn to be angry and embarrassed. "You should be thanking me for what I did to you, *friend*," Clifton taunts him. "You survived the end of our world because of me. None of your brethren were as fortunate. Dragons are long gone."

Cherno flinches, as if Clifton had struck him. "What happened?"

"As far as we can tell, it was massive solar flares—not the weak kind that we have now, that threaten power sources. No, these were massive flares that carried radiation and melted polar ice caps in hours. The entire planet became a giant storm for decades. Our cities sank beneath the seas in a matter of days. The famine that occurred afterward wiped out your species and most of ours. Radiation proved to be too much for us. We survived it, but—"

"But what?" Cherno demands.

"Prolonged exposure to that kind of radiation reduced the strength of our powers. We can still heal ourselves, but the traits that made us extraordinary waned."

"I once witnessed you raze a temple of gold and stone with your bare hands. Can you still do that?"

"No. My powers are gradually returning, but none of us are what we once were."

"Show me what you can do," Cherno growls through clenched teeth.

Clifton glances around at the table. He focuses on my sweaty water goblet. Condensation drips from it onto the gleaming mother-of-pearl table. Ice cubes float on the surface of the half-full glass. With a deep exhale, Clifton moves his manicured hand above the rim of the goblet. His handsome lips turn down, and his brow furrows. The clear rim buckles like a wax candle consumed by a flame. The ice melts away. The water boils, steam rising from it. The goblet loses shape, and the stem folds over, spilling the hot water onto the table, over the edge, and onto the floor.

When Clifton glances up, Cherno has a hideous scowl on his face. "That's it? That's what you can do?"

"It's much better than it was. I've been doing experiments with a new drug—"

"We're doomed," Cherno growls, picking up a chair. He hurls it across the room in rage. It crashes into the far wall and shatters into pieces.

"Calm down, Chernobian," Clifton orders in a clipped tone. He puts his arm out protectively and pulls me closer to his side. "Technology, new weapons, and information are our strength and magic now. Harness them, and the world's yours."

Panting with fury, Cherno retorts, "Someone has knocked you off your hill, Cassius! I have lived with this new evil for the past three years." He tears at his hair. "I go to my death willingly rather than return to that madness!"

I leave the protection of Clifton's arms, go to Cherno, and clutch his elbow. "I won't let him get you. I promise. I'll do whatever it takes to keep you from Crow."

"The only thing that will keep this new world from crumbling into another one of those lost kingdoms out there"—Cherno's massive arm sweeps toward the watery empires outside—"is power. Do you have that kind of power, Roselle? Are you a death-harbinger? Because if you're not, we all die."

I turn toward the table we vacated. Concentrating on Cherno's napkin, I lift it with only my mind into the air and mimic the flight of a butterfly. Then the other napkins in the room join it, floating up from tables and fluttering in place.

"We need more than that from you, Roselle," Cherno urges. "Crow will snap your spine like a stick with those parlor tricks."

I clench my teeth and try harder. Tables rumble and break free from their bolts in the floor. They levitate and spin in a whirling dance. The dishes and cutlery bounce up as well, hovering above the tables, then twist in a howling vortex that encompasses the entire dining room—except for the eye of the storm, which we're standing in. The chandeliers swing. The napkins fly around now, more like a murder of crows than butterflies. The chaos stirs a breeze through our hair. The intensity of it is staggering. I've created a maelstrom—and I'm being cautious. I wonder, *If I were really to let loose, would I rival the Lord of Raze and Ruin of old?*

A tug—like the feeling of my heart unraveling—distracts me. Through the debris of floating chairs and half-eaten morsels, I glimpse the sea outside. Hawthorne's there, against the glass, pounding on it. He makes no sound. His screams are silent, but they're traumatizing nonetheless.

The tumultuous cyclone I've created crashes to the ground. Glass shatters. Metal clatters. It's deafening, but it's not as shocking as the fury of silent pounding from Hawthorne's fists as he tries to break through from the sea.

I stagger over shards of porcelain and jagged metal, slipping and getting back to my feet, until I make it to Hawthorne and the glass wall. I scream his name. My palm splays on the cold surface, and I slam against it, mirroring Hawthorne's actions. He recognizes me—or maybe he doesn't. He's shouting something else now, telling me something, but I can't hear him. I place both my hands on the glass and force it to move. A crack streaks over the surface.

Before I can break it apart, Cherno tackles me from behind. His strong arms snake around me, collapsing my lungs.

I gasp for air, hollering breathlessly, "It's Hawthorne. He's here. Let him in! It's Hawthorne! Hawthorne!"

Chapter 12
The Vanity of Kingdoms

Hammon and Edgerton shout orders into their wrist communicators at the same time. "We have a possible breech, level one dining area," one of them says. "We need all available maintenance personnel here now. Be ready to seal the hatches around the main dining area should the wall fail to hold."

Reykin and Clifton try to calm me while Cherno holds me in a death grip. I plead with them, "You have to let him in!"

Reykin's intense eyes bore into mine. "No one's there. Roselle, we're at the bottom of the sea! No one could survive out there, not even Crow's cyborgs!"

I stop fighting and close my eyes. A sob catches in my throat, but I can't cry, because I have no air. I look again. Reykin's right. Hawthorne's gone. No one's there.

Something daubs my skin. Opening my eyes, I see Reykin dabbing at my nose with a napkin. "Let her go, Cherno," he orders. "You're going to hurt her." Blood seeps into the linen in Reykin's hands. He folds it, finds a clean spot, and dabs again.

"If I let you go, Roselle," Cherno says in my ear, "will you promise not to try to break the glass wall behind us?"

"Yes."

The pressure eases, but Cherno doesn't let go. He sits us on the ground beneath the cracked panel.

"Who am I, Roselle?" Reykin asks.

I try to focus. "You're Reykin Winterstrom. Firstborn—from Stars."

"That's right." He gives me a relieved smile. "And who's this next to me?"

Following the gesture of his hand, I glance at Clifton. "Firstborn Clifton Salloway from Swords . . . I mean he's Cassius . . . I don't remember him telling me his real last name . . ."

Reykin smiles. He wipes my lip with gentle strokes of the napkin. "Maybe we should call him Cassius Ruin—would that work?" He's devastatingly handsome when he smiles. Too bad he doesn't do that often. And that we fight all the time.

Behind me, Cherno growls in my ear, "You need to hone your power if we hope to defeat Crow. I will work with you to make you stronger."

Reykin takes my hand. "We should get out of this room until it's secure."

Clifton evaluates the window behind me. "It should hold. It's meant to withstand an avalanche of falling rock."

"I'm sorry," I whisper past the growing lump in my throat. "I thought I saw Hawthorne. I'm not sure what's happening to me. I need to talk to Ransom Winterstrom."

Clifton crouches next to Reykin. "I can arrange that, Roselle. He's aboard one of my vessels. I can take us to him. Go to the infirmary here. Have them make sure you're okay. We can leave as soon as you're ready. Does that work for you?"

"Yes," I say.

"I'm going with her," Reykin announces. "I need to see my brother as well."

"You're welcome to join us," Clifton replies.

"Wherever Roselle goes, I go," Cherno says, glowering behind me.

Clifton seems annoyed by the thought of Cherno joining us, but he nods. "We will leave in a few hours."

I decline to answer questions from the medical staff in the *Sozo One*'s infirmary.

It's too hard to explain that I have a device in my head that may be making me hallucinate. It's pointless. They don't understand Ransom's technology. They don't know why my nose bled after I tried to break the transparent wall in the dining room. They want to run tests—scan my head, see what's going on in my brain. But I refuse. I don't trust anyone but Ransom to do that.

When their backs are turned, I slide off the exam table and sneak out of the medical center into a hallway. Still a bit dizzy, I put my hand on the wall and hurry through the twist of corridors, trying to stumble back to my room. When I find it, I breathe a sigh of relief. Once inside, I close the door. Rogue isn't here to greet me. Reykin gave my puppy to Phoenix to take care of while we toured the vessel. The mechadome's probably walking Rogue around one of the simulated sundecks.

I go to the bottom bunk. Slouching on the thin mattress, with my elbows on my knees, I bow my head and hold my face in my hands. Sobs wrack my body. I can't keep them in. Tears roll down my cheeks. Snot runs from my nose. Wretchedly, I use my sleeve to wipe my face, and then I tug my boots off and throw them across the room in rage.

I don't know what anything means or what's happening to me. Was that Hawthorne I saw? Was it a phantom of my imagination—my guilt torturing me? Or worse, was it Crow playing games with me? Whatever this thing's doing in my head, it's rendering me one of the most powerful beings in the world, but vulnerable to Spectrum's control. I'm changing, and I'm powerless to stop it.

I slip under the thin blanket and pull it up to my chin as I curl into a ball facing the wall. Damp spots speckle my pillow.

The door of my room opens. "Roselle?" Reykin's voice calls softly.

"I'm fine," I reply. "I just need a moment. Can I just . . ." I hold my breath so that my tears don't betray me. It's no use, though. My breath catches, and a torrent of blubbering pours out of me. I have to stop crying in front of Reykin. I swear he's going to think that it's all I do now.

"You're not okay," Reykin replies, closer now. His tone is one we would use with wounded soldiers in battle—gentle and sparing.

"I will be in a minute. I just need . . ." My throat closes tightly again, and it's hard to swallow back my tears.

The mattress dips as he sits beside me. He has his back to me, and his voice is a little muffled when he replies, "I really can't leave you, Roselle. I swore to myself that if I found you, I'd never leave you again."

"You didn't *leave* me, Reykin. Leaving me would've been jumping from the platform at the Silver Halo. You did the brave thing and stayed with me until they tore us apart."

"I'm coming in." He pauses, as if implying that I should say something if I object. I don't respond, and Reykin crawls under the blanket with me. His fingers touch my hair, smoothing it away from my neck. His arm curls around my waist, and he presses his rugged body to mine, spooning me. A large, calloused hand covers my trembling one. He rests his head on my pillow. His nose touches my nape. Soft, sweet-smelling breath tickles my neck. My breath catches in my throat. My body tingles with deep-seated awareness of him. His fingers thread through mine as he snuggles me closer still, our thighs clasping together, his languid body heat seeping through my uniform. The warmth of his hand stills my shakiness.

A million thoughts of Reykin bombard me at once, confusing me. I have that empty-belly feeling of fear. I'm not afraid of Reykin—I mean I *am*, but it's not a threat that he'd hurt me physically. Anyway, I all but begged him to promise to kill me if my mind was ever overcome by Crow or Spectrum. The gut-wrenching ache I feel now stems from my belief that when he truly sees me for what I am, he won't love me. How can he? I'm everything he dreads. And I want him to love me. I want it desperately. I have a forever kind of love for him. After a while, my tears subside and my throat doesn't ache quite so much. I sniffle, lulled by Reykin's body.

"I dreamt of you," I whisper.

"You did?" He sounds surprised.

"I don't remember any other dreams except that one."

"What was it about?"

"You were holding me, like you are now, except we were in your room, at your home—where you took care of me. In my dream, you said something to me."

"What did I say?"

"You told me to lead my army." I sniffle and turn over to face him.

"That sounds like something I'd say." He has a small dimple in his chin that hides when his beard grows in a little. It's present now.

"I'm not the same person you knew, Reykin."

"I don't care," he replies with a breathy laugh. "I'll love the person you are now, if you let me."

"I might be losing my mind," I whisper. Another tear runs from the corner of my eye. I dash it away with my sleeve.

"You said you saw Hawthorne in the water, right? This is the second time this has happened."

I sniffle. "The first time was just a glimpse. It was like catching someone with the corner of my eye. This time was different. He was in the window, screaming for me to help him, only I couldn't hear him because he was on the other side."

"Did he look like he was in the water, or did he look like he was inside the glass?"

"He looked . . ." I have a clear image in my mind of what I saw. "He looked like he was inside the glass."

"And, you're sure Hawthorne's dead?"

My heart races. "Yes. I found his body."

"And there's no way he could come back to life, like you did?"

"I don't know."

"I can think of two scenarios that make what you saw 'real'"—he lets go of my hand and uses air quotes to highlight the word—"and not a trick of your imagination."

"I'm listening."

"Okay, the first is that Spectrum is breaking through to your mind, somehow, and trying to get you to sabotage the ship, or manipulate you into returning to them, or killing us all. If that's the case, Hawthorne is a simulation meant to strike you where you're most vulnerable."

I feel myself growing paler. My hands resume trembling in full force. I push them beneath the blanket to hide them from Reykin. He can probably feel my body quaking in fear of Spectrum's gaining access to my mind again.

"What's your second scenario?" I ask.

"The second one is that it really *is* Hawthorne, and he's desperately trying to contact you from inside Spectrum. Within the artificial intelligence, he's still alive—or at least he thinks he is. Either way, you're not losing your mind."

"If the second one is true, I've trapped Hawthorne inside Spectrum forever. He has no way of escaping if he exists only inside it."

"If my theory is true, Roselle, there's another problem."

"What?" I dread what he might say next.

"A version of you could still exist inside Spectrum."

"Like a backup?"

"Yes. Spectrum could retain a version of everyone—depending on how it works. If you disconnected from Spectrum, it just wouldn't have the latest *version* of you."

"Would the me inside know that she's not . . . me? Would she think she's real?"

"Maybe . . . or maybe not. If Hawthorne's trying to contact you on the outside, maybe he knows that there's a different you, somewhere else. This is all theory. I don't know how it all works. We need Ransom."

If I'd hoped that Reykin's theories would put my mind at ease, I was sorely mistaken. This is worse than losing my mind. Somewhere there might be an imprisoned version of me attempting to survive in a world she may or may not know isn't real. And she's me, but everything that has happened from the moment I awakened would be different for the two of us. She'd have experiences that I don't, and vice versa. We've diverged, she and I.

"This is all speculation, Roselle," Reykin says in a soothing tone. "If a version of you were in Spectrum, she might not be a conscious entity. She could just be part of the collective, without self-awareness."

"I want to believe that, Reykin, but Cherno said something earlier that makes me think that Crow kept some of us separate from Spectrum's collective conscious. Cherno said he saw me in 'the box'—some sort of palace in the AI's world. Maybe I don't know about it because I never *uploaded* what went on in there into my body—into my brain. Maybe I left the other Roselle there with all the putrid memories of what we've done."

"We need answers," Reykin says, determined. "Are you ready to get them?"

"The answers, or Hawthorne and the other version of me? Because the answer is yes to both."

"You're operating under the assumption that an alternate version of you would be autonomous and would want to be saved."

"Crow's in control of Spectrum. Tell me, would you want to be saved if it were you?"

"Yeah," he sighs, "I'd rather be erased than be in any conscious state where Crow could manipulate me at will. Let's start by getting answers from Ransom."

I wait for him to move, but he doesn't. He just stares at me. "I dreamt about you, too, Roselle, but it wasn't just once. It was every night."

"You did?" For a second, my world doesn't feel so utterly bleak.

"I've been given a second chance, and I won't squander it. I need to tell you something—to explain things. I told you before that I didn't care about anything until you came into my life. You remember that day on the battlefield—when we met?"

I nod.

"I couldn't take this world any longer. The *ache* for the family stolen from me! Their slaughter was . . . horrific. Census sent death squads to kill my little brother. I tried to stop them—so did my father. They executed my dad quickly—a shot to the head as he tried to defend my mother. They made me watch. I listened to my mother's screams. I listened to her cries. My little brother, Radix . . . He went out with a whimper. Just one. They hit him and his skull cracked. My mother was last. They tortured her and dragged her body off with Radix's.

"After that, I was a ghost. My heart was dead. I lost control. You found me when the lifeblood was draining out of me. It was a relief to be dying, listening to the wind rustling the nearby reeds. Just before everything went dark, this beautiful dream came walking up to me, and she gave me her heart."

My tears flow unchecked.

"So when you told me I cared about you," he goes on, "the morning I found you alive with Hawthorne, after I thought you'd *died*, I was so angry, because you didn't understand the depth of what I felt for you. I didn't just care about you—I don't exist without you. If your heart stops beating and you die, I do, too. But instead of telling you that, I lied and said I didn't care about you."

"You're a complicated man, Reykin," I whisper.

"I'm in love with you, Roselle. You don't have to love me back—I mean, why would you? I've never given you a reason to. All I've ever done is be mean to you so that you wouldn't see how hopelessly lost I was whenever I was near you."

"You weren't always mean to me," I say.

"Mean enough," he replies, looking tortured.

"I'm afraid to let myself get close to you. If I lose control of my mind, I could kill you—or worse. And there's worse, Reykin. There's so much worse than dying."

"I know."

"We're never going to survive this. You know that, right?"

"I know that."

"I love you, Reykin."

His arms tighten around me. "Are you telling me that because it's the end of the world?"

"Yes, but I do mean it."

He kisses the top of my head. "Then I'll find a way for us to win."

We board a small, lightning-fast underwater vehicle with the Salloway logo emblazoned on the side. Once we launch into the sea, I quickly lose sight of Edgerton's vessel. I'm afraid that I'll never see him or Hammon again. I barely got a chance to speak to them and never even met their daughter, Rosie. Despite my anxiety, I'm so tired that I nod off in a comfortable chair by a round window. A hand touches my forearm and startles me awake.

"I'm sorry, did I scare you?" Clifton asks.

I rub the sleep from my eyes, sit up, and find a cashmere blanket has been laid on me. "You?" I ask, indicating the camel-colored covering keeping me warm.

"Your friend Reykin did that," he replies.

"Where is he?" I ask, looking over my shoulder for him. The cabin's empty except for me and Clifton.

His head tilts toward the forward cabin. "Reykin was curious about this ship, so he went to the control room to ask questions. He's kind of nosy, but he took Chernobian with him. I feel as if I should pay him for that."

I frown and glance at Clifton. "You're not going to hurt Cherno, are you?"

He shrugs. "Depends on how he assimilates to our world. Killing him doesn't seem to work anyway. I tossed him in a tar pit last time, and he just came back."

I nod and worry the soft fabric of the blanket. "You know, you shouldn't surprise me when I'm sleeping—I might . . ."

"Cut off my head?"

I grimace.

He grins. "What, too soon?"

My eyebrows knit together. "I'm not sure why you think that's funny. Don't you know I'm dangerous?"

"You say that like it's a bad thing." His smile could melt snow.

"It is a bad thing when I'm not sure what I could do at any given moment."

"You're afraid Crow and his technology will acquire you again?"

"'Acquire.'" I frown. "I hate that word, Clifton. The Sword military *acquired* me and forced me into their infantry as a secondborn soldier, you *acquired* me to sell weapons for Salloway Munitions, The Virtue *acquired* me to be a participant in my brother's downfall while I mentored Grisholm, and you made a contract with him to *acquire* me as your chattel in an arranged marriage."

"You're my fiancée, not my chattel."

"Technically, I'm Clifton Salloway's fiancée, not Cassius the Sacker of Cities' betrothed."

"Technically, Clifton is my name, too—it's my middle name."

"Would you have told me who you were before or after our wedding?"

"Would you have believed me if I did?"

He has me there. If he had showed me his power, I'd have thought it was some sort of technology, not divine genetics. "No," I sigh. "Probably not. It's a good thing we're no longer engaged."

"Excuse me?" All amusement is gone from his expression. "What did you say?"

I look him squarely in the eyes. "I'm breaking our engagement. I assume you'd want to forgo the nuptials anyway, seeing as how I have a device in my head that could activate at any moment and instruct me to separate your head from your body again."

"You assume wrong. Where I'm from, what you did could be construed as a lover's quarrel, and I'm adamant we keep our agreement to wed."

"You're not serious."

"I've never been more serious," he replies.

"What do you want from me? You don't need me to take down the Fates Republic anymore. The government's power was eradicated with its Clarities. What you want me for—to kill Crow—I don't know if I can give to you. The best I can do is fight Crow, but I don't know if he can die or be defeated anymore. He's not anchored to a physical form. I don't even understand what he's made of now. Energy? A mind algorithm? Trying to destroy him may be as futile as trying to snuff out the stars. What we have now is a war to end all wars."

"What do you mean by that exactly, Roselle?"

"Three different life-forms now dominate our planet. The beings we consider to be of 'normal' intelligence and biology, the beings like you, who consider themselves to be gods, and the AI beings who may or may not need a biological form. Evolutionary-wise, I doubt you'll all agree to coexist."

"You forgot to include yourself in that, Roselle. You encompass them all."

"Or none of them."

"Why wouldn't you want to marry me?" he asks.

"Maybe I'm afraid of you."

"Are you?"

"I was," I admit. "You controlled my life and threatened my family."

He frowns. "I was protecting you. Your family wasn't worthy of you."

"And I'm protecting myself now."

He's disconcerted. "Are you protecting yourself, or are you leaning into the punch?"

My eyebrow quirks in question.

"Are you walking away from me so it doesn't hurt as much if you trust me and I fail you again?" A haggard look shows on his face. "I didn't see Census or Crow coming. None of us did."

"I don't blame you for that. I actually find it comforting that you're not omnipotent."

"Why's that?"

"I like knowing I could hide in the gaps between your control if I had to."

"From me? It'll never happen. I'll always find you. I know you love me."

I sigh. "Maybe I do, but it might be like how an orphan loves anyone who's the least bit kind to her."

"I loved you when no one else was worried about you."

"You don't love me."

"I do."

I'm unnerved by the bend this conversation is taking. I don't know what his play is here. What does he really want from me? "Is it because you thought I might be her?"

"Who?"

"Roselle—the goddess you knew."

"No," he replies with a half laugh, half frown. "She's long dead. I thought you might be *like* her physically, not the real *her*."

"Cherno thinks I am her."

"Cherno has been in a tar pit for centuries."

"Did you love her?"

"Not like you think. I respected her."

"Were you lovers?"

"Uh, no." He gives me a dubious look. "Everyone speculated that we were. She was probably the most beautiful woman I'd ever met—cunning and brave—but I was smarter than to get involved with her in that way. She wasn't like you."

"Why do you say that?"

"She was . . . fierce. Ruthless when it came to her enemies, even more so when it came to matters of the heart. She demanded blind loyalty, even if she wasn't willing to return it. If you loved her, she swallowed you up. She was the exact opposite of you."

"You don't know what I'm like now."

"I know *exactly* what you're like."

"No, you don't. I *killed* the person I thought I loved most in the world, and I was awake when I did it—not manipulated by an AI. I'm not the same person you knew. I have only one objective now, and that's to find a way to annihilate Crow. I'll destroy anything that gets in my way, including you. Don't love me. I don't have a future. I only have a purpose."

"You're *my* purpose, Roselle St. Sismode—from now until eternity."

Lights flashing in the window to my side distract me from Clifton's stern expression. I glance out at the sea.

"What is that?" I ask.

"That's my other vessel—my home in the sea. I'm bringing Ransom here for you to meet with him."

Clifton's other vessel is unlike anything I've ever seen before. It's a round, floating fortress—a black sphere dotted with lights. I feel as if I'm a modern astronomer discovering a new world. Surrounded by dark water, the underwater ship reminds me more of a space station than something on our own planet. A port beneath the equator of the fortress slides opens. Our small, torpedolike craft travels toward the cavernous hatch in the belly of the sea station.

"What do you think of my boat?" Clifton asks, his cheek inches from mine as we stare out the window.

"That isn't a boat, Clifton. It's a planet in the sea." Other orbs connect to each other by segmented walkways that undulate in the ocean currents. The interconnected fortresses don't seem to be moving, just hovering above the seafloor.

"It's kind of a boat—each sphere can move autonomously . . . so boats."

We enter a huge hangar. Inside, it's a colossal warehouse of seawater.

"Not a boat," I say. Our tiny vessel latches on to a dock within. The hatch closes. Water sucks into pipes while air pumps into the hangar.

"They're underwater habitats. They can go places, but we mostly float around in the same area. I built this first sphere because I needed privacy for classified projects. There was little of that when operating in any of the Fates—and, after what happened to my world, I felt the need to build something with preservation in mind. We have seven spheres in total, each owned by private investors—many of whom you've met already from our interactions with the birds." By "birds," Clifton is referring to the clientele who used to purchase weapons from us.

"Does Valdi Kingfisher own one?" The kingpin's real name is Firstborn Valdi Shelling, but the scar-faced man was first introduced to me by his bird name. He owns the Sword social club in Virtues.

Clifton chuckles. "He was my first partner in the venture."

"Is Valdi a god?"

"Barely. He possesses immortality, but little else. His money and influence are his only powers now, whereas once, he was the strongest being I knew in terms of raw, physical prowess." He gives me a side-eyed glance. "Would you like a tour of my sphere?"

"I would," I reply, my curiosity piqued more than a little. Clifton's always full of surprises.

We meet Cherno and Reykin in the control room and disembark the elegant commuter ship together. We walk across a large docking room adorned with drainage pipes, hatches that lead to metal hallways, and warehouse spaces that are larger than the ones in the Trees of the Stone Forest Base. We emerge from one hatch and out into a bright, sunlit street. The door behind us closes and assumes the facade of a windowed storefront in an odd world. An exquisite window display exhibits quaint doors from throughout history. Other attractive shops line a pristine avenue. The next store is an ancient apothecary, with colorful vials and bottles meticulously labeled in scrawling ink. I bend to examine them closer.

"These remedies are interesting," Clifton says, leaning near my ear, "but you may want to stay away from the hair-growth one."

"Hair growth?" I wrinkle my nose at him. "Why would anyone want to grow more hair?"

"People used to lose their hair."

"Really? How?"

He nods with a small grin. "It just fell out."

"Weird." I straighten and look around, taking in the full vista of the avenue.

The impact of a long-ago kingdom hits me and steals my breath. The lush landscape before me is a mixture of old and modern—of urban and oasis. Vines cling to spiraling buildings that jut up twenty stories or more. Their facades, made to appear like ornately carved stone, have ledges with various types of statues. One dragon-shaped sculpture, with massive gilded bones, snakes up the frame of a skyscraper across the river.

"Do you like it?" Clifton asks.

"It's breathtaking," I reply.

"It's Gildenzear." Cherno's voice holds a breathless note as well.

"I call it New Gildenzear," Clifton replies satisfactorily. His eyebrows waggle a bit when he glances my way again.

Cherno smiles grudgingly. "You've captured Icarnus's likeness rather well"—the dragon-man nods in the direction of the dragon sculpture—"although she had a bit more flesh when I knew her."

"You knew the dragon?" I ask, my eyes widening.

"She wasn't a pleasant creature," Cherno replies, "but she was very beautiful."

"She was also—*often*—very hungry," Clifton states dryly, "and as I recall, we were her favorite snack."

"A dragon's gotta eat," Cherno mutters. His stare lingers on the carving. "Look at that tail!" His appreciation is clear. It must be hard to be the only one of your kind left, even if he no longer resembles the kind of dragon on display here.

Clifton takes my arm in his. Reykin stiffens but says nothing. We wander along the edge of the river. White lilies dapple the water that runs parallel with this street. Reykin walks on my other side.

"This is a mere copy of Gildenzear," Clifton says. "Some of the monuments I salvaged from the originals and reconstructed them. The rock was preserved due to the depth, temperature, and lack of sunlight where the city lies now. We harvested it from there and did some reconstruction, but this is a modern version of what used to be."

We spend the next hour or so journeying through Clifton's marvel of design and engineering. The considerable girth of this sphere probably elevates the sea level. New Gildenzear's integrated magnetic system, Clifton informs us, repels against the planet's molten metal core and keeps it from crashing onto the seafloor. The indoor metropolis seethes with city dwellers. It has streets with pedestrians, automated scooter-like transports, and a large monorail.

"Who are all these people, Clifton?" I ask.

He tips his head toward Reykin. "Ask him."

Reykin gives me his half smile. "They're mostly rescued thirdborns."

"Wait"—I touch his arm—"I thought you didn't know each other." I look from him to Clifton and back. "Didn't you just meet at the Halo Palace?"

"We did just meet," Reykin replies. "I never knew who he was, and he never knew who I was. Only Daltrey knew us both. It's how we keep from compromising everything if we get caught. The less people know about each other, the better. Details don't circulate. When I explained to you that we took care of thirdborns, this is what I meant. In most cases, I didn't know where they went. I just knew that they'd live. Obviously, not all thirdborns came here. Some were integrated into Fates because you provided us with new monikers."

"They seem happy here," I comment.

Laughter floats to us on the gentle breeze. Some couples hold hands. There's energy in the air around us. Even their clothes are unique and vibrant, with all the colors of the rainbow woven into creative designs that would enthrall a Diamond-Fated fashionista.

"They're safe, as safe as I can make them," Clifton replies. "I'd like to keep them that way."

We've strolled at least six blocks already when I finally notice that the simulated sky isn't congested with hovercrafts or other airships but instead is clear and pristine—blue and hopeful—like the airspace above the Halo Palace when I lived there.

Clifton pauses to gaze up as well. "You get used to not having airships."

"I prefer it this way," I say.

"I manufacture airships, and I prefer it this way, too. It's hard to control an idea once it gets out. Once a dream originates, it becomes, in a way, inevitable."

He takes us toward the center of the sphere. Most of the straight avenues lead to it. The streets that don't are concentric circles that surround the center. Formal garden paths of pebbles and loamy earth and grass lay out before us in an enchanted inner sphere. Lush foliage with pink flowering trees teems with bees. Pollen teases my eyes. A gentle breeze stirs my hair. We pass through an archway of stone into the inner courtyard of a building so gorgeous that it makes Grisholm's at the Palace of Virtues seem quaint by comparison.

"Is this where you stay?" I ask. We cross a stone bridge over a tranquil pond and climb steep stone stairs.

"Yes, and you're my guests. You'll have rooms in my home. Arrangements have been made for Ransom Winterstrom to join us here. It's my understanding his vessel will be arriving shortly."

A temple to a god isn't an unfair way to describe Clifton's not-so-humble abode. The stairs lead to an open-aired portico with large cauldrons on either side of the entrance. Walls of black stone run with water. Stone pillars—with twisting rose vines studded with large white blooms—support the main floor. Inside the magnificent stone structure, enamel tiles with pale roses on them cover the floor.

We find our way through to another lush garden. At its center sits a round, dark-stained, wooden table that must be hundreds of years old. Clifton shows me to a seat at the table and orders tea from one of his staff. The young man bows and walks away silently. Reykin sits beside me. Cherno gravitates to the seat beside him. The dragon-man lifts an unlit candle from the table and studies it for a moment before pursing his lips and blowing. The wick ignites, and Cherno sets the ceramic candleholder back with a gentle hand.

Helpless to resist a smile, I try to hide it behind my hand. A tea set is brought out, along with a light repast. Reykin peppers Clifton with questions about his city. I'm content to listen to them. After a few minutes, labored footsteps approach. Ransom walks into the room with robotic steps. Clad in a Gates of Dawn uniform, he looks like a rebel. He has a brace on his left knee and a slight grimace on his face. Sweat beads on his brow and upper lip. He smiles at Clifton and bows his head in greeting.

"You have a lot of stairs," Ransom quips, wiping his brow with a small kerchief. He's pale and in pain but vastly improved from the last time I saw him.

The chair next to mine scrapes against the floor. Reykin stands and turns to greet his brother for the first time in years. Initially, the two just stare at each other. Reykin snaps out of it first, reaches for Ransom, and clasping him around his shoulders, draws his brother in for a tight hug. Ransom's face scrunches up like he's fighting tears. I look away and lift my tea to take a sip. I set the delicate cup down before glancing at Clifton. He's watching me. His strong hand reaches out and covers mine. He gives me a little squeeze, as if he knows I was desperate for a reunion like this with my own brother, and when it happened, I was too late to change our destinies.

"I missed you," Reykin says when they release each other.

Ransom uses his kerchief to wipe the mist from his eyes. "Yeah, me, too."

"You got big!" Reykin's a hair shorter than his brother. They look so much alike—same vulpine shape to their faces, same aquamarine eyes, dark hair, jawline, and complexion. It makes me wonder if their other brothers resemble them, too.

"Naw, you shrunk," Ransom replies with a gravelly voice.

"Would you like to sit?" Reykin asks, offering his chair to Ransom, who nods and takes a seat.

"Here, Reykin. Sit next to your brother." I pop up from my chair and move to the other side of Clifton. Reykin sits in the chair I vacated. An attendant enters and pours Ransom a cup of tea before leaving again.

"How are you feeling?" I ask Ransom.

"I have a massive headache that won't go away, but I don't care, because the voices in my head are gone. I don't have to inject beta-blockers anymore. It's just me in there now." Ransom gazes at Cherno, and then at me again. "You two got me out of the Sword Palace."

"Reykin helped," I reply, smiling in his brother's direction. "He showed us the way to the beach and brought a rescue team." I leave out the part where Daltrey tried to kill us.

Ransom looks shocked. "I didn't believe it when I woke up in that vessel with those soldiers—the Gates of Dawn. I thought I was deep inside Spectrum and it was a ploy to get me to talk. I sometimes still don't believe I'm out of there—beyond Spectrum's control. I didn't think it was possible, but I can't feel its signal. I thought they'd be able to get to me anywhere, but the depth we're at doesn't allow for it. We're out of range for the piece-of-crap implant in my brain." He has the vulnerability of a lab rabbit who just escaped the pen but isn't sure which way to run yet.

"I think I may have had some contact," I say, "not with Spectrum exactly . . . but maybe an individual who's trapped inside." I select an almond sliver from a bowl in front of me and eat it. It has a honey coating. I take a couple more.

"I'm not surprised," Ransom replies, lifting his teacup to his lips. His hand trembles. "Your implant should dominate all the others. It was made to create avenues in your mind that access and expand your cerebral cortex. What we need to do is work on infiltrating Spectrum so we can reverse engineer its existing world to suit us."

"That sounds great," I reply, "if I can live long enough to master the implant in my head."

"What contacted you, and what did it want?" Ransom asks. "You're sure it wasn't Spectrum's ploy to entrap you?"

"I'm not sure about anything. What I know is that I've seen Hawthorne twice in the span of a day or so. Both times he appeared in a reflective surface. The second time, he looked to be calling my name, but I couldn't hear him."

"So you don't know what he wants."

"Yes, I do," I reply. "He wants me to get him out of Spectrum."

"Does he know he's dead?" Ransom asks. He reads my surprised expression and adds, "I saw him in the morgue when I checked on your body."

"I don't know if he knows he's dead." I take a deep breath. "So I really was dead—drowned in the throne room?"

"Yes," Ransom replies. "I thought all was lost when I examined you on the slab."

"You didn't know I could come back to life?"

"Roselle, I don't know a lot. I have theories, but even I couldn't imagine you obtaining immortality."

"She's a god," Cherno replies. "It's in her blood."

"I don't understand what you mean, Cherno." Ransom shakes his head. "I don't even understand how you're awake."

"I'm a god, too," Cherno explains. His head flits, almost birdlike. "I melted the implant in my brain."

"I think what Cherno is trying to say," Clifton translates, "is that whatever you implanted into Roselle's brain has activated latent genetic traits she inherited from her ancestors."

Ransom catches on with a dubious look. "Like immortality."

"And telekinesis," Reykin replies.

"What you're talking about are called atavistic traits. If someone is born, let's say, with fur on his face like a wolf-man, some consider it an ancestral trait from a previous evolutionary state."

"Well, there's the science behind it," I say.

"But that means your ancestors were really gods," Ransom says.

"Like Cherno," I reply.

"No," Clifton denies my example with a frown. "Not like Cherno. You have no dragon in you. You're a god like me, but I think Ransom gets the point."

"So . . . you're immortal and you have telekinetic powers?" Ransom asks me with a growing smile.

I nod at him, my look serious. "I'm sort of a freak."

"From what I've seen so far, I'm pretty sure everyone here's a freak. I mean, look at this place." Ransom lifts his hands and gestures at the odd opulence around us. "And what's so great about normal?" He shrugs. "When it comes to the brain, we're all unique. If I were to slice your brain and Reykin's brain into pieces, they'd be significantly different, on many levels—biochemically, the numbers of dendrites and axons, the gaps between neurons, the neurons themselves, you name it. I could map your brains and create a clone that exactly matches them, down to the atoms that make them up. But if I were to put your implant into Reykin's brain, I'd get a different result, because you've had different experiences."

"So it's twofold," I state. "Nature and nurture."

"Yes," Ransom agrees. He seems to have relaxed a little and settled into the conversation and his surroundings.

"Can you make another implant like Roselle's?" Reykin asks.

Clifton leans forward. A deep frown creases my lips.

"Maybe," Ransom replies, caught off guard. "But who would want one? Anyone who gets the implant would face possible integration by Spectrum—and that's *if* everything went well and the body didn't reject it, *and* I was able to make all the right incisions in all the right places. It's a gamble. I took it with Roselle because I had no choice. My Census overlords were going to make her a Black-O whether I performed the surgery or not. I thought this way she'd have a chance.

"For the first few hours after her surgery, I thought she was going to die. The implant didn't seem to be responding, and her vital signs dropped significantly. I thought we were both dead. I knew that as soon as Crow found out what I did to her, I'd be tortured, forced to give them my research, and then slaughtered. But after Roselle's initial setbacks, she steadily improved. I burned everything—all my research—after that. Hiding Roselle's reports was dangerous. I swapped out scans with other subjects' images. It became a cat-and-mouse game. And then when she did integrate into Spectrum, I lived in daily fear that we'd be discovered. But Roselle's device hid itself, by design—I'd written protocols for it to regard Spectrum as a threat and to imitate standard VPMD protocols whenever it was singled out for testing. It did it so well that I thought my technology was a failure, because after a while, *I* couldn't tell the difference when I'd test her. I wasn't even sure she would awaken from Spectrum. It's not something I want to bet on again without a battery of tests and research."

"But it could be done?" Reykin asks with a calculating look.

My frown deepens.

"Maybe," Ransom replies, but he seems confused. "My mind has been a little fuzzy since the escape from the Sword Palace. I'm having a hard time remembering some things. I was unconscious for a long time."

"It's probably only temporary," Reykin says, trying to reassure him.

"Yeah . . . temporary . . . ," Ransom echoes. "If you want another prototype like Roselle's, I'll need a lab, and that's just the beginning. Re-creating just my work environment will take time. The vital equipment isn't exactly lying around, or something I can just throw together."

"Forget about another implant." I give Reykin a withering look. "What we need is a way to reverse engineer Spectrum. If we can't destroy it, maybe we can succeed in pulling individuals out of the AI."

"You mean steal them from the collective?" Ransom asks.

"To start. What if we could disconnect them from Spectrum, like you and I are now?"

"They'd still exist inside Spectrum—a version of them will exist."

A painful ache hollows my chest. I stare at Reykin across the table. He was right. "So I'm still in there," I say.

"Most of what you were is in there," Ransom explains. "Remember I told you I blocked Crow from seeing pieces of your memory? I succeeded. He didn't get everything in his Spectrum version of you. He knows almost nothing about you and Reykin."

"What about *Roselle and Reykin*?" Clifton asks. His gaze shifts between the rebel and me.

I'm a little surprised Reykin didn't explain to Clifton in all this time that I've been spying for the Gates of Dawn. From the moment Reykin returned me to Clifton's ship, just after the Gates of Dawn soldiers captured Edgerton, Hammon, and me in Stars, I was technically a Gates of Dawn operative, even if I didn't understand it right away. But I realize now that Reykin would never tell a soul about what conspired between us, or about my participation in espionage—nor would Daltrey.

The Gates of Dawn and the Rose Garden Society are adversaries in a different sort of game. They are friendly when the occasion arises to protect thirdborns, or to shelter me when I was secondborn, but they never have the same ends in mind. Clifton likes the Fates Republic. He wants the status quo—he just wants to rule it with me. Reykin wants its annihilation. He wants freedom from the Fates Republic for all of us. Reykin would protect every hint of knowledge about me to keep me safe.

"Did you work with Reykin as a Gates of Dawn spy?" Clifton asks.

"Everyone has secrets, Clifton," I reply. Turning back to Ransom, I try to keep my emotions in check. "So I'm in Spectrum—a version of me—and Hawthorne is, too."

"Yes. I couldn't delete you. You were Crow's personal punching bag within Spectrum. He'd know the nanosecond you went missing. I knew they were coming for me. I injected a prototype virus into the copy of me to erase my Spectrum backup. I'd already manually erased memories in my backup over time. This was just an extra precaution. It's why I'm still alive. They were torturing me for my research, how I developed not only your implant, but also the virus I used to erase myself from their world."

With my suspicions confirmed, that bleak feeling returns. "What do I . . . What am I like in there?"

"You're like you, except there the physical laws that govern us don't exist. It's an alternate universe. Some of it is unexpectedly exquisite, but most of it is horrifying."

"I agree you *do* need a lab, Ransom," I urge, "but the focus should be on finding ways inside Spectrum's world. Ones we can lock down when we're not using them. In the meantime, we must disrupt their operations out here in the real world. We also need you to redevelop the virus you used to erase yourself from Spectrum."

"I can't go to the surface," Ransom warns. "The moment I return to dry land, I run the risk of reintegration. My device can't fight them like yours can, not now anyway. I can work on something that might help me stay autonomous, but I fear I'll always be a liability in that regard."

"Your lab will be here—New Gildenzear," I reply. I focus on Clifton to see if he objects. He doesn't. "This will be our base of operations. From this moment on, we're a family. We do things as a family. That means the Rose Gardeners and the Gates of Dawn are no longer separate entities. We pool all our resources, and our only goal is the survival of . . . anything that isn't Spectrum. We have to be ruthless and single minded in our purpose. There are no rescue missions from this moment forward. Our only goal is the eradication of Spectrum and our survival."

"What if Spectrum takes you back?" Reykin asks.

I meet his stare. "Then I'm Spectrum, and you erase me from existence at your first opportunity."

Reykin scowls. He turns to his brother. "Once we get your lab, Ransom, how fast can you build another prototype implant like Roselle's?"

I shoot to my feet, my chair scraping against the floor. "Can I have a word with you, Reykin?"

Reykin pushes up to his feet, staring down at his brother. "You map out the Base in the Fate of Seas and give me a detailed inventory of the equipment you need, and I'll get it for you."

"But it's guarded by Black-Os," Ransom replies with a doubtful look.

I walk to Reykin's side and link my arm with his. "Excuse us," I say. I tug Reykin from the tearoom and walk him through the main floor of Clifton's abode. Outside, near the cauldrons, I let go of his arm.

"What are you doing?" I ask.

"Exploring options," he replies coolly.

"You're not going to volunteer to get implanted, are you? Because that would be stupid."

He points toward the house. "You know your buddy's going to do it—the god. Why aren't you yelling at him?"

"He's smarter than that. Clifton isn't going to risk messing up his mind for all eternity."

"I wouldn't count on that. And why am I stupid for wanting to help and protect you?"

"You're not. I'm saying I don't want to lose you. An implant is a way into your mind. If Spectrum takes control of you, or if Crow kills you . . ." I turn away, take a deep breath, and then exhale. "Listen," I go on with a gravelly voice, pointing my finger at the ground, "I need you on the outside. I need you out here to attack the targets I'm going to set up for you when I'm on the inside. It will be a two-pronged attack. I'll control the Black-Os. You'll control the Gates of Dawn. We'll coordinate strikes on Spectrum's factories and bases. We'll be a team—you and me."

"What if you need help on the inside?" he demands.

"Hawthorne's in there. If I know him, he's waging war. I need someone I can trust to have my back out here."

"Why are you so frustrating?" he asks.

"Because I'm right."

"You're not right. You just think you are."

"Is there a problem?" Clifton asks, joining us.

"Nope," I reply, crossing my arms and glaring at Reykin.

Reykin frowns and asks Clifton, "Was the other Roselle—the ancient goddess—this obstinate when you knew her?"

"Oh"—Clifton shakes his head ruefully—"they're not even the same caliber weapon when it comes to that."

I narrow my eyes at them. "I'd like to view rooms that will make a suitable lab space for Ransom, and a weapons-testing facility for me, if you don't mind, Clifton."

"I have what you need here. We can get started straight away."

"Perfect."

I leave them, reenter Clifton's cavernous house, and retrace my steps past potted palms to the tearoom. When Clifton and Reykin arrive behind me, Clifton guides us all to elevators that take us to a lower level. Cherno ducks his head to fit inside. I press up against Clifton and glance at Reykin on our way down. His jaw's rigid. His jealousy, a dark frown. His blue eyes, seduction.

And I'm the stubborn one?

The elevator doors open to a hive of open-floored levels populated by nonuniformed technicians working on various engineering projects, from vehicles to weapons. The environment hums with activity and energy. Ransom's eyes grow wide when Clifton shows him to an unoccupied laboratory with rooms for testing and equipment.

"Now all we need are your lists," Clifton tells him, "and a detailed understanding of the island where you were based. I can relay messages to the surface to get comprehensive images of the operations there."

"I'll get started right away," Ransom replies with an eagerness I haven't seen in him before.

"And I will study your maps," Cherno states emphatically.

Clifton smiles with satisfaction. And why wouldn't he? He'll be acquiring the kind of technology that could make him a truly powerful god once more. The thought gives me pause. He makes a gracious gesture with his hands. "First I'll show you all to your quarters so you can get settled here in New Gildenzear."

As we follow Clifton out, I fall behind with Ransom. "Just to be clear, Ransom," I say softly, "if you touch Reykin's brain in any way, I will murder you. I will chop you up in little pieces and feed you to the sea."

Ransom slows, but I never check my gait, moving ahead of him, and past Reykin, to join Clifton.

Chapter 13
Superposition

Reykin bursts into my new bedroom just as I'm shrugging on my training shirt.

Fear triggers a burst of energy from my palm. I restrain it just enough so that it strikes the stone wall near Reykin, missing him. Loud cracks spider over its surface. The handcrafted vase on the bureau shatters, and a puff of dry clay lingers in the air. The noise grates my raw nerves. My heart, thrumming wildly in my chest, settles a little when I realize I'm not under physical attack and didn't hurt the firstborn Star.

Reykin glowers from the doorway, acting as if he didn't just do something extremely stupid by barging in like that. "Did you threaten to kill my brother?" he demands, taking an uninvited step inside my room. He sweeps his dark hair back in agitation, knowing he almost lost his head.

I cringe inwardly. He's not angry that I almost killed him. He's livid because I threatened his little brother. "Don't scare me like that, Reykin," I growl, avoiding his glare and gathering my discarded Gates of Dawn uniform from the bed. "I could've crushed you by accident. I don't have the kind of control that I need." Having him this close to me isn't helping to calm me. My attraction to Reykin rages in an unrelenting swirl of unfulfilled desire. I turn away and go to the closet to drop my dirty clothes into the conveyor shoot, which whisks them away.

I straighten the new training outfit that Clifton's assistant provided me. It's dark, with clean, elegant lines, red roses, and a thorny vine embroidered on the sleeve. When I emerge into the airy bedroom, I notice that Reykin's closer, assessing my huge bed. I blush a little. Its base looks like an altar to a god of dreams. My skin feels taut. Thoughts of the two of us entwined in it flitter through my mind. I try to conceal them with a mask of irritation that matches Reykin's. He needs to go, soon. I can't pretend to be indifferent to him for long.

He turns away, even more annoyed. "Did you threaten to chop Ransom into tiny pieces and feed him to the sea?" he demands, his voice low and bitter.

"I might have said something like that."

"Something like that, or exactly that?"

"Exactly that."

"He's terrified of you, Roselle. He just got out of that hellhole!"

"Ransom has nothing to fear from me if he doesn't put an implant in your head. If he does, well, he won't live long."

"Who do you think you are? That's my choice, not yours." Blue fire snaps in his narrowing eyes.

"You're an idiot. I can't take my implant out, and you want to put one in? I can't even deal with your stupidity." I gather my training bag and sling it over my shoulder. "Are we done here? Because I have to go train." I start to move past him, but his hand latches on to my elbow.

"I want you to apologize to Ransom," he says in a low growl.

"No," I reply, and I wrench my elbow from his grip. His eyes widen, a little surprised that I'm that strong. He has no idea. I could crush him.

I take a step toward the large opening in the wall that leads to an outdoor patio. The fake sun indicates it's midafternoon. I want to get some training hours in before I sleep tonight.

"Who are you training with?" he asks.

"No one."

"If you wait for me, I can train with you."

"No, you can't. I could hurt you."

He scoffs. "You've never beaten me before."

"I'm different now, Reykin. I don't even know how powerful I am. I won't let you get anywhere near me until I do—until I know I can control it. Where did Clifton put you? I'll come find you when I'm done, if there's time before dinner."

"Cherno has the room next to mine, on the other side of the 'temple,'" he replies, calling out the house for what it is—an elegant shrine to a wealthy god. "My bed doesn't look like yours."

My eyebrow arches. "No?"

"No."

"Huh." I try to hide my smile at his provocation. "I was thinking of asking Clifton for a bigger one myself. I'm not sure I'll have enough room in this one. You know how I do battle in my sleep."

A grudging smile flickers across his sublime lips—lovely, and gone in seconds. "I do know. You talk a lot in your sleep, too."

"I recall you telling me that. You should warn Clifton, too. He might not want his room so close to mine."

"Would it bother you if I said that to your fiancé?"

"I told Clifton he isn't my fiancé."

"Did you? Because I don't think he got the message."

"He's a god. I don't think people tell him no very often. He'll figure it out."

"If you don't want me to train with you, I'll contact Edgerton. We need his ship here at our disposal. As soon as we work out a plan, I'll be going to the Fate of Seas."

You're not going anywhere without me.

"Will you get my puppy and my mechadome for me?" I ask.

"Of course."

"When are we meeting to discuss strategy?"

"We start plans tonight—after dinner."

"I'll see you at dinner, then." I make a move to leave.

"Consider that apology to my brother. Threats of violence are no way to build a family."

"It worked in mine."

"Did it?" he asks. "You were close to them, were you?"

His sarcasm isn't lost on me. "Okay, you make a strong point. I'll think about it."

"And also, consider that it isn't the technology that's fearsome. It's the individual wielding it."

"I'll consider it, if you'll consider that the technology could wield you."

I duck out the door, leaving him behind. I search the grounds for a suitable place to train and choose a lea overlooking a small pond. It's deserted except for a pair of gray cranes. A cherry-blossom grove and a stone wall conceal it from the rest of the city.

I set my training bag down by a mossy tree trunk. From it, I retrieve three drill instructor devices: a silver one, a blue one, and a red one. Manufactured by Salloway Munitions, the autonomous hexagonal drones have the size and weight of a grapefruit.

I pitch the first one into the air, and above my head it hovers, twirling and scanning the terrain. The next two do the same, finding angles around me to best mount an attack. I withdraw two Dual-Blade X-Ultras from their sheaths. They're the newest versions of advanced Salloway weapons, created by Clifton at some point while I was a monster for Crow. Holding each fusionblade in one hand, I ignite them at the same time. Sizzling energy erupts from the strike ports.

"Initiate warm-up program," I command.

The drones swarm me with their fusionblades ignited in training mode. If I'm struck, it will burn, but I won't lose a limb. At first I use both blades together, swaying them like a rolling wave, a tide to defend the assault from three different angles. The familiar sound of the weapons clashing calms me, and I fall into a rhythm, able to predict the next few moves from each pivoting device.

Frowning at the simplicity of their moves, I give another command: "Initiate advanced sparring program—highest-level assault, multiple weapons." The three devices careen, whirl, and come at me all at once, a barrage of fusionblades and fusionmag pulses at low-energy training levels. I can hardly move without being burned somewhere on my body. It motivates me to move quicker. I blur, sliding and tumbling over the grassy hill, pursuing the bots.

After a little while, it's as if I tap into their symphony. I read it like notes on a page, predicting the next several movements, and I become a virtuoso, the maestro to their opus. Their weapons wend and twirl. I bend and whirl and send the curl of a fusionmag pulse back at them. Movement behind me distracts me. I *feel* Clifton and another powerful male approaching me. Their presence is unmistakable.

Because my mind is on them, the heat of a glowing fusionmag pulse from the winking eye of the silver drill instructor skims over my cheek. The sting of it has me hissing. Something manifests in my mind—a singular focus. It reaches out and captures the steely silver device by directing a different kind of energy at it, one that I draw from subatomic particles. I disrupt the silver bot's algorithm, and the whirling device calms and hovers at eye level, unable to break my spell, like a snake before a charmer. The blue one beside it twists and throws a fusionmag pulse at me. I squint at the silver drill instructor, and it moves to block the shots from the blue one.

My mind takes over the silver one completely, and now instead of fighting the other two drill instructors physically, I fight them mentally, using the silver drill instructor as my weapon. In a few breaths, I attack the red one with several lethal-level fusionmag pulses from the silver one. The red drill instructor emits dark roils of smoke and crashes to the lawn in a fiery pile of melting metal. Mentally infiltrating the blue drill instructor, I pit it against the silver one in a battle to the death. Within seconds, it's over. Lumps of metal spark on the lawn.

"It would appear you need better drill instructors," Clifton says from behind me.

I turn and find him leaning against the trunk of a cherry tree, his arms crossed over his chest. Pink petals have fallen on his head and shoulders, like floral confetti anointing a hero returning from battle. Beside him, Valdi Kingfisher stares at me with an approving smirk. I extinguish the fusionblades in my hands and sheath them in holsters on my thighs. I'm sweaty and dirty. The glow of the setting sun rests behind me.

"If I'm not mistaken, Roselle," Valdi says, his deep voice permeating the air, "you controlled those drones with your mind rather than with voice commands." The red scar on his cheek seems darker in this light.

"They're not programmed to attack each other, Valdi," Clifton replies with a satisfied grin. "In fact, they're programmed to *avoid* striking one another."

I ignore their elation. "I need something else, Clifton. Something more difficult to control. Do you have anything like that?"

"You could always take over Ransom's mind and make him spar with you," Clifton jests. He isn't serious, but he makes a good point. Ransom has a device in his head. I need to be able to infiltrate Spectrum devices and control them at will. Too bad Ransom's isn't a VPMD.

"Clifton, can you capture someone with a VPMD implant and bring her here?"

His amused look lingers. "We have some Numbers and zeroborns here already, Roselle. We've been taking hostages for testing. It's cruel, but necessary. We're studying them, trying to find a way to dislodge the implants without killing them."

"Why is that cruel?" I ask.

"We don't give them a choice. They're awake down here, Roselle, at this depth. They know who they are—what's happening to them."

"They're conscious?"

"Yes, but they still have implants, so we can't trust them. We keep them incarcerated."

"*You* trust *me*, and I have an implant. Why don't you incarcerate me?"

"You're a goddess," he replies simply.

His logic is flawed.

"What do you plan to do with an implanted subject?" Valdi, the thuggish god, asks.

"I plan to re-create a small, regulated version of Spectrum—one I control."

"How will you do that?" Valdi asks.

"I may not have upgraded Spectrum's protocols and technology into my mind, but that doesn't mean the rest of them haven't. They'll have pieces of it hidden inside them. I plan to interface with them, find those pieces, and create my own gateway into Spectrum."

"This doesn't sound like the Roselle I know," Clifton says proudly. "The one who's always giving me lessons in ethics." He likes me ruthless.

I walk to my bag, lift it to my shoulder, and sling it over. "I plan to be ethical about it. I'm going to ask for volunteers among the implanted hostages you provide."

"Why would they volunteer?" Clifton asks.

"Because I'd wager that all of us would rather die than go back. Now if you'll excuse me, I need to get ready for this evening."

"I'll accompany you, Roselle," Clifton offers.

"No, you have a guest, and I know the way." I turn to leave.

"Whatever you need, Roselle, you'll have it," Valdi says. "Check your wrist communicator. The Rose Garden Society has extended funds to you."

I touch my wrist, fondling the gold band Reykin gave me. "What do I need money for, Valdi? I earned more working for Clifton than I can spend. Anyway, the world's ending. It's all meaningless now."

"It has ended before," Valdi replies. "It will rise again."

"You're a god, right?" I ask. "I mean, the bird names were code for gods, right?"

"That's right." He grins from ear to ear. "You're our hummingbird. It fits, doesn't it?"

"Tell me, Kingfisher, would the gods do something different with it—with the world—if given another chance?"

"I don't know," he answers with a lift of his eyebrow. "Give us that chance to find out."

I turn and move toward the house, wondering how the gods will behave after they evolve into the most powerful beings in the universe once again.

A silky yellow gown has been draped across the snowy coverlet on my bed. I touch the exquisite fabric with the backs of my fingers. Apparently Clifton intends us to dress formally tonight. I check the time on my wrist communicator and find I need to hurry if I want to shower before-hand. In the bathroom, I strip off my training outfit and step into the shower. Water flows over me. The abrasions on my arms shrink and disappear—healing unnaturally fast. The bruises on my thighs lose their bluish hue. The speed of my recovery elicits a shiver from me, despite the heat of the water.

I lift the silk robe from the hook by the shower door and step out of the water. It turns off. Shrugging into the robe, I towel-dry my hair and move to the vanity.

A menagerie of hair ornaments decorates the shelves above the marble surface. I seat myself before the vanity's holographic program, and my image appears along with a menu of hairstyle options. I choose a style reminiscent of glamorous Diamond-Fated actresses from a bygone era.

A hole slides open in the surface of the marble countertop. An orb levitates out of it, circles me once, and then hovers behind my head and begins to style my hair. First it sucks up the tresses, swirling them in waves to dry them. When it lets go, my hair falls around my shoulders in cascading ringlets. The orb circles again. A hole opens in its metal veneer, and a wide-toothed comb emerges on a thin arm. The comb smooths my hair as it moves around me. When it's finished, the comb retracts, and the hole disappears. The orb shuffles around me once more, lasering off my split ends. After it finishes, it returns to its compartment inside the vanity. Following the automated instructions from the holographic program in front of me, I use golden-hummingbird combs to hold my curls back on one side.

The vanity comes fully stocked with makeup, too. I use the holographic display to select a more sensual rendering of makeup than I'm used to wearing, to cover the slight burn that still lingers on my cheek. When I'm finished, I leave the bathroom and reenter the bedroom. I dress in the salacious undergarments and yellow frock that Clifton has provided. They're somewhat more complicated than my combat armor. Lifting the fabric, I discover it feels almost as light as air. The gown itself has a plunging V neckline, and a train sweeps the floor. I slip on canary-colored high heels.

A male attendant around my age comes to collect me for dinner. He offers me his arm, and I take it, allowing him to guide me from my room. His bicep trembles a little. I pretend I don't notice his fear of me. Neither of us attempts to make conversation. After a considerable walk, we come to a massive rectangular inner courtyard framed by stone columns and a wraparound, arching portico. A stream wends through a grassy lawn. Recessed stone steps descend to a courtyard and a growing crowd of gowned and suited guests gather on the black-slate dance floor beneath fanciful hovering lanterns.

The lamps cast a warm, golden glow over the candlelit tables beside the dance floor. The fake sky has grown dark. Stars abound in a cosmic rendering of night that rivals anything I've seen in the real sky. The temperature is just warm enough to forgo a wrap. I thank the attendant, and he disappears from my side. I stroll a bit under a myriad of intricate buttresses. The dark tiles of the eaves bear rose emblems. Pausing, I reach out and lean my palm against a stone column, scanning the growing crowd of elegant guests in the courtyard below.

My heart thumps faster when I spot Reykin nursing a cocktail by the outdoor bar. He's standing beside Ransom. Attired in dark suit jackets, the two gentlemen's snugly tailored coats have silken sheens from shoulders to waist, but the fabric changes to black leather from waist to hem. They resemble the aristocrats that they are. The lanterns' glow cast Reykin's hair with a midnight gleam, like moonlight.

If Reykin is bothered by this surprise dinner party, I can't tell. He smiles and chats with his brother with a familiarity that I wish I'd shared with my own. Ransom, on the other hand, isn't as comfortable. He's less used to this type of affair than I am. He has a shell-shocked look as he scans the crowd. He holds his drink like a shield. It feels impossible to interact with strangers right now. I've never been one for small talk, and it's always been frowned upon in a secondborn. My job has been to listen, not talk. If I talk, it's usually for training purposes, or demonstrations, or to explain myself to an authority figure. I've been a mind-controlled prisoner for months. Why am I being subjected to a dinner party, now, in the middle of the world collapsing?

I feel Clifton approach—sense his energy. "There you are," he says, so close behind me that his warm breath tickles the curve of my ear.

I'm surprised to find that I'm angry with him. Furious, really. We have so much to plan and strategize. There's no time to waste with a frivolous party. None.

"What is all this?" I ask, not bothering to look at him. In truth, I'm attempting to get my anger in check.

"This is a surprise party, to welcome you to our community, Roselle. Do you like it?" There's a sensual softness in his voice. It's a tone he's been using with me ever since we became engaged.

"No." I turn around to face him. My breath catches a little. Clifton's the personification of sophistication. His skin, flawless. His dark suit, impeccable. His smile, glinting.

His grin fades when he sees my scowl, but then he scans the rest of me, and it returns in full force. "Reykin said you'd hate a party."

"Reykin was right. What were you thinking? We need to plan an invasion—a counterattack against a formless, ever-evolving enemy. Don't you get that? Crow grows more powerful by the second—and you want to have a dinner party?"

"You think this is my first war? It isn't. Your reaction is exactly why you need a party. It's your first evening here. There will be many months ahead when we'll be forced to talk strategy and find solutions to complex problems, but it doesn't have to be tonight. Tonight's special. You're alive. That's something to celebrate."

"You do realize Spectrum could infiltrate my mind at any time and turn me into an assassin again. I could annihilate your entire guest list."

"Not my entire guest list. I'd stop you, after I let you clear out some of the less desirables."

I glower at him.

"I'm joking, Roselle." He grins and places his hand on my waist. "Ease up a little."

"It's your head, Clifton."

"C'mon"—he squeezes my waist—"I want you to unwind."

"Why? I'm your hired gun, like before, aren't I? That's why you brought me here."

"I brought you here because I happen to like you. Why's that so hard for you to understand?"

I sigh. It's because I still feel secondborn, but it's more than that. I feel truly nihilistic. None of this can last. "I've been on the other side of this war—Spectrum's side—where people don't come back. A part of me is still there. I'm a ghost in your world."

"I *want* you to come back. Will you at least try?"

His earnestness persuades me. "I'll try."

Orchestral music filters to us from the band on a higher tier of the courtyard. Beautiful people find partners and begin to dance.

With his hand still on my waist, Clifton gives me another gentle squeeze. "May I please have the honor of a dance? Don't say no," he orders when I frown. "I've been dreaming of this moment for a long time now . . . Please?"

"One dance," I reply, attempting to suppress my reluctance.

He takes my hand. "You should never put a limit on fun, Roselle."

I gather the train of my gown and descend the stairs with him. "Where's Cherno?" I ask as we pass guests openly gawking at us.

"He declined my invitation to dinner, called me an irritating man-child, and said something about how I should postpone mating rituals until after we kill Crow. He ordered me to have an unbelievably large quantity of food sent to his quarters, and then he told me to go away."

I should've done that.

We linger by the edge of the dance floor until the song ends with a few soft notes. Together, we step onto the black-slate floor, my heels clicking on its glossy surface. The first strains of a dramatic melody begin. I know how to perform all the steps to this song. I was taught quite a few dances, having been prepared for the unlikely event that I'd one day be firstborn. Now I am, but the distinction isn't meaningful anymore. I am The Sword to a dead fatedom.

These thoughts lead me to remember Gabriel, as I last saw him—lifeless in the tower room of Balmora's Sea Fortress. I haven't really mourned for my brother yet, and the pain of his death aches like an open wound. Tears feel overindulgent, though. Everyone has lost someone. No one has been untouched by the conspiracy to transition consciousness into a collective power. It's a different world now.

Couples move aside to give us room at the center of the floor. Clifton's hand remains in mine, and he places his other one on my waist. I rest mine on his shoulder. The tempo of the music surges, and Clifton sweeps me in a dizzying arc. The train of my gown flutters out, like a canary's wing. We conquer the dance floor as if we're weapons on a killing field, with calculation and precision. Other dancers fall back, watching. When we're the only couple on the floor, Clifton handles me like a well-seasoned warrior. I see it in his eyes, in his mind. I'm an extension of him, the fusionblade of a swordsman. The air between us electrifies. I smile, not from pleasure, but because I'm no one's weapon but my own.

As the music winds down, I deviate from the routine and force him to kneel on one knee before me or risk losing his balance. Clifton, hiding his frown, takes my hand in his and compensates by lifting it to his lips and kissing it, all of which comes off as horribly romantic. He's clever, I'll give him that.

As he stands, he bends near my ear and whispers, "If you wanted me on my knees, you had but to ask."

"I'm not your toy, Clifton," I reply under my breath, smiling as if he's the wittiest creature alive.

"Not yet, but the evening's young." The innuendo isn't lost on me. A tinkling of bells summons us to dinner. "Come join me." He offers his arm, and I take it. "I have friends you should meet."

Clifton escorts me to the largest table in the center of the garden sanctuary. Fireflies flitter near the stream, their glow receding with the ignition of every candle and torch. Clifton introduces me to the gathered guests, two of which are Valdi and his wife, Edwah. I remember Edwah as the very lovely Snow Queen from the night of the Gods and Goddesses Ball. She retains her icy demeanor, appraising me as one would a rival. A stunning jealousy emanates from her. I'm sure at one time she could've turned me into an icicle.

Some of the gods I meet own spheres like the one we're in, small universes where they can wield the kind of political power they once held in the past. It's possible I'm being a little dramatic. I haven't a clue how they conduct their lives. I simply don't trust any of the them to do the right thing when given absolute power.

Clifton pulls out a chair for me at the main table, and then he settles into the seat beside me. Thorny rose vines twist and climb up the crystal vases of the centerpieces. An excessive display of roses erupts from the top, spewing vibrant blossoms of molten red and ashy white.

At an adjacent table, the Winterstrom brothers flank a beautiful blonde goddess. Ransom's nervous and fidgety, while Reykin's relaxed, or seemingly so—I'm not sure he's quite as calm as the image he projects. His superior air allows him to fit in with the egocentric creatures surrounding him. Whether the assembled gods believe he fits in is another matter. They have their own hierarchy. It intrigues me. They're fixated on both Reykin and Ransom, plying them with questions and animated chatter. Especially the sultry, exotic-looking goddess sitting between them. Her attention never wanes from them, but Reykin's been watching me.

The woman leans closer to Reykin and murmurs something with a toothy grin. I strain to hear what she's saying, but it's no use. At my table, a youngish-looking man with dark eyes regales me with a story about the first time he'd met my supposed relative, the goddess Roselle. Dinner is served. Clifton leans closer to me and whispers, "We've scheduled a thunderstorm tonight. Would you care to watch it with me?"

"You're gonna make it rain?" I ask with an uptick of my eyebrow.

"I am. Changing weather makes this place feel real."

"I hope your invitation extends to me as well, Cassius?" the goddess next to Valdi asks with a sultry smile. Her use of his godly name makes me feel that much more like an outsider. They've known all along who and what he is. Did they think it was amusing that I hadn't a clue?

"Edwah, you and Valdi are welcome to join us, of course," Clifton replies.

I listen with only half an ear to more flirtatious banter between Clifton and Edwah. I'm much more focused on what the lovely goddess seated between Ransom and Reykin is saying. She touches their sleeves with her fingertips, leaning close to one and then the other as she talks. Reykin doesn't seem to notice. He's trying to pretend like he's not watching me. Ransom notices, but he shrinks from her, unused to the contact. She doesn't understand that he's spent the last few years in a hell she can't even imagine. Her touch probably feels like a soldering iron to him.

The plates are cleared. The goddess covers Reykin's hand with hers. Something shifts in me. My eyes narrow. I blink, and suddenly I have a different perspective. I gaze down at my body and find it isn't mine—it's Ransom's. I glance across the courtyard and find myself still seated at the table beside Clifton. I'm still conscious in my body as well.

I've split.

I'm Ransom and Roselle at the same time. It's not even confusing, and it takes very little effort. I search Ransom's mind for him. He has receded to the background, but I get impressions of him—fear, in echoes that lack intensity, and memories of me that I don't remember at all. Goose bumps rise on his arms. I reach for Ransom's water glass and take a sip. It tastes different with his taste buds, diminished somehow. I frown.

"Is something wrong, Ransom?" Reykin asks.

I gaze at Reykin with both Ransom's eyes and my own. But it's Ransom's voice that answers, "Excuse me, I wasn't listening." I mean to assure Reykin that I wasn't eavesdropping on his conversation. I bite Ransom's lip in consternation.

Reykin says gently, "Nesunna asked you if you'd tested your RW1 Device on anyone besides Roselle?"

I tilt Ransom's head in their direction. Nesunna has a doe-eyed, innocent look on her youthful face. Cynically, I wonder how many eons it took the angelic blonde to perfect it. In an instant, I know everything that Ransom knows. I sift through data in his mind. He doesn't remember much about the device he created, or even how he implanted it in my head. He has purged almost all these memories. The last time he purged seems to be after he spoke to me on the airship, on the way to the Sword Palace.

The information isn't gone, though. He couldn't bring himself to delete it. He buried it inside me. In my device. It was in the upgrade he gave me. *I'm* the only person who knows how to make a replica of my implant now. He has a code. It will unlock his secrets in my mind.

I whisper that phrase now: "Winterstrom five, dead or alive." Ransom derived the phrase from his acute longing to know what had become of his siblings.

The vault in my mind springs opens, and with it comes a chaotic swirl of knowledge. I can't call what's in my brain a device anymore. It's a part of me, a living, growing organ—a neuro-enhancement that has adopted and adapted my DNA. In fact, I've already modified the new organ several times, upgrading it subconsciously. I can even make another one if I want to—a much better version—with the information Ransom has given me, and my own knowledge of my physiology. It'd be so easy.

Reykin nudges Ransom's elbow with his own. "Ransom?"

"He doesn't know how to construct another RW1," I murmur with Ransom's lips. "He doesn't remember."

"Who doesn't remember?" Nesunna asks with a confused smile.

"Ransom. He doesn't know how to make you a powerful goddess again. He purged all his memories of designing my implant. He can probably re-create the research. He may be able to get back to where he left off. He's brilliant, but it'll take him a long time, unless I give him his knowledge back. That was his insurance policy. Ransom knew Crow would keep him alive indefinitely, to get his hands on the technology."

"Roselle, what are you doing?" Reykin asks, swallowing back his growing anger.

"I don't know," I answer with his brother's voice. I can make Ransom's body mimic my voice if I want to, but I don't. It'd scare Reykin even more. "I suddenly found myself inside Ransom. I couldn't hold my mind back from taking over his."

"You have to get out of him. Right now, Roselle!" Reykin seethes.

I narrow my eyes at him. "Ransom has done something similar to this to me many times. He let others control me, too."

"I don't care. Get out of there now!"

My shame heats Ransom's cheeks. Reykin's lips twist in disgust.

"Ransom had a special access code to me—to my mind," I blurt out. "He programmed me to ask him a phrase—a passcode. 'Am I yesterday?' I would say. He'd respond, 'You're the future, Roselle.' That's how the implant in my head would know it was him and let him in completely. My mind won't allow Ransom to access me now even with this code, not since I died. The embedded neural implant has truly become part of me. I'm my own person now."

Reykin grimaces. "Roselle, leave him alone," he growls, and his anger sparks my own.

"And I just unlocked all my own secrets," I seethe at Reykin. And without waiting for his reaction, I do as Reykin demands. I leave Ransom.

Chapter 14
Cherry Bomb and Winterstrom

Ransom returns to awareness in his own body.

From my seat next to Clifton, I see Reykin bend near his brother and ask him if he's all right. I lift my napkin from my lap. "Please excuse me," I say. I push my chair away from the table and stand. "I need to stretch my legs."

Clifton frowns at the abrupt change in my demeanor. "I'll come with you," he replies, and starts to stand.

I put my hand on his shoulder. "No, I just need a moment to myself."

Reluctantly, he sits back down. "Don't be too long. The storm will begin, and you'll get caught in the rain."

I don't answer him, but hurry toward the stone steps without looking in Reykin's direction. Inside the walls of Clifton's temple, I traverse hallways lit by fiery cauldrons. After crossing the main foyer, I escape down a steep set of stairs. The lovely bridge over the pond leads to a stone archway. Once on the other side of that, it's just a short walk to the public streets.

Streetlamps cast a soft glow on the sidewalk. Storefronts with imaginative displays offer a distraction from my chaotic thoughts. I can't shake the guilty feeling that I've done something horribly wrong. Shame, intense and savage, bears down on me. My intrusion into Ransom's mind was inadvertent, but I should've tried to leave it as soon as I realized what happened. Instead I took over his consciousness—deliberately stole his thoughts, his memories, and his insight into what I am. That makes me no better than Crow. It doesn't matter that Ransom had done the same to me. He did it to survive and protect us. I did it because I could.

I stroll slowly, allowing the train of my dress to drag on the pristine, polished stone of the sidewalk. Passersby recognize me immediately and give a wide berth. I don't care. It's not like I'm looking for acceptance here. None of this is real anyway. It's a temporary world, with temporary people, meant to serve immortal gods for as long as it lasts. And it can't last. Not with Crow conquering the people, land, and manufacturing facilities on the shores above us. It's only a matter of time before he gets here, unless I somehow get to him first.

As I walk, my feet start hurting, but it doesn't matter. This is the most freedom I've had in ages, and I don't want to waste it. I pull off my heels and carry them, peering into restaurants and shops filled with patrons laughing and sharing their lives together. A crack of thunder breaks overhead. The dark sky roils with clouds. Flashes of lightning move across the landscape. People scatter from the sidewalks and streets, moving indoors. Parts of the sidewalks open, forming grates to catch the rainwater.

The first drops patter my hair and face. It's cool. It smells like real rain. Quickly, my dress dampens and plasters to my body. I jump in the small puddles forming in my path. Within a short time, I'm almost back to where I began walking, having made an entire loop around the sphere of New Gildenzear—on this level anyway.

A brightly lit candy store catches my attention. In the window jars of every size and shape contain colorful arrays of confectionary, whimsically leaping and careening on conveyors of air. The jouncing display is highly entertaining. I watch it for a time before peering through the

Amy A. Bartol

glass door into the shop. At crowded tables, patrons eat ice cream from glass boats with long silver spoons.

I wonder if they have crellas.

Before I know it, my hand wraps around the heavy brass door handle. I enter the shop. Lively conversations die almost at once, except for the children's, which continue babbling with happy abandon. Water drips from my hair and chin. A young woman behind the counter straightens from her work arranging the display case. Slender and tall, she wears a clear plastic apron over her clingy candy-striped uniform. Her hair, dyed in pastel shades of pink, purple, and blue, has been teased to resemble cotton candy, giving her extra height. Blue and lavender eyeshadow sparkles as her eyes round in surprise when she sees me. Her sugary smile fades for a moment before it returns with extra exuberance.

"Hi! Welcome to Madam Goria's Candy Emporium! My name is Grenadier. What can I getcha?" She runs her hand over the top of the glass case in an exaggerated "Behold!" gesture.

I stand dumbfounded before the array of elaborate sweets. "Do you have crellas?"

Grenadier looks crestfallen, and her bottom lip sticks out in an animated pouty face as she replies, "No." She quickly brightens. "Buuut we have candy and ice cream! Would you like to try something?"

"I'm not sure. I've never had candy before."

Her eyes widen again. "You've never had candy?" Her long blue-painted fingernails cover her O-shaped lips.

"I was told it's poison," I reply sheepishly.

She leans across the counter and whispers conspiratorially, "Well, it's not great for you, but it's delicious. Just dive in." She straightens again and gives me an expectant look.

I stand awkwardly for a minute, hopelessly lost in the options.

"What looks good to you?" Grenadier prods with growing excitement, as if she's trying candy for the first time, too.

232

"I don't know."

"Well, these here are Blobfish Jellies—they have a strawberry tang to them." She points to pink, gelatinous masses that look like melting, fleshy heads adorned with gigantic noses and black eyes. "Or you could try our Glucose Atlanticus." Grenadier indicates the blue dragon-sea-slug-shaped candies, next to the blobfish. "They have a lemony sour sting that's a little painful if you're not used to them. Or! You could try the Treacherous Tidal Waves! When you bite into one, an ocean of flavor gushes into your mouth."

I see the confections in a way that I wouldn't have before my implant. Before, I would have seen colors and shapes. Now, like Phoenix, I can see the molecular level. Which is interesting, but it doesn't tell me how any of it will taste.

Grenadier quirks her eyebrow and points. "Or maybe Black Licorice Eels? Or Seahorse Sandies? Blowfish Gum?"

"What's your favorite?" I ask with a grin.

"Me?" She lays one hand over her heart dramatically. "Oh, I *love* me some cherry bombs! They *never ever* let me down."

I sigh, relieved. "I'll try one!"

"Comin' right up!" Grenadier uses a vacuum-like device to select a small red hard-candy ball from a tall glass jar. She levels it toward me, and the vacuum spits it into my hand. She waits with anticipation.

I put it to my lips and lick it, testing the flavor.

Grenadier giggles and says, "You don't eat it like that. You put it in your mouth and suck on it."

"Oh," I say before popping the candy into my mouth. My eyes widen. *"Ohhh!"* A faint echo of a memory from Ransom surfaces. He's had these before as a child. I try to suppress the memory, wondering how I purge it from my mind.

"Right?" She grins. "How many do you want?"

"Two?" I feel completely greedy.

She frowns. "Two? No one gets just two." She fills a glass jar with cherry bombs before sealing it and handing it to me. "Here, would you like anything else?"

I shake my head, gazing at the crazy amount of candy in my hand. "No." I reach my wrist communicator under the scanner and pay for the candy. "Thank you," I murmur, still sucking on my cherry candy.

"Anytime," Grenadier replies, patting her cotton-candy hair. "Come back soon!"

It's still raining outside. I exit the shop and stand beneath the striped awning. A hum tingles under my skin, a low trill, like a thrill of desire. I recognize its source. Reykin. Looking around, I find him leaning up against the building across the street, his hands shoved in his trouser pockets. His white dress shirt clings to his broad chest. He's been watching me.

The firstborn pushes away from the wall and crosses the street. Water drips from his sharp jaw as he stops in front of me. I straighten, ready for another verbal assault for threatening his brother. Instead he says softly, "I'm sorry."

"For *what*?"

"For treating you the way I did tonight. I was wrong. Ransom explained some things to me that I didn't know."

"What things?" I ask, still shocked that *he's* apologizing.

"Things that he's done to you—allowed to be done to you. You tried to explain it to me, but I wouldn't listen. I don't know if I can forgive Ransom after what he's told me. I love my brother, but forgiveness is . . ." His jaw tenses. "He said he's been expecting you to enter his mind since you woke up. It's something you had to do to unlock secrets he hid inside you. He thought when you did, you'd destroy him, but you didn't."

"No, I didn't."

"Why not? I don't know if I'd have had that kind of restraint."

"I know why he did it," I admit. "I would've taken the deal had he asked my permission, in that moment, before he implanted the device. It was desperation, survival, and revenge—things I understand. If he hadn't done it, I'd be killing for Crow now. Forgive him, Reykin, for your sake and his."

"But he didn't ask your permission. Are you saying the end justifies the means?"

"It has to."

He exhales deeply. "So instead of killing my brother for revenge, you decided to go for candy?" He gestures toward the store. Rainwater has turned his already-dark hair inky.

"I went for a walk. The candy was a happy accident. They didn't have crellas, but they had these." I lift the small jar in my hand. "Would you like to try one?"

He bends his face slowly toward mine. My stomach does somersaults, and my heart feels as if it's melting as he presses his mouth to my sticky lips and tastes the cherry bomb on my tongue. My knees weaken. I drop my shoes, and my arm curves around his nape. He's so warm, an inferno. Shivering, I lean into him. Reykin's hand slips into my hair and clutches me. The candy explodes in our mouths in a stunning array of sweetness.

We break apart, me giggling, Reykin with a smile. "Well," I say breathlessly, "now I understand the 'bomb' part."

His look sobers me. Tenderness slackens his sharp edges. My heart aches in recognition, thumping more wildly. Our fervors match. The adrenaline he ignites in me—fear and desire, always those two together, like a Reykin cocktail—slips through my veins. He *can't* feel that way for me. He needs to remain vigilant. My mind's growing, and with it cracks keep splitting open in the veneer of who I was. Beneath the fissures lies a surging, ruthless energy, straining to get out. Reykin can't see it yet, but it's there. I can be thousands of people at once. I've always been a weapon, for someone or something, but now a formidable goddess has awakened inside me.

"Will you do something for me?" I ask.

"Anything," he says with a sultry look that makes me want to kiss him again.

"Will you wait for me?"

"What do you mean?"

"You're rushing to judgment with me. I'm not . . . trustworthy . . . I can't accurately predict where this is going or what I may do."

His smile deepens. He doesn't believe me—he doesn't understand. "Roselle, I think you need to worry less about—"

"No. Hear me out. I understand Spectrum on a level I didn't before now. Everything's evolving, Reykin."

One corner of his mouth raises in confusion. "Explain what you mean."

I think about how to describe a difficult concept in simple terms. "Okay, once, we were all individuals. Spectrum could only control someone with an implant—a VPMD. It wasn't the AI it is now. It was basically a capable computer. Soon, though, it became self-aware. It found that by collecting more minds, it'd have more options—more ideas to harvest. Spectrum grew more efficient and based its core values on resourcefulness, which sounds great, right? But if more is the end goal, then it can never be satisfied."

"I understand that," Reykin says. "Like you, I've witnessed it in action. It'll keep implanting VPMDs into everyone it catches to control them."

I shake my head. "No, it won't. It's too efficient for that. It won't be long before Spectrum won't need implants anymore. It'll be able to interface with someone, like you, for example, by reaching out to you telepathically and scanning your entire genetic makeup and your brain's unique neural pathways. Spectrum will read you, and then Spectrum will *own* you. It'll control you on a neurochemical level—firing your neurons at will."

"So when it finds us, it'll control us. End of story?"

"Not quite the end. It will keep evolving. When it does, it will simply absorb an intellect and discard the shell. It won't be concerned with your body anymore. You'll be part of the collective."

"Why? What does it want?"

"It's looking for something, but it's not very interested in this little world. It wants more."

"How do you know this?" he asks.

"When I captured Ransom's mind at dinner tonight, I saw Spectrum through his experiences. It gave me insight, but when I used the passcode I found in Ransom and unlocked memories he'd hidden inside me, everything about Spectrum began to make sense. Spectrum is evolving quickly, but so am I. I can infiltrate minds in ways Spectrum can't yet—I can do it with, or without, a VPMD."

"You can do *what*?" His hands go to my arms and squeeze.

"In theory, I can hack the brain of someone who's not implanted with a VPMD."

"In theory. You haven't done it yet?"

"No, I haven't tried yet, but it's really elementary."

"You think it's elementary because the implant in your head is growing?"

"It's not an implant anymore. It's part of me."

He shivers. The door behind me opens with the sound of a tinkling bell. A crowd of boisterous people files out. Their happy chatter makes my revelation seem far worse. Suddenly I foresee that one of them is about to slip on the pavement. I push past Reykin. "Sorry, he's going to fall," I say, noticing the confusion wrinkling his brow.

Ahead of me, a slim man slips on the slick sidewalk. I reach out and catch his elbow before he tumbles all the way to the ground. He turns to me. "Whoa, thanks," he says with an embarrassed grin. "It's slippery."

"You're welcome," I reply. His friends laugh and tease him as they walk away.

"What was *that*?" Reykin asks with a shocked frown.

Amy A. Bartol

"I have this predictive element developing right now. I'm aware of subtle cues in my environment that give me a sense of what might happen. I could hear the man's shoes didn't have much of a tread, and based on the way he shuffled toward the door, there was a high probability that he was going to slip on the damp sidewalk."

"You heard his tread? *While* you were talking to me?"

"I can multitask."

He leans his face near to me and presses his lips against my temple. The scent of him and the exquisiteness of his lips turn my insides to butter.

"I have a plan," I whisper.

I link my arm in Reykin's and tug him gently. We walk in the rain past the closing shop fronts.

"What's your plan?" Reykin asks.

"I have to find Hawthorne."

His shoulders stiffen. "Why?"

"He's alive."

"What do you mean? You said you accidently killed him."

"I'm talking about the Hawthorne from your theory. The one in a different world from ours. You were right. He exists, and if I know him, he's with me." I tip my head to the side. "The old version of me. They're technically dead here, but they're alive if you think about it. Spectrum's world exists, so they do, too—unless Crow has killed them, but I don't think he'd willingly give them up. He enjoys hurting them too much."

"They're programmed for pain?"

"Reykin, it isn't *programming* anymore. Wherever Hawthorne is, he's *real* in that world. He feels love, horror, desire . . . The most tragic aspect of his predicament is his endless potential for pain. Crow can make Hawthorne's life a torment that never ends."

"What do you mean by 'wherever he is'? He's inside Spectrum, right?"

238

"Like I said, it's not an elaborate computer anymore. It's like it punched a hole in our world and leaked out."

His brow furrows. "I don't understand."

"It's creating a new world—an alternate universe. It's stealing pieces from this world to do it. Ransom has been there. He knows. He killed his copy there, and when I say 'killed,' I mean it's not how you think about erasing a program. The other Ransom existed. He was alive in that world. Destroying him was like murder. Do you understand?"

"How can a copy be real? By definition, it's a reproduction—a fake."

"Let's call the other world Spectrum. As I said, it's not a computer or a sophisticated program like I once thought. It's an alternate universe, a new world with similar properties, but with its own unique features. It won't always conform to the laws of nature we expect."

I know this is distressing for Reykin, but he's shoving aside his fear and trying to grasp what I'm telling him.

"You've seen glimpses of Hawthorne here in our world," he says. "On the *Sozo One*."

"Yes. He's trying to break through to me. He's using quantum physics. Whether he knows that or not is a different matter. He's probably using the other Roselle and doing it through—"

"I don't need to know how. What I want to know is, does he look like he's in control, in this other world?"

"He's using Roselle to see—to witness his message—and then they're communicating that visual image to me, through her, because of our connection to each other."

"Because she's your copy?"

"Yes. She's me. The old me. Our paths deviated the moment I awoke in my capsule on the way to the Sword Palace to join Crow, but she's still me."

"Couldn't it just be Crow using a likeness of Hawthorne to get to you?"

"It could, only Ransom's memories tell me otherwise. He's been there. He's the one who lifted Roselle out of the collective and made her self-aware there. He's given her knowledge she needs to make others like her self-aware, too."

"They can rebel?"

I make a face. "They can *resist*, but their whole world *is* Spectrum, so the only ways they win are by annihilating their world, which means they cease to exist, or a hostile takeover—a transition to a state like Crow's, merging with Spectrum, or . . ."

"Or?"

"Or, they do what Crow did and get a new body in this world to inhabit."

"If Roselle gets a new body here, then . . ."

"Then there's two of us in this world. We'll have the same mind up until a point, but some of her memories have been purged, and I have a RW1 implant, so we're different in a lot of ways. She's more like the old me."

The one you love, I think with a stabbing ache in my chest.

"How do you feel about that?" he asks.

I'd like to ask him the same question. *If he could choose between us, who would he pick? The old Roselle, or me?* Emotions flash through my mind at light speed. Integrating with my alternate could be an option, but she'd lose her autonomy. She'll never go for it. If I destroy Spectrum, I destroy her and Hawthorne. If I somehow rescue them both, then there will be another me around. She won't know who Reykin is, because Ransom erased all those memories in her to protect Reykin, but she will have a raging "heart-on" for Hawthorne, who may or may not be in love with his former girlfriend.

"It's complicated," I say.

"How do you plan to talk to Hawthorne?" A subtle change is taking place in Reykin. He's withdrawing. Not physically—he's still holding my arm—but he's not looking me in the eyes. His are hooded and . . .

sad. I don't understand. Emotions just aren't my strong suit. I have a ton of them, but I don't understand them.

"I have to go up to the surface and dry land to talk to Hawthorne," I say. I point toward the sphere's sky, where the rain's turning into a fine mist. "Spectrum will completely lose interest in this world soon, if it hasn't already. It's going to take what it wants, then annihilate us on its way out."

He nods, but I know he's far from calm. Jagged fears must fill his mind, slicing him apart inside. "You can't go to the surface until you figure out a way to resist Crow and Spectrum," he insists. "When you do, we'll go together. For now we should get some rest. I'll walk you back."

I refrain from telling him again that Crow is Spectrum and vice versa. He'll get it eventually.

He lets go of me, and I instantly feel cold—bereft. I try to shake it off. After all, didn't I just warn him to be vigilant around me—to not get close? I thought I meant it, but right now I'm not so sure. Aren't I supposed to be evolving? Why do I have all these ridiculous emotions? Why this angst, and this raging libido?

Reykin ushers me across the street and along the path to Clifton's home in silence, lost in his own thoughts, which I need to remind myself not to reach out and capture. That . . . would be rude. My heart thumps wildly. The ache to do it—to shove my way into his mind—keeps breaking over me in waves.

When we finally reach my room, I hurriedly say, "Okay, well, thanks. Good night."

I slip inside and close the door in Reykin's face. I lean my forehead against the thick metal between us. And wait.

And wait.

Reykin's still there. He's not walking away. *Why isn't he walking away?*

The door slides open again. He stands over me, so near that I shiver, yearning to snuggle into his heat. The intensity of his look—I hold my breath. It's the look he had when I first met him on the battlefield. He was torn apart, as broken on the inside as he was on the outside.

"I've thought about what you told me—what this means," he says, his voice soft. "Spectrum can create endless worlds with versions of you in all of them . . . but the only one I'll ever want is standing before me now. It's you, Roselle. It's always you. It's what's in here"—his finger reaches out and touches my temple—"and in here." He traces his finger to my heart.

His hand slides down my side, searing my skin beneath the silken fabric of my yellow dress. He catches my waist in a firm grasp. I'm instantly feverish. His other hand entwines in my hair.

He bends down, and his lips meet mine. "I love *you*, Roselle." His urgent whisper muffles against the curve of my bottom lip. "Nothing and no one can replace you."

He deepens our kiss, his tongue brushing mine. I wrap my arms around his nape. We cling together, an explosion of desire ricochets through my body, and a soft groan stirs from my throat.

His fingers react, clutching my hair. The golden comb tumbles out. Wet tendrils spill over my shoulder. Another rush of yearning pumps through my veins, quickening with every beat of my heart.

My need for him startles me. In my darkness and unending despair over the tragedy I've awoken to—and the unrelenting guilt for what I've done—I'd forgotten what it feels like to *live*, to be *alive*, to emerge from beneath a drowning pool of desolation and take a gasping breath.

Reykin is that breath. He's air. I need him to survive.

He slips a silken strap of my dress from my shoulder. His mouth moves against my bare skin. Sensual lips savor my flesh. Goose bumps rise, and a heady hunger claws my insides. His arm moves under my knee. He lifts me up and cradles me against him. The door behind us closes automatically as he moves toward the bed. He sets me on my feet next to it.

I reach for the buttons of his shirt and undo the top one, and then the next, until the fabric parts, revealing his powerful chest. His scar— a thin, red line—cuts from his collarbone, down the side of his chest, and over the rippling muscles of his torso. Gently, I trace the scar with my finger. His skin quivers and his breath hisses as I trail lower, to the waistband of his trousers.

He draws closer. His hand moves to my other strap and slides it over my shoulder. The damp silk catches, and then the gown runs down my body like liquid and pools at my bare feet. My salacious undergarments remain. He exhales deeply and takes a step back, studying me. His aquamarine gaze caresses my curves. The scant, intricate fabric of my undergarments seems harder to take off than they were to put on.

I raise my eyebrow in challenge. Either this kind of undergarment isn't new to him, or Reykin's really good at puzzles. He reaches out and touches the small, sparkly jewel between my breasts. The fabric ignites like a fuse and burns away, without heat, in a puff of smoke, leaving me utterly naked.

I take a step nearer, but his hands go to my shoulders, staying me. "Let me look at you."

I've been naked in front of soldiers, in locker rooms on Bases, more often than I care to think about. This is different. This is intimate.

A heat creeps over my cheeks. "You've seen me without my clothes before," I remind him. He rescued me from his allies, fended them off. Afterward he bathed me and tended to my wounds.

"Then I couldn't see past your bruises. I wanted to kill them for what they did to you, Roselle. Daltrey wouldn't allow it, so I had to settle for beating them, the way they'd beaten you."

I freeze. "Why would you do that? They were your soldiers. They were just doing what soldiers do."

"You were surrendering—defenseless. That wasn't a battle. Their lives weren't in jeopardy. You didn't even fight back. It was just blind cruelty."

I move a step closer to him and rest my hand against his heart. It thumps wildly in his chest. "You're not a cruel man."

His hand covers mine. "You're wrong. I am, but only to those who hurt what I love."

"I love you, too."

"You're just saying that because it's the end of the world, but I don't care. I'll take it." He leans down to kiss me.

I reach a finger up and press it against his lips. "I'm not." Our eyes meet. "Reykin, I'm saying it because it's true. It's the beginning of *us*. We won't let anyone or anything tear us apart again." My finger drops from his mouth.

Something snaps inside him. Heat and passion sharpen his gaze and features. Firm lips press to mine, devouring me. Wherever his skin touches me, I burn. His hand slips down my abdomen. My back arches. I kiss his neck, and the salty taste of his skin mixes with the scent of lemongrass, the combination irresistible. My teeth graze his neck. A soft gasp of his breath against my ear sends a shiver down my spine.

We know each other's rhythms. We learned them in combat, but now we torture each other to exquisite heights of pleasure, every throbbing ache drawn out to ratchet up our torment until a pinnacle of raw exaltation leaves us both satiated and soothed.

Reykin's fingers stroke my temple as we cuddle. We want to stay awake, to preserve this moment for as long as possible, but the last few hours' haze of ecstasy gradually dissipates. A soft, worried sigh escapes me.

His fingers caress my hair. "What's wrong?"

"Clifton," I reply.

"Are you going to tell him about us?" His voice is casual enough, but his breath slows as he waits for my answer.

"He already knows. He was by the door earlier . . . when you were doing that thing with your tongue."

He tries to hold back his chuckle and fails. His chest heaves with male pride. "You mean the thing that made you scream my name over and over?"

"Yes, that." Thinking about it makes my toes curl, but my heart sinks.

He finds my hand. His fingers entwine in mine and squeeze. "So he knows about us. Is that going to be a problem for you?"

I tilt my head up and meet his eyes so he sees that I'm not hiding anything. "No, it's not, but I would've told him in a kinder way than by screaming out your name in the heat of passion, though. Clifton didn't deserve to find out like that, but the way it happened between us tonight was spontaneous. Secretly, I wanted it to happen, but neither of us planned it."

"You're glad it happened?"

"Reykin, given our feelings for one another, it was inevitable. It's just . . ."

"What?" He shifts so we can see each other better.

"How do I stop it all from ending? I see the signs. We're in the blur. What's happening here is different from what's happening in Spectrum's alternate universe. I'm not sure how long it plans to keep us."

"To keep us?"

"To let us live. I feel tension. Crow and the collective want me desperately—want my power, my traits."

"Why not just destroy everything now?" he asks, his features darkening.

"Because of my potential for *more*. Spectrum cannot look away if it believes it can be stronger with me than without me."

Thoughts of Hawthorne invade my mind, but I suppress them. It's too much right now. I'm a traitor, that much is clear, but not to my own heart. It loves Reykin—every shattered, ugly piece of it.

Reykin's limbs coil with mine. "Sleep," he whispers. "We'll make plans after you rest."

I don't think I'll be able to sleep, but wrapped as I am in his arms, drowsiness overcomes me. I sleep, and I dream. I dream of stretching into dark matter, of multiplying the stars.

Chapter 15
Fugitive Motel

I awaken in the middle of the night, feeling a sizzle, low and dull, in my head.

Reykin breathes softly beside me, asleep. I untangle our bodies. He snuggles my pillow to him. I flitter out of bed and pad off the altar-like dais. My mind reaches out in the quiet. A smoldering feeling of flame and moonlight echoes back to me. It's the sensation I associate with Cherno. He's near. I wrap a silken ivory robe around my shoulders and tie it at the waist before creeping to the glass wall.

Cherno's eyes flicker, two flames dancing in the darkness. He's resting on a lounge chair within the walls of my private patio. It's sort of comforting. My curiosity piqued, I slide open the glass and step outside. The dragon-man studies me while I cross to the seat beside his. I perch on the cushion, which is still a little damp from the rain, and wait for him to speak first. He is clutching a large dragon scale. The metallic veneer shines in the simulated moonlight.

"I get edgy when I don't know where you are," he mutters with a low rumble. His long talons smooth over the texture of the scale. "Spectrum assigned me as your bodyguard. Even though I don't have a device rattling around inside me anymore, I still feel responsible for you."

"I don't mind you checking on me." I ease against the backrest. "What have you got there?"

His sharp eyebrow quirks. "I took a walk to that building—the one with the dragon on it. This was in a glass case in the lobby."

A smirk forms on my lips. "You stole it?"

He looks somewhat surprised by my insinuation. "It's not as if it belonged to them. I knew this dragon, and since I'm the only dragon here . . ."

"So . . . property rights don't apply to you?" I try to hide my smile and fail miserably. A giggle slips out. "Why did you take it?"

"It's *my* past."

"Why do you want it, though?"

"I'm the only one of my kind. No more dragons . . . and it appears that humans are next."

Extinction. We're on the precipice again. Soon people won't exist— not in their original form.

"We have to stop Crow," I say with an apparently contagious shudder, as Cherno shivers, too.

"How long, do you think, until he gets here?" he growls.

"Soon."

"Then let's prepare."

"I may have a plan." I stiffen, feeling Ransom near. "I have another visitor."

"Who is it?" Cherno growls.

"My technician."

His scaly nose wrinkles with disdain. "I've been avoiding him."

"Why?"

"I have this intense impulse to kill him."

"Has he done something to you, Cherno?"

"He's done something to *you*."

I grin. "Do you have feelings for me, Cherno?"

"I find you physically repulsive, Roselle," he replies with another shudder.

I snicker. "Don't kill him. Make us a fire. I'll go let him in." I rise from my seat and return inside. Reykin isn't in bed. Among the twisted sheets, there's a depression where he had been, but he's gone. So are his clothes.

Maybe he's not ready to tell anyone else about us?

I open my door just as Ransom raises his hand to the intercom. "Come in, Ransom." I gesture with a sweep of my arm. He's disheveled, in sleeping attire—a dark robe and slippers. Exhaustion hollows out his eyes. "Cherno and I were about to discuss a plan."

"The dragon's here?" he asks, gulping. "Isn't it late for that?"

"No. We should already have met tonight instead of having a dinner party."

"No argument here."

"We're just in my garden." I direct him outside without further explanation. Cherno carries material made to look like real wood from a stack in the corner to the grate of the fireplace. Curling red heat sparks from his mouth, and he blows on the pile. Flames engulf it, causing snaps and hisses. Filters cover the chimney, converting the smoke back to breathable air. "Have a seat," I tell Ransom, indicating a chair.

Ransom sits. Cherno sits as well, but I pace.

"I have a plan for the box," I say, using the name Cherno coined to describe Crow's torturous world.

Ransom grimaces. "You know about the other world now. You have my memories of it. I came here to thank you for not killing me." Apparently he's been stricken by fear of my reprisal.

"You shouldn't thank me for that. I have no plans to kill you. I promise. I'll never chop you up in little pieces and feed you to the sea, no matter what happens."

The frown lines around his mouth deepen.

"We're family, Ransom," I explain. "All of us. You gave me a weapon, and I intend to use it. I need you."

"You don't need me. Not anymore."

He's right. I don't. I only said it to make him feel more at ease. "It's true, I don't *need* you, but you're still an intelligent man. Your ingenuity makes you an asset. Without you and the chances you've taken, we wouldn't have this opportunity now, so I thank you for that."

Ransom relaxes against the seat. "What's your plan?"

"We locate all the external gateways to Spectrum and decimate them."

"The implants *are* the gateways—internal gateways," Ransom replies.

"Spectrum's moving everything it wants off site . . . or more like off-world. Think of it like cell division. Spectrum's a malignancy that grew from us, but now it's autonomous. It plans to kill us on this plane and keep replicating its worlds with the copies of us that it retains. It'll also search for new worlds to invade."

Cherno frowns. "To what end?"

"We're just a small part of a bigger whole. Let's call Spectrum a gang of pirates. They built their world from ours. That's their pirate ship, and all their flags are flying now. When they locate another world—another ship—they'll latch on to it, tie up to the side, and pillage. But they're still anchored to our world, too, and like pirates, they take hostages, who become part of the crew. The pirates see no advantage in allowing other ships to go free once they've been plundered, and I'm afraid they'll burn the other worlds as they sail away. I want to find these tie-ups—the *anchors* keeping us tethered to Spectrum's ship—and destroy them before they sink us."

"The Fate of Seas Base has an anchor for sure," Ransom replies. "I've seen plans for something I could hardly understand—"

"I know. I found them in your memories. I haven't told your brother yet. We talked, but I didn't want to overwhelm him. I want to ease him into what we're facing."

"You understand the designs I saw?"

"It's not that hard. I'd show you telepathically, but I'm afraid of melting your brain."

Cherno chuckles. "You won't melt mine."

"True." I push the designs from my mind to his. He grunts as the transmission sears his frontal lobe, but the information disseminates. He clutches his head in his hands. "That's brutal, Roselle."

"The information, or the process of learning it?" I ask.

"Both," he grumbles.

"Do you want to help us?" I ask Ransom. Firelight shifts over the side of his face. He nods silently. I reach out and touch his temple with the tip of my finger, where his technician's implant lies, and upload information onto it. "Before you leave tonight, I'm going to bury this deep so you won't remember it until the right time."

"When's the right time?" Ransom asks.

"We'll know soon. There's another matter."

"What other matter?" Cherno asks.

"The gods . . . They want their powers back. They'll be more agreeable if they believe we're working to get equipment to create the neuro-enhancements they need to achieve that goal."

"Are you going to do that?" Ransom asks.

"Do you want more gods in this world?" I counter.

"No," Cherno replies with a scowl. "I was worried when I found them powerless—when I thought we needed them—but now I'm delighted they're weak. They're not all good."

"That's an understatement," I reply. "It's only a matter of time before they achieve their goals on their own. We're going to need their help—at least some of them. Clifton for sure."

"Do you know how to give him back his powers?" Cherno asks.

"I'm sure I can improve upon the powers Clifton has now," I confirm, "but whether it will get him back to the level he once was remains to be seen. I'll approach him soon. For now we keep this to ourselves. We use the excuse of needing equipment to create new implants. Meanwhile, we wait for Crow. He'll come looking for us."

"Why're we waiting for him? Why not be the aggressor?" Cherno asks, rising and pacing before the fire.

"We have to appear weak, and we need misdirection. I want Crow's focus on other things when I enter Spectrum."

"You're going to kick down Spectrum's door?" Reykin emerges from the shadows. I knew he was there, listening in the darkness, but I'm still not sure why he doesn't want them to know he was with me.

"Yes, Reykin," I confirm. "And I'm not going to knock first. I have to teach the other me how to take over her world."

Chapter 16
Entanglement

The next few weeks are fraught with emotional turmoil.

Clifton knows about Reykin and me, having stumbled upon us that first night, but no one else does. Reykin leaves the decision to disclose our ever-expanding relationship in my hands. He believes it's my right. His opinion is that we should shout it to the ether and let everyone else deal with the consequences, but I'm much more cautious. I understand what it means. It elevates Reykin to a prime target—for Crow or any of my other enemies, and I do have them. The longer I put off the gods, the more that rift grows. If they want to get to me, it will be through Reykin. He's my strength, but also my weakness.

Clifton pretends not to know. It's disconcerting. I need to speak to him about it, but he finds reasons to change the subject whenever we're alone. Today I plan to corner him. I dress carefully in a lovely summery frock to match the weather Clifton decided on for today.

As I near my bed, I receive a low whistle. "You are so beautiful." Reykin's voice is deeper from sleep. "Where are you off to so early?" He's propped against a slew of pillows, one hand tucked behind his head. The blanket has slipped down, revealing his bare chest.

"I have some things to discuss with Clifton." I go to Reykin, intending to give him a peck on the cheek before I leave, but he captures me around the waist, hauls me into bed with him, and proceeds to cover my face with kisses. Rogue joins in, licking my face and reducing me to giggles. "Enough, you beasts!" I laugh, playfully pushing them off me and struggling to my feet.

I straighten my hem and back away. Phoenix brings me my strappy heels, and I put them on. "Are you working in the lab today?" I ask Reykin.

"Yes. The simulator's nearly perfect. Ransom and I are fine-tuning the training terrain."

"How soon until it's ready?"

"We're running a test. After that we should have you view it to see if it aligns with your memories of the Base in the Fate of Seas."

"I'll meet you in the lab, then."

"Stay for breakfast." He pats the bed next to him. "We can have Phoenix bring it to us here."

I groan, wanting to crawl back in. "How about we have lunch together there?"

"Naked lunch?" he asks with a growing grin.

"I'll see you later," I reply with a chuckle.

When I enter the tearoom, Clifton's already there stirring a tiny silver spoon in a porcelain cup. He rests the utensil on the saucer and rises as I take the seat across from him. Impeccably dressed in a linen suit, he wears his hair combed to the side, showcasing his gorgeous profile.

"Ah, you're here," he says as a greeting, but his smile is warm as he sits once more. "You do realize that gods hate to be up this early in the morning? We're all self-indulgent nighttime beings."

"That must've been hard for you as a Sword Exo officer," I reply.

"As an immortal, one must play a role when one's overpowered and outnumbered."

"Is that what your life is, a role?" One of his staff brings me a gold-rimmed cup and pours tea into it. Steam swirls into the air, bringing with it the scent of jasmine. A tiered plate full of breakfast delicacies is set down beside me. I thank the man before he departs.

"Change is a constant," Clifton answers at last. "I adapt. As your mate, I'll help you evolve with our changing world."

The small sip I just took chokes me, and I cough and sputter, setting down the cup. "As my what?"

"You know we're meant to be together, Roselle." His green eyes twinkle with mischief.

"I know that you know about me and Reykin." *There. Honest and direct.*

"Of course I know about him. I'm just not sure *you* do." He takes a sip from his cup, watching me over the rim. "He's temporary."

I frown. "I'm going to marry Reykin."

His smile doesn't falter. "Reykin's mortal. You're not aging, Roselle. I've had your blood tested. Your cells regenerate. That makes you immortal. You're a god. In theory, you'll even outlast me, if nothing external destroys you. And let's face it, how long after Reykin dies until you're ready to love again? You're more resilient than most." He smears butter on a piece of toast and takes a bite.

I force a smile. "My love for Reykin will last forever."

Clifton swallows. "You felt the same for Hawthorne, didn't you? It hasn't been very long since he died. Weeks—maybe months. Don't look so sad, Roselle." He frowns. "I admire your resiliency. I do. I love everything about you. You're unjaded. Optimistic. And clever—you're so clever. Crow doesn't stand a chance against you."

"Your confidence in me is absurd, where Crow's concerned."

"It's not misplaced."

"You're wrong about Reykin, too. I *will* love him forever."

Clifton leans back in his chair, studying me. "You don't even know what forever is. What are you, twenty? To you, it's a hundred years, maybe two. I'll give you those years with your mortal. It's only fleeting seconds in our time, but I plan to be your constant companion. There's nothing you can ask that I won't give you."

"In exchange for what?"

"In exchange for my getting my powers back," he says. "I know you can do it, and if you do, I promise to guard Reykin for the rest of his life. I'll keep the other gods from interfering in your lives. After he's gone, and there's no reason for us not to be together, then you consider my offer to be your mate."

"And if I say no?"

"Why would you? I mean you no harm—either of you. I don't want to live in a world where you don't exist, so I'll protect you with my life. I've waited for you for so long, Roselle. I want your lionhearted devotion. I can wait a little longer for you."

"I don't think I'll ever love you like that, Clifton."

"You let me worry about it."

"I don't even know if I can restore your strength."

"You can do it," he replies, sounding doubtless. "You need me. I can protect Reykin when you can't. When you go inside Spectrum, he'll be vulnerable."

"I'll let you know my decision soon, Clifton." I rise from my seat and step toward the door. Clifton reaches out and takes my hand. He brings it to his lips and kisses the back before letting me go.

Slipping into someone's mind isn't difficult. The hard part's not hurting the person. I stand inside a circle of six volunteers, controlling them through their implants. It's different than what Spectrum does. The ones I'm working with aren't integrated in a collective. They don't communicate with each other. I'm just manipulating them like puppets.

It's taken me days to learn how to maneuver them separately. They're not as easy to control when they aren't integrated—like when I simply ordered the soldiers in the detention center back in the Sword Palace. The Spectrum algorithm made sense to me then, like a musical composition, but because these volunteers are not driven by AI, I need to tell them what to do, every movement. If I don't, they can't get from point A to point B on their own. Inhabiting them all at the same time takes practice. When I first started, they all moved the same way at the same time, like synchronized swimmers. I'm better now. But their bodies are much weaker than mine. Slower. Not at all nimble. It's frustrating.

We've gathered in a large arena formed of safety glass and illuminated by bright-white lights. Reykin and Ransom created this training facility together. They improve on it almost daily. Located on a lower level of Clifton's sphere, it's been almost home for the past several weeks.

Standing on the opposite side of the glass barrier, Ransom activates the holographic walls. The arena transforms into a three-dimensional world pieced together from satellite imaging of Crow's island Base in the Fate of Seas. I've used Ransom's memories of the interior of some facilities to construct a profile of what we can expect to find inside the Trees that contain Spectrum's labs. The minutiae—from routes, to the equipment we need in each facility, to the best places to plant incendiaries, to extraction points—are tweaked constantly as we work out simulated scenarios.

"Strike!" Ransom orders, his voice an echo from the mountain range in the distance.

In this simulation, we're outside a Tree on the Fate of Sea's Base. Waves crash against the piles of rock erected as breakers. Tall lamps illuminate the night, detailing cracks in the pavement where weeds grow through. Steel military trucks loom. Out-of-date air-barracks dangle from the Tree branches.

Reykin, Cherno, and Clifton, playing the roles of villains in our scenario, attack my circle of volunteer soldiers from different angles. The VPMD-implanted squadron surrounding me brandishes fusion-blades, but it's really me. They aren't self-aware. My intellect possesses all of them. Reykin strikes first, burning one of my middle-aged soldiers with a swift blow to his forearm. His weapon falls from his grip, his fingers tingling. I can feel a dull echo of the pain in my own hand, and it only serves to annoy me. Frustration makes me growl.

Cherno snatches another one of my soldiers from his feet and tosses the burly combatant aside with ease. I counter the dragon-man's aggressive move with a fusionmag attack from a female volunteer. Without even a grimace, Cherno absorbs the low-energy pulse with his thick skin.

Clifton, outfitted in tactical armor he created himself, fires simulated missiles at my volunteers. According to the sparkling fallout, my soldiers should be nothing more than vapor. All my adversaries rush me at once. Growling through my teeth, I lift my palms and send out bursts of energy to repel them. Heat gushes from my fingertips. Cherno and Clifton hurtle backward and come to rest in a heap at the far end of the arena. I don't use the same strike on Reykin, because he's mortal and decidedly more breakable. Instead I erect an invisible barrier between us. When he runs up against it, he hits it hard and glowers.

Reykin gnashes his teeth, rubbing his nose, and then his forehead, which bore the brunt of my blockade. "This isn't the plan we discussed, Roselle."

"I'm improvising."

"You're supposed to be keeping us back with your soldiers." He places his hand on his nape and kneads out the kink in it.

"This is a dumb plan, Reykin. The volunteers don't possess the musculature to do what I want as quickly as I need them to do it. They'll get hurt."

"That's not the point, Roselle. The point of the exercise is to practice using them, because Crow will, too. What happens when he throws a hundred thousand at you at once? You won't be able to keep his forces back without using Black-Os, zeroborns, and Numbers of your own. You know this. Do the math."

"There are other strategies to consider. I can turn *his* tide against him."

"Can you? You know that for sure?"

"Using living shields is cowardly."

"Crow *is* a coward. You need to fight him with his methods, so you must train. The sheer numbers of his arsenal will drown you in bodies if you don't. Let's go again." He calls out to the sky and lifts his finger in the air, twirling it in a circle to indicate that Ransom should reset the program. Clifton and Cherno have gotten to their feet.

"We're not going to beat Crow in a ground war. I can't face him like that," I implore. "I might win, but everyone else will lose. Everyone. There won't be many left standing. I've run the scenarios in my head over and over. It's bloodbath after bloodbath without end, until the annihilation of life as we know it, or until Crow kills me. We need to find another way. It has to be unorthodox—something he won't expect."

The lights come up, and the terrain around us changes. A snarl of dark and destructive energy digs into my mind. Crow's essence slips inside the facility. It makes my heart race and my stomach roil. Sweat breaks out on my upper lip. The Trees in our simulation begin to melt and bend, and the screech of metal against glass fills the air. My hairs stand on end. Ransom has entered the arena now, too. He drags the sharp edge of a long-handled knife along the lab wall, but it looks as if he draws it through the air.

"This is *your* lair, Roselle?" Ransom's mouth moves, but it's Crow's perfect elocution that tumbles from it. "Submerged in a watery grave-yard, among the ruins of another lost civilization. You hide like a little girl who's petrified of monsters." He slowly strolls nearer with a mania-cal leer.

My expression remains taciturn, but fear slides icily from the base of my brain down my spine.

"Imagine *The Sword* too afraid to face me." He drags a fluttering hand above Ransom's heart in mock fear. "Your ancestors must be disgusted by the way you've deserted your people."

I turn my attention away from Crow and let the barrier between me and Reykin disintegrate. Reykin moves to my side. I frown at Ransom, but it's Crow in there—I know it.

"How did you find us?" I ask, surprised that my voice doesn't quiver.

"I'm omnipotent."

"No, you're not."

"I came looking for Gildenzear—for the home of the gods—and look what I found instead!" Crow turns to Clifton. "If it isn't Clifton Salloway. You're a very nimble fellow, Clifton. I didn't expect you to run away so quickly that evening of our coming-out party at the Silver Halo. And *abandon* your *fiancée*? Did you even try to help Roselle, or were you too busy scurrying to your airship?"

Clifton doesn't answer him, but a blush stains his cheeks.

Crow's attention shifts again, this time toward Reykin. "And here's another of the failed leaders of the resistance! The Winterstroms are reunited." Crow chuckles, making Ransom's face look eerily like Crow's own. "Firstborn and secondborn living in harmony. One big happy family . . . except you forgot the other two brats in your disgusting tribe. What are their names again? Rettis and Reign?" From Ransom's mouth come the tormenting pleas of young men's voices. They beg Reykin to save them. Their chilling voices freeze the marrow in my bones.

A sardonic smirk curves Reykin's lips. "You don't have them. You scraped Ransom's brain for information, but I never told him where they are. It's just a parlor trick. It shows your weakness, not your strength. You're afraid of us. We're set to hunt you into extinction, *Agent* Crow, because, after all, it's your turn."

"I'm immortal. I'll pluck all your stars from the sky and melt them down—starting with this one." He throws his head back and his arms wide, indicating Ransom as his intended victim. The knife in Ransom's hand glints evilly. Cherno and Clifton creep nearer to us. I hold up my hand, signaling them to stay back. Ransom's posture straightens, and Crow's voice grates the air: "I may not have your brothers yet, but I will. I'll kill everyone just to get to them. Who'll stop me? You?" Ransom eerily seems to delight in Crow's superiority. "You're hiding in a bubble, leagues under the sea—afraid to face me. But this time I'm going to rip out Roselle's heart and show it to her. Just like I'll rip out his."

I knew Crow could reach this depth. He just hadn't known we were here, until now. Spectrum created worlds—it'll be nothing to infiltrate this vessel now that it's been located. My mind scans the sea around the sphere. Crow's submarines encircle New Gildenzear. We don't have much time before he's inside.

"I'm coming for you, Roselle." Crow raises Ransom's hand and angles the knife toward the technician's chest. I raise my palm. The downward thrust of the knife almost reaches the fabric of Ransom's uniform, but within the span of a breath, I yank Ransom's body to me telekinetically, pull until his forehead reaches my palm, and expel Crow from Ransom's mind with a brutal pulse.

Ransom convulses. I hold him to me with little effort, but fear turns my own knees weak. His muscles stiffen. Saliva drools from his mouth and courses down his chin and onto my shoulder. His skin takes on a deathly hue before he goes limp in my arms.

"Ransom," I whisper. Gently, I lower his unconscious body to the floor. On my knees, I lean over him, smoothing the dark hair back from his face. Worry that I might have fried his brain wrinkles my forehead. Reykin kneels, too, saying his little brother's name over and over.

Finally, Ransom gurgles, coughs, and opens his eyes, gasping for breath. He squints and hisses, touching his forehead with a shaky hand. "What happened?"

"Are you all right?" Reykin asks. The look of relief on his face replaces one of raw fear. Cherno and Clifton stand around us, listening.

"My head feels like someone set it on fire." Ransom grimaces.

"Crow broke into your mind," Reykin says, touching his brother's arm lightly.

Ransom groans. "Did I hurt anyone?"

"No, you did exactly what I asked you to do when we came up with contingency plans for Crow taking possession of you," I say. "It worked, but unfortunately it means that it's time for us to go now." I help Ransom to his feet and glance at Clifton. "Crow's ships are here. He has docked his vessel, and he's inside, on the main level above. Are you sure everyone's gone?"

"I love this place. It's been my home for a while now."

I frown. "Clifton, focus. Have you made sure that everyone is gone?"

"Yes. Everyone evacuated to the other spheres weeks ago, and they scattered throughout the sea. My staff left yesterday when you told me you sensed that Crow was close."

"Good. It's time to go."

"You're sure the transporter device is sound?" Clifton asks, raising his golden eyebrow.

"You're asking me now?" I can't help the exasperated smile that crosses my lips. "Isn't it a little late to question me now, what with Crow storming your temple?"

"I suppose it is," Clifton says. He gazes at the machine I built for the occasion. Reykin and I worked on it with Clifton's engineers. Inside the center of the archway's steel frame, foggy blue air undulates. A cool draft emanates from it. The surface moves in concentric blue waves. I march my volunteers into the transport, where they vanish one by one.

"Cherno, will you help Ransom through?" I ask.

"No." Cherno crosses his arms over his chest. "I'm not leaving here until you do."

I glance at Reykin. Before I can say a word, he crosses his arms, too. "Don't even ask, Roselle. You have to leave before me."

"You're both stupid," I reply, letting Ransom lean on me. "Don't forget to incinerate the place on your way out."

They both grin evilly. "We won't forget," Cherno replies, holding up an ignition switch.

"I can make it on my own, Roselle," Ransom says, pulling away.

"You're sure?" I ask. He nods and walks unsteadily toward the transporter, dematerializing after he steps into it.

"Shall we go together, Roselle?" Clifton asks, presenting me with his arm. Something in his expression reminds me of the night our engagement was announced. The way he's looking at me now is the same way he looked at me then—like I'm his.

"Thank you, Clifton." I take his arm and slide mine into the crook of his elbow. Together we walk through the archway of the transporter, arriving almost instantly aboard the *Sozo One*. Hammon greets us in the cargo bay, where I had the mirror of the other transporter installed a few days ago.

She's holding Ransom's arm, helping him toward the waiting medical staff. My volunteers are also being examined. Ransom's loaded onto a hoverstretcher. I know he's okay, but they want to make sure he's not inhabited anymore. He's not. As soon as he awoke from Crow's control, I disabled his temporal-lobe device. Spectrum can no longer infiltrate him. I haven't told him yet, but I will. When Crow attacked Ransom's mind, Ransom delivered the false information I had planted inside him. Seeds of misdirection. Crow will believe that I plan to bring my army to the Fate of Virtues to face him. With any luck, he'll shift his forces there.

Clifton leans his mouth near my ear. "Have you come to a decision yet?"

"Yes. I'll do it. I'll restore your strength if you promise to protect Reykin."

"Done. When will you heal me?"

"Before our mission this evening. I'll meet you in your quarters. We'll do it there. Tell no one."

If he's surprised, he doesn't show it. "You have nothing to worry about, Roselle. You can trust me."

"I hope so," I reply.

"Please excuse me while I go to the control room to witness the demise of my home."

"You'll build a new one—a better one."

"I already have plans to create something lovely for you," he replies softly. He kisses my cheek, offers a slight bow, turns, and faces Hammon and bows to her as well. "Ladies," he says, and heads in the direction of the control room.

Hammon gawks after him. "He's something, isn't he?" she says with a glazed-over look.

"Yes, he is."

Her attention returns to me. "I've sent your other people on to the infirmary to get checked out. Rogue and Phoenix are in your quarters. Where's Reykin?" Nervously, she stares at the transport apparatus behind me.

"He and Cherno have this chivalry thing going on, where they each have to be the last to leave a dangerous situation. They can't help it. Plus, they wanted to blow up Crow together."

"Completely understandable," she replies.

She leans her shoulder against the vessel's transparent wall. We both stare at the ocean outside. Hammon worries a strand of her long dark hair. It reminds me of when she was a mechanic and we waited for airships to return to the hangar.

"Clifton gave us the signal before you arrived," she says. "My man's about to open fire on Crow's armada. And if I know Edge, he's grinning from ear to ear."

She points. Through the glass, I can just make out the enormous sphere of New Gildenzear in the distance. It's the only sphere around.

Behind me, Reykin and Cherno materialize from the portal. In the next second, New Gildenzear explodes, crushing Crow's vessels surrounding it. We all stare at the rush of displaced seawater pushing outward from the blast. When it slams us, it rattles the ship uncomfortably. We lean with it, and the force passes quickly. The vessel stabilizes.

"You got him?" I ask Reykin.

His strong arms wrap around me and lift me off my feet. His mouth covers mine in a searing kiss that leaves me breathless. "Yes," he whispers against my mouth.

"You do know that Crow's not really dead, right? We need to kill *all* of him. That was just one needle in a very large haystack."

"Stop ruining this for me," Reykin says, kissing me again.

"Ugh, take your slave elsewhere, Roselle," Cherno comments, pushing past Reykin and me. "Let me enjoy our victory without losing my lunch."

Reykin sets me on my feet. I watch Cherno's retreating form. When I glance at Hammon, I see she has tears in her eyes.

"Hawthorne's dead, isn't he?" she asks. "You'd never kiss Reykin if he were alive."

My hands fall way from Reykin. "It's . . . complicated, Hammon."

"Just because he has an implant, that doesn't mean we give up on him!" Hammon growls. "We're working on finding a way to turn the devices off."

"Hammon, I'm not giving up on Hawthorne. He's with me . . . I know he is, but not here—not in our world."

"What does that even mean?" she asks, dashing away tears with her sleeve. "Is he dead?"

"It means we have to help him. I'm going to find a way into their world. I'll explain it to you on the way to the Fate of Seas."

Rosie uses a small paintbrush to smear red dollops of pigment on Phoenix's dull metal veneer. We picked her up from the *Sozo One's* daycare facility and brought her to my room. Sitting on the floor next to Hammon, with our backs against my bunk, I pet Rogue intermittently, and Hammon strokes her daughter's hair as we talk.

"So Hawthorne's alive in another dimension—inside Spectrum?" Hammon asks me for the fourth time in as many minutes.

"Yes, an alternate universe."

"I don't think you're right about the word you used."

"Which one?"

"You said you 'murdered' Hawthorne in the Sword Palace. You didn't. He drowned."

"I might still be able to save him, Hammon."

"The Hawthorne in the other world?"

"Yes."

"What about Reykin, then?" she asks. "I love them both, you know? Reykin has done so much for me and Edge—and Rosie. He's in love with you, Roselle."

"And I'm in love with Reykin." I draw my knees up to my chest. "It's different than what I felt with Hawthorne. I know I can live without Hawthorne. It was hard, losing him when he Transitioned to first-born, but I did it. Things have never been the same between us since. I wanted it to be, but it just wasn't. Maybe it could be again—if things were different?" I think of him in another world, a different set of circumstances. "I don't know. But here, with Reykin, we just fit." I swallow hard, past the lump in my throat, forcing back tears.

"Like Edge and I fit?" Hammon asks.

I nod.

"This is all so confusing, Roselle. My mind doesn't know how to deal with it. Even with all the scary things you've explained to me, this world is still better than when we met as secondborn soldiers. I never had control of anything then. But I have more freedom now, with Crow ravaging our world, than I did when everything was normal—when they owned us. It's a sobering thought, isn't it? But our odds of living through this aren't good, are they? Even I know that." She holds Rosie's little green sweater in her hand, plucking at the soft fabric.

"No, they're not good odds." I watch Rosie deface Phoenix with broad strokes, and I wonder what a Winterstrom toddler would look like with aquamarine eyes and a paintbrush in her hand.

"I've gotten to be a mother, Roselle. I'll always be grateful for that." Tears cloud my eyes. "You're great at it, Hamm," I whisper.

"You're leaving tonight?" she asks, wiping her tears from her cheeks. Trepidation raises the tone of her voice. She tries to hide it by clearing her throat.

"Yes."

"Do you think that's . . . wise? It sounds terrifying, Roselle. You're talking about going to an alternate universe. Maybe there's another way?"

"I can't think of another way, not one with a chance of winning. With this plan, we have a sliver of hope."

"You'll be alone, though? I mean, they don't make enough chets for this, do they?" She isn't kidding.

"I am scared, but my threshold for terror has expanded a bit. Fear that Crow's growing stronger supersedes my fear of the unknown."

She wrings her hands. "If anyone can do it, it's you, Roselle. You're brave like that."

"I don't feel brave. I feel backed into a corner with nowhere left to run." I never intended to be this honest with her. I should spare her this. She doesn't need to know. I'm not sure why I'm telling her. Maybe it's because we've been this desperate before, and we faced it together.

"When we left the Fate of Swords for Stars," she says softly, "we only had a loose idea of how we'd survive."

"It's the same now," I agree, "except the scale is a little different. Now it's all humankind that Crow intends to kill instead of just us."

"I guess I'll have to stop taking it so personally," she jokes.

A smile spreads across my lips. "Yeah, it's nothing personal."

Impulsively, Hammon throws her arms around my shoulders and pulls me to her for a fierce hug. Her voice quivers as she says, "You come back, okay?"

"Okay."

"And when you find Hawthorne, will you tell him I miss him?"

"You know I will."

Chapter 17
The Anchor

Churning waves break against the heavy gray rock of the shoreline.

Rusty steel Trees on the Fate of Seas Base loom like an ancient, dark forest in the last gasps of winter. Moonlight shines off the bygone models of the few air-barracks still swaying in the wind on the monstrous branches above. Corroded metal grates creak. It's the disguise of a ghost town, but I wonder why they bother to keep up the facade when they believe they've won?

I cling to the slippery stones, pushing upward and dipping down with each swell. Finding a foothold, I ease out of the water. My black, temperature-controlled wet suit and mask acclimate to the air, making me invisible to infrared and motion detectors, not to mention keeping me warm, a bonus thanks to the engineers at Salloway Munitions.

Reykin, garbed in a similar wet suit, stands beside me. I flash him the hand signal we came up with so that he knows I've retained control of my body. It's a concern. I haven't been back on terra firma since I escaped from the Sword Palace. My fear that I could be reacquired by Spectrum the moment its frequencies reached me wasn't far-fetched. I hear the siren call of those frequencies, but I can tune them out like white noise.

A small band of elite soldiers joins us—among them Cherno and Clifton. Cherno's discernible because of his size, even in a wet suit and full facial mask. He towers over us, staying by my side.

I kept my deal with Clifton. We met in his quarters. He didn't believe that I could heal him by running my hands over him, but I was doing way more than that, manipulating the very particles that comprise him. He's beginning to believe it now, though. He keeps flexing his hands, and his strength appears to be improving by the minute.

Clifton trained the squad himself. They're well-seasoned fighters with the bonus of being immortal, so the person I'm most worried about is Reykin.

Salty air mixes with a noxious chemical scent that stings when I inhale. My adrenaline level ratchets up a few notches. Filters in my suit engage, siphoning off anything lethal, but the atmosphere practically crackles with energy. I can taste it and feel it pressing against my chest. But it's unusually quiet. No patrols. Nothing to indicate that the island has inhabitants. I reach out with my mind and scan for life, but the hazy electricity muddles my senses.

We move across the grounds to the Tree used for research and development. Other buildings on the island manufacture VPMDs, but the one looming ahead is where I was made a Black-O.

My mind reaches out and decodes the lock on the security door. It slides open, and I don't break stride. Inside the Tree, stillness. Containment tubes no longer gurgle with misshapen creatures. Those tanks have been replaced with state-of-the-art ones. The beings inside are hard to discern at first. The growing organisms curl in on themselves, in various stages of development. The farther I walk the path between them, the more my stomach aches.

I stop at a tank a few rings in and study the small child inside. His hair is white blond, finer than corn silk, softly floating in an amniotic fluid. He appears to be around four years old. So is the one next to him, and the one next to him, and on and on. The small boys resemble

269

youthful versions of Crow—thousands of them. A shiver slips down my spine.

"Where is everyone?" Reykin whispers in my earpiece.

"I think they're either dead or they've been moved off-world," I reply.

This facility appears fully automated. Sophisticated machines tend to the living organisms. As I move, the electricity in the air grows more saturated. I follow it, looking for its source. The path ends at the security entrance leading to the underground Census bunker. I signal to my team, indicating my intentions to enter.

Reykin's arm extends to me and touches my side. His voice in my earpiece whispers, "No stairs. They've been filled in. Do we proceed?"

"We don't have a choice," I reply softly. "What we came for is down there. I can feel it."

"I don't like it," Clifton chimes in. "It feels like a trap."

He's right, but I need to get inside Spectrum. "It's what we came here to do, Clifton. I can go alone from here."

"I'm coming with you," Reykin answers without hesitation.

"You and you," Clifton says, pointing at a couple of soldiers, "stay here." That leaves eight of us to continue.

Reykin nods, slips ahead of me, and inspects an elevator car before allowing me to enter it. The rest follow us inside. Cherno has to duck when he steps in. Silence punctuates our descent through the island's gray rock, until Reykin says, "My vision wear isn't working. Can anyone else *see*?"

"Negative," Clifton responds.

"I see fine," Cherno states.

"I do, too," I reply. "Energy's thick down here. It might be disrupting your tech. Those who can't see should head back to the surface."

"I'm not leaving you," Reykin replies.

I take his hand and squeeze it. "You can stay with me until I find Spectrum. Then Cherno and Clifton can help you back."

"I said I'm not leaving you."

The elevator slows to a stop. The doors slide open. More darkness. We step off the lift. "What do we do, Clifton?" the tallest soldier asks. "I can't see past my nose."

"You're doing better than me," Clifton replies. "I can't see my nose."

The soldier reaches for his mask and pulls it away from his face. Instantly, several black orbs drop from slots in the ceiling. The military hardware floats above us. Lethal red lasers burst forth and cut the unmasked soldier into pieces. Blood sprays on the soldiers closest to him.

"Nobody move," I order. With my mind I seize control of the orbs and scramble their programming. They fall from the air, hit the floor, and roll off in different directions. "Okay, clear," I whisper. But then I see movement in the long hallway up ahead. Shadowy creatures slither forward in the darkness. "Wait. Something's here."

"I see them, too," Cherno says.

"What are they?" Clifton asks.

"Bermin," Cherno replies.

"Bermin? That's not possible. They've been extinct for centuries," Clifton says in a salty tone.

"Well, they aren't anymore," Cherno mutters.

"How big?" Clifton asks.

"About your size."

"What are Bermin?" Reykin asks.

"You know what bats are, right?" Clifton asks with a grimace.

"Of course," Reykin replies.

"This is their much older, much bigger, much thirstier cousin," Clifton says. "They're winged, nocturnal carnivores who dine on blood, and you're their favorite delicacy. How many, Cherno?"

"In this hallway? I count thirty. They smell blood. It's emboldening them."

After cursing under his breath, Clifton orders, "Get back on the elevator, Roselle. We need a plan before we can advance."

"Cherno, what are Bermin afraid of?" I ask.

"They hate the light."

"Roselle, get back on the elevator," Clifton insists.

"I can handle this," I say. I create a glowing sphere of light in my palm and project it. The orange-sized ball glows golden and glides slowly down the hallway. "This way." I lead the team down the corridor. The Bermin stay on the outskirts of the light, hissing and fighting each other to get closer to us. Involuntarily, gushing spurts of energy inside me surge outward at the ones nearest us. They vaporize, and the others retreat with gut-wrenching shrieks.

"What was that?" Clifton asks. I hear the grin in his tone.

I'm weaker after the rush of energy. "I don't know. I didn't mean to do it. It was—"

"A defense mechanism," Clifton finishes for me.

I shrug. "I don't know. Could the goddess Roselle do anything like that?"

"No," Clifton replies. "You've surpassed her powers tenfold."

We come to the end of the hallway. A steel door separates us from whatever's on the other side. A supercharged field of energy seeps through the minuscule gaps in the frame. Beside the door, a holographic panel projects a glowing dark crow. Its eyes eerily pivot toward me. Telepathically, I ask it what it requires.

Without speaking aloud, it says, *I was first, soft and pure, but in water, I couldn't endure. What am I?*

"Sabah," I say aloud. Crow's sister's name.

The steel door opens soundlessly, revealing an arena-sized, onyx room with enormous rings in the center of it. The rings appear to be made of golden light, like halos. They spin into the illusion of a sphere in the negative space.

"What is that?" Cherno asks me.

"It's an anchor."

Chapter 18
Introspectrum

The anchor gyrates so fast that the others don't see its rings. To them, it's a dimly glowing sun.

"Why do you call it an anchor?" Reykin asks, gazing at the radiance.

I pull my mask off and push back the hood of my wet suit. My long hair tumbles down my back. I smooth it away from my face. "It's holding the two worlds together. Without it, they'd drift apart."

"It's time to weigh anchor, then," Reykin replies.

I shake my head. "Not yet. We need to find all the anchors and destroy them. Otherwise it's futile. We also need to flush out Crow, preferably in this world so he can't hide out and return after restoring himself to power."

Reykin yanks off his mask. "I'm coming with you," he growls, knowing he's in for a fight.

"You don't have a key." I tap my temple with my finger.

Reykin ignores me and cases the glowing anchor, circling it. When he returns to my side, he exhales deeply and then walks straight into the anchor. I lose track of him for a second, until he emerges unscathed on the other side. The frustration etched in the lines of Reykin's face when he glares at me would be funny if this were at all humorous. It isn't.

"I'm going now," I say. "Do what we planned. Retrieve the explosives from the *Sozo One*. If I don't return by daybreak, detonate this anchor. I'll find another way out."

Reykin holds my elbow. His body tenses. "You can't go alone."

"We don't have a choice. If I'm not back—if there's trouble—"

"I'll wait for you." He grasps my cheeks and places an urgent kiss on my lips. I kiss him back. We drift apart, and my lips curl inward to savor the taste of him.

I walk forward into the light, piercing the air and shredding the veil, and I slip inside. My hair lifts toward the tear in the fabric. The seam knits back together, concealing the real world. The resonating hum of the vortex vibrates my body. A rush of power stretches me, yanking with a force that feels like it will pull my face off. My cheeks wrinkle and pool.

Behind me, the onyx room vanishes. I'm rendered deaf, unable to hear even my own breathing. My forward motion pauses, and then I'm standing in a pastoral landscape, familiar in a primal way. Doors open ahead. I pass through them and emerge in a thriving city by the sea, adorned with romantic, impractically ornate structures. Hovercrafts dodge in and out of traffic lanes. People are everywhere.

I turn and glance back. A set of silver doors with holographic crests of the nine Fates of the Republic closes over the threshold. I take a step back from the portico, onto a city sidewalk behind me, and I look upward. The anchor resembles a skyscraper here in Spectrum's world.

I turn again and face the city, smelling the salt air coming off the water. Gorgeous structures perch near the shore and reach into the stratosphere. Across the street from me is a particularly breathtaking building. Beautiful carved sculptures of blackbirds flank the opaque glass of its front entrance. However lovely its facade, the vibe coming off it feels threatening. If I had hackles, they'd be rising, but it's all I can do to keep from shivering. The building is another anchor, but the cold air coming off it leads me to speculate that it isn't an anchor to the world I just left. It feels shrill and ominous—its aura, grave. With my pulse quickening, I turn from it and scurry away up the sidewalk.

How many other worlds are you destroying, Crow?

Beads of sweat form on my upper lip. Glancing to my left and right, I find I'm amid uniformed men and women resembling people from my world. They wear black from head to toe. Tiny soaring holographic blackbirds project from their lapels. My armored wet suit stands out, but I'm not catching their eyes at all.

No one around me speaks through their mouths, but they're communicating intricate details for the next phase of Spectrum development. I slink past.

After a few blocks, I begin to lose my fear of the people. They don't seem to notice that I'm here, let alone that I'm different. Masses stream around me. I attempt to bump into one woman, but she deftly avoids me.

Emboldened, I reach out and touch another's shoulder as she walks by. She doesn't turn to look at me, but simply keeps walking. I shove a man and get the same result—he keeps moving as if he didn't notice. I stop and stand in the middle of the sidewalk. I'm not exactly invisible— they clearly *see* me enough not to bump into me, but none appears to realize who I am or that I'm not supposed to be here. They have the glazed-over looks of extremely busy robots.

My shoulders sag as I relax a little. I have no idea how to find a needle in this haystack, or rather a thorn—a Hawthorne. He's been trying to find me. So maybe he'll be somewhere he thinks I'll look for him? The first place I think of is Lenity, Hawthorne's home in the Fate of Virtues. Does it exist here? How do I get to it if it does?

I rub my temples. "I wish I could bring Hawthorne's house to me."

Suddenly everything around me grows hazy, shimmering like a sun-soaked mirage. Off balance, I lean against the blue slate of the nearest building. Lawns begin to flicker up ahead, so green they almost glow. The intricate architecture of the Trugrave estate fans out before me, overlaying the cityscape.

The air shifts, turning heavier. I trudge ahead, my footfalls becoming laborious, as if I'm trekking through swamp water slushy with ice. I gasp and shiver. As I reach the edge of the ghostly estate, I find I'm also smack in the middle of a hovercraft lane in the city. Wind from a speeding silver vehicle passes through me just as I duck into the idyllic countryside.

Gravel crunches beneath my boots. My hand goes to my heart, which is racing from fright. Panting, I study the new terrain's lush panorama. This is how I remember Lenity. Wasting no time, I hurry to the flyway in front of the impressive home. As I do, the heaviness of traveling between the veils dissipates.

The once picturesque building is destroyed. Broken glass mars the rosette window. The front archway no longer has a security field. Something moves just inside. I enter the dim foyer. It's a cow, standing on the floor's embedded pyrite swords. Its black eyes gaze at me as it chews, and I wonder if it's a program—a sentinel keeping watch—or if it has a mind appropriated from some person. I'm not curious enough to find out.

I just want to locate Hawthorne. My heart sinks. I don't feel his presence here at all. That doesn't stop me from checking inside.

I enter the great room and gaze up at the vaulted ceiling, now a home for nesting birds. I tread lightly. It smells like death in here, and the reek of decay grows more pungent the closer I get to the study. I'm not shocked to find the remains of people inside. The corpses of Census agents lie mangled on the rug in front of the gargantuan fireplace. I examine the faces of the cadavers and sigh with relief. No Hawthorne. I wander around to make sure, but judging by the too-small clothing in the closets, I'd say he's never been here. I drift back out, past the munching heifer and onto the gravel flyway.

Relief and frustration war inside me. I try to think of the next place he'd be. Maybe our old air-barracks on the Stone Forest Base in Swords? A shiver creeps down my spine. In my world, it's now a Sword-soldier graveyard. Here it might still be a bustling Base. Either way, my instincts tell me Hawthorne wouldn't hide there. I scrap the idea and consider where he'd think I'd go to look for him. But then I pause. I'm looking at this the wrong way. The question isn't, "Where would *Hawthorne* go?" The question is, "Where would *I* go to hide in this world?" Wherever Hawthorne is, he's with *me*—if I'm still alive here.

I know where I used to hide as a child. Maybe there? Closing my eyes, I envision Westerbane Heath in Forge—the park next to the Sword Palace. As I open my eyes, the gardens and common appear as a shivering overlay of Hawthorne's estate's grounds. I slog toward the phantasm ahead of me. Thickening air hampers my steps. Cold envelops me as I plod through the gap in the weave.

The need to trudge lessens and finally disappears, but I'm lightheaded as I arrive in the Fate of Swords park. It is terrifyingly different than how I remember it. Westerbane Heath is empty of visitors. The well-worn paths wind in on themselves, the shrubbery shifting into new patterns as I watch. I gaze up at an ever-changing sky. It moves in unlikely and upsetting ways. Upon closer inspection, I see that it's composed of thousands upon thousands of bodies, floating and tangling in obscene ways, like a pit of vipers newly hatched. A dull hum sets my teeth on edge.

Ahead of me, the Tyburn Fountain looms with gloomy shadows. My throat tightens with dread as I approach. The statues on its peak move in slow-motion combat, savaging each other. The effigy of Tyburn, God of the West Wind, is particularly gruesome, slashing at the metallic shape of Hyperion with vicious snarls, cutting into bronze flesh. Water pours from the gaping wounds in Hyperion's chest and abdomen. I travel around the structure, cautious lest the gazes of the sculptures turn to me. Mist dampens my skin.

Tyburn's lover, Roselyn—a bloom in her hand and a crown of bronze roses on her head—points the way to the secret door in the side of the fountain. I creep nearer and ease into the frigid water. I shiver, my attention fixed to Roselyn's face. When I'm abreast of her, her pert smile broadens to a grin.

I gasp.

"Shh." She brings her finger to her lips, admonishing me. The hairs on my nape stand on end, but I twist the bloom of the rose in her other hand, to the west, opening the door.

I hoist myself inside. One concrete slab remains open while the other, within the chamber, lies shut. The walls and floors of the obelisk-shaped interior are covered with small swords. I find the one that is exactly west and press it. The sword moves inward and locks in place. I quickly press the other swords that complete the code. The door across from me rumbles open, and the one near Roselyn closes. I scurry inside the newly exposed tunnel. The passageway spirals downward. As I move forward, the door behind me closes.

I wonder at the level of detail in this alternate universe, until I realize that Crow would know this place, having picked my brain and Hawthorne's, too. But still, Spectrum has scraped and assembled a world of such mind-boggling accuracy that I'm filled with a scary respect that soon threatens to change into a feeling of complete hopelessness.

How will I defeat something so advanced?

Traversing the tunnel, I emerge through another stone door into Tyburn's Temple. The alabaster figure of the masculine deity glows in the dimness. Round walls show distress, and cracks splinter around the stained-glass windows. Dry leaves stir over the intricate inlaid floors. Soft drumming makes me hesitate. I peek around the statue's elbow to find that the temple has been converted into a large maginot kennel. The gigantic cyborg wolfhounds wag their tails, creating the drumming sound. They're all the older versions, the same cyborgs I grew up with.

When they see me, they come to me, seeking affection. Silently, I pet the many heads, stroking muzzles and gazing into their expressive eyes. Their bodies are thin, as if they aren't being fed very often. Worry creases my forehead.

I consider, on a molecular level, what I used to feed the maginots. Everything I need to build their food is in this room and the surrounding landscape. With my mind I draw the atoms and subatomic particles near.

In front of us, a trough assembles, like the one we used to feed them when I was young. Inside it, cuts of meat materialize. The maginots whine and limp toward it, wagging their tails. Voraciously, they chow down the food I assembled, and I stand in wonder.

I pass the feasting maginots and go to the spiral staircase. I tiptoe up and enter the observatory. This floor overlooks the quiet forest. The floor plan resembles the one below, with gorgeous tiling, elegantly carved statues, colorful windows, and a balcony that wraps around the domed room.

I pause in the center of the chamber. Hawthorne lies next to the other Roselle on a small, thin mat. His body spoons hers, and my heart squeezes in pain at the sight of them. I'm not sure why. He thinks he's with *me*. Only she isn't me. Not anymore.

I have no business feeling this way. I murdered Hawthorne. Up until this moment, deep down, I still believed he was dead. I knew that this version of him could exist in theory, but the man I knew and loved died. I killed him, and yet here he is in a different form. It's confusing and heart-wrenching. My stomach roils with anxiety.

I clear my throat. Hawthorne and the other Roselle startle awake. They sit up with the fluidity of soldiers, ready to fight. Then they spot me. They don't have the robotic look of everyone else I've encountered here, which assures me they're no longer part of the collective.

"Roselle?" Hawthorne breathes, gazing from me to the other Roselle and back.

"Hi," I reply with a tight smile. I take a step closer.

"Stop!" Hawthorne orders. His hand moves to the fusionblade sheathed on his hip. "Who are you?" he asks, gripping the weapon. But he doesn't ignite it.

I glance at the other Roselle. She's studying me. She's not surprised to see me. She's just . . . sad. My eyes shift back to Hawthorne. I want to ask him who he thinks I am, but as far as he knows, I could be anyone in this world. I could be Crow, disguised as me. Spectrum would know anything we know. And what it doesn't know, Roselle won't know either.

"I received your message, Hawthorne," I begin. "I'm sorry that I couldn't get here sooner. It's been . . . difficult."

"You got my message?" he asks, stunned. "What did I say?"

"I don't know. I couldn't hear you. I only saw you. Could you see me? I was on a ship beneath the sea."

Hawthorne looks skeptical. "We sent the message on a loop. It was supposed to keep broadcasting continuously, but we think Crow destroyed it soon after it was sent."

"I saw it twice," I reply. "I couldn't hear anything you were saying. I just saw you shouting. We had theories that this world might exist—"

"Why do you look like Roselle?" Hawthorne growls.

"She's a copy of me."

"You're the original?" He's skeptical.

"Yes. This world is Spectrum."

"So you're saying you're the *real* Roselle from a *different* world? If that's true, wouldn't you have been here before, for Spectrum to copy you?" Hawthorne growls and points to the other me.

"You must've believed that I existed, to have sent me a message, Hawthorne. I don't remember being here. I know I was, but I left all of it behind when I awoke."

Roselle takes a step toward me. She raises her hand and shows me her palm. "Do you have a scar on your hand—a star?"

I nod, showing her my palm.

"Can you tell Hawthorne and me how you and I got it?"

"Why? You don't know, and apparently neither does Hawthorne."

"If your story makes enough sense," she replies, "I might be inclined to believe you."

"Okay," I exhale. "It happened the first time I deployed. They air-dropped me near the battlefield in Stars. I was supposed to tag wounded enemy combatants and mark them for death. I found one. He was Gates of Dawn. I was required to beacon him—mark him for death by drone strike. I did, but I wanted to give him his sword back so he could defend himself. His name was Reykin Winterstrom—a firstborn Star. He'd rigged his sword to burn anyone, other than himself, who touched the hilt. It scarred me—us—with his family's crest. I beaconed him for a med drone and stayed with him until it arrived and patched him up. Afterward I fled. The Gates of Dawn army was almost on me. If Hawthorne hadn't come when he did, I would've been captured and executed."

"Why don't I know this?" my copy asks.

"Ransom Winterstrom, the secondborn technician who implanted me with a Census device, is Reykin's brother. He purged your memories of Reykin—the espionage we perpetrated for the resistance—and the familial connections between them."

"Ransom Winterstrom freed me from the collective," my alternate states.

"He told me that," I reply.

Hawthorne growls at me, "I figured out most of that. Spectrum could fill in the blanks from what I knew," he says to Roselle. "This doesn't prove anything."

I try again. "I went back to Stars—after Hawthorne became first-born. Hammon was pregnant. Crow was going to kill her. Reykin saved us. He and Daltrey Leon got Hamm and Edge new identities as first-borns in the Fate of Seas." I direct my gaze at Hawthorne. "Hammon said to tell you she misses you."

Hawthorne swallows. His voice turns gravelly: "All things you could have made up, knowing what I already know."

"In my world, Gilad is probably dead," I say.

Hawthorne looks shocked.

"Census attacked our Bases the same night as I was taken from the Silver Halo, by Crow and his Black-Os. Only a few Trees survived, and Spectrum turned the rest of the Sword soldiers into mind-controlled monsters. Gilad probably never had a chance."

Hawthorne shakes his head. "We've been to the Stone Forest Base—doing recon. They're filled with Crow's Black-Os."

"Not in my world—in my world they're graveyards."

Hawthorne's face pales.

"I believe you," Roselle says, stepping closer to me. "Whatever's in my head—the implant—it doesn't work. It's dead or something. When I woke up, Ransom told me my implant isn't a VPMD—that it isn't normal. He said it's organic material, but it's dormant in this world. He said it couldn't survive here. We had a conversation. It was so brief—and I was confused—and then he was gone. That was a while ago. How long have I been in here? When did Ransom upgrade me to 'ghost status' in this world?"

"Ghost status?" I ask.

"We call it that," Hawthorne replies, "because we feel like ghosts here."

"Have I been here years?" Roselle asks. "It feels like years."

"It's only been a handful of months," I reply.

"After I woke up in the Sword Palace, the box, I found I was no longer a prisoner of it," my alternate says. "Ransom kept telling me, 'Free them all,' before he left. When he was gone, so was Crow. I searched for Hawthorne first. It took a while, but I found him in the morgue. He wasn't dead. He was just lying there with his eyes open—but vacant. When I touched him, he awakened."

"What happened to her?" Hawthorne asks me. "How could she do that? I was part of the collective, until she touched me."

I meet his eyes. "Roselle and I diverged. I woke up from Spectrum's control in our origin world, but Spectrum had made a copy of me." I gesture toward Roselle. "Ransom came back here looking for the copy of me. He upgraded her. Then he erased the Spectrum copy of himself. He only exists in the other world now."

Hawthorne cringes. "He came back and murdered himself?" He moves protectively to shield Roselle from me.

"Yes, but you don't have to worry. I don't plan to do that. I need Roselle. I need both of you."

"So you're real . . . and we're not." His dark look borders on madness.

"You exist. I saw it in Ransom's memories, but I didn't fully understand this place. Not until now. It *is* real. Spectrum has created an alternate universe. It's not a program. And Crow, whatever he is, owns it."

Hawthorne swallows hard. "We haven't seen Crow in days. We were told he was raging when he found us missing. He left soon after and hasn't been back. He destroyed the control room and the beacons Roselle insisted we try to send to you. I have to be honest and say I thought Roselle"—he indicates my copy—"my Roselle, her, was insane about that, but what isn't insane here? So I trusted her, even though I thought she was—not wrong, but . . ."

"Hawthorne thought the original world didn't exist," Roselle finishes for Hawthorne, "that the one we're in now was the real one."

"You believed the red sky and all the creepy things in it were part of our world?" I ask Hawthorne.

"Now it sounds stupid, but yeah. It's no more stupid than an alternate universe I never knew I'd entered."

"Fair enough," I reply. "I assure you, our original world exists, and it's being decimated by Crow."

"It can't be as bad as it is here," Hawthorne replies. "Every breath here is a new form of violence. Every day, an execution. Death and resurrection and more death." He sounds mad, and that's how I know he's sane. If he didn't, I wouldn't trust him.

"May I come closer?" I ask Hawthorne.

"Where's the other me?" Hawthorne asks. "Why didn't I come here with you?" His questions still me. My stomach sinks.

I should make up a lie, but I can't. He'll find out later, maybe from Crow, and then it will be worse, if that's possible. I square my shoulders. "You couldn't come, Hawthorne. You died. You only exist here."

He swallows hard, processing it. "I died? How?"

"You . . . you got caught up in my plan to kill Crow, and when you did, I murdered you."

Hawthorne's jaw tenses. A look of betrayal shines in his eyes for a second, then recedes. He nods. "You're a soldier. You did what you had to do."

I snarl and tears cloud my eyes. "Don't forgive me. I can take your anger right now—your hate—but I can't . . . Just don't." Holding back tears is nearly impossible, but I do it.

"I know you're her." He nods toward the other Roselle. "But you're different—harder."

"Ruthless," I reply.

"Yeah. I can feel that. I can't say I don't like it, Roselle. I do, but I know *her*." Again he gestures to the other Roselle. "To me, *she's* the real one. Maybe she's your soul. I don't know. I could get to know you, but I love her."

Betrayal that I have no right to feel cuts me deep, as does his idea that I'm soulless without her. I'm not. I swallow past the lump in my throat. "I understand, Hawthorne. I'd never take her from you. I want to bring you both back to our world, but I need to figure out a way to do it. In the meantime, I need your help."

"Tell us how we can help you," Roselle offers, looking me in the eyes. It's so strange—looking at myself—I forget what I was about to say for a few seconds.

"Remember when we uploaded the virus into the maginot," I ask, "at the Sword Palace the night we were honored for bravery?"

Roselle's brow furrows. "Yes, Mother tried to have us killed that night. I remember uploading the virus—I just don't remember where I got it."

"You got it from Reykin Winterstrom. It was a program designed to infiltrate the Sword industrial systems. We're going to do that again, except this time you're my virus. You're my warlord here. I want you to seize control of this world by any means necessary."

Hawthorne frowns and crosses his arms over his broad chest. His shirt's torn and grimy, the armpits stained with dried sweat. His hair's limp and unkempt. Dark circles hollow out his eyes, and his cheeks are beginning to sink in a little. He gazes at Roselle, who resembles his state of decline.

"Don't take this the wrong way," Hawthorne says, "but don't you think we'd have done that already if it were possible?"

"I do, but it wasn't possible until now. If Crow's a god in this world, then I'm a goddess. I'll give you the tools you'll need. I'm going to make you gods here."

Hawthorne's lip twitches. "You're gonna make us *gods*? If you're a goddess, then we could really use some food, new clothes, and a shower."

"The maginots are hungry, too," Roselle adds.

"I already fed the maginots." I raise my hands and concentrate on the things I require on a molecular level. Everything I need lies at my fingertips—I just need to assemble it. I get to work, first providing food. I construct an elegant cart, like the one I'd seen at Hawthorne's estate, and fill it with the kinds of delicacies I became accustomed to at the Halo Palace. The cart hovers to a stop in front of Hawthorne and Roselle. Their eyes have grown to a size that rivals the tea-service saucers. Pastries and fruit cover the three-tiered tray. They look at each other with wary frowns. Then they glance at me with suspicion.

"I know." I shrug. "It's weird, but it's real. See?" I move to the cart, take a bite of a cherry tart, and chew demonstratively before swallowing. "Safe."

That's enough for Hawthorne. He lifts the closest thing to his hand, a croissant, and shoves the entire thing in his mouth. Roselle does the same with a scone. They both chew, roll their eyes, and make small groaning noises as they ravish the trays, dropping crumbs everywhere. I know that kind of hunger, and it pains me to see it in them. I move around the room, filling in cracks in the plaster and repairing broken panes of glass. I create a large brass tub with handheld showerheads. A bed comes next, and a wardrobe of clothes, and another with weapons and armor.

The air in here feels taut, supercharged. The maginots below begin to whine. I'd keep going, but I need to let the atmosphere rest, give it a chance to rebalance.

"I'll leave you two to shower and change," I say. "I'll wait for you outside in the yard." I walk to the gray doors and out onto the balcony. Climbing up on the stone ledge, I jump two stories to the ground below and land on my feet.

Above me, Hawthorne calls, "You're freaking me out!"

I glance up and see him gripping the stone railing. A small smile forms at the corner of my mouth. "You ready for an upgrade, Trugrave?" I ask.

"I'm ready for a shower. Please don't die while I'm in it."

"I promise," I reply so he can hear me, and then add, under my breath, "I can't die."

It's not long before Roselle and Hawthorne join me in the yard. They're both garbed in light armor with Sword-soldier tagging that I provided. It's better than any armor they've ever had, and it's fitting because Roselle is The Sword in this world. I push away the maginot who has gently caught my arm in its massive maw.

"He looked like he was about to eat you," Hawthorne says.

"Funnyface would never eat her—me," Roselle and I say at the same time.

286

"This is weird," Hawthorne says with a chuckle.

Roselle ignores him. "Do you have a plan?" she asks me.

"I do. I want to see how you wake someone up from the collective."

"I'd show you"—she gives me a sheepish look—"but I can't find any more of them on the ground, so to speak. When we awoke a few days ago, the sky was red, and everyone was gone . . . up there." Roselle points to the sky.

"All the food was gone, too," Hawthorne adds. "We've been starving ever since. I thought I'd go insane with the noise the groaning sky was making."

I want to ask him again why he'd think this world was the real one after *that*, but I don't. "Okay, we'll get to them soon. First I'd like your permission to go inside your heads. I think I can improve your situations if I do, but I won't try without you saying it's okay."

Hawthorne glances at Roselle.

Roselle nods. "She's me, Hawthorne. If you trust me, then you should trust her."

"You heard her when she told us she murdered the other me, right?" he asks.

"How did Hawthorne die?" Roselle asks.

I explain what happened, how Hawthorne drowned, and how I came back to life—twice.

Hawthorne frowns. "You didn't murder the other me. You tried to kill Crow."

"That's intent. The fact remains that I did kill you. You're dead."

"I'm not dead. The other Hawthorne is dead. I'm very much alive."

"You are," I agree.

"He'd be okay with it," Hawthorne says. "If he were me. He'd only regret that it didn't work."

I feel like I'm dying inside. I push back my tears. "I can't talk about this now. Will you give me your permission?"

"Yes," Hawthorne says, relaxing his shoulders. "Whatever you're gonna do, it's better than starving to death here."

"I'm going to touch you," I say. He nods his okay, and I move to him. I reach up, slide my hands over his freshly shaven cheeks, and rest my palms on his temples. His scent is the same. My heart aches, but I push that aside and focus. He has a VPMD implant. Of course he does—he's a copy. Roselle must have somehow scrambled parts of it when she freed his consciousness from the collective, because it no longer accepts Spectrum's signal. I can feel the frequency of the signal streaming around us. I wander a little in his mind, taking its measure. "That fantasy you've got going on in your head—the scenario with Roselle and me and you—it's never going to happen, Hawthorne," I tease him.

"A guy can dream." Hawthorne grins, unashamed. He fights the impulse to wrap his arms around me and ravish me . . . but then a thought occurs to him, and he stops smiling. He's worrying about me. Not the other Roselle—me. He's afraid that I'm alone without him. He still loves me, and he's getting a sense of my sorrow.

"I'm okay," I say aloud.

"No, you're not."

"There's a lot you don't know, Hawthorne."

"Can you show me?" he asks. He raises his hand with the intent of putting it on my hip. He stops himself, balling it into a fist.

"What do you want to know?" I ask.

"Everything."

"No, you don't."

"Yes, I do."

I pull my hands from him and sigh. "Let me . . ." I pause, considering how best to say this. "I want to reorganize your mind to make it . . . more efficient. Faster. I can remove your VPMD implant, but it'll collapse your brain if I don't create something to take its place. I want to give you an implant like mine. It's organic. It will grow with you. It's sustainable, but there are side effects."

"What kind of side effects?"

"You'll obtain abilities you may or may not want."

"Like what?"

"Like being able to jump off balconies without getting hurt . . . and if you do get hurt, you'll heal, even after you die."

"You're saying it will make me immortal?"

"Yes, you might not be able to die. And in this world," I whisper, "that might not be a good thing."

"I'll be like you?"

"Similar, but I can't accurately predict your abilities or how they'll manifest. There are infinite possibilities based on your unique brain and DNA."

"I could degenerate into an evil monster like Crow?"

"I don't think so—not with your personality. I think it'll make you more . . . you."

"But you don't know for sure."

"No, I don't. Roselle's much easier. I can predict what she'll be like—basically me."

"If I die, she's alone here?" Hawthorne asks.

"She's alone here with a billion or so mind-controlled Crow underlings. And there's more. The way I came in . . . It didn't feel like it was the only world that this one's anchored to. I think there might be other worlds Spectrum is exploiting."

"You're kidding me?" he asks with growing anger.

I shake my head.

"Then do it, on one condition," he says. "I want to know everything that's happened to you since I saw you at the Halo Palace right after you left my room."

"You mean the night you thought I was a Fate traitor? You don't remember anything that's happened after that?" I ask. "You don't remember seeing me after Gabriel died?"

Amy A. Bartol

"No, and you wouldn't tell me anything about how you were taken by Spectrum." He gestures in the direction of the other Roselle.

I glance at her. She nods once, agreeing to his terms. "You're sure you want to know?" I ask. "It doesn't matter. It's the past. I haven't figured out a way to time travel, or we wouldn't be speaking right now."

"I need to know," he insists.

"You don't—you only think you do."

"Please?" He gives me an imploring look.

I sigh. "First I upgrade your implant. If you want to know after that, I'll show you."

"Then I agree," he says.

"I think you should lie down."

He indicates the grassy lawn. "Here?"

"Yes."

"What if Crow comes?" He glances over his shoulder at the forest.

"You said you haven't seen him in days, right?" I reply. "Let's hope he stays busy."

"That doesn't make me feel good," Hawthorne gripes with a sigh. He lies down on the ground. Roselle kneels on one side of him. I take the other.

"This probably won't either," I say under my breath.

He grimaces. "Awesome."

I hand him a handkerchief that I manifested. I give another to Roselle. "Here. Just in case."

"Just in case what?" Hawthorne asks.

"It could get messy. I've never done this before."

"You're killing me," he grumbles.

"Let's hope not—*I'm kidding*," I add when he frowns. "It's going to work." I place my hands on his temples again. My palms glow with golden light. "How do you feel, Hawthorne?"

"My head feels hot."

"Does it hurt?"

290

"No, it's just pressure and heat." Silver liquid drips from his nose and ears. "Is my nose bleeding?"

"Not exactly. I'm dissolving your implant. It's coming out."

He grunts and lifts the handkerchief to catch the liquefied implant. Roselle does the same, sopping up more of the tepid, metallic ooze. When it's done draining, I take my palms from his head and rub them briskly together, concentrating on creating a seed that will grow into an interfacing organ—a neuro-enhancement.

"I don't feel well," Hawthorne slurs, and closes his eyes.

"You will," I assure him soothingly. I lift a glowing orb of light near his face. It floats upward and disappears inside one of his nostrils.

"Is this working?" Roselle asks in a hushed tone. She's on the verge of panic.

My hands touch his temples again. "Yes. It's perfect," I reply with a reassuring smile.

Hawthorne doesn't open his eyes for several minutes, but when he does, they're a much brighter shade of gray, bordering on silver, but steelier. "I'm beginning to really like that there's two of you. I can tell you apart now. Your eyes glow." He points at me.

"Yeah, that's my implant working. Hers is practically dead. We have to bring it back to life."

I go to help Hawthorne sit up, but he waves me off. "I feel different. Stronger."

"That's what we want."

"How are you going to bring her implant back to life?" he asks, getting to his feet. He flexes his hands, gazing at them as if they belong to someone else.

"I have to stop her heart and restart it—give her a reboot."

"What? No way! Absolutely not," he growls, glaring at me.

"It's going to be easier than what I just did to you. Trust me. I can speed up her implant's growth, too—make her stronger in a shorter amount of time, because we're running out of it. I need to return to the anchor I came through, before dawn in my world, or I'll have to find another way out."

"How do you know when that is? It's daylight here."

"I have an internal clock."

"Is the anchor going to close?" he asks.

"Not exactly. We have plans to blow it up. It's complicated. I'll explain it all to you, but let me do this first."

"You're going to leave us?" he asks.

"My world needs me. I can't stay here. I have a plan, but it involves both of you being as strong as possible."

"I trust you," Roselle says, lying in the spot that Hawthorne just vacated.

Hawthorne begins to kneel beside her, but I stop him. "You can't hold her hand," I say. "This requires sending electrical charges through her. I don't want them to touch you. I also don't want you to freak out. Can you do that?"

"What?" he asks. "Not freak out?"

I nod.

"I honestly don't think I can watch her die and not freak out."

I get to my feet and lead him away, to the steps of Tyburn's Temple. "You don't have to watch. You said you want to know everything that's happened to me, right?"

Hawthorne nods grimly.

"I'll show you. Are you ready?"

"Yes," he replies.

"Sit on the steps." He does. I place a finger to his temple, like a finger gun, and pull the imaginary trigger, sending thousands of my memories into his mind at once. He grunts, and his eyes start darting back and forth, as if he's dreaming with them open.

I slip away, back to Roselle. Kneeling beside her, I meet her stare. "This shouldn't hurt, because it will kill you almost instantly. Close your eyes."

She nods and obeys. I rest one of my palms on her forehead. The other covers her heart. My hands heat up, and I send pulses of energy into her. The moment I stop her heart, I send a neuro-enhancer into her organic implant. Then I strike another burst of energy into her heart, restarting it. Roselle's back arches, and she gasps for breath. She gazes at me. Her eyes, I suspect, are as blue as mine now. I take her hand.

"It's okay," I say soothingly. "I've got you."

She just stares at me in awe.

A fierce growl of pain issues from Hawthorne, startling both me and Roselle. He rises to his feet, his hands in fists, looking murderous. He marches to the edge of the woods and slams his fist against a tree trunk. Cracking noises issue from it, and the tree topples over in a flurry of broken branches and falling leaves.

"What's happening?" Roselle demands, alarmed. "What's wrong with him?" Sitting up, she clutches my hand.

"Nothing's wrong with him. He's angry. He deserves to be. I just showed him everything that's happened in my world. He's processing it."

Another tree meets a similar fate. For several minutes, we sit and watch Hawthorne tear the forest apart. I'm trying not to be upset. In truth, I feel somewhat hopeful. Hawthorne's already super strong, and we need that. We need it desperately. I tell myself he doesn't have to forgive me. He just needs to help me defeat Crow. I know I'm a liar, though. We watch Hawthorne slump against a tree and slide down, holding his head in his hands.

"Can you wait here, Roselle?" I ask.

She nods, pulling her knees to her chest. I rise, cross the yard, and sit beside Hawthorne.

It's several minutes before he speaks. "You *had* to kill me, Roselle," Hawthorne growls, choking back emotion. "I was a monster."

"If there'd been anything I could've done to save us *and* kill Crow, I would've done it," I whisper. My throat's too tight to speak louder.

"You love Reykin more than me." It's a statement rather than an accusation.

"I don't know how that happened. Truly, I don't. Reykin and I saved each other's lives during the war."

"He forced you to spy for them—for the Gates of Dawn."

"Yes, but look closer. Reykin taught me I was worth more—my life had value other than as someone else's property or as a soldier. He expected me to fight for myself—for *my* life—not to uphold the power of a corrupt government. Then Census and Crow changed everything. They took you and changed you. I tried to save you, but I couldn't. Reykin prevented me from choking on your loss . . . His hope is infectious. The way he looks at the world is unique. I need him, Hawthorne. He makes me better."

Hawthorne turns and hugs me. I hug him back. "Reykin makes you happy," he says softly.

I swallow a sob. "I don't even know what happiness is, Hawthorne. I think I was happy for a moment when I was with you—before you became firstborn. Reykin makes me sane. One day maybe he and I can be happy together. I hope so. I'll fight for it."

We let go of each other. "You said you have a plan?" he asks.

"I do. You need to create chaos in this world. You and Roselle must seize power from Crow by creating an army, and force any pieces of him that you find to retreat into my world. I'll set traps for him there. We must kill all of him if either world has any hope of peace. You need to suss out the anchors to every world you can find here, control them, and eliminate them one by one. He can't be allowed to hide or come back. I don't think you want whatever he's cultivating on the other side of those anchors coming here to nest. We'll keep one anchor open between our worlds. Only one, so we can monitor it at all times, until we decide to close it."

"There's an anchor in the Sword Palace. Now that you've shown me through your memories, I know what it looks like. Should we keep that one?"

"Can you secure the Sword Palace?"

"I think so. It's empty now. Like I said, Crow hasn't been here in days. He must be distracted—or we're not a big enough problem to come looking for now."

"You will be soon. You'll have to be careful. Look out for Roselle—she's The Sword here."

"I'll protect her."

"I know you will." I get to my feet and offer him a hand up. He takes it, squeezes it, and then lets it go when he's standing. We move back toward Roselle.

She walks into Hawthorne's arms and hugs him. "What was that all about?"

"I'll tell you later," he whispers in her ear, squeezing her tighter.

"You better," she replies, smiling.

I tip my chin and stare up at the slithering sky. "I have an idea how you can get them down." I manifest a golden bow and a quiver filled with golden, shimmering arrows. I select a sharp one, nock it onto the glowing string, and pull it back until it's taut, aiming it toward the sky. When I loose the arrow, it travels up and into the collective above, dislodging a slew of mind-controlled people. They plummet to the ground, dropping around us like fallen, wingless angels. They bounce and groan but appear unscathed.

I glance at Roselle. "Show me how you wake them up."

After dislodging potential soldiers from the sky for a few hours—awakening them from the collective, reassuring them that they'll be okay, reorienting them, and seeing to their needs—it's time for me to go. I'm cutting it dangerously close.

I teach Hawthorne and Roselle how to fold space, and together we force the anchor city and Tyburn's Temple to meet so we can punch through from one to the other. Ahead of us, the metropolitan street where I entered this world lies like a misty veil over the round chamber of Tyburn's Temple. I walk seamlessly through the veil. Hawthorne and Roselle join me on the sidewalk. Quickly we set off in the direction of the anchor building I originally came through.

"This is it." I gesture toward the silver doorway with the nine Fates holograms. "I don't know if you won't be able to use this after I leave. Reykin couldn't come here. It may be because he doesn't exist in this world, or because he doesn't have an implant to act as a key—I don't know for sure. You'll have to find the other anchors to our world. I'll be looking on the other side as well. If you need me, send me another beacon. I'll return if I can. Stay away from this building once I go through the anchor. It could explode."

"What about *that* one?" Roselle points to the crow-adorned building across the street.

"I don't know what's in there, but it feels very . . . wrong."

Roselle cringes. "I feel it, too."

"If this is an anchor, then maybe that is, too," Hawthorne says.

"Yes, but to where?" Roselle asks.

"Build your army, and then find out," I advise. "I have to go now. I'll return as soon as I can." I start to walk toward the doors.

Hawthorne grabs my arm, hauls me back, and lifts me off my feet to hug me fiercely. "I still love you," he whispers.

A sob catches in my throat. "I still love you, too," I whisper back. "Take care of Roselle."

"I promise."

He sets me on my feet. I grasp the handle of the silver door, open it, and slip through.

Chapter 19
Breaking My Chains

The onyx room's in shambles.

It's a bloodbath. Pieces of soldiers lie shredded on the floor. Blood spatters the walls. Nothing moves except for a lump of scaly flesh in the corner. Cherno wheezes, laboring for breath. Disoriented from traveling through the anchor, I stumble to him. I kneel beside the dragon-man and place a shaky hand on his forearm, finding it colder than normal and slick with congealing blood.

"Cherno," I whisper.

He opens his eyes. The flickering flames within them are mere embers now. "It's Crow," comes Cherno's guttural response. "He's here."

"Whose bodies are these?" I can't bring myself to say his name. If Cherno tells me that one of them is Reykin, I'll go insane.

"They're Crow's clones. I slaughtered some of them. But there are too many. They took the others and left me for dead." Blood oozes from abrasions in his skin. He's been descaled along his forearms and chest.

It takes several frantic beats of my heart to crush the rising panic. *Crow has Reykin!*

"Did you stop your heart and play dead?" I ask.

Cherno nods and groans. "It wasn't hard." He lifts his hand, and I see the gaping wound in his abdomen before he covers it again and coughs. Tar-black blood specks his lips.

My mind races. "I can help you." I pull some of the surrounding energy to me and funnel it into Cherno, stoking his internal fire and beginning the healing process.

He hisses. Smoke streams from his nostrils, but he's still too weak to stand.

"How long ago did this happen?" I ask. My hands jitter, and my guts are turning to butter. I don't know if I can do this without him.

Cherno pants in pain. "Not long."

"Does Crow know where I went?"

"Yes. Retreat inside Spectrum. Find another anchor."

"If I do that, all of you die. Where are they?" I wipe his cheek with my hand, even though I know he finds my flesh repulsive.

"I never made it out of this room. Leave. Now."

"I'm not running, Cherno. The monster in my head is as strong as his. I'm breaking my chains. Stay here. I'll be back for you."

He points above us. "Roselle, he told me there are thousands of him up there."

A Crow army—the narcissist.

I shiver with dread. "He doesn't know how to murder me and make it stick."

"You and I know there are worse things than death." Cherno winces, trying to rise. He groans and slumps back against the wall, puffing and holding his gaping wound. It's knitting itself back together, but it'll be a while before he can stand. He stares into my eyes, beseeching me to leave.

I shake my head. "I have to fight him now."

"Roselle, in case I don't see you," Cherno grumbles, "it's been a pleasure."

"Knowing you has been mine, dragon." I rise from his side and creep to the door.

"Roselle," Cherno calls. "You might need this." I turn and find him holding my St. Sismode sword, the one Crow took from me on my Transition Day. He tosses me the fusionblade. I catch it and stare at my family's crest on the hilt. It feels like a toy in my hand, compared to the other weapons I have at my disposal. "I couldn't let him keep it, once I knew it was yours."

"Thank you, Cherno." I ignite the blade. Golden energy sizzles from the strike port.

I open the door with my mind, and close it once I slip out of the onyx room and into the dark hallway. The light of my fusionblade illuminates the carnage in the corridor. Bloody membranes of Bermin slick the floor. Shrieks from the grizzly, man-sized bats lament the light that allows me to escape. I traverse the passage and curse under my breath, knowing the elevator is the only way out, unless I go back to the anchor.

I step inside the elevator and extinguish my fusionblade. Emboldened by the darkness, Bermin surge forward in a rush and flutter of wings. I pull myself through the emergency door in the ceiling, slam the hatch closed, and lie on top to keep the crazed fiends inside from breaking through. I wait until I've trapped several of the bloodthirsty creatures in the elevator, then, with my telekinetic power, trigger the car to rise. It speeds toward the surface.

As we approach the main level of the Tree, I cringe and turn my face, panicking that I miscalculated. The elevator stops with enough room so I'm not crushed. Below, the doors roll open. The Bermin's bloodcurdling screams are cut short almost immediately as fusionmag pulses flood the elevator car. The scent of burning flesh assails my nostrils.

Someone enters below. No chatter. I hold my breath. The weight of a couple more bodies sways the car. The holographic sensor triggers on the control panel. Whoever they are, they intend to send the car back down. Their weight leaves the elevator, one by one. The doors slide closed. I open the hatch and swing down, easing gently to the floor.

With my mind I seize control of the elevator again. I exhale deeply . . . and then I slide open the doors.

A hundred or more Crows stand around idly in the shallow Census bunker. The three that entered the elevator slink away with their smoking fusionmags, their backs to me. I raise my fusionblade, jam the strike port so it doesn't extinguish, and hurl it at the one in the middle. It tumbles end over end until it reaches a Crow and slices through him vertically. He falls apart, his guts sliding down his crumpling legs. Using my mind, I draw the sword back to me like a boomerang and catch it in my palm with a loud *smack*.

"Roselle!" all the Crows say at once. A chorus of ninety-nine maniacs.

Fusionmags rise and aim at me in synchronization. They all fire at once. I hold up my palm and send out a single pulse of energy. It catches the fusion energy careening at me, reverses its direction, and amps up the severity of the charges. Lethal energy burns holes through the Crows' armors and enters their bodies. The lethal charges bounce around, frying most of their molecules, and the Crows melt into piles of molten flesh.

I turn the corner and run through the Tree's warehouse, past empty containment tanks. Near the exit, I come to a skidding halt. Ahead, hundreds of Crow clones, armed with fusionblades of various kinds, stand shoulder to shoulder. Several rows deep, the army of psychopaths blocks the way out.

One of the Crows steps forward a few paces. He wields a fusionblade, twisting it in patterns of sizzling golden energy that match a demonstration I once did for a training video. Stroke for stroke, his form is perfect. His smile's ominous.

"What have you have been doing inside Spectrum, Roselle?" the copycat Crow asks.

"I thought I'd take a vacation," I reply, hoping to buy myself some time. "It's a very interesting landscape you've constructed—creepy, but interesting."

"We're just getting started. We're on the verge of filling Spectrum with creatures from other worlds."

"How fun for you—like your own personal zoo, with more slaves to torture, I presume?"

"It's a utopia, Roselle. We thought you'd be intelligent enough to realize that. We offer paradise. Once you've been inside Spectrum, everything here seems so *dull*. The Fates lack vibrancy, wouldn't you agree? We find it all rather boring."

"Then leave."

"Oh, we intend to. We just hate loose ends. Some day you might discover a way to harm us. We would find that . . . rude."

"At the risk of sounding impolite, Crow, I promise to do more than just harm you."

"I offered to make you part of our world."

I scoff. "As your personal punching bag."

The Crows behind him take a step forward, wielding their fusion-blades in intricate maneuvers. "Everyone needs a hobby, Roselle. Torturing you is ours. We're going to dissect you, to see how you tick. We need your self-healing. It's the only reason we haven't decimated you."

"You can't have it," I seethe.

"We take anything we desire."

"I learned a little something new while I was on holiday in Spectrum."

"Oh?" the Crow in front asks with a cock of his head. "What's that?"

I fold space, like I did inside Spectrum, leaping invisibly across the distance between us, and arrive a sword's breadth in front of him in only a blink. Swinging my fusionblade, I slice off Crow's head. While his body crumples, I answer, "This."

The battle begins. All Crows rush me at once.

I fold space, jump through it, swing, carve, cut, kill. Five Crows die with only a few thrusts of my sword.

Fold again, disappear inside, reappear behind them and slice, plunge, hack, slaughter. Ten more topple.

Stagger, fold space, rush through it, materialize outside the tight sphere of confusion they've balled up into, and slash, hew, lacerate, splice, maiming and murdering Crows as I go.

Panting hard, covered in flecks of blood, I snarl and cut through the last one. But I glance behind me, and a thousand more Crows file out from around empty glass capsules. Dread filters with icy fingers through my veins.

There are too many.

Above my head, a small legion of stingers buzzes like a hive of angry bees. The drones extend the barrels of their fusion cannons. As they circle the warehouse, they open fire on the gathering Crows. The clones scatter. Pulsating rounds scream through the air, pounding everything with searing energy. Pieces of bodies vaporize before my eyes. I crouch, unsure where to run. They're everywhere. The burning smell of flesh scalds my flaring nostrils. Screaming from the disfigured clones fills the warehouse. I cover my head with my hands.

The ear-piercing squawk of a thousand dying Crows dissipates, leaving just the hum of the stingers above me. My hands slip from my head.

Bootheeled steps echo through the warehouse. I straighten and stand as Flannigan Star walks toward me from my left. To my right, another Flannigan Star appears from the shadows and heads in my direction. Dressed in all-black combat gear, they have similar hairstyles—a bob cut at a sharp angel—that accentuate their pointy chins. Neither possesses the star tattoos that accentuated the peaks of the original Flannigan's eyebrows, but other than that, they look like her. They stop in front of me.

My heart pounds wildly in my chest. "Flannigan . . ." I pause and then add the plural, "*sss* . . . ?"

They tilt their heads with the cocky smiles I know from the original Flannigan. "Yes," they say in unison.

"Do you control those drones?" I ask, pointing to the machines hovering overhead. They reach out and pull me toward the closed hangar door, which we crouch beside, the two Flannigans flanking me.

"We control the drones," whispers the one on the left. "We want to help you."

"Why?" I mouth.

"The Crows murdered our sister."

"Who?" I ask.

"Flannigan Two," they reply in unison. "She poisoned a bunch of them, and the new Crows retaliated."

"I thought she liked Crow."

"Crows are monsters," the Flannigan on the right hisses.

"And you are . . . ?" I ask, trailing off.

The one on the left points to herself, saying, "I'm Flannigan Five." She nods to the one on my left. "That's Flannigan Nine."

"We're the only two left," Flannigan Nine explains.

"For now," Flannigan Five adds. "The Crows keep remaking us, hoping one of us will love them. It'll never happen."

"They're pure evil," Flannigan Nine states with a shudder. "We have to stop them."

"We should send the drones," Flannigan Five suggests.

"No," I reply quickly. "My friends might be out there."

"The stingers are only programmed to seek and destroy Crow."

"Okay," I relent. "At least it's a plan. I'll open the door, and you send out the stingers." I meet their stares to make sure they understand and agree. They nod. "Ready? On three. One. Two. Three!"

We all lean away from the door. Using telekinesis, I slide open the heavy metal barrier. It squeaks and rumbles. The hum of the army of drones above us amps up. In a diamond formation, they whoosh past us, rocketing out of the Tree with pulsating bursts of ammunition.

In seconds, the humming falls silent. Then, with a sound like heavy metal raindrops, they strike the pavement.

And then, silence.

I move forward and peek through the open doorway. Before me, thousands upon thousands of snarling, blond-headed, blue-eyed beasts await. Between them and me stand Reykin, Clifton, and the soldiers we brought with us last night. They're on their knees, bound and gagged. Reykin struggles when he sees me, trying to get to his feet. Welts and bruises mar his handsome face.

Slowly, I walk forward. Stingers litter the ground in front of me in a jumble of useless metal.

Flannigan Five reaches out and grasps my elbow. "What are you doing?"

"I have to face them," I reply.

"You can't win!" Flannigan Nine warns.

"No, I can't lose," I reply. *Because if I do, it's over.* I shrug off her hand. "Stay here. Don't come with me."

"We'd rather die than go back to them," Flannigan Nine replies.

"They're sadistic," Flannigan Five adds.

"I can't protect you!" I hiss. "Stay. *Here.*"

I move forward alone, into the dawning light of a beautiful, clear morning. Seagulls squawk above us, mocking my pain with their shrill laughter. Looking for the spokesman, I scan the Crow clones. The cult of personality reveals itself to be the Crow standing just behind Reykin. He steps forward. The rest remain still, evenly spaced.

"That was some display, Roselle," he says. "You're more and more resilient by the day. Those jumps you do through space . . . impressive. You must teach it to us."

"Let my friends go, and I promise I will."

A devious smile broadens Crow's lips and lightens his eyes. "We plan to let them go. It's only you we want. They can remain here and die with the rest of the trash. We were going to ambush you inside Spectrum, Roselle, but we thought this way would be more fun. You get to say good-bye to them—and we get to watch."

"I think this would've been more fun in Spectrum," I reply. "The rules are different there—more flexible. You were afraid to follow me there, weren't you? Afraid I might dominate you in your hellish paradise."

He snickers. "I don't expect that this will be very fun for you, here or there."

"You'd be surprised by what amuses me these days."

"Do you find this funny?" He grips the handle of his fusionmag and withdraws it from his holster. He aims it at Clifton's head.

I stumble forward, screaming, "Wait!"

Crow fires. I raise my hand and send out a pulse, deflecting the shot. It veers toward one of Crow's clones and strikes the creature in the chest, dropping him to the tarmac.

Crow lets out an uncertain, hawkish laugh. "My, Roselle, you've certainly evolved since I *last* killed you."

"You have no idea."

"Why are you protecting this supposed *god*?" Crow taunts. "You know my shot wouldn't have killed him. He would've grown another head, wouldn't he have? Like he did before. And anyway, you don't love him."

"You don't know who I love."

"I know you. You could never let yourself love Clifton . . . Oh, I'm sorry," he tsks, "his real name is *Cassius*, isn't it? No, you could never love *Cassius* after he left you to die at the Silver Halo and flew away unscathed, like a coward. He's the God of Ruin all right. He'll always ruin everything. You can forgive him for that, but you could never trust him again. And what's love without trust, eh? Love is a wasted emotion."

"I thought you had a thing for Flannigan?"

"I thought I did, too, but Flan poisoned us with cyanide one night, so I had to let her go."

"You let her go?"

"Off the rooftop of the Halo Palace's *Upper Halo*." He chuckles. "As it turns out, the only thing we truly love is hurting you, Roselle.

And it's so easy, too, because you love foolishly, deeply, and with your whole being."

"What made you like this?" I ask, trying to understand why he has fixated on destruction, and on me. *Was it because he could never break me?*

"You know what made me this way! It started when I was treated like a worthless piece of garbage by my own family. They *hated* me. I was secondborn—disposable. But I planned to discover *true* power. It happened when I was killing Sabah. As I tugged my sister beneath the water, something spoke to me. It was dark, and I could see it clearly. It knew my name. It knew everything about me. It knew I was secondborn, and what that meant. It told me it was from another world, and that if I let it inside me, it would help us transform into gods. I believed it. We finished killing Sabah, together, and then, piece by piece, we began to claim everything that belonged to us."

I shiver, unsure whether to believe him. Or is he completely insane? "You don't have to destroy our world. You can resist being a psychopathic terrorist. You can change."

"Why would I ever want to change, Roselle?"

"Crow, what do you *want*?" I shout through gritted teeth.

"I want to watch you suffer."

He raises his fusionmag and aims it toward Reykin.

"No!" I scream, and rush forward, thrusting out my palm. Crow raises his hand, somehow blocking me, and triggers his weapon. A blistering pulse strikes Reykin in the back of the head. Pieces of him hit me, like dirt on a grave. I manage to catch what's left of my love's collapsing body. The next moment is a blur. White-hot energy snarls from my hand, straight at the laughing Crow in front of me. It tears through him, creating fissures in his veneer. The energy passes through him to the other Crows behind him. They all electrify, flaming into thousands upon thousands of burning pillars on the seaside.

I drop my hand and cradle Reykin's nearly lifeless body in my arms. He slumps, and I lay him on the ground. Kneeling, I bend near his ear and whisper not words, but frequencies. The waves generate a magnetism, coaxing the scattered molecules from the pieces of Reykin, returning them to him and reassembling like a neurological jigsaw puzzle.

I ignore the acrid smell of the burning bodies around me. I'm singularly focused on Reykin. The blood on my face slips away, returning to him. My head feels like it may explode at any moment, but I don't stop whispering, finding all the ways he fits together. When I have all his atoms reassembled, I rub my hands together, creating a seed—a neuroenhancement like mine. The glowing nucleus floats up and disappears inside Reykin's nostril to bore through his nasal cavity and penetrate his cerebral cortex. There it will grow, like mine has, transforming him into a being like me. Immortal. If I'm not too late.

Clifton kneels by my side, having broken free of his bonds. "What can I do?" His gaze is on Reykin's unconscious face.

I'm trembling and weak. My hands won't stop shaking. "Get Cherno. He's still in the anchor room. He needs help." I look at the metal shackles restraining Reykin, and they crack and fall away.

"You need help," Clifton replies softly.

"Get Cherno," I seethe.

Clifton nods grimly. He calls one of his men and orders the others to contact the *Sozo One.* Everything's fuzzy. I have no idea how long it takes for the hoverstretcher to arrive. Or how Reykin comes to be on it. I vaguely register clutching his hand and stumbling next to him. Then I realize Hammon's talking to me, draping a blanket around my shoulders in the wide corridor of the *Sozo One.* The infirmary lights dim on Hammon's command. I walk, holding Reykin's hand. Once we reach a private compartment, the physicians work around me, because I won't let go of him.

They cut away Reykin's armored wet suit and clothes. He's covered and bandaged now, but his abrasions are rapidly disappearing. The physicians perform scans and whisper words like "miraculous" and "astonishing." Cherno's thick growls sound from an adjacent room. He's yelling at Clifton.

Amy A. Bartol

Periodically, people talk to me, but I can't understand what they're saying.

Finally, Hammon shoves me into the bed with Reykin and orders everyone to leave us.

Tears slide down my cheeks unchecked. I snuggle against Reykin's warm side, feeling an uncanny déjà vu. Hawthorne feels like a lifetime ago. Now I just need Reykin to wake up.

The rocking of the vessel lulls me, and I close my eyes. When I open them again, I'm staring into Reykin's, their aquamarine literally glowing. I blink.

"Did it work?" he asks.

"Did what work?" My voice is gravelly.

"Did you find Hawthorne and the other you?"

"Yes," I whisper. "Hawthorne believed his world was the real one, but I managed to convince him otherwise."

"Everything else go well?" he asks.

"Yes. You were right. There is another me. She's going to build an army and help us defeat Crow."

He looks around at the walls, the ceiling, the bed we're in. "How did we get here?"

"It's a long story."

"Why don't I have any clothes on?"

"That's a longer story."

"The next time I wake up in bed next to you, without any clothes on, you have to be naked, too," he says, pulling me toward him and kissing me.

"Deal," I whisper with a little sob, but then I kiss him back, passionately.

He pulls away when he realizes I'm crying. "Hey"—he cups my cheeks tenderly—"shh, what's wrong, Roselle?"

"Nothing. I'll tell you later. Just kiss me."

Reykin smiles and accommodates.

308

Chapter 20
My Own Life

One Year Later

He holds his hands over my eyes.

We traipse through fragrant grass and wildflowers. "Where are you taking me, my love?" I giggle and sway. My hands lift to his forearms to steady myself on the uneven terrain. Around us, I hear the nickers of horses. The loamy scent of sod fills my nose. A crisp breeze stirs my hair, teasing it against my cheeks.

"Only the most special place in the entire world," Reykin replies.

"Where's that?" I ask, holding back a giddy smile. We come to a stop.

"Our new home," he says. He lifts his hands from my eyes, revealing a magnificent sunrise. A gorgeous state-of-the-art building lies before us. Its impressive stature is nestled within homey gardens, flanked by a barn and outbuildings of a similar style that add to its warmth and appeal. It's a marvel of architecture and design, simple and sophisticated all at once.

Reykin wraps his arms around my swelling waist and gently strokes my baby belly. "We can come here when you're able to take breaks," he says, "from official Sword business at the Palace. Do you think Dune will like it?"

I grin, watching the horses as they graze a meadowland that stretches to the horizon. "This little guy will love it," I assure him, "especially if his father teaches him to ride those horses one day." I tip my cheek so that it rubs against the short bristles gracing Reykin's jaw. My hands slip over his. "When did you do all of this?"

"I have this next-level ability to multitask," he teases, "thanks to you."

"Are we in the Fate of Stars?" I ask. Something seems familiar, but I can't quite figure out why.

"Yes. We're in Stars. It's where we first met. This is the spot where a tiny Sword soldier stumbled alone across a battlefield and had the courage to save her enemy's life instead of take it. And in that moment, she saved the world."

Tears spring to my eyes. I turn in his arms.

Reykin lowers his mouth to mine and kisses me. He murmurs against my lips, "I love you, Roselle."

The last time we were here, Reykin's heart and spirit were both broken. In a way, mine were, too. Now we have each other. Forever.

"I love you, too, Reykin," I whisper back, feeling a happiness I never imagined possible.

Epilogue
Reverie

Finding and destroying all the anchors between worlds proves to be arduous.

Crow hid them everywhere, amassing them like a Sword second-born hoarded chets. Only one anchor from our world to Spectrum's remains—the one inside the Sword Palace. Roselle and Hawthorne stanchly guard it in Spectrum while Reykin and I secure it in our world.

Today's an auspicious occasion. It's Transition Day. In the past, secondborns were given to the government on this day, but now it's the day that both of our worlds gather to celebrate the end of Crow's reign of terror. We've outlawed the practice of enslaving secondborns and abolished limits on the number of children a family can have. This year, the Transition Day gala's being hosted in Spectrum's Sword Palace by The Sword and her husband, the Fated Sword Hawthorne Trugrave.

Roselle's title, like mine, has some of the hereditary power of our mother's position, but we're both striving to change the ways our worlds are governed. We are the sole Clarity in each of our worlds, the other eight Fates here having lost their leaders. Reykin has some interesting ideas about holding elections, allowing everyone to have an equal voice. He's drafting an outline for his idea, which he calls "self-governing" and includes the abolishment of implanted monikers. He wants every individual to decide how to contribute to society, instead of mandating duties through a caste system. Due to Reykin's diligence, we've got a multitiered plan to implement these and other much-needed reforms soon.

I've been preoccupied with tracking and annihilating Crow in all his iterations. It's been several months since anyone has sighted him in the Fates. Spectrum's universe is a little tougher to gauge. Many more anchors to other strange worlds exist inside Spectrum, and new ones are discovered now and then. It keeps all of us busy.

Roselle and I stroll together near the edge of the Round Ballroom. The white skirt of her gown brushes against the gold of mine. We greet guests in her Sword Palace. Our matching crowns and Sword broaches sparkle in the light of ornate chandeliers. We've just returned from putting my son, Dune, and her daughter, Flannigan, to bed in the nursery. It's still amusing to see people stare at us. They treat us like twins, which is taboo enough where we come from, and no one but our husbands really grasps that we were the same person for the first two decades of our lives. She has all my memories, except for the ones of Reykin and the others that are solely mine from after our split. People have taken to calling her Rose, to cut down on the confusion, but I still call her Roselle. It's not confusing for me, or her.

"Where's Cherno?" I ask her.

"He asked me to give you his regards," she says. "He's traveling off-world, to the universe with the dragons. He said something about searching for Crow. I told him that we've cleared that world, but he wanted to make sure."

"Hmmm." I smile, thinking about Cherno's history as a full-blooded dragon, but I keep it to myself. I'm glad I gave him a key. Maybe he can find peace with his past.

Reykin and Hawthorne join us, both men looking handsome in their formal Fated Sword uniforms. It's strange, but I'm all broad grin and giggles when Reykin wraps his arms around me from behind and nuzzles my throat, sending a thrill of pleasure through me.

"What plans are you two Swords hatching?" Reykin demands with a gentle growl.

"I was just about to ask your wife where Clifton has gotten to," Roselle says, and grins at Reykin while Hawthorne slings his arm around her shoulders.

"He gave me his apologies," I reply. "He had to leave early. Ransom contacted him. They've had a breakthrough extracting the VPMD implants from their test subjects. He's on his way back to our Halo Palace to oversee the trial. He said to tell you they'll share their findings with you soon."

"That's exciting!" Roselle replies. "I feel sort of bad for him, though—working on the holiday."

I snort. "Don't feel too bad for him. He took Flannigan Five and Nine with him. They keep him super busy." Roselle and I both burst out laughing.

"We have news, too," Hawthorne says, glancing at his wife.

"That's right," Roselle says soberly. "There's a newly discovered anchor to a world that we haven't been able to clear yet." She tips a crystal goblet of punch to her lips and sips it.

"Which one is that?" I ask.

"They call it Earth," she says, her eyes following the dancers who twirl around the floor by us. "We don't think Crow ever made it there, but we can't be sure yet."

"What an odd name." I sigh. "Why would anyone name a world after dirt? Anyway, I can go with you and help. I'll be able to sense if Crow's hiding there."

Reykin's arm remains around my waist as he moves beside me. "Your ability to locate Crow is uncanny, love, but you can't go this time." He takes my hand and squeezes it conspiratorially. "You're pregnant again. You need to take things easy and let someone else handle it.

Besides, you don't want our secondborn daughter to arrive in a world with a funny name, do you?"

"Why not? She's bound to be a rebel, just like her father."

"All of them will be rebels," Reykin replies.

"How many children are you planning on having?" I ask.

"A dozen at least, and we'll let them choose if they're Stars or Swords or Diamonds, or—"

My heart flutters wildly for this man. "Let's just have this second one and see how it goes." I pause, thinking. "In fact, let's only ever say second *one* and never say second*born* again."

"Excellent idea," Reykin says close to my ear, sending a shiver of pleasure through me, "and we'll only ever call our other children, the third *one*, and the fourth *one*, and the fifth *one* . . ." He takes my cup and sets it aside before leading me out onto the dance floor with him. There, Reykin sweeps me into his arms, and I know without a doubt that I've never been more alive, more in love, or more beloved.

Glossary

air-barracks. Kidney-shaped dormitory airships that dock on the military Trees in Bases like the Stone Forest. They transport troops and house them.

The Apiary. An outwardly decrepit-looking military Base on an island near the Fate of Seas. A Census stronghold.

birth card. Enacted by Greyon Wenn the Virtuous, birth cards are a rudimentary way to give permission to a couple to have a child. A couple is issued a card, like a license, which allows them to have a baby.

Black-O. A Census soldier enhanced with advanced military-grade artificial intelligence technology embedded in his or her brain. Each soldier is subject to mind control by programmers and handlers who are often Census agents. *See also* VPMP.

Black-O mode. The state of being a Black-O soldier. It can entail being mind-controlled by a third party or using artificial intelligence to solve problems, follow commands, and complete tasks.

Bermin. Ancient, human-sized, bat-like creatures. They're carnivores who dine on blood mostly from humans. Thought to be extinct, they have been genetically brought back into existence through genetic engineering.

Brontide Mountains. Also known as the Brontides, they were named for the sound they make—it's the shudder of distant thunder. The tectonic plates beneath them shift, which makes the rumbling noise.

Burton Series-7 fusion cannon. A fusion-energy cannon designed by Burton Manufacturing. The weapon was originally used as a lightweight fusion rifle, but the Series-7 was redesigned for use as a prosthetic device to physically enhance a soldier. It's a First-Tier Option for Soldier Augmentation in Agent Crow's journal called the *Transhumanism Directive*.

Burton Rapier. A jetlike aircraft used in combat. Usually black with bulky fairings at the air-compression ports.

Burton Weapons Manufacturing. A Sword-Fated weapons manufacturing company owned by Edmund Burton and his firstborn son, Malcolm Burton.

Census. A branch of the government comprising agents whose mission is to hunt down and kill unauthorized thirdborns and their abettors. Their uniform is a white military dress shirt, black trousers, black boots, and a long tailored leather coat. Their Bases are underground beneath the Sword military Trees at Bases like the Stone Forest Base and the Twilight Forest Base.

Census Transition Day. The day at the Opening Ceremonies of the Secondborn Trials when Census massacred the attendees and revealed their plans to initiate a new world order—one controlled by Census. Also referred to as "CTD" and "CT Day."

chet. A nonaddictive substance that is used to relieve tension and induce relaxation. Looks like a white stamp.

Clarity. The leader of a Fate.

Class 5Z Mechanized Sanitation Unit. A robot designed to repair and maintain sewage and septic lines. Phoenix was one of these robots but has now been enhanced by Reykin Winterstrom with AI and weapons.

Cliffs of Agamaya. A location of one of Hyperion's temples. Hyperion is a demigod, known as the God of Water.

Copperscale. A defensive textile or fabric developed by Salloway Munitions Conglomerate that acts like armor. It can conduct an energy pulse, fusion or hydrogen, away from the wearer.

crella. A type of donut.

CTD. Census Transition Day. *See* Census Transition Day.

CT Day. Census Transition Day. *See* Census Transition Day.

drill instructor devices. A hexagonal device the size of a grapefruit created to aid in weapons training. The device can be programmed in several different functions to train a soldier in both attack and defend modes. Manufactured by Salloway Munitions.

Amy A. Bartol

Dual-Blade X-Ultra. A fusionblade designed by Roselle St. Sismode for Salloway Munitions Conglomerate while she was a secondborn Sword at some point before Census Transition Day.

Exo. A rank in the firstborn Sword military. It is higher than all of the secondborn ranks. Only the Admiral and Clarities are higher. Black uniforms. Clifton Salloway is an Exo.

fatedom. The realm of a Fate, like a kingdom.

Fated Sword. A title given to the spouse of The Sword (the Clarity of the Fate of Swords).

Fates of the Republic. Also known as the Fates Republic. A society comprising nine Fates or "fatedoms." The Fates highest to lowest in the caste system are Virtues, Swords, Stars, Atoms, Suns, Diamonds, Moons, Seas, and Stones. The leader of the Republic is the Clarity of Virtues.

Firstborn Sword. The title of the firstborn son or daughter of The Sword, which is the acting Clarity of the Fate of Swords. Gabriel was the Firstborn Sword. Roselle bore the title after Gabriel died.

flyway. A path designated for hover vehicles or aircrafts. A road or designated zone for flying or driving a vehicle.

Forge. The capital city of the Fate of Swords. The Sword Palace is located in Forge.

fusionblade. A fusion-energy-driven laser-like sword. The sword resembles a broadsword without the expected weight. Fusion cells reside in the hilt of the sword and create a stream of energy when engaged. The hilt is constructed of a metal alloy and usually personalized with a family crest or some other distinctive marking. The St. Sismode family is the originator of the fusionblade.

fusionmag. A gun-like weapon that fires energy in bullet-shaped pulses.

gaolgahl. Cherno's word for "oubliette," which is a deep dungeon with a trapdoor in the ceiling.

Gildenzear. An ancient region beneath the sea that was once ruled by Roselle the Conqueror and given as a gift to Cassius, the Lord of Raze and Ruin.

heartwood. An escalator-like machine that carries occupants up or down levels through a vertical tube within a Base Tree.

hovercar. A wheelless vehicle that is propelled above the ground by various means.

hovercycle. A wheelless motorcycle.

hoverstretcher. A self-propelled stretcher that is automated and floats above the ground. It carries wounded people from one place to another.

Hyperion. A demigod, known as the God of Water.

kill tallies. Black line tattoos that extend from the outside corners of the eyes to the hairline of a Census agent, denoting the number of thirdborn kills the agent has amassed. The marks can also be found tattooed on the neck or temples of an agent.

maginot. A canine-like cyborg that resembles a wolfhound. They patrol the grounds of the Sword Palace, acting as sentinels.

medical drone. An automated robot with a silver metal casing. It's shaped like a cylinder. It uses a blue-lighted laser scanner to x-ray wounded soldiers in combat by hovering over their bodies. It has mechanical arms, which project from its underside, that can administer medication and perform triage. The drone is summoned by a red-blinking "medical-drone beacon" or "med-drone beacon." The beacon emits a high-pitched sound, prompting a drone response. Once the drone performs triage on a soldier, it inflates a hover-stretcher with a homing mechanism in it. It places the soldier on the hoverstretcher for transport to a rescue airship.

medical-drone beacon. Also known as a "med-drone beacon." A red, disc-shaped device the size of a thumbnail. It blinks and emits a high-pitched frequency that summons a medical drone. The device is placed on wounded soldiers who need medical attention from a medical drone.

memory mapping. The process of accessing a subject's memories and brain activity and cataloging them for remote-viewing purposes. Another step in this process happens when the information from one person's brain is grafted onto another brain, essentially allowing for a sort of brain transfer.

moncalate. A tool used to surgically implant a moniker beneath the flesh.

moniker. A symbol implant each person receives at birth to denote class/caste. It is a brand that covers a holographic chip. The chip is loaded with the person's identification and other vital information, such as rank, family members, fatedom, status, and so on. The holographic chips can be activated by checkpoints manned by security personnel. They are used to track people entering and leaving districts, to process secondborns, to denote firstborn status, and more.

neuro-enhancers. A general term that alludes to a broad range of enhancements and capabilities brought on by VPMDs.

New Gildenzear. The orb-shaped sea vessel owned by Clifton Salloway (Cassius) that resembles the ancient city/kingdom of Gildenzear in a time of gods.

Numbers. The newest term for Zero Fates or zeroborns. They are VPMD-implanted civilians who are not intended to perform military functions unless a need arises and Spectrum decides to use them "in the moment." They mostly perform whatever task Spectrum designs for them. They do not function consciously. Outwardly, they are robotic, exhibiting no emotion or personality.

phantom orb. A small, silver, ball-shaped device that provides resistance to infrared scanners and pings from Virtue-class stingers. It cools a person's body temperature to camouflage the individual from detection.

Platinum Forest Base. A Sword-Fated military Base consisting of tree-like structures that air-barrack ships dock upon. It's located in the Fate of Stones.

remote-viewing. The process of accessing and viewing a subject's memories at will, with or without their knowledge or permission.

Rose Garden Society. A secret club dedicated to the preservation and welfare of Roselle St. Sismode. They have a vested interest in seeing her become The Sword (Clarity of the Fate of Swords). One of the most influential members is Clifton Salloway (firstborn Sword aristocracy), an arms dealer who owns Salloway Munitions Conglomerate. Members are called Rose Gardeners.

Rose Gardener. A member of the Rose Garden Society.

Roselyn. Tyburn's lover, known for wearing roses in her hair. Her statue is part of the Tyburn Fountain, located in Westerbane Heath. She points to the secret door that leads inside the secret passage to Tyburn's Temple on the grounds of the Sword Palace.

RW1 Device. Short for "Ransom Winterstrom One." A biotechnology device created by Ransom Winterstrom and implanted into Roselle St. Sismode.

Salloway Munitions Conglomerate. A Sword-Fated weapons manufacturer owned by Clifton Salloway. Headquarters is in Forge, the capital city of the Fate of Swords.

seraphinian. A poison.

Sozo One. An underwater vessel. The Greek word *sozo* means "save" or "saved."

stingers. Sharp-nosed security drones that catalogue and ping monikers. They scan for unauthorized personnel and for soldiers that are in the wrong areas for their service level access. They are weaponized.

Stone Forest Base. A Sword-Fated military Base consisting of treelike structures that air-barrack ships dock upon. It's located in the city of Iron in Fate of Swords near the border of the Fate of Virtues and the Fate of Atoms.

strike port. A part of an energy-powered sword such as a fusionblade or a hydroblade. The access point or source from which a fusionblade glows with golden energy. On a sword, it is located at the end of a hilt.

Transition Day. Historically, a day in early autumn that happens annually, when eighteen-year-old secondborns are required to report to a processing base set up by the Fates of the Republic government in order to be indoctrinated into governmental service. Sword-Fated secondborns report to the nearest "Golden Circle" just outside of each Forest Base for processing on this day. Their families, for a multitude of reasons, bring their Sword-Fated secondborns to these Bases years too early, as young as ten years old. One reason is that parents fear their secondborn will harm their firstborn in order to gain power and position in their society. Some parents don't want to grow attached to their secondborn, because they know they will have to be given up later.

Tree. A tree-shaped military building used by Sword-Fated personnel. Firstborn officers and high-ranking secondborn officers reside in apartments or air-barracks in glass Trees, while subordinate soldiers reside in apartments or air-barracks in concrete and steel Trees.

Trial Village. The name of the area in the one-mile circle at the center of the secondborn training camps. It's an exclusive area for aristocratic firstborns to socialize and find food and entertainment within the Secondborn Trials atmosphere.

Tyburn. A demigod known as the Warrior of the West Wind. He defeated Hyperion, the God of Water, and gave water to his people.

Tyburn Fountain. A fountain in Westerbane Heath. The fountain depicts the God of the West Wind, Tyburn, defeating Hyperion, the God of Water. The fountain contains a secret passage that leads to Tyburn's Temple on the grounds of the Sword Palace. The statue of Tyburn's lover Roselyn, part of the fountain, points the way to the hidden door.

Tyburn's Temple. The domed, gray stone building located on the grounds of the Sword Palace in the Fate of Swords.

VPMD (Virtual Perception Manipulation Device). A system of automated and biochemical devices implanted in the brain that can alter reality, including enabling mind control, hallucinations, and false memories. In elite cases, it can stimulate biochemical reactions that enhance one's senses and physical makeup.

VPM Agent or VPMA (Virtual Perception Manipulation Agent). A Census agent who manipulates a VPMP (Virtual Perception Manipulation Participant).

VPMP (Virtual Perception Manipulation Participant). An individual who is implanted with a VPMD (Virtual Perception Manipulation Device) and is subjected to mind control or other applications of the device. *See also* Black-O.

Westerbane Heath. The public park on the west side of the Sword Palace in Forge, the capital city of the Fate of Swords. The park contains the Tyburn Fountain, an ancient monument to the warrior-god, Tyburn.

Whetstone. One of the main thoroughfares in Forge, the capital city of the Fate of Swords. It passes through Old Towne.

whisper orb. A ball, usually metallic, that, when activated by touch, produces an iridescent sphere of light capable of containing sound frequencies. They can come in several different sizes.

Zero Fates (also Zero-Fated). Individuals who have Black-O monikers.

zeroborn. A person manufactured in a laboratory and implanted with mind-control technology. The person isn't "born" in the traditional sense. Noncombat zeroborns have red monikers. Black-Os have black monikers.

zeroborn mode. The state of being mind-controlled.

Acknowledgments

To my readers and bloggers: Thank you! The outpouring of love that I receive from all of you is mind blowing. Your generosity toward me is humbling. You make me want to write a thousand books.

Jason Kirk, you're a maestro. Thank you for teasing creativity from me with your thoughtful notes and your poetic mind.

Tom Bartol, you're my best friend. I cannot imagine my world without you in it. I love you.

Max and Jack Bartol, I count myself as the most fortunate person in the world to have you both in my life. Thank you for knowing when to let me write and when to rescue me from my computer.

Tamar Rydzinski, one of the best days of my life was when you agreed to be my agent. Thank you for always having my back.

Amber McLelland, your help with this novel was invaluable. Thank you for beta reading it and for your amazing insights. Team Reykin!

Thank you to my publishing team at Amazon Publishing and 47North, who worked on this project every step of the way. I'm forever grateful.

About the Author

Amy A. Bartol is the *Wall Street Journal* and *USA Today* bestselling author of the Kricket series, the Premonition series, and the two previous novels in the Secondborn series: *Traitor Born* and *Secondborn*. She has won numerous awards for her writing and been nominated for several more. She lives in Michigan with her husband and two sons. For more on Amy and her work, visit her website, www.amyabartol.com.